SEARCH AND DECEPTION

Peter J. Marzano

Swan Publishers
Durham, Connecticut

For book and story information visit **www.peterjmarzano.com**.

Publisher's Note: This book is a work of fiction. Any references to historical people, actual places, and events are used fictitiously. Any names, characters, places, and incidents are used solely within a product of the author's imagination. Any resemblance to actual people, living or dead, or to businesses, companies, events, institutions, or locales is entirely coincidental.

First editing: Samantha De Divitis
Final edit and formatting: Rita M. Reali
Cover design: © 2022 Peter J. Marzano
Final cover Assembly: Al Esper Graphic Design
Cover Photo: Trevi Fountain by Peter J. Marzano
Cover Photo: Mezquita interior by Peter J. Marzano
Cover Photo: Street sign on building by Peter J. Marzano
Cover Photo: Zaanse Schans windmills by Peter J. Marzano

Ordering Information:
Quantity sales: Special discounts are available on quantity purchases of more than 20 books by schools, book clubs, corporations, associations, and others. For details, visit peterjmarzano.com or email pjmau-thor@gmail.com.

Search and Deception / © 2022 Peter J. Marzano – 1st edition

ISBNs:
Paperback: 978-1-7366827-2-2
Ebook: 978-1-7366827-3-9

Swan Publishers

Books by Peter J. Marzano

Litany of Sorrows

Search and Deception

Dedications

*To my high-school teachers for their lifelong commitment to education,
their examples and spiritual guidance, especially
Irish Christian Brother Ted Dausch, Reverend Monsignor Thomas Bergin, and Jim
Marini.*

***

*To my Monsignor Farrell High School 1968 classmates — all of whom are awesome
friends.*

***

*To my parish pastor, for his guidance during my teenage and young-adult years,
Reverend Monsignor Paul (Andriaccio) Andrews.*

***

*To my brother-in-law "Harry" Coyle, a NYC firefighter who responded and
worked inside the WTC Twin Towers on 9/11 and miraculously survived.
And to other NYC firefighters, including Uncle Ray Dolan, and neighbors
Fireboat Captain Frank Tracy, Fire Marshal Richie Grassia, and Captain Warren
Dunton.*

***

To neighbors who were notable examples as good fathers and husbands.

Larry Tickle, Larry Summerhill, Joe Grassia, Joe Labita, Al Shultz,

Jack Hoffman, Gene Ammann, and Bill Jordan.

***

*To my son and daughters, Peter, Tricia, Kathy, and Shawn,
their spouses, Solie, Mark, Alan, and Stephen, and to my eleven grandchildren,
Layla, KC, Mark, Isabelle, Brayden, Ryan, Kate, Gavin, Allie, Stella, and Matthew.
How awesome and memorable was our family trip to Ireland!*

Acknowledgments

Again, another huge hug and thanks to my dear wife, Kathleen, whose patience and support allowed me to focus on this, my second book.

Thank you to my alpha readers: Al O'Leary, Susan Ciani, Stephen George, and especially my dear sister, Patricia Marzano-Smith, whose flower garden is awesome.

And thank you to my beta readers: Denise Stemmler, Christine Kopyt, Leo Rohan, Andrew Militano, Dr. Chris Gostout. Your feedback has been so valuable.

Thank you to my editor, Samantha De Divitis, and to Rita Reali for her final editing and formatting of the manuscript. Thanks to Al Esper for his help with the cover. And a huge thank you to my good friend, Curt Hockemeier, whose proofreading skill is greatly appreciated.

Donation

Ten percent of profits from the sale of this book, *Search and Deception*, will be forwarded to the **Adenoid Cystic Carcinoma Research Foundation (ACCRF)** to help in the effort of finding a cure for this uncommon cancer that affects the lives of hundreds of thousands of people around the world. It will be sent on behalf of our daughter, Shawn Elizabeth George, who suffered from the disease.

Author's Note

Readers expressed how much they enjoyed *Litany of Sorrows*, a historical fiction story about young lovers that begins with World War I and runs through World War II. People loved most of the characters – especially Katrina for her good heart – but despised Karl for his cruel actions.

Many said the ending was perfect and reviews were very positive. But over the next several months three of every four readers asked me these questions: "What became of Katrina, Luca, and Brian?" or "Did you write *Litany of Sorrows* with the intention of writing another book?" Some encouraged me to write again. "This is a great story; you can't stop now! You need to write more!"

My honest answer was, "No, I didn't plan to write a sequel." But many high-school friends, the old boys from the *Monsignor Farrell Class of 1968*, urged me on. As winter approached, I put away my golf clubs, and being a fan of neither the cold nor outside sports, I sat at my keyboard, listened to the silence... and began writing once again. Like *Litany of Sorrows*, I was pleased as the story developed – and surprised as dialogue between characters emerged.

Search and Deception answers questions readers asked and reveals much more. It discloses Brian's hidden career and reveals the struggle between Brian and his wife, Grace – whose hidden secret and resulting depression encompass struggles childless women sometimes face. Such challenges can crush a couple's spirit. Just writing about their experience saddened me.

And incredibly, as my writing of this story was being finalized, Russia's malicious, unconscionable, and horrific invasion of Ukraine commenced. Sadly, the parallels between Hitler's desire to expand the German homeland, and Putin's expansion of Russia are uncanny. May the Ukrainian people succeed in their struggle for a safe and independent country free from Russian incursions.

Will we ever learn from history?

– Peter J. Marzano

"The only thing that we learn from history is that we learn nothing from history."

Georg Wilhelm Hegel, German philosopher

27 August 1770 – 14 November 1831

Germany

SEARCH AND DECEPTION

Prologue

I t was a frigid March afternoon when the adult O'Sullivan children returned to their mother Sheila's home from her burial. After a family brunch, all four siblings gathered in their mom's bedroom. The twins, Tricia and Kathy, hovered over the open hope chest, pulling out miscellaneous items. The youngest sister, Shawn, kept track of who would get what. Methodically, the sisters retrieved birth and baptismal certificates, old photos from each of their weddings, and linen christening gowns with the names of each grandchild carefully embroidered by their mother. Brian, the eldest of the four, sat nearby, watching, and nodding his approval.

As Kathy reached for the final item, the chest's bare wooden bottom tilted. Mother's hope chest was deeper than it appeared. On inspection, she determined a thin piece of lauan plywood fit so perfectly there was no room for fingers to grab it. Brian went to the kitchen and returned with a serrated knife. He slid its blade down along the edge and, with a twist of the handle, lifted.

Shawn grabbed the piece and lifted the false bottom. "Look! It looks like a musical instrument case. And what's inside that big box?"

Tricia, the older twin, nicknamed "the boss," took charge. She pulled out and opened the case. Inside was an old mandolin. She passed it to Brian, who placed it on the bed and returned to his seat.

Next to the mandolin's case was a cardboard box. Kathy lifted it up and out, and Shawn removed the cover. The siblings stared at an old, dark, leather-bound book, about five inches thick. Embossed on its cover were the words, "*Unsere Lutherische Familienbibel.*"

Brian set his small glass of Laphroaig scotch on the nightstand and sat up in amazement. He translated the cover's German words, which meant, "Our Lutheran Family Bible."

"Correct me if I'm wrong but aren't we Catholic?" asked Shawn in confusion.

The twins looked at Brian, in silent question. Shawn lifted the Bible and slowly opened its thick, heavy leather cover. Immediately inside she found a delicate piece of parchment paper. Gently unfolding it revealed an elaborate drawing of a family tree, four pages wide and two pages long.

Brian, a career European-history and art professor, translated the document using the little German he knew. He told his sisters the words above the family tree said:

The von Richter Family History
The Duchy and Kingdom of Wurttemberg
Since MCCLXV Anno Domini

Tricia stared at her brother. "BJ, what's this Bible doing here, and where did it come from?"

He shrugged. "How should I know?"

Absent of an explanation, Shawn carefully refolded the page showing the family tree. Then, turning to the next page, she found an envelope tucked deep into the binding. Pulling it out, she noticed the envelope was addressed, *"To Brian."*

Seeing his name, their brother reached for it and opened it. Inside he found a folded letter with beautifully scripted handwriting from a broad-tipped ink pen. Dated March 1, 1951, it started:

To my Dearest Son,

I'm not sure how to begin. Many years ago...

Brian scanned the page slowly, silently. His sisters watched intently, waiting for a reaction. For a minute, he thought his just-deceased mother, Sheila, had written the letter. As he continued down the page, he stroked his chin. After another moment passed, his blue eyes sparkled with tears. He put the first page of the letter down on the Bible and, wiping his eyes, continued reading. His sisters watched as his expression changed. Moments later, the tears rolled down his cheeks.

Tricia peered over his shoulder. "Brian, what is it? What's the letter say?"

When he started on the third page without a reply, Tricia grabbed the first two. Brian wept openly. Kathy and Shawn remained silent but watched for their sister's reaction.

Concerned by the silence, Brian's wife, Grace, entered the bedroom and asked what was happening. He continued reading the last page, then stopped. He looked up at them and said,

"Dear Jesus... I remember when the pretty lady with the beautiful blue eyes visited us. This... this letter... it's... it's from her. She wrote this. She says she's my birth mother.

"Apparently, Mom and Dad adopted me during World War II."

CHAPTER ONE

Hidden Letters

The mood in the bedroom grew heavier. Still shocked at the discovery of his adoption, Brian again wiped away his tears, silently reflecting on the contents of his birth mother's letter. His heart ached. His sisters, equally upset by the discovery, huddled around and group -hugged him. Though initially comforted by their affection, he suddenly felt alone. He stood and, with a growing sense of unsettling detachment, stepped back, shedding his loved ones. He glanced at his wife and sisters and left the room.

He walked through the kitchen, grabbed his keys and ski jacket, then headed outside. His three brothers-in-law, engrossed in the University of Connecticut vs. Syracuse basketball game, were unaware of the unfolding drama and never noticed his leaving.

Outside, the day was cold and grey—fitting weather for his mother's burial earlier that morning. After getting into his car, he began driving along Hylan Boulevard, toward the Point at Great Kills Harbor. Many years earlier, he and Grace would go to this very place to be alone and enjoy each other's company. Grace joked about its being their "happy place." But during the last twenty years, Brian occasionally visited the Point when facing unexpected challenges. Grace had begun calling the Point "Brian's retreat." It was his place to be alone and to think. Now, with his mind spinning, he again needed its solitude and comfort, to reflect on the letter he'd just read.

What a terrible day it's been—and no day is ever fitting to learn of one's own adoption.

When he arrived, he parked facing the water and shut the engine, welcoming the quiet of the seashore. Brian stared at the waves rolling from the Atlantic Ocean into Raritan Bay. Exiting the car, he walked onto the sand and let the freezing wind bite his face. To his far left, he saw the towers of the Verrazano-Narrows Bridge. Ahead and to the right, across the bay, the New Jersey Highlands.

How could it be? How turbulent and painful could her circumstances have been to walk away from a child? From me*! How pained the lady with the blue eyes must have been. And they never married? What happened that she didn't mention in that letter?*

Off in the distance, a container ship slowly moved across the bay toward the Kill van Kull—the old Dutch name for the water separating Staten Island from New Jersey. Distracted momentarily, he watched as the huge vessel entered the narrow waterway. Just then, a seagull swooped down within a foot of his head. Its flight into the strong wind gusts coming from across the bay startled Brian. Only feet in front of him, the bird hung virtually motionless in the wind. Then with a quick twist, it flew away. Its departure let him return his attention to his birth mother's letter.

If only I'd known about her sooner. Why did Mom and Dad keep this hidden from me all these years? Surely, they knew I'd find the letter someday. There's got to be more to this story.

A sudden blast of freezing air brought on a blinding snow squall. The icy flakes began pelting his face. He turned back to his car with tears and snowflakes frozen on his cheeks. Reprieved from the bitter cold, Brian started the old Saab and headed back to his mother's house.

In her brother's absence, Shawn paged through the old German Bible and discovered several more onionskin pages hidden in its last book, Revelation. They seemed to be post-scripted addenda to the mysterious letter. Each contained detailed information revealing terrible circumstances. The details exposing the woman's emotional pain outlined a full litany of sorrows she experienced. The sisters and Grace took turns reading the addendum letters, shocked by the details Katrina Amorino-Luciano had written, and worried over the new find. The twins suggested Shawn be the one to give them to Brian, as they'd always shared a special connection.

After learning of the letters, and feeling bad for Brian, the three brothers-in-law left the house for a local bar to drown their own sorrows. UConn's 58 to 55 loss to Syracuse in the Big East tournament had ended UConn's 13-game post-season win streak.

An hour and a half later, Brian had yet to return. Grace, anxious about his whereabouts, paced back and forth with an eye on the front window.

Five minutes later, she spotted him pulling into the driveway. She quickly walked into the bedroom to let the sisters know their brother had returned.

He came in through the side door; the old screen door with the maladjusted cylinder slammed shut behind him. Seeing no one in either the living room or kitchen, he went to his mother's bedroom, where he was met with silent stares and concerned faces.

"From the looks of your long faces, something else is going on and it can't be good."

Shawn moved toward him.

"What's in your hand, Little Bear? More shocking news?"

She nodded.

He raised his chin, closed his eyes for a moment, and inhaled deeply. Letting it out slowly, he prepared himself for the unknown.

Shawn handed him the onionskin pages, the last of Katrina's writings.

Taking them, Brian settled into Dad's old recliner next to his parents' bed. "Can one of you get me another scotch? One ice cube, please."

He pulled his glasses from his shirt pocket and slid them on. Grace and his sisters was stood motionless, watching him read. The room was silent.

Brian slowly took it all in. *My God, how could he do that?*

As he finished reading, his tears again flowed freely. Looking at the ceiling, he spoke aloud, "Oh God, what a terrible ending! I can just imagine the scene. Poor Katrina!"

"BJ, I found those extra pages in the back of the Bible after you left. Along with several letters she sent Mom and Dad. We've all read them, and we're heartbroken." Shawn hugged her big brother. "You need some time alone. We'll leave you and Grace here and we'll go clean up. It's getting late and we'll need to leave when the guys return."

After her sisters-in-law retreated to the kitchen and to gather the children from the upstairs playroom, Grace watched her husband. Brian let the new information sink in and he wiped his eyes again.

"You left without your cell phone and there was a call while you were gone," she said at last. "I heard it ringing and found it on the counter a moment too late. I saw the caller's name. Erick Schmidt. Who's he?"

Brian breathed out a sigh and shook his head. "It's nothing. He's a colleague."

"Don't all your colleagues and friends know we buried your mother this morning? I think it's inappropriate for anyone to bother you today. They should leave you alone."

"Did you catch the phone number he was calling from?"

"No, just his name."

"Well, Erick is a colleague from overseas; he wouldn't know Mom died."

She cast a perplexed look at her husband. "What's he calling about?"

Brian shrugged. "It's probably nothing."

"That's what you say all the time, but it always turns out to be something. Next thing you always say is, 'I need to go overseas to a conference.' I'm tired of your conferences, Brian. I'm tired of a lot of things." She gave a headshake of frustration. "This has been a long day, and it's all very disturbing. Can we go home now?"

"Of course. Get your coat. The girls can wrap things up here."

"What do you plan to do with that Bible and this other thing from your mom's hope chest? It's a mandolin, right?"

"Yes. We'll leave it here for now, but I'll take the Bible and those letters. I need to read them all again, perhaps even a third and fourth time, to take it all in."

As he entered the kitchen, Shawn handed two bottles of scotch to him. "Here, take these. Mom had them tucked away in the hutch."

As Kathy and Tricia approached, Brian looked at his trio of sisters. "I love you three very much. Regardless of what we learned here today, you're truly my sisters. We still have lots to discuss regarding the disposition of Mom's house and everything else that's here."

"Relax, BJ, Tricia will make a plan for us to deal with everything."

Brian kissed each sister goodbye. He and Grace put their coats on and ducked into the cold. After putting the Bible, letters, and scotch in the Saab's trunk, they drove away. Still annoyed, Grace reclined her seat and closed her eyes. In the angry quiet, Brian recounted flashes of the day's events during the hour-long ride home.

The burial in St. Peter's. The bitter cold and snow flurries. My seemingly wrong DNA test results. Going through the hope chest. It's interesting I never saw my birth certificate, nor my baptismal certificate. The false bottom! The antique mandolin. The old leather-bound German Bible. Her first letter. The letter Shawn found in the Book of

Revelation – my God, of all places for that to be! Everything Katrina went through, then her efforts to find me. I'm sure she must have thought I ignored her all these years. I can't even begin to believe I was born in Germany, given up, sent here to the States, and adopted. If all that's true, then the results of the DNA test were right. And to top off my day, Erick calls. That can mean only one thing. What lousy timing! Grace is going to have a fit.

CHAPTER TWO

Katrina's Letters

The mid-week drive south on the Garden State Parkway was faster than usual. For Grace it was a long day and her nagging myalgia was now accompanied by a severe migraine headache. Her silence on the drive home offered no consolation to Brian's emotional day.

It was 7 o'clock before they arrived in the village of Spring Lake. Once inside their classic Dutch colonial home, Grace quickly changed and went right to bed, without so much as a "Goodnight."

Brian stepped into the study to open three days' worth of mail. Once finished, he opened the old leather-covered Bible, looked at the family tree and reread the letters his birth mother sent to his parents.

In the first letter, postmarked in Rome in October of 1950, Katrina identified herself as their son's mother.

My child was born during the war. His grandparents received word that their son, a high-ranking soldier and the child's father, was killed in battle. As a single parent, I couldn't support the baby, so I gave him up for adoption.

Katrina wasn't specific with dates, the child's birthplace, or any other details in her letter to avoid suspicion. In another letter she explained she entered a cloistered convent after giving the child up for adoption. She eventually left and married a kind and gentle man who was formerly a priest. Brian sipped his scotch as he continued to read through his birth mother's letters to the O'Sullivans.

Before Christmas 1950, Katrina wrote:

My husband will be traveling to New York City for business meetings this coming spring, the week before Easter. I'd like to join him on the trip and visit you both. And with your permission, perhaps I may briefly see the child. I have no intention of announcing myself to him, but we have an old musical instrument from his grandfather that may be of interest to him later in life, especially if he should someday learn about his adoption. Surely a visit will calm my soul and reduce my anxiety, constant worries, and sorrows for the child.

Very sincerely yours,
Katrina Amorino-Luciano

P.S: With your permission, my husband and I also would like to make a small contribution toward a college fund for the child during our visit.

Brian saw that his mother, Sheila, kept penciled copies of her own notes sent in reply to Katrina. One acknowledged their willingness to have Katrina visit during a school week. In another, Sheila wrote:

Even though just eight years old, young Brian is tall for his age. He attends the local parochial school around the corner from our home in Astoria, Queens. He is bright and is a good student; he has an A in every subject of his schoolwork and aspect of his behavior. Brian shows a keen interest in his father's workbench and in picking at his father's guitar.

When Brian finished reading the exchanges between Sheila and Katrina, he thought more about his upbringing. *All my life I've been Joe and Sheila's kid. Learning I'm adopted doesn't change my childhood. And it doesn't change who I am now—who I've become. If Dad and Mom were still alive, I'd ask them why they kept all this from me. But they're both gone. And I suppose my birth mother is deceased as well. Well, I need to move forward with my life, and with this information. I'm German and Italian, like the DNA test showed. I'll need to look that over again tomorrow.*

He checked his voicemail before heading to bed. Most were brief, messages of consolation from fellow professors and a few people in the art business. But the last message, the one from Erick that arrived while he was at the Point, surprised him. He finished his scotch, shut off the office lamp, and headed to bed.

As he settled under the covers, Brian thought about flying into Amsterdam. *What could Erick want? Whatever it is, it can wait until morning; I need a good night's sleep. Grace won't take this trip well, especially with how she's been bugging me to retire from the university. I'll give him a call first thing tomorrow.*

Then his thoughts returned to his birth mother's letter.

CHAPTER THREE

The Message

The next morning, Brian woke still feeling tired. Sleep last night was uncomfortable. With so much on his mind, he never reached a deep sleep. He tried recalling a disturbing dream, but it disappeared quickly. He stood and stretched and looked out the bedroom window. It had snowed overnight. Enough to cover the grass but not enough to stick to pavement. Some early spring hyacinths were a few inches above the snow.

He sat in a small chair adjacent to his bed and reviewed all that had happened yesterday. Brian's heart still ached from his mother's passing and yesterday's incredible discovery of his adoption. He remained stunned at the revelations. He recalled every detail of Katrina's letters, especially those Shawn discovered while he was gone from the house. He wondered how it all happened. Learning he was adopted had cast a sudden and unexpected empty space in his life.

He then reached for his phone and listened again to Erick's message. The voice message was brief: "Hey Brian, catch the next flight to Amsterdam."

Brian replayed it several times just to listen to the tone of Erick's voice, which often revealed more than his words. Brian realized a second message had come in sometime overnight.

"Hey BJ, an interesting situation has developed and we need you here right away. It might be the breakthrough we've been seeking the last few years. Your presence here will make a difference. Call me when you wake up. We need to move quickly on this."

Brian had successfully concealed his role as an Interpol agent from Grace for the last twenty years. While he was being recruited, the lengthy position description explained why keeping a spouse in the dark was necessary. In fact, secrecy in all matters was a key condition of employment. Brian acknowledged this and faithfully kept Grace blind to his undercover activities. Secrecy was for her protection as well as his own maneuverability. Income from his secret line of employment was deposited directly into his private savings account in a small branch of the Staten Island Savings Bank near his mother's house.

Brian's role in Interpol was to use his knowledge as a history professor, and his degree and interest in art history, to help identify and recover missing art. He and Erick Schmidt had become acquainted at conference meetings at which lost art was discussed. Both were focused on identifying and recovering art stolen by Germany's Gestapo and SS during World War II. Eventually Erick, an Interpol agent living in Amsterdam, recommended Brian to the agency. After Brian became an agent, he was assigned to work with Erick. The two would meet in Europe sporadically. They never met on a regular schedule or in any set pattern. Brian would tell Grace he was attending an art conference, history conference, or a special meeting to support his academic responsibilities and position as a history and art-history expert.

On the occasions when real art exhibits were held, Brian would invite Grace to join him and attend. Side meetings during conferences and other visits with Erick always remained a secret. But in the past decade, the glamor of attending European meetings with Brian had worn off for Grace. She complained she found them boring, and they left her with little or nothing to do.

CHAPTER FOUR

The O'Sullivans

Brian's thoughts turned from Erick's message to his parents, Joe and Sheila O'Sullivan, whom he'd loved dearly. They'd been fun, warm, loving, hardworking... and very generous. He finished college without debt, and they'd even gifted him a sizeable down payment on his and Grace's first home.

Surely, I can still call them my parents. It's odd: I'm missing Dad even more now, with Mom gone.

Thinking of his parents, Brian lost track of his surroundings. His dad's life as a NY City firefighter was exemplary. Sadly, he smoked all his life and died from lung cancer in 1980. He was fifty-six. His mother, Sheila, was a small Irish-looking woman and the best mom a person could have. Her corned beef and peach-apple cobbler were extraordinary. But her best was the Irish soda bread. She'd make six loaves at a time to be given to family and friends and sometimes a few more for the children's school teachers. Sheila's death was from a stroke suffered while driving home from daily Mass in her old, blue 1972 Datsun 510 with 234,000 miles on it. The stroke happened on New Dorp Lane. It caused her to side-swipe three parked cars, then, careening off them, she ran head-on into a moving city bus.

The kettle's whistle finally brought him back to reality. He poured boiling water over the grounds in the French press and waited a few minutes for it to brew. It was 6 AM and Grace was still asleep. He opened the front door and reached for two daily newspapers. *The New York Times*, which he found lying atop the *Wall Street Journal*, was soaking wet from the snowfall. He returned to the kitchen, opened it along the counter to dry, then pressed and poured his coffee. Brian munched a piece of crusty Italian bread as he read. The date at the top of the front page of the *Journal* was Friday, March 9.

I wonder what's happened that Erick wants me there so quickly. I know he'll expect me to stay at least two weeks. Now is not the time for this. Between Grace's unhappiness and classes in session, it's just not a good time for an extended trip.

Brian had always excelled in school. A tenth-grade trip to the Metropolitan Museum of Art in Manhattan piqued his curiosity, and he developed a strong interest in art, which far exceeded his childhood desire to drive a fire truck like his dad.

BJ, as family and close friends often called him, majored in European history, and minored in art history at St Peter's College in Jersey City. At NYU in Manhattan, he earned dual master's degrees in European medieval history and European art history. He earned his doctorate in European history at Rutgers. There, he rose through the ranks and became a professor in the history department. Focusing on the European Middle Ages from 475 to 1500 A.D., from the Dark Ages to the Enlightened Age, he published several papers on the period and was considered an authority. After additional studies and another well-received paper, Brian found himself in a circle of society comprising academics, art historians, art dealers, and wealthy collectors. Despite the new social level brought by his work, he remained close to his parents, sisters, and nieces and nephews, seeing them as often as possible.

Brian eventually married Grace Daly. Grace was born east of Cork City in Tivoli where her parents owned and operated the quaint Belvedere Inn. After their untimely deaths in a car accident, Grace immigrated to the U.S. while still a teenager, and lived with her aunt and uncle in a large Irish community in Bay Ridge, Brooklyn.

In 1970, two days after McSorley's officially opened to women, Grace was there with former college friends, celebrating her birthday. She and Brian backed into each other in the crowded bar, spilling ale on her blouse and on his shirt. Both turned, ready for confrontation, but instead found themselves instantly attracted to each other. Grace reminded Brian of his mother, but her long flowing red hair made her appear much feistier. His tanned skin and dark hair reminded her of a movie star. Drawn to each other in an instant, they laughed and began dating days later. The short drive over the Verrazano Bridge to Bay Ridge proved convenient. They dated for three months before becoming engaged. Marriage followed almost as quickly. They rented a small house in Tottenville and, a year later, purchased an historic Dutch colonial.

Grace had worked for Catholic Charities in downtown Brooklyn after graduating from St. John's University. After they married, she left Catholic Charities to take a position as a social worker on the women's side at Mount Loretto. It was a good use of her education and an easy commute from nearby Tottenville. Their new home offered BJ easy access to his work at Rutgers, as well. As they had no children, Grace made herself available to travel to Europe with BJ. Unfortunately, Grace hadn't been able to get pregnant during the early years of their marriage. Specialists offered alternatives, but unfortunate circumstances prohibited her from carrying. Eventually Grace and Brian resolved themselves to the reality their nieces and nephews would be the children in their lives.

Two years later, Brian suggested they consider adoption, but Grace remained cool to the idea. Adoption became an ongoing issue between them for the next few years. Then one night, Grace eviscerated Brian in an argument over the subject, and they never again discussed adoption. But the argument had a massive impact on their relationship. Brian believed the argument changed her outlook on life and even how she felt towards him. He wondered why she was so resolute in her position.

Soon afterward, Grace again changed jobs to become a social worker at an elder-care home. BJ continued teaching and traveling to Europe. Over the next decade, his presence and stature in the art community grew, and he was recognized not just as an authority but as an expert. His trips to Europe became more frequent. Every so often, one of his trips came up at the last minute. Grace increasingly found her husband's "irregular meetings" annoying, even disturbing. And she wondered about them and about Brian's behavior while he was away.

Brian was halfway through the morning newspapers when he heard Grace coming from their bedroom. After a quiet and unsociable hello, she poured herself a cup of coffee, cut a stale seeded bagel, and put it in the toaster. Earlier, Brian had gone into the garage and called Erick. After learning more about what was happening, he called the airlines to schedule a flight to Amsterdam. He knew Grace wouldn't take this news well, but he had no choice.

He waited for her to sit and be settled before he broke the news. "Grace, something's come up and I'm needed in Amsterdam. Two pieces of art known to have been missing since World War II have recently been identified in a German soldier's journal that just turned up. I've been asked to research and validate the information and help to recover the two lost pieces of art."

"Oh? And why would *you* be involved in something like that? Here you go again, running off on short notice. When is this going to stop? I'm beginning to believe you've fallen in love with a woman over there. Maybe she comforts you better than I do. Maybe she's been able to give you a child. Is that it? Maybe you have several children?"

"Come on, Grace, you know it's nothing like that."

She retrieved her toasted bagel and brought it to the island.

"I've reached a point in our marriage where I just don't know anymore. Frankly, I don't even care anymore. But why does it have to be you who runs to Europe all the time? So many other people are art historians who can, as you say, 'validate a painting' or recover lost art. Why must it be you?"

"Grace, you know my position is very respected. I'll do what needs to be done and be back as soon as possible."

"Let me remind you, the last time you left you were supposed to be gone for a week. It became two weeks, and then three. And it was very upsetting when I couldn't reach you because you claimed you lost your phone. Make this the last time you leave, Brian. If you're not back in a week, maybe I'll go take my own trip."

She slowly buttered her bagel, then looked up at him.

"Listen, you've talked about retiring, Brian. Promise me this will be your last trip."

Brian nodded. "It's on my radar, Gracie. I should be able to retire in six months, before the fall semester begins. But right now, I can't make any promises. I need to fly out tonight. I have a car picking me up and taking me to Newark later this afternoon."

"Brian, I'm serious. This is it. Make this your last business trip to an art conference, or to do this 'art validation' stuff, or I'm leaving you. I swear, you'll come back, and my things will be gone. Or maybe I'll stay here and just get rid of all your things."

She started crying. "If you really love me, Brian, you'll call whomever you must and submit your retirement papers. Get it done today before you leave. Let me know you won't be going back to Europe again."

Still crying, she stood and left the room, her bagel uneaten.

Brian was conflicted. Home life had become increasingly difficult over the last ten years. He thought perhaps it was just part of growing older, or maybe it's what happened when marriages lose their spark. He saw Grace's wavering moods and depression had worsened. He wondered whether recent changes in her antidepressants were working – or if she was even taking the pills. Perhaps his mother's sudden death had intensified her irritability this morning, since the two of them had generally spent a fair amount of time together.

Brian went upstairs to pack. He thought about his daily work as a professor. It was fresh and stimulating. His work with Interpol was even more interesting and exciting. *Home life with Grace isn't anything near what it used to be. When was the last time we made love?* He couldn't remember. The spark was indeed gone.

The limo pulled up to Brian's house right at 3. His cold, meaningless goodbye hug with Grace left them both feeling sad and empty.

The past two days hadn't been easy for Brian – first the death of his mother, then the revelation about being adopted. Grace's threat certainly didn't make him feel any better.

If only she understood. This will be the last time. When I return, I'll be able to let her know what I've really been up to these past twenty years. Then maybe she'll understand. But for now, my work with Interpol must remain a secret.

He made another call to Erick during the ride up the Garden State Parkway and New Jersey Turnpike to the airport.

Erick shared more details. The case they'd been working on for the last few years was not just warm, it was now hot. "We have two parts to this lead. Initially, I'd been looking through old records found in an apartment in Munich a year ago. The records discuss how the Nazis would sell or trade paintings and sculptures they took from Jews for those favored by Hitler such as works by Johannes Vermeer. They hoped to have them placed in the *Führermuseum* Hitler was preparing.

"I decided to have Nina compare the latest information recently uncovered against some old files. It wasn't long before she found a match. What's the American phrase? Finding a needle in a haystack? It was a hunch and a long shot. With this luck, I should be taking a chance on the Irish Sweepstakes—if it was still running.

"The persistent rumor about Hitler's gifting art to Generalissimo Franco is a hot topic again in many art circles. In the last year, the focus has been on two paintings from a high-end home in Paris owned by Jews, right on the Avenue des Champs-Élysées. Just before the Germans entered Paris and marched to the Arc de Triomphe, the SS and Gestapo went through every house along that street to sweep for sharpshooters. Rumor has it that these two paintings, owned by the Lieberman family, were confiscated by the Gestapo. But they somehow never made it back to the salt mine in Altaussee, Austria, near Hitler's hometown of Linz, which is where he planned for the massive *Führermuseum* to be built. Instead, it was decided they'd be given to Franco in Spain. So, one or more people had to bring them down to where Franco was living at the time."

"Fascinating! Tell me more."

"The second part of the lead is a diary we've acquired. I'll tell you more when you arrive, and I'll share those details then. By the way, how is Gracie? Was she upset with your sudden leaving?"

"Upset would be an understatement. She wasn't at all pleased with my flying off to Europe again. It's been a rough few days on this side of the pond. You had no way to know, but my mother died earlier this week – we buried her yesterday."

"Oh, sorry to hear that, BJ. Deeply sorry."

"There's more. But I'll share it when I get there."

"Okay. I'll see you as you exit customs."

CHAPTER FIVE

Amsterdam

Brian took the 8:30 PM flight from Newark and arrived in Amsterdam the next morning. His transit through customs was quick.

The female agent who'd seen him on his last arrival recognized him and greeted him with a smile. Five minutes later, they were in Erick's old Benz, heading to his place.

"Good to see you, BJ."

Brian ignored the greeting. "This better be good. It's only been five weeks since I left you."

"I'm sorry about your mom's passing. What happened? You never mentioned she was ill. Was her death unexpected?"

"She had a stroke while driving. Sideswiped three cars on a busy street then hit a city bus head-on. The EMTs who arrived on the scene said the stroke killed her—she was dead before hitting the bus."

Erick's face paled. "I'm so sorry to hear that. How are your sisters taking it?"

"The twins are upset with Shawn and me. They thought Mom was too old to be driving. Shawn and I advocated for her independence. Mom was sharp, conversed well, and showed few signs of being ninety-four. She visited my father's grave two or three times a week in her old junk of a car."

"That's too bad, BJ. And no doubt Grace is upset about your coming here again. It's unfortunate. Your life at home has to be uncomfortable."

"Between the frequency of my visits this past year and my having to stay weeks beyond my initial plans, she's convinced I've got a second family in Europe. So, my friend, tell me what's so important you had to have me return so quickly?"

"An old German woman around seventy years old visited an antiques dealer in Leipzig three weeks ago. She identified herself as Elsa and told an interesting story. She claimed her German-Russian mother cooked for the Nazis in the early nineteen-forties inside the Bendlerblock building, where several departments of the German Wehrmacht, including the Abwehr intelligence agency, had been headquartered since 1938. It's also where a group of German officers attempted to kill Hitler in July of 1944. She said her mother also worked twice a week as a cook in Hitler's *Führerbunker*.

"She went on to say when the Russians entered Berlin in the Battle of Berlin in the last days of the war, Nazi officers evacuated the Bendlerblock building and scattered. Her mother stayed behind, where she was subsequently discovered, held, and interrogated by the Russians. Her mother stayed on as head cook at the facility because she could speak Russian, the language of her grandfather.

"Six weeks ago, her mother was dying and revealed to Elsa that she had found the diary of an SS Nazi officer who left the building in a hurry, and she'd kept it hidden among her things since the war ended. Only in her last days did she feel it was safe to reveal the existence of the diary, hoping it might be worth something and benefit her daughter. The mother, whose name was Hilda, died a few days later. Elsa waited a week, then went to the antiques dealer, hoping to sell the diary.

"Fortunately for us, the antique dealer in Leipzig who made the purchase is an old Interpol agent named Kristofer Bronn, who worked with my father, Gunter, at Interpol after the war. Bronn was forced to retire a dozen years ago—I'll explain why later. Kristofer looked the diary over carefully and offered the woman a hundred Euros. She was happy and took the money. Kristofer called me last week and I drove to Leipzig several days ago to pick it up. He wanted five hundred Euros claiming it contains particularly valuable information. I told him we could do two fifty now and, provided it can be validated as original and we agree there's value, we'd spring for the difference."

"So, is the diary genuine?"

"I had Nina test the ink and paper. We're confident we have a genuine World War II-era diary on our hands. I've looked it over closely, page by page. The entries are extremely orderly and full of references. It begins with the SS soldier's reactions to his training at the SS officer school in Bad Tölz. His first post-training entry is about being selected to participate in Kristallnacht. Additional entries focus on activities with the Wehrmacht's construction arm, run by Organisation Todt, helping to build Nazi camps. He even got to meet Fritz Todt.

"It looks like he was promoted numerous times along the way. He briefly ran a death camp, where he made horrific 'improvements' by injecting oxygen into the cremation furnaces, and later provided strategic military guidance to senior Wehrmacht field generals in Germany. He even met with Kesserling in Italy to discuss the German defensive lines set up to hold back the advancing U.S. 5th Army. And get this: His last entry says,

'Headed to the Führerbunker for the extraction. The Plan needs to work. Proud to be the Chosen One.' The date of his last entry was April 30, 1945.

"But here's the specific reason I called you. Several entries are of interest to our unit's search for missing World War II art pieces. They suggest the SS soldier who wrote the diary was given a special assignment to bring two pieces of art to Spain. From the entry, it looks like Hitler was gifting them to Generalissimo Franco. At the time, Spain was neutral but leaned toward the Axis Powers. Politically, Hitler wanted Franco to remain a friend, so he was sending the valuable gifts to ensure that friendship. The diary indicates the officer was to pick up the paintings in Paris, from the Gestapo who'd taken them from a wealthy Jewish family. He was to meet another officer there, then bring the pieces to southern Spain. It also appears the person in southern never showed and so he carefully hid them and waited for additional orders.

"Later, he writes, 'The art is now safe and hidden. I stayed until the arch and the ceiling were repaired, then I eliminated all the workers on the project. Other than this diary and my radio message back to Berlin, there is no record of the location. The Spanish had the right idea with the Alhambra Decree chasing all Jews from Spain in 1492.'"

"Very interesting, Erick. So have you figured out where this art might be?"

"Right now, my first guess is the Alhambra, an old fortress from when the Moors had full control of Andalusia in the twelve hundreds and thirteen hundreds."

"Who else knows about this diary?"

"Nina, of course, because she assessed the paper and ink. She's fluent in German and is reading it 'as is.' "

"Anyone else?"

Erick gave a nod. "I ran the story about the diary up the ladder to Pieter Van Deusen. He knows Bronn. He told me to call Wilhelm Mueller, who replaced Hobson."

"Yes, What a shame about John. He was always a good boss. Damned pancreatic cancer."

"Mueller and I spoke about the diary. He was intrigued and asked for a copy. Nina was just finishing an English translation. When I finished reading it, I brought a copy to Mueller. The next day he expressed significant interest in supporting our efforts to find the art, and immediately approved my suggestion for a trip to Spain. Yesterday he said he's having the diary translated into Italian for two other agents who'll be joining us in the investigation."

Brian's eyebrows rose. "Really? That's a surprise. Who are these Italian agents? Do you know them?"

"Yes. Uh, well, I know *of* them. Paolo Luzzi and Antonio Gozzo. Both have been in Interpol for over twenty years and have been partners most of that time. But they've got rather an interesting reputation."

"How's that?"

"Some folks have wondered about them, including Bronn, who sold me the diary."

"Wondered what?" Brian pressed.

"Some in the agency believe they're dirty and have done side deals."

"Side deals?"

"Yes. Bronn believes they've stolen and then sold some of the art they've recovered."

"I see. That twist complicates things. Did you share with Mueller your hypothesis on where the art might be?"

"Not yet. Well, kind of. I told him the art might be in southern Spain. But that's all I've said. Nina has a few ideas herself. I thought it'd be best if we discussed where it might be hidden."

"Good. What's our next step? And when do we start?"

"I asked Nina to make another copy of the English translation for you. When we get to my place, you can take a day to go over it and reach your own conclusions. Maybe you can use your old Irish intuition and come up with the city and exact location of the art. But the diary implies it's well hidden and won't be easy to find."

"Good work, Erick. There's more to tell about my 'Irish intuition,' but right now I need a little shuteye. I've been finding it getting harder to sleep on these overnight flights. I'm physically exhausted, not to mention emotionally shot. I'll head right to bed when we get to your place."

"Nina will be by later. You'll want to hear what she has to say about the diary. She has good insight as to where to start. She made a list of churches, including some that were formerly mosques in Andalusia's largest cities."

Brian sighed. "That's great, but right now, I need sleep. Have her come tomorrow morning."

Erick pulled up to his place and, after moving three misplaced bicycles, parked out front. Brian grabbed his suitcase and, using the spare key Erick gave him, went inside. He started up the steep, narrow stairs to the second-floor spare bedroom when Erick called to him, saying to use the downstairs bedroom during this visit. Brian came back down the few steps and went in the direction Erick indicated. He pulled the window shade, took off his shoes, and collapsed atop the bed's plain grey comforter. He was asleep in moments.

In the kitchen, Erick called Nina to ask her to hold off on her visit but got no answer.

Twenty minutes later, the doorbell rang.

Getting no response, Nina knocked at the front door and, finding it not completely closed, let herself in. "Hello? Erick? It's Nina. You asked me to come by. Erick? Are you home?"

Erick tugged the pull chain and exited the half bathroom. "Hi, Nina, I tried calling you earlier. BJ's had a tough week. His mother died unexpectedly and was buried two days ago. He's sound asleep. You'll need to come back tomorrow morning .We can brief him on all your findings then."

"I'm sorry, Erick. I left my apartment early and went shopping before coming here. While I was out, I realized I left my phone at my apartment."

"No worries."

"I'll leave the English translation here now and I'll see you in the morning. By the way, I brought Leo some cat treats."

"Thanks, Nina. As usual, he's hiding. If he shows himself, I'll give him the treats and mention they were from you."

Nina grinned. "Sounds good. Take care, Erick. See you tomorrow."

Erick went into the pantry just off the kitchen to put away the cat treats as Nina made her way toward the front door. She scanned his living room and foyer walls before leaving, shaking her head in disbelief. *Erick's flat is so plain. How can an art expert have plain white walls, absent of any hanging art?*

Just then, as she went to step out the open front door, Erick's beautiful Persian cat came running toward her. The regal cat stopped and looked up at Nina, purring. As she bent down to greet the silken-haired animal, it bolted out the open door and down the street. Nina immediately ran outside and looked around, but she couldn't see the Persian anywhere.

Oh, no! What do I tell Erick?

CHAPTER SIX

Miss von Scholz

Nina von Scholz, Interpol's youngest art and art-history expert, grew up in southern Germany in the town of Ravensburg. Her parents were old enough to have seen their small industrial town aggressively bombed by Americans during World War II. Nina's father, Rolf, followed in his father-in-law's footsteps, becoming a skilled machinist and helping to rebuild the industrial town's reputation to revive the area's economy. Her mother, Greta, worked as a nurse at the nearby Friedrichshafen Hospital, where Rolf's father had been the administrator in the 1930s and 1940s. A substantial inheritance on her mother's side allowed Nina to grow up privileged and receive an outstanding education.

Nina took an early interest in art, and her parents supported her request to attend college in England, where she studied art history at Oxford and at the Royal College of Art. Her studies there and her final research paper focused on items stolen by Nazis during the war and what was found—including art recovered by the American team of soldiers called the Monument Men.

Upon graduating and returning to Germany, Nina worked in a Munich art gallery for a dozen years before being recommended to Interpol by a friend of the family. Recognizing her talent, they quickly recruited her and made a handsome offer, which she accepted. She was delighted to learn about the research work accomplished by the unit to which she would be assigned. They were focused on recovering art stolen by Germany and its Axis allies during World War II. It was the same subject she'd written about in her final college paper.

Her primary responsibilities at Interpol were to research and catalogue all paintings above a certain value known to have been owned by families of any nationality prior to the war, and which remained missing. But unlike her research efforts in college, she now had financial resources and a generous budget to conduct detailed investigations. Nina's work required her to travel often, to follow and evaluate leads. Besides the work itself, she especially loved when her teammate agent Brian O'Sullivan came to town.

Brian represented many things to Nina. She found his life experience, his professorship, his international status, and his ability to engage in high society highly attractive. She also found him personally attractive. Although old enough to be her father, there was something unique about his good looks: his darker skin color which always seemed tanned, his almost-black hair and, most especially, his piercing blue eyes. On more than one occasion, in the privacy of her bedroom, she thought about being with him sexually.

***

Keeping the door open with her briefcase, Nina returned inside. Erick came to the door, wondering why she was coming back into the apartment.

"Gosh, Erick!" Nina exclaimed, flustered. "I opened the door to leave, and your cat came up to rub against my leg. It purred and looked at me, then ran outside, like it was afraid of me. I'm so sorry! What should I do?"

Erick waved away her fretting. "It's okay. It's not the first time Leo's bolted like that. Let me go next door and tell my neighbor the cat is out. Solmaz cat-sits for him when I'm gone more than two days. He likes her and will come back into the house for her. They get along great—I think it's something to do with their Persian heritage!"

"By the way, Erick, why do you call your cat 'Leo'?"

"Besides art, I'm a fan of Greek history. Leo's full name is Leonidas."

"Gosh! Your interests always surprise me. But, my friend, while I have the chance, I must tell you, the inside of your house is so plain. How can you be an art expert and have nothing hanging on your walls? It's a *non sequitur.*" Not waiting for an answer, she shrugged. "I'll see you tomorrow."

Erick smiled. As Nina departed, he walked next door and knocked at Solie's door. He told her the cat had just run outside.

"No problem. I'm sure he'll come to my door within the hour."

"Solie, I need to pick up a few things at the market and will be back in twenty minutes."

"Oh, look, Erick! Here she comes now. Come here, sweetheart!"

The cat looked up and ran straight into the woman's house.

Erick looked on in amazement. "Darn, how did you do that, Solie? Maybe you should keep him."

"*Him?* Erick, don't you know? Your Leo is a *she.* Ah! Maybe that's been your problem all along. She resents her name. I call her 'Bashful' when we're together. She likes that."

"I had no clue, Solie. But I've never been able to figure out women! You're all much too complicated for me."

CHAPTER SEVEN

Morning Coffee

Erick rose earlier than usual the following morning. He realized he'd forgotten to pick up coffee for his French press. He put on his coat and headed to the store.

It was a pleasantly brisk morning for the time of year. His brief walk took him beside Vondelpark, where the green tips of tulip plants were just emerging from the dark earth. After a quick hello with the shopkeeper, he picked up a pound of dark-roasted Colombian coffee, ground for a French press, along with two Irish-style breakfast sandwiches, and a quart of orange juice.

On arriving back at the house, he found his front door closed but unlocked. Inside, three fragrant coffees and sweet pastries waited on the counter. Several loaves of sliced French bread sat beside them, and Nina stood at the stove. .

"Good morning, Erick. As you can see, I'm taking you up on your month-old challenge to 'someday cook at your place.' I decided to make a delicious breakfast for you and Brian. He let me in then jumped in the shower. You have syrup, right?"

"Nina, you seem awfully full of energy! It's a bit early for you, isn't it? And yes, the syrup is in the pantry."

"I can't wait to tell Brian what I've discovered in the diary."

As if on cue, Brian emerged from the bathroom, a towel tucked around his waist, momentarily forgetting Nina was present. The image of Brian in that towel reminded her of Sean Connery in an old James Bond movie. She was delighted and a bit aroused, seeing him like that.

"Good morning again, Nina. It smells good in here. What are you making for breakfast?"

"It's your favorite: French toast and I'm using real French bread."

He smiled. "Perfect!"

Erick stowed his just-purchased bag of ground coffee in the refrigerator, then grabbed the maple syrup from the pantry.

"Good morning, BJ. I hope you're well rested by now."

"I am."

Brian finished dressing, then returned to the kitchen for his favorite breakfast. *She is such a sweet young lady to remember my preferences.*

He poured a cup of coffee and sat just as Nina set a hot serving of French toast in front of him.

"Nina, that looks delicious." He inhaled deeply. "I can smell the cinnamon and vanilla. Thanks! Let's enjoy our breakfast, then we can get into the reason I'm here. I can't stay in Europe long. Grace isn't happy. My trips have become a huge issue recently, and she's pressing me to retire. But let me put that aside for now; I'll tell you both what's happened in the last few days back home in New Jersey.

"After my mother's burial, my sisters and I headed back to her house for brunch, and to go through some of her things. We started with the hope chest. My sisters parsed through the memorabilia, finding birth and baptismal certificates and a ton of old black-and-white photos that never got put into albums. We even found an old Brownie camera with a roll of partially exposed film in it. God only knows what's on it!

"Meanwhile, one of my sisters went to the kitchen for a moment and brought back mom's unopened mail. One item was addressed to me. It was the results from one of those new DNA tests. I opened the envelope and read the contents. It said I was part German and part Italian, and a few other things, including four percent Jewish. We all laughed at the obvious mistake made by the company. My mother always said I was 'dark Irish' with a lineage back to the days when the Spanish Armada crashed off the Irish coast. So, my DNA results seemed to be mistaken.

"We continued going through her hope chest, but never found my birth certificate. When the hope chest was almost empty, my sister noticed the wood on the bottom moved and tilted. The chest had a false bottom. We got a serrated knife, shoved it down the side, and pulled up. The knife grabbed the edge of the thin lauan plywood, and I was able to pull it up.

"Underneath was an old mandolin dating back to the late eighteen hundreds and a box containing an incredibly old German Bible. The inscription was in gold leaf, embossed on the leather cover. Translated into English it read, 'Our Lutheran Family Bible.'

"We were all stumped, asking ourselves where these items could have come from. My sister opened the Bible and inside the cover was a folded page with the drawing of a huge family tree. Translated, it said something like, 'The von Richter Family History, the Duchy and Kingdom of Wurttemberg, Since 1265.' We wondered what it was doing in our mother's hope chest.

"Shawn refolded the family tree page, turned to the next page, and found an envelope addressed to me in beautiful script handwriting. In the envelope was a letter from an Italian woman named Katrina Amorino-Luciano. She began by apologizing for what she was about to tell me. She wrote that she loved me very much but conditions in Italy during the war were extremely difficult. She said she had me out of wedlock and, sadly, gave me up as an eight-month-old infant. I was sent from Italy to the United States for my protection – and a better life. Subsequently, I was adopted and raised by the O'Sullivan family in Astoria, Queens, as Brian O'Sullivan.

"She went on to explain how sad she was to have given me up. She said had she been more patient and trusting in God's providence, she could have kept me with her. She felt her impetuous decision was the biggest mistake of her life—a pain she carried every day.

"It was shocking to discover that my O'Sullivan parents were not my natural family, and instead, I'd been brought up by people who adopted me. I felt sad and betrayed with this new truth. I went for a drive to clear my head, and when I returned, there was worse news. My birth mother had written several additional pages of what had happened to her. She began with how she fell in love with a handsome young German skier and left her nursing job in the Italian Alps to go live with him in Friedrichshafen, Germany.

"The guy, Karl von Richter, was drafted into the SS before she arrived at his home in Langenargen—a small hamlet on Lake Constance. His parents had connections and she landed a nursing job in Friedrichshafen. He wrote to her saying he was involved in Kristallnacht. Later he got involved in constructing the death camps and took on several special Nazi assignments.

"Katrina spoke highly of Karl's mother, an Italian woman, and she learned of Karl's Nazi activities from his father, who worked in a factory.

"Uh, Nina, is the French toast burning?"

"Oops. Sorry!" She turned back toward the stove and flipped the darkening slices. "You've completely captured my attention with this story, Brian."

"One night, Karl unexpectedly returned home to Langenargen, drunk and high on amphetamines," Brian continued. "He raped Katrina. Nine months later, I was born. Eight months after that, she left her administrative job and returned to her parents' home in Lecco, Italy. Keep in mind, this was while the war is going on, and she had a ton of courage to drive across the Alps – even in the springtime, because sudden snows can be so unpredictable.

"A week after she arrived home, she gave me up to a priest in Brescia with the last name DiBotticino. Through connections, they shipped me off to New York City.

"I know from our family history that my parents, the O'Sullivans, had tried to have a child for some time. What I didn't know was they'd applied for an adoption through Catholic Charities. They'd just figured she couldn't get pregnant. Besides Katrina's letters, my mother Sheila also left a note in the Bible. Apparently, two months before I arrived in the States, Mom found out she was pregnant with the twins. Then a few years later, her pregnancy with Shawn was another surprise."

"Oh my God, Brian! You learned all this just a few days ago?"

He nodded. "That's what kept me awake on the plane ride here. It's why I've been so tired. I can't get over what this woman, Katrina – my real mother – went through."

"BJ, that's quite a story. Nina, would you pass me the syrup?"

"Erick! You're so cold at times."

"Sorry if I appear that way, but of course I care. What's happened is a terrible thing—but please, I just need the syrup."

"This is unbelievable, Brian. I feel so sorry for you and for Katrina." Nina dabbed at her eyes. "You have me in tears. Your sisters must be upset, too."

"I'm not finished, Nina. Katrina's story goes on. When she gave me up to the priest to be sent to the United States, she said goodbye to her parents in Lecco and, with the priest's permission, left to join a convent in southern Italy.

"Katrina was deathly afraid of Karl. She said she'd expected a loving and warm relationship with him—that's why she moved to his house. But she said he became radicalized with all of Hitler's propaganda in the SS Officer Training School in Bad Tölz. As an SS soldier, he focused more on killing Jews than fighting in the war. To get as far away as she could, she entered a convent in Bernalda, in the province of Basilicata, where her mother's cousin was the Mother Superior.

"As the war ended, Karl finished an assignment in Berlin and tried to find her. In Rome, he found the priest who shipped me to the U.S. By then, the priest was a cardinal in the Vatican. Karl ended up killing him—his name was Giovanni Cardinal DiBotticino. Before killing him, Karl learned from the cardinal that my birth mother, Katrina, was hiding in the Bernalda convent.

"Oh my God! No! He's going to find her!"

"A week later, Karl made his way to the convent, gained entry by lying to a nun, and then confronted Katrina. There was a heated exchange of words. Katrina told Karl off. She also told Karl that he was not Otto von Richter's son. It was a secret told to Katrina by Karl's mother, Valentina – who would have been her mother-in-law had she and Karl married. The secret Valentina told Katrina meant Karl was three-fourths Jewish. In that heated exchange, Karl became terribly upset, believing Katrina was lying and had hidden me somewhere in the convent. He was shouting and openly threatened to kill a few nuns until she told the truth about where I was. Then unexpectedly, a small nun whose job was to answer the front door of the convent, reached for a shotgun hidden in a closet to shoot Karl. The nun shot him in the convent's foyer, killing him instantly."

"Oh my God! Brian! What you're telling us… your real father was killed right in front of your birth mother! It's an incredible story. Erick, pass me some tissues, please."

"BJ, are you okay, mate? This is some heavy stuff you're telling us!"

"I'm okay. But I keep going over it in my head."

"Do you want to take a break?"

Brian shook his head. He took a sip of his coffee. "My mother, Katrina, later wrote the extra pages so I'd know the whole story. There are more details, and marital issues between Karl's parents, I haven't told you. Katrina undoubtedly suffered emotionally from all her experiences."

"Do you know what became of her?"

"Yes and no. A priest at the parish in Bernalda oversaw the church and convent. He was a kind man, but not cut out to be a priest. After Karl was shot, Katrina and that priest, Luca Luciano, began getting serious about each other. They each eventually left religious life and got married."

"Wow! And then what, Brian? Do you know any more?"

"Katrina wrote that Luca entered the wine business and did well. In the last part, she wrote they moved to Positano. Then they moved to the west side of the Sorrento peninsula. A few years passed and Katrina grew heart-sick about having given me up. Luca financially supported her efforts to find me. An old connection inside the Vatican put her in touch with a priest in the New York Archdiocese. She learned the details of my adoption, wrote to my parents in late nineteen fifty and flew to New York to visit the next spring. I was eight years old at the time. I remember she came to our house one day, just before Easter. She brought us cookies and had the most beautiful blue eyes."

"Just like yours, Brian. You have the most beautiful, sparkling blue eyes," Nina observed. "She must have been a beautiful-looking woman too—it's probably why you're so handsome."

He blushed through his dark complexion.

"By then, Luca had become remarkably successful. He gave my parents a huge sum of money for my education and to buy themselves a house in the country—which they did when they moved from Astoria to Staten Island."

He pulled the letter from his pocket and unfolded it.

"The last thing Katrina wrote was this:

'Son, when you learn about these things, please come find me. Luca and I now are financially very well off, and you deserve a large share of what we have. I've asked your adoptive mother to let you know about all of this when you are between 40 to 50 years old. That will be time enough for you to understand and then come find me. There's something else waiting for you, too. Love, your mother, Katrina'

"The last part she wrote absolutely crushed me. Imagine, she's been waiting all these years for me to find her. She must think I don't love her or am angry with her. Here I am turning seventy-one this coming summer. I feel so bad. And of course, I feel bad for her, too. She must think I've ignored her all these years. God only knows if she's even still alive."

"Oh, Brian. That's so sad!" Nina got up and gave Brian, still seated, a hug.

"BJ, my good friend, it's no wonder you're exhausted. You just described an incredible sequence of events that would break most people. Learning of being adopted is never easy, but learning about the challenges your birth mother faced brings your situation up two or three levels. What an incredibly strong woman she must have been to endure what she did!"

"Brian, do you know how old she was when she had you?" Nina asked. "Maybe she's still alive?"

"I have no idea how old she was, whether she's still alive, or where she could be if she *is* still alive. I have some information about the wine business she and Luca owned. Katrina wrote her letter, and most of the addendum, on onionskin paper. But the last two pages of the addendum were written on letterhead with the name of the wine export company Luca ran. It was someplace in Positano and then moved. On the very last page, directly under her signature, she put one thing that's puzzling. It's a set of numbers I've memorized: 10-28-14-16-18-0. If I had to guess, I'd assume it's a code, a bank-vault combination, or a combination lock of some sort."

"Searching for your mother won't be easy after all these years. But it sure beats looking for lost art."

Erick stood and turned to Nina. "Nice job on breakfast. I'd like you to use the rest of today researching the company Brian thinks is the link to Katrina and Luca's wine business. With luck, we'll help BJ find a link to his past. I suggest we reconvene early tomorrow morning and discuss where Nina's investigations will lead us. Tomorrow will be a busy day."

"Thanks, Erick. Nina, the company is Luciano Wine Exports, initially based in Positano. If it grew and needed a larger warehouse, the company might have moved to Naples or even north to Rome if Luca began traveling internationally."

"I'm on it, Brian. I'll work on this now. When we meet tomorrow, I'll review the details of the SS soldier's diary with you. One entry might lead us to a few possible locations in Spain."

"Thanks Nina. Erick, I'm headed out to the park to catch a little sun.

Hopefully I'll screw my head back on straight and walk off that delicious breakfast." He patted his midsection.

"Brian, you hardly ate while you were talking."

"The little I had was tasty, thank you. Maybe we all can have dinner together tonight?"

Brian left and headed to Vondelpark, a few blocks from Erick's apartment on Johannes Verhulststraat. Early tulips were already colorful in a few places. The spring weather in Amsterdam was warmer than expected and he'd brought all the wrong clothing. The sky was clear and deep blue. It reminded him of the lady with the blue eyes and how pretty she was. And then he remembered she was his real mother.

Dinner for three never materialized that night. Erick remembered he had a date with his boyfriend. And Brian, still tired, opted for an early night's sleep.

Their ditching her left Nina disappointed. That afternoon she'd made progress learning about the Luciano Wine Exporting Company and wanted to share it with Brian. Saddened about dinner, she made a Bibb lettuce salad for herself. She read a bit, set the alarm, and fell asleep to pleasurable thoughts about Brian.

CHAPTER EIGHT

The Revelation

The next morning, Nina arrived early at Erick's, again riding her bicycle. She put down the kickstand and after locking the wheel to the frame, approached his front step. He and Solie were speaking on the steps next door.

"Really, Erick? Your request is a surprise, and I'll need to think about it. And you realize, if I take Leo, there'll be no women left in your life."

Erick gave her a coy look. "Solie, you already know that would be okay with me. The only woman I ever fell for was years ago. I was in the seventh grade when a girl named Greta grabbed my attention. But then in high school, I awoke to a new way of thinking. You understand where I'm coming from, right?"

"Of course. As for taking Bashful permanently, I need some time to think it through. Wait! Here's an idea. Perhaps you can remain a good uncle and provide a little something, like a small monthly allowance for her? The commitment also would help you remain emotionally attached."

"That's a great idea! It's a deal. I'll give you monthly cat support. It'll be enough for a full food allowance for Leo—uh, I mean Bashful."

"Okay, Erik. I have commitments today and tomorrow morning, so I can take Bashful later tomorrow. She'll be a wonderful companion. Thank you! You're really a wonderful and caring guy with a big heart."

Having overheard the exchange, Nina smiled. She made her way up the steps and continued in through the apartment's partially open door. She found Brian seated at the table and greeted him with a light kiss on the cheek. *Gosh, he looks great this morning. He's shaved and he smells good.*

Her kiss surprised Brian, but he enjoyed the affectionate attention. *The way things have been, I needed that.*

"Good morning, Nina. How are you this morning?"

"I'm well. I have lots to tell you."

A moment later Erick came back inside, carrying Leo and looking gloomy.

"Are you okay? You look kind of down."

"I'm a bit sad. I know it'll be best to give Leo to Solie, but I'll miss him—I mean her."

"Erick, chin up. I'm sure Solie will let you visit whenever you'd like."

He poured a cup of coffee and returned to the table. "BJ, can I top off your cup?"

"Sure. Erick. Maybe you can make some toast and more coffee for all of us, and we can chat while it's brewing."

"BJ, I told you I set up a meeting for us today at noon with our new boss, Wilhelm Mueller. He texted me a minute ago. He wants us to come in at one instead. That gives us extra time to go over Nina's findings before we all leave for our meeting. Nina, you still plan to come with us, right?"

"Absolutely. When I went home yesterday, I started investigating the Luciano Wine Export Company. And Brian, I thought more about your story and made notes. What you said about Katrina caught my attention. I looked through that soldier's diary again, page by page. I found many similarities to the story you told us about your birth mother and the diary in our possession."

"Really? Like what?"

"Several instances in your story about Katrina and Karl von Richter match with the diary."

Concerned and feeling BJ's emotions were still fragile, Erick cleared his throat and gave her a direct look, attempting to pause her speculation. When she continued, he spoke up.

"Nina, I know you think the world of BJ, but perhaps your imagination is running away with you on this. There must be a thousand German SS soldiers whose service responsibilities line up with that diary at one point or another during the war. You do realize that, right?"

She fired a glare in his direction. "Erick, I understand your point, and your concern for Brian, but the similarities kept me up half the night. Let me go over a short set of entries that make my case. Here's the first one: 'Enjoyed the training, much longer than expected. Off to cause trouble for the Jews. Missing K but duty calls.' "

"That means nothing."

"Well, the next entry says, 'Helped Eicke design some improvements at the concentration camps using oxygen to enrich the flames like we did at the factory.' "

Erick shrugged. "Where's the coincidence in that comment?"

"Brian told us Katrina's letter talked about how Karl and his father worked in a foundry."

"Okay, go on."

"The next one, dated December 23, 1941, says, 'Quick trip to Italy. Stopping to see Katrina. How long has it been?'

"Right after that, in the next page, he writes, 'Last night was a huge disappointment. Why is she suddenly a bitch?'

"These last two entries clearly point to the possibility that the diary in our possession is the diary of the soldier who was with a woman named Katrina. While the next entry does not relate to Katrina, it's the reason we are here this morning. 'Headed to see General Franco and deliver two of Der Fuhrer's newly acquired art pieces to keep his ally happy. Haven't worked with Hockemeier since Kristallnacht. Should be fun to catch up.'

"And then, a few days later, he writes: 'Hockemeier a no show. Will get it done. Like Fritz Todt's tunnel project, I'll eliminate the workers to limit knowledge of the location of these paintings. They may be worth a million Reichsmarks or more. I need to remember this place. So many colorful columns and arches. It's confusing. But that will keep them hidden.'

"On the next page the next entry says: 'Finally complete. Art is safely hidden. Ceiling repaired. Eliminated all workers. No record of location except this diary and these words as a clue: "Look up! Der Fuhrer checkmates Franco in the uniquely colorful arch." ' "

"Then he added, 'The Spanish had the right idea with the Alhambra Decree chasing all Jews from Spain in 1492.'

"The next one, several pages further, on is one of the longest entries. It shows what appears to be a change of heart by the diary's author. He writes: 'Implementing the Fuhrer's Final Solution is not always easy. The smell of burning flesh is nasty. The bodies keep piling up too quickly. Shooting and burying the bodies is the fastest way to deal with the carnage. But seeing Ruth, my first love in her nakedness with the other women, then seeing her being shot and falling into a ditch, has continued to bother me. It's unexpected. I need a change from here. Perhaps a quick stop in Friedrichshafen and Langenargen. I'm sure Mother, Father, and Katrina will greet me as a hero.' "

"Nina, I see now where you're going with these entries you've collected," Brian said. "It does seem like they're making a connection."

"Brian, there are three more entries in the diary connecting the dots; two show that remorse is growing in his conscience or subconscious. But the last entry is our best link. He writes: 'Leaving the Bendlerblock in a few minutes. Headed to Der Führerbunker. Bringing him to freedom will be my last and most important assignment. Proud to be the Chosen One. Ah, Hilda was terrific. For a few minutes, she made me forget the war. Now I must get my things and hurry.'

"Erick, the woman who turned in the diary to Kristofer Bronn said her mother, Hilda, worked in the Bendlerblock building complex in Berlin. Don't you see the connection? I think it's him! I believe the author of the diary is possibly Brian's biological father. He might be the man who raped Katrina."

Still wanting to protect Brian's feelings, Erick spoke up again. "Nina, you're bright, and great at researching and assembling bits and pieces of puzzles. It's why you are on our team. But we'll need more proof to validate your hunch. BJ, what are your thoughts?"

"From the last letter my birth mother wrote that was stuck in the back of the Bible, she identifies her rapist, my biological father, as Karl von Richter. Does his name appear anywhere in the diary?"

"Well, almost. Inside the diary's front cover are the initials 'KvR.' Then on the back cover it's written, 'Property of KvR, Langenargen.'"

"Gosh, BJ! That sure seems like a match."

"Nina. You're on to something in connecting all these entries. Thanks a bunch."

"Anything for you, Brian. Anything."

Erick then took the lead. "BJ, as I see it, we have three mysteries to solve. The first is the entry by KvR, referring to his delivery of two pieces of art to a hiding place in a building in Spain—someplace with colorful arches. It seems the art pieces were intended as a gift from Hitler to Franco, who claimed Spain was neutral but leaned toward Hitler and Mussolini.

"The second is determining the diary's author. Now, it appears to have been written by Karl von Richter, Katrina's boyfriend-turned-rapist. If so, he is your biological father.

"The third mystery is based on the story you told us about the letters buried in the old German Bible Katrina sent you. We need to determine what happened to the Luciano Wine Export Company and see if we can find your birth mother. It's a long shot, but by my calculation and with some luck, she may still be alive."

"We have our work cut out for us – and it better be quick. As I said yesterday, Grace is very unhappy. She doesn't know I've already officially retired from the university and am filling in for two colleagues on sabbatical. I also must decide – soon – how much longer I remain with Interpol. If I take too much time on this trip, I might come home to an empty house."

Nina, almost thirty-five years his junior, suddenly wished that would happen. She knew Brian's search for his natural mother could take a few months, which would likely cause Grace to leave him. She also wanted to help him find Katrina, if she's still alive.

"Brian, I researched the Luciano Wine Export Company yesterday. The information online is incomplete, so I sent a few emails to people in Naples and Rome, requesting information. I'm hoping to hear back from them this morning."

"BJ, today's meeting with Mueller is to get his approval for an exploratory trip to Spain to pursue the lead on the art pieces noted in the diary."

"Erick, you're certain I should go to today's meeting and then to Spain, right?"

"Yes, absolutely, to both. We'll need your skills, and we'll implement your ideas to search various locations for the art. And Nina, since we have an extra hour, why don't you head back to your place now. We'll pick you up on the way."

"Okay. I hope I'll find a reply to one of those emails from yesterday. And Brian, when the two of you stop to pick me up, please come in to my apartment for a few minutes to see how I've decorated my place. It's such a stark contrast to Erick's."

"I heard that, Nina! Don't lose my Leo again on your way out."

"Erick, have you already forgotten? Your Leo is now Bashful."

She gathered her things, then leaned and gave Brian another gentle kiss on the cheek. *He's so attractive and smells so good. Hmm.*

CHAPTER NINE

The Hague

As soon as Nina left, Erick and Brian pulled out their laptops. Erick's recently upgraded internet service now offered Wi-Fi inside his apartment, eliminating the need to plug into the wall.

"It's about time, Erick. You know Wi-Fi's been available at least ten years."

"Not in this neighborhood, my friend. The local internet carrier finally offered it here last month. Ha! Remember sliding a thin modem card into your PC's card slot for a twelve-hundred-baud connection? And then dialing into an internet service provider like AOL? It seemed like a miracle back then as cumbersome as it was!"

Brian laughed. "Yes! And when flying in to an airport, remember the race off the plane? We had our choice: Run to the bathroom or run to the bank of public phones to make a long-distance call to retrieve a dozen voicemail messages. We first dialed a ten-digit 800-number to log in to our company account, then ten more digits to reach who we were calling, then another seven digits so the company could keep track of our individual calls. It was painful! I've kept my little Motorola pager and my dial-up modem card as 'techno' memorabilia."

He sighed. "That's enough reminiscing about technology for now. Erick, what do you know about these two fellows from Italy that Mueller has assigned to help us?"

"I know of them but haven't met either one in person. I called a woman in the office to get the skinny. Paolo Luzzi is sixty-four. His partner for the last dozen years is Antonio Gozzo. He's maybe late fifties to about sixty. Luzzi spends some time in Italy and most of his time in Malta. She said he's also bragged about some tie to the Vatican. By the way, have you ever seen the Vatican art collection? It's magnificent!"

"I was invited there before I joined Interpol. The Vatican collection is extraordinary. The complete collection is better than any single museum in the world. So are Luzzi and Gozzo trustworthy?"

"Good question. They've been Interpol agents for over thirty years. They were supposedly vetted, like us. Luzzi had several good discoveries that brought him some notoriety back in the late nineties. I know less about Gozzo. Since then, as you Americans say, it's been 'slim pickings.' Much of the valuable art that's still missing was maliciously destroyed by the German high command as they withdrew back toward Germany and then to Berlin. Thank heavens for the quick actions of the American Monument Men, or we'd all be visiting Moscow to view the most precious statues and paintings."

"And Mueller, our new boss? You've had contact with him in the last few years when I was back in the States. What's he like?"

"Well, here's where it gets sticky. He's in his thirties and very bright. His father, Klaus Mueller, was Director of European Operations about the time you joined Interpol. Most thought he was connected to the underworld. Rumors implied he was dishonest, but nothing was ever proven. Bronn, the art dealer in Leipzig who bought the von Richter diary, worked with my father on an Interpol team long ago. Bronn suspected Old Man Mueller was up to something, but they could never prove it. Kristofer Bronn was wrongly forced out of Interpol when Klaus Mueller learned about an effort to initiate an internal investigation against him. My father's deep connections made sure Bronn received his pension upon leaving. As for Old Man Mueller, some say he died unexpectedly while working on a case down in Sicily, because he crossed the wrong capo. Others say he is a capo and has a villa in Malta.

"When young Mueller arrived at The Hague, he had connections left and right. He came up through the ranks quickly and was assigned to our unit when Hobson left. He's been supportive of our activities since being assigned to our Art Reconnaissance sector. He brings new energy to our efforts. I kind of like him, but deep down, I don't trust him because he's Klaus Mueller's son. The apple doesn't fall far from the tree—especially rotten apples on crooked trees. Rumor in the division has it he's in line to take over European, Middle Eastern, and African operations next year. You're planning to be gone by then, right?"

Brian nodded. Then both returned to their laptops and began looking at maps of southern Spain, imagining where von Richter could have hidden two paintings intended as a gift to Franco.

"Where do you think Spain's Franco hung his hat during the nineteen forties? Maybe that's near where the art was hidden?"

"Good question, Erick. Maybe that's where we start looking. What time do we need to leave for our meeting?"

"The meeting's at one o'clock. It's an hour to get there. We need to leave here by eleven thirty. It's a simple ride along the A4, but there's always construction, and we need to get Nina first."

Some thirty miles away, at Interpol's National Central Bureau within The Hague—the administrative and royal capital along the western edge of the Netherlands, bordered by the North Sea—Wilhelm Mueller prepared to meet Luzzi and Gozzo. He planned to turn over copies of KvR's diary, translated into Italian.

As Mueller looked out his window, overlooking the International Court of Justice and the International Criminal Court, where the trials of Nazi soldiers and party members were held after World War II, his hands-free intercom buzzed.

"Yes, Ursula?"

"They're here."

"Good, bring them in."

He stood and greeted them warmly, handshaking and arm grabbing.

"Come in, come in! Please. Thanks for coming in this morning. Antonio, how was the flight from Rome?"

"*Bene.* Good, very good. *Grazie.*"

"And you, Paolo? Did you come through Rome or fly straight from Naples?"

"I left Naples and had one stop in Milan. We landed here within minutes of each other."

Without pausing, Paolo got straight to the point. "We got your call, saying this is a hot case. Why did we need to come so quickly? What are the details?"

"Please sit, let me explain. One of our agents here in Amsterdam who covers the western European countries was contacted by an old friend of his, an art dealer in Leipzig, who came across a German soldier's diary."

"Wilhelm, there are hundreds of those—if not thousands—floating around Europe. What's so special about this one that you called us in from Italy?"

"Erick Schmidt sent a copy to me to read while he was having the diary's age tested."

"Go on."

"The diary's author, a German SS officer, refers to delivering two pieces of art to Generalissimo Franco during World War II. The art was to be delivered somewhere in southern Spain, according to the diary. The author implied he should have had another SS officer helping him, but the guy didn't show for some reason. The diary's author decided to hide the art.

"Based on our department's 'Still Missing' art list, there were two paintings a Jewish family claims were taken by the Gestapo as the Germans marched into Paris. It appears Hitler may have acquired and immediately parted with these two pieces, intending to use them as gifts to show his good faith to Franco who, at the time, was teetering on Spain's being Axis-friendly or remaining neutral. If these art pieces are the same two stolen from the Lieberman family, and I believe they may be, I can tell you each painting is worth over ten million Euros. These paintings need to be found and brought back here.

"Now, let me explain why I've called you both here. First, the investigation team pursuing this is Schmidt who brought this to my attention, Brian O'Sullivan, and a young woman whose name escapes me for the moment. You both have met Schmidt in the past but probably not O'Sullivan. He is a strait-laced art professor with all sorts of credentials. He's been Schmidt's partner for the last eighteen years and is nearing retirement. In fact this could be his last job.

"Schmidt said an old antiques dealer bought the diary from a woman who claims it was in her mother's possession since the war. The dealer called Schmidt, saying it referenced art, so Schmidt purchased it. He and the woman assistant have gone over the diary cover to cover. She apparently is an ace with research and discovery. Schmidt sent me a text an hour ago, saying there's additional information from the diary's review. I'm waiting to hear what that is when they come in today."

"What time are they due here?"

"At one. Here, take these copies I had translated into Italian. What I'd like you to do now is to take thirty minutes to read the soldier's entries and make notes. We'll have time for lunch before they arrive. While we eat, you can tell me what you think and give me your impressions.

"One more thing. You both have known my dad and worked on cases with him over the last twenty-five years. I happen to know you were working with him in a very discreet way and he put a good amount of money in your pockets with side deals. I've known about the two of you since I was a teenager, and I've been aware of your activities with him without your knowing.

"So, here's the real reason I've called you both in on this case. Listen closely. After looking this situation over, although we haven't worked together like you did with my father, I think this case can be a huge score for the three of us. Paolo, you're near retirement, and Antonio, I'm sure you wouldn't mind retiring soon, as well. I plan to move up in the organization after Pieter Van Deusen retires, then retire with a similar pension. Can I count on the two of you to join me in handling this situation, or should I say this opportunity, as you both have with my father in the past? The three of us will be set for life. Are you in?"

Shocked by the openness of the conversation, Luzzi and Gozzo looked at each other, wide eyed. Gozzo shrugged.

Then Luzzi turned to Wilhelm. "*Certo!* Uh, certainly! Of course, we're in. It'll be like old times. We had fun working for Klaus and we made a little extra money for ourselves on the side. But we must be careful. It'll be a race between us and the other team to find the art. But of course, we'll do whatever it takes to win like in the past."

"Great. Take the translated copies of the SS officer's diary. Ursula will bring you down the hall to an office. It's eleven fifteen now. You have thirty minutes to read and take notes. Then we'll head across the street to grab lunch, go over your thoughts and discuss our next steps."

CHAPTER TEN

Paolo and Antonio

P aolo Luzzi was born on the western shore of Lake Garlate, south of Lake Lecco. His father was one of thousands of Italian men dragged unwillingly into World War II by the German Wehrmacht. They fought bravely in Anzio and along other German defensive lines in Italy against the advancing Americans and the Allies. Badly injured in the horrific fighting south of Rome, the elder Luzzi survived with shrapnel buried deeply in his legs and other parts of his body. He suffered greatly and died in 1947 when Paolo was six months old. In 1951 an unexpected illness took Paolo's mother's life, and the youngster was left to be raised by his elderly grandmother.

In 1953 his mother's nursing-school classmate visited. Upon arriving, she learned of Sophia's death two years earlier and saw quickly the grandmother couldn't properly care for young Paolo and herself. Sophia's friend took them both into her home to live with her. Within months, the grandmother passed away, but Paolo remained with his mother's friend and grow up in her home. His guardianship was made permanent when Katrina and Luca adopted Paolo in 1954. Young Paolo did well in school, but delinquent neighborhood kids influenced him and led him into trouble.

The family moved several times before his teenage years as the step-father's business grew, and Paolo never adjusted well. During his teens, he became even more troublesome and defiant, openly rejecting his loving adoptive family. Sent to boarding school in England when he was sixteen, Paolo matured, slowly becoming more responsible. He finished his formal education and earned degrees in history and art with high honors. Years later, aided by Paolo's father's broad business connections, Interpol recruited him.

Antonio Gozzo's mother and her husband left Italy for the United States in 1939 and settled with relatives in New Haven, Connecticut. A year later, the family moved to Hartford when her machinist husband joined the Colt Firearms Company. Sadly, on July 6, 1944, he and two sons died in a tragic fire during an afternoon performance of the Ringling Bros and Barnum & Bailey Circus.

In those days, circus tents were customarily waterproofed by soaking the canvas fabric in a mixture of paraffin wax and gasoline. It was standard procedure for circus workers to stand outside the tent with buckets of water to quickly distinguish any flames.

On that day, a flame, possibly started by a discarded cigarette, quickly spread along the tent's side wall. People inside the huge tent panicked and began running for their lives. Within minutes the raging fire grew to engulf the entire big top. In another minute it had collapsed on top of hundreds of people still trying to get out. One hundred sixty-seven people perished in the flames or by being trampled to death in the mad rush to escape. More than seven hundred men, women, and children were injured.

After the tragedy, Antonio's mother immigrated back to Italy with her remaining children. She remarried and Antonio was born in Milan in 1953. Throughout his childhood he often saw his mother break into tears for no apparent reason. Only years later did he fully understand why.

Paolo and Antonio were twenty minutes into reading their copies of the Nazi soldier's diary when one of the entries caught Paolo's attention. Another seemed even more familiar. The third struck a nerve. He shifted in his seat. He continued to read and, as he scrutinized additional entries, the connection dawned on him. Paolo let out a sharp gasp of realization. When Antonio looked in his direction, Paolo disguised the sound as a cough. He stood up and paced for a moment, stroking his chin.

This can't be a coincidence! I've heard my stepmother's sad story. It's unbelievable that this Nazi soldier's diary should arrive in my hands! I'll keep this to myself for now.

CHAPTER ELEVEN

The Meeting

Erick, Brian, and Nina arrived at headquarters minutes before their scheduled meeting. They signed in at the front desk and were given badges. Then they passed through the metal detector, they were subsequently escorted to the elevators with a security guard by their side.

Once inside the elevator car, Nina rolled her eyes. "It's been a while since I've been here but being walked to the elevator isn't ordinary."

Erick whispered as the lift ascended to the third floor. "Shh! Be careful what you say. I hear the new guy's a stickler for security. This elevator could be bugged."

As the door slid open, a guard greeted the trio and walked them to the Director's office suite. Ursula buzzed the intercom.

"Sir, they're here."

The Director paused his conversation, stood and opened his door.

"Come in! Welcome. O'Sullivan, Schmidt, and uh, yes, Miss von Scholz. Glad you could all come. O'Sullivan, it's nice to finally meet you in person."

The Director shook their hands. Mueller's few-seconds-too-long hand grasp made Nina uncomfortable.

"Allow me to introduce Paolo Luzzi and Antonio Gozzo. As you may know, both have been with Interpol for many years. I have complete confidence in their skills, and I've asked them to participate in this search for the lost art pieces."

The team members cautiously greeted one another with suspicious nods and handshakes—the men all looking at each other's eyes. Nina took a side look at Mueller and silently sized up the new Director: tall, maybe six foot three, blond, handsome, and close to her age. But something about him immediately made her mistrustful. *I don't like him. Something's wrong with this picture. The diary is* <u>*our*</u> *team's find and we should get to do the field research. I can't say why yet, but these two unshaven Italian guys give me the creeps.*

"Let me begin. As you all know, we're here today to focus on two missing pieces of art. Thanks to Agent Schmidt and his connections we are in possession of a diary of a World War II SS officer. Thank you, Miss von Scholz, for validating its authenticity and for the English translation. I subsequently had the document translated into Italian for the benefit of our associates.

"We see in the diary a substantial number of entries spanning the author's career—right up to his last assignment—when he loses or misplaces the diary. At one point in his years of service, the author—whom we shall call 'KvR'—has an assignment to deliver two paintings to Generalissimo Franco somewhere in Andalusia.

"As you well know from your study of European history, Franco was only slightly friendly to Hitler and the alliance between Germany and Spain was teetering. Hitler thought himself a charmer and, after striking a treaty with Russia, believed he could have a similar treaty with Spain. An alliance would be important, and Hitler wanted a closer personal friendship established with hopes it would remain in place for the duration of the war.

"Over lunch, Luzzi, Gozzo, and I discussed the possibility of the paintings' being taken by Hitler's SS or Gestapo days after the occupation of Paris. Instead of being sent to Germany, Hitler directed they be transported directly to Franco. This gift of valuable art to Franco would have been a symbol of that commitment. For some reason, the SS soldier KvR decided to hide the paintings. Maybe that was his original directive—to hide them until such time as a communication arrived in Berlin from Franco. Or perhaps something came up and a commander in Berlin ordered KvR to not make the delivery. In any case, we know – or, I should say, we *believe* – KvR hid the two paintings. From the database of missing World War II art Miss von Scholz manages, and from the comments about when they were taken, these could be the two paintings stolen from the Lieberman family.

"So, gentlemen, and Miss von Scholtz, here is my plan: I'm asking both teams to research and determine the city where the paintings were delivered by KvR, and to discover specifically where he hid them. Then we must retrieve both paintings and return them here."

Erick chimed in. "Director, we discussed another idea in the car on our way here. The SS soldier may have had his own plans of what to do with the paintings after the war."

Director Mueller nodded. "O'Sullivan, what do you think?"

"Well, Director, there are many possible scenarios of what might have happened. The first challenge for all of us is determining in which city KvR most likely hid the paintings, then determine precisely where. Nina's list of paintings that have yet to be discovered is a reliable source to confirm our findings once we uncover the art. But as you know, many paintings remain in secret locations – including those that have been hidden among private collections. We've concluded the paintings referenced in the diary are likely those stolen from the Lieberman family living in Paris. We will make every effort to find the art as quickly as possible. For personal reasons, I need to return to the U.S."

The Director engaged the intercom. "Ursula, is Philippe here?"

"Yes, Director, he's waiting for you."

"Have him come in."

Philippe stepped into the room, having been instructed by Ursula to remain silent. Nina looked him over. Tall, with fair skin and long, light-brown hair and a small, thin moustache, he looked French. She sat up, straightened her shoulders and, raising her chin, tossed her long dark hair back. *Hmm. He's cute, but seems young and naïve.*

"This is Philippe Peugeot. He's new with Interpol. He'll join Paolo and Antonio's efforts in the search. He's not as skilled as Miss von Scholz, but he understands our work. Now, two final things: First, I'd like you all to jump on this case without delay. Report your findings to me every twenty-four hours. Second, I believe in incentives, so I'm offering two months' bonus pay to each individual on the team that recovers the art. You all have your work cut out for you. Good luck."

Everyone stood. After acknowledging each other, Erick, Brian, and Nina left the Director's office.

Before Paolo and Antonio could leave, the Director stopped them. He turned to Philippe. "Are we all set?"

"*Sì.*"

"Good. I know assigning Philippe to help you is unusual but allow me to explain. Philippe is my nephew. He's been with Interpol less than a year.

I briefed him yesterday on the case. I told him that agents O'Sullivan and Schmidt have been under internal investigation for some months, as suspected art thieves. I told Philippe they need to be watched closely without their suspecting anything. In fact, Philippe began his work on the case this morning. He'll assist in the search by keeping track of Schmidt and O'Sullivan and will always keep you both apprised of their whereabouts."

"*Grazie,* Wilhelm."

"Philippe, while we are here together, please review your plan."

"*Signori,* after O'Sullivan and Schmidt left Amsterdam this morning to come here, I entered Schmidt's house and placed the newest style of miniature GPS tracking device inside the lining of each of their laptop bags and inside the lining of their shaving kits. I've also placed a listening device in the den, two devices in the kitchen—one under the table and one in the overhead light fixture—and one in each bedroom. I also planted GPS devices in their personal belongings. I will listen to them and I expect to give you details of their movements to aid in your search for the art pieces. Those two will have no advantage on you with these devices in place."

Paolo nodded his approval. "*Bravo,* Philippe. Wilhelm, we will call you later today. *Antonio, andiamo.*"

Both left smiling, believing they had the upper hand and a special deal in place with Wilhelm, reminiscent of the deals they did with his father, Klaus. On the way out, Ursula let them know she had made hotel arrangements for them near Schiphol the night.

Philippe remained behind for a minute. "Uncle, as I was leaving Schmidt's apartment, a cat ran out of the house. It skittered through my legs and took off running. I looked around outside for a few minutes, without any luck."

Uncle Wilhelm shook his head. "I don't understand why I let my sister talk me into hiring you. Now get out of here."

CHAPTER TWELVE

Zaanse Schans

Brian, Erick, and Nina were silent on the drive back from The Hague. Brian was recalling his last conversation with Grace. Erick was focused on the chance for a bonus to buy some art for the walls in his apartment, and Nina was thinking about Brian.

As they approached the western side of Amsterdam, Erick turned to Brian. "Have you ever visited Zaanse Schans?"

"No."

"Let's take a few minutes. It's slightly out of our way, but we need to relax a bit before we dive into this search."

Erick parked the car, and as they began walking. The scene felt reminiscent of a hundred years earlier, when windmills like these had been used to grind grain. The air blowing off the waterway felt fresh and chilly, and the scene was highlighted by a beautiful pair of white swans, floating in the blue water.

"Brian, these windmills are reminding me of Don Quixote and his search for glory and adventure in Spain."

"That'll be us this week, searching for the glory of finding those paintings."

He thanked Nina for her work on the diary, and then he and Erick discussed their trip to Andalusia, telling Nina she'd play a key role in helping to unravel the mystery. She smiled in appreciation of the recognition.

Feeling invigorated after their brief diversion, the three returned to the car. Twenty minutes later, they pulled up to her apartment.

"Thanks again for including me. I'll see you both later. When will you pick me up?"

"We'll be by at seven. Tonight we'll decide whether we should work together or split up to cover more ground. Either way, we should leave first thing in the morning. Nina, you have a knack for solving puzzles; we'll trust your intuition on where to begin."

They returned to Erick's. As Brian headed inside to call Grace, Erick saw Solie emerge from her house with the cat in her arms.

"You're so careless!"

"What do you mean?"

"Do you have another guest? I saw a handsome young man leave your apartment this morning as I left for my meeting. When I returned, Bashful was sitting at my front door. Is he one of your, uh, close friends? If not, maybe you can introduce me?"

"Brian and I left early this morning," Erick replied with a snappy edge. "I'm certain Leo was inside when we left. Can you describe the young man?"

"He was tall, slender, fair skinned, with brownish hair."

Erick's eyes squinted in suspicion. "Was he wearing a Navy peacoat?"

"Yes. He's really cute."

"Uh, yes, he's a friend passing through town. He probably let Leo out by mistake."

"Okay. Don't forget, your Leo is now my Bashful. It's official."

Solie turned and went inside to her apartment, carrying Bashful.

Waving goodbye to his cat, Erick turned and entered his apartment. As he opened the door, he heard Brian's elevated and exasperated voice from the guest bedroom.

"Gracie, I'm going to say it again. I'm in Amsterdam . I'm staying with my associate, Erick Schmidt. We need to travel to Spain tomorrow for perhaps a week. I might have another week's worth of business before I return home to New Jersey. No. No, Gracie. I'm not living with a woman. Erick and I aren't a couple. No, I don't want you to come here. Gracie, there's nothing to be concerned about. Please Gracie, just stay home and be patient. I can explain more when I return home. Yes, dear. I'll let them know I'll be finishing at the university at the end of this school year. I promise. And I'll be finishing my other projects as well. Grace? Grace?"

Shaking his head, Brian carried his laptop to the kitchen table. He pulled up maps of Andalusia, the southern province of Spain, bordering the Mediterranean Sea.

"Problems, BJ?"

"It's Grace. She's threatening to fly here. She said she's thinking of leaving tonight. Then she hung up on me."

Erick put a finger to his lips and wrote a message on a piece of paper and slid it in front of Brian.

We had a visitor in this apartment while we were at the Director's office. From my neighbor's description, it was Philippe. He was here after we left, and accidentally let Leo outside.

"Let me get coffee going for you, BJ. You like the dark roast, right? While it's brewing, you can start looking at where we should fly to tomorrow, based on Nina's ideas." He continued writing.

Don't say anything of importance until I figure out if any electronics have been planted here in the apartment. They might be watching us, too.

Brian gave him a thumbs up. Erick put the water on and went to a closet for a device to pick up electronic signals. He continued the bland dialog as he searched the apartment.

"What do you think, BJ? Based on Nina's review, where should we head to?"

"I'm thinking the SS officer would have had to fly into a major city. Your thoughts?"

"I agree. Nina gave us useful information on where Franco was holed up in the early nineteen forties when the two paintings should have been gifted to him from Hitler. By the way, BJ, I'm glad the weather's been good for your visit so far."

The needle on the device Erick was using indicated he should check the kitchen table. He bent down and spotted a tiny listening device adhered to its underside with a gummy substance. He pulled it down and showed it to Brian. He wrote another note.

Don't say anything. We can use finding this to our advantage. There might be other planted devices. Let me continue to look while we chat. Just don't mention what I'm doing.

Erick searched his bedroom and the guest room where Brian was staying. He found GPS devices in his and Brian's laptop bags and both their shaving kits. Two more audio devices had been placed in the nightstand lamp in Erick's bedroom and in the small den's desk lamp.

I think I've found all the listening and GPS devices Philippe left. I'll look some more. Continue talking about the coffee and the weather. In a few minutes we'll take a walk to Vondelpark and discuss what's happened here. Something's rotten in the Agency and I'm sure Wilhelm is behind it.

Brian gave another thumbs up as Erick put the small collection of GPS and listening devices on the table, letting them sit in the open.

"Here. You take milk in your afternoon coffee, right?"

"Right. Thank you, Erick. You know, you should settle down. You'd make someone a good partner."

Erick sighed. "I have my eyes on a good friend. We get along well and enjoy being together. But frankly, I'm concerned about someday having issues like you have with Grace. It makes me think that making a relationship permanent makes it harder, not easier."

"Great coffee, Erick. Thank you." Brian savored a sip of the warm beverage, then set the mug down and pushed back his chair. "I'm headed to the park for a walk. I'll catch you later."

"Okay. I'll head our shortly myself, to pick up some cheese at the corner market. See you when you return."

They left the house a few minutes apart, in case they were also being watched. Erick found himself checking to make sure the cat remained inside as he left, then remembered Leo was now living next door with Solie. He felt sad, as if he'd lost a good friend.

Brian walked to the end of the street and stepped into an alcove of a deeply set doorway. He stepped forward as Erick approached within a few feet. He'd grown anxious thinking about the devices being planted in the apartment. Grabbing Erick's coat by the collar, he yelled, "Damn it! What in God's name is going on, Erick? What was that all about?"

"Relax, BJ. Just relax. Here's my best guess. Years ago, several folks in the bureau suspected Klaus Mueller — who, aside from being a terrific art expert, is our new Director's father — of being a thief. Those suspicions were never proven. At that time, agents conducting investigations would find historical art pieces in back rooms of antique shops. Some of those art pieces would be returned to their rightful owners. But some pieces thought to be held in a small collection remained missing, even after the rest of the paintings in that group had been found.

"Some in Interpol believed Klaus would take one or two select pieces from a group, hide them for himself, and then sell them later via the illegal market into private collections for top dollars. He eventually retired, but it was easy to see he was living far better off than the income earned from his position would provide. Then Klaus went missing, but along came his son a few years back. He, too, was extraordinarily successful at finding paintings, statues, and other art pieces.

"In fact, Wilhelm discovered two paintings right inside the Palace of Versailles. Both had been stolen from Dutch Jews here in Amsterdam. I remember reading Wilhelm's report. It said, 'I followed a hunch and discovered the two pieces hidden inside a hollow wall.'

"Wilhelm similarly *discovered* a few more art pieces shortly afterward. Some speculated the small statues and paintings Wilhelm would 'find' were originally found by our director's father. In other words, Klaus would find two paintings, report having found one, and keep the second piece for himself or sell it to an art collector. Then years later, when Wilhelm got into the business, it's rumored Klaus ratted on several private collectors and told his son where to look for and eventually find the stolen art. These so-called 'surprise discoveries' in several private collections launched Wilhelm's quick advancement. While it's all speculation, I'm growing more certain we're dealing with a new boss with a shady family history. It's likely he'll try to repeat what his father did, even though none of it is proven. And by the way, I've never believed the rumors Klaus died. Nor was he knocked off by the Mafia. I think he's on an island somewhere in the Mediterranean, getting daily massages. Klaus is alive and well and, as an art lover, still holds onto a few paintings—worth millions—that he's retained hidden for himself."

"So, Erick, where does that leave us? Why would those devices be planted in your place and in our shaving kits and personal computer bags? It's worrying me and making me very anxious that we are being spied on" He paused. "I'm sorry for grabbing your collar and yelling at you like that."

"No worries, BJ. You've had a tough week. As I see it, the discovery of the SS officer's diary and its reference to two art pieces has opened the door for Wilhelm to follow in his father's footsteps. This situation is not to be taken lightly. Back in the day when Klaus was in charge, there were two Interpol art agents who went missing and were never found.

"Jesus, Mary, and Saint Joseph!" *Oh my God, I just sounded like my mother!*

"Finding the GPS and listening devices in my apartment lets us conclude there's a scheme underway linking Wilhelm, Luzzi, Gozzo, and young Philippe—who's obviously not yet perfected his undercover craft. Those two Italians looked surprised when he was introduced, so the connection must be Mueller and Philippe. But that doesn't exclude Luzzi and Gozzo from the scheme since they stayed behind when we left. We need to somehow take advantage of Philippe's mistake and use it to our advantage. Perhaps we play along and misdirect them. I'm not sure yet how we'll do that, but it'll get more dangerous for us as we head to Spain. And trust me, devices or not, they'll be following us. It might be better to let them follow us for a bit and then mislead them as we get closer to finding the art. Understand, my friend?"

"My God, Erick. My twenty years of work in the agency has been all about verifying newly uncovered art. But this is making me nervous. I feel like a character in a mystery novel!"

Erick nodded gravely. "I agree. This situation has suddenly turned dangerous. And with our Director being Klaus' son, I'd put nothing past him."

"So where do we go from here? What's next?"

"Nina's already put together a list of the three southern Andalusian cities where the paintings are likely to be: Seville, Cordoba, and Granada. At first, we can split up and each take a city, checking out places on her list. As we discount places we've searched, we can proceed to another targeted city and focus on places there.

"Second, Nina texted me a few minutes ago. She has more information for you on what happened to the Luciano Wine Exports Company. You'll want to spend time exploring what happened and determine what became of Katrina and Luca.

Brian nodded. "Yes. That's important to me."

"Of course. And when we get back to the apartment, I'll go through your things again to see if there are any more hidden devices. My detector's battery had run out of juice, and I had to plug it back in. If I find more devices, we'll need to visit Solie's apartment to chat before we meet Nina for dinner. For now, I'd like to keep her unaware of what's gone on today."

Brian rubbed his hands down his face. "Wow. This is getting intense. Maybe I'll retire from the agency first thing when I get back …"

The ringing of Brian's phone interrupted him.

"Hello? Grace, is something wrong? You've decided what? No. You're where? Oh, Grace, please don't come to Amsterdam. I'm leaving here first thing tomorrow morning... Grace, wait, you need to listen. Do you understand, I'm not going to be here in the—Gracie!"

Brian frowned at his phone. "Darn it. She hung up!"

"You sure have your hands full, my friend."

"She's on her way to Newark and flying overnight. She'll be here in the morning. Once she has her mind made up about something, it's tough to change her thinking!"

Once they finished their chat, Erick headed back to his place while Brian headed to Vondelpark for a walk. He had to sort through this latest episode with his hotheaded and impetuous Irish wife.

CHAPTER THIRTEEN

Planning

Brian hoped a lengthy walk several times around the Vondelpark loop would clear his head from Mom's death, his being adopted, Katrina… and Karl. And yesterday's revelation from Nina's research that the diary's author might have been Karl seemed to make it all worse. Now his thoughts were twisted even further by Grace's hasty decision to fly to Amsterdam. On the brief call, she again accused Brian of having a secret life. He began heading back to Erick's.

She's right. I do have a secret life! Now, how do I get her to wait and behave in Amsterdam while I'm gone?

Back at the house, Erick's recharged electronic monitor turned up another listening device, on the floor near the front door. It was no doubt dropped by Philippe. Erick had just finished his second sweep of the apartment when Brian returned. Erick quickly wrote another note and held it up as Brian made his way into the kitchen.

I found another GPS device on the floor at the edge of a carpet. Everything is in the center of the kitchen table. Now say, "Erick, I need to run back out to the drug store for some aspirin."

Brian spoke aloud as requested, and together they exited the house. "What now?"

"Our friend Philippe's error has given us a good opportunity. I have a plan. Let's sit here on the porch for a few minutes and I'll explain."

"I have a plan, too. When Grace called earlier, she said she went through my old Rolodex, and found your name and address, so she'll be headed here. She told me, 'I'll see you at your boyfriend Erick's in the morning. I'm going to get to the bottom of your charade and your double life.' So, we need to be gone before she arrives tomorrow. When she gets here, I'd like Solie to be here to greet her and let her in. I'll leave a note for

Grace explaining we're in the middle of a project and I'll be back in a week. I'll leave her the key you gave me to use. No doubt, she'll stew over my absence, but we don't need her complicating matters."

"I like your idea, BJ. Now here's what I have in mind. We put the listening and GPS devices in an envelope and get it set up for the morning's mail pickup. The mail man will be here to pick the envelope up after we leave but before she arrives. The GPS trackers' movement will confuse Philippe. We can go on our way, and we should be free of the two Italians following us too closely."

"Sounds good. Let's visit Solie. I'll explain about my mother's death and tell her Grace decided to come to Amsterdam after all and ask if she'd please welcome Grace into your apartment. I'm writing a note to leave for Grace: 'I'll be back in a week. Use your credit card freely, go splurge!' Hopefully, she'll like that, and shopping in Amsterdam will provide some fun for her. And Solie can give Gracie the apartment key I have after she lets her in."

Solie hardly knew Brian. She'd only occasionally seen him coming and going a few times since she began renting next door a year earlier. She welcomed them both in. Erick approached Bashful, who turned and walked away. Solie then graciously agreed to Brian's request and told him not to worry. The two then returned to the apartment, opened a bottle of wine and, for safety, used a series of back-and-forth notes to plan for the next day's journey. Meanwhile, the devices remained in the envelope in the center of the table.

Dinnertime approached and upon arriving at Nina's place, Brian rang her doorbell. When she answered, she gave him a huge smile and, grabbing his arm, ushered him inside for a quick look at her apartment.

He was impressed with her small art collection as well as the interior's colors and fabrics. "It's well done, Nina. You have good taste."

"I'm glad you like how I've decorated. I don't understand why Erick's place is so dull."

Brian shrugged. "We're all different. Erick's place is fine for Erick, or he'd change it."

As they turned to leave, Nina couldn't hold back anymore. She planted a big kiss on Brian's cheek.

He turned, looked in her eyes and smiled.

"Thanks Nina. It's been a tough week and I sincerely appreciate your warmth."

"Brian, I have some good news for you! That wine-exporting company you asked me to investigate? I uncovered some interesting information."

"Great! Tell me about it over dinner." They stepped outside, got into Erick's car, and headed back toward his apartment.

CHAPTER FOURTEEN

Luciano Wine Export Company

Earlier in the day, Erick had made a reservation at Restaurant Bellavista, his favorite Italian restaurant on Johannes Verhulststraat, just down the street from his place. Well known for its chef who developed his culinary skills in Cortona, Italy, it was an excellent choice. The wall décor was exclusively scenes of Tuscany and its largest cities.

The three were greeted and seated in a quiet corner; it was perfect. Nina, bubbling with enthusiasm about her findings, was waiting to share her news. Brian asked the server to bring a large sparkling water for the table and a bottle of 2005 Brunello.

"Brian, please, can I tell you now?" she pleaded as the server left their quiet corner table.

"Sure, Nina. We don't want you to explode here at the table! Tell us what you know."

"I received several emails when I got back to my apartment after today's meeting." She shook her head. "No, let me start at the beginning. The Luciano Wine Export Company was incorporated in 1947. Officers of the company were Luca Luciano and Katrina Amorino-Luciano. Their initial place of business was Positano, with a small warehouse in Naples. Two years later in 1949, the business address was restated as 12 Via Abbazia in Montechiaro on the west side of the Sorrento Peninsula. I looked up the address online. It's a magnificent location with wonderful views. It's no longer a private home; it's now a beautiful bed-and-breakfast called Villa Denise. I'd love to stay there!

"Next, in 1952, the business and warehouse addresses both changed to Rome. Using an app, I saw the new warehouse location in Rome was four times the size of the original one in Naples. The Luciano Wine Export business was flourishing. I saw three tax returns and the business income was growing incredibly—more than doubling each year. I'm guessing several new distribution channels opened in European countries. Luca Luciano must have had his hands full exporting wine from Italy, because the records show the business significantly expanded again in 1960. At that time, he added warehouse locations in Johannesburg, South Africa; Long Island City in Queens, New York; and Toronto, Canada.

"Now the next two facts are really interesting. In 1971, the name Paolo Luciano is added to the list of officers of the company. But two years later in 1973, the corporate records show the third officer's name is changed to Paolo Luzzi-Luciano.

"Brian, could it be? Could it really be that the Paolo Luzzi-Luciano, an officer of the Luciano Wine Export Company, is the same as the Interpol agent Paolo Luzzi we just met?"

"You're stepping way out on a limb to assume they're one and the same. Luzzi might be a common name – like Schmidt or Jones. If we look it up online, there might be a dozen Paolo Luzzis in Italy. Right? Did you try that?"

"I did."

"And…?"

"Well, I came up with fourteen people with that name."

"See? There's a slim chance it's the same person."

"But that also means there's a slim chance it *is* the same person!"

A trace of a smile crept across Brian's face. "I love your enthusiasm, Nina."

"Thanks Brian. Let me tell you more and maybe you won't be so skeptical."

"Sure, go ahead."

They paused as the waiter poured the wine and took their orders. Each selected a salad and a protein with pasta. Erick and Brian chose grilled scallops. Nina ordered the grilled chicken. Brian requested a side of anchovies with his salad and another order of bread. He began mixing olive oil, grated Romano cheese, and ground pepper for dipping. As he stirred the ingredients together, he drifted off while staring at the mixture, mesmerized by the facts Nina had just presented.

Erick spoke up. "Go on, Nina. What else do you have?"

"On July thirteenth, 1989, a Naples newspaper headline reads, 'Luciano Wine Export Company to be acquired for fifty-three million U.S. dollars.' Then, on July fifteenth, 1989, Luca Luciano suddenly died."

"What happened next?"

"Good question. Luciano Wine Export Company disappears. There's no trace of the deal being finalized in the limited information I received. No record of any distribution of money, nor where Luca Luciano was buried, nor a place where Katrina Luciano now lives—if she's still alive. It all becomes a dead end. I'll need more time to go through additional records.

"So, Brian, here's what I think might have happened: First, Luca and Katrina adopt Paolo Luzzi and change his name to Paolo Luciano. Paolo reaches legal age and becomes an officer of the company. Two years pass and he decides to add Luzzi back to his legal name. This doesn't sit well with Luca. The deal to sell the company is approaching. A lot of money is at stake. Then Luca's sudden death causes turmoil as the deal's about to close. From there, I see several possible scenarios. I can only guess Paolo Luzzi-Luciano, being an officer of the company, tries to, or *does*, gain control of the company as the deal is about to close. If he did gain control, he's rich and we're not dealing with the same Paolo Luzzi. But if there's a snafu… and something held up the deal, then we're dealing with someone who is frustrated, not happy and, as Erick has described, has been involved in crime. Right now, the latter scenario seems to fit the profile of who we know as Agent Paolo Luzzi, who subsequently—and conveniently—drops the Luciano part of his name."

"That's all very plausible. What about Katrina? What do you think has happened to her?"

"From what you've told us, Katrina was seventy-five years old in 1989, while all of this was happening. She may be trusting her adopted son, Paolo. On the other hand, maybe she didn't trust him, or maybe Luca didn't trust him, and that's why things went down differently. By the way, if she were alive, Katrina would be ninety-eight now."

Erick listened patiently, then spoke up. "BJ, you said in the note she left you, she promised you money. Some of what she wrote implied she and Luca were very well off. I'm curious about that because her note to you was in 1951, many years before sales at Luciano Wine Exports skyrocketed. And

BJ, as you shared her story with us, you mentioned a series of numbers beginning with 10-28-something in the letter Katrina left to you. What could that be about? You need to find out what happened to the money she promised you. Additionally, if Nina's right about the growth and sale of the wine-export company, and Paolo Luzzi was indeed held at arm's length so as not to influence the deal's closing, despite Luca's death, there could be millions of dollars in your name sitting someplace, waiting to be claimed. Wow! I'm doubly concerned now, because if Nina's right about Agent Luzzi being Paolo Luzzi-Luciano, he might want you dead and out of the picture."

Nina gasped. "Dead? Oh no, Brian! Erick, that's crazy talk!"

"That's a lot of speculation, Erick. He still doesn't know I'm related to Katrina. So, even if he *is* the same Paolo Luzzi-Luciano person, he can't be wishing me dead—at least, not yet."

"Brian, this is making me nervous. What if he finds out more about you? What if he starts to dig into your past?"

"Nina, we weren't going to mention this, but given what you've uncovered, I need to share something. Erick's apartment was broken into earlier today by someone we believe to be Philippe Peugeot—the young fellow who showed up late at our meeting at headquarters. He planted several listening devices throughout the apartment, and several GPS-tracking devices in our laptop cases and shaving kits."

"Oh no! Why would he do that?"

"I'll tell you more as we eat. But for now, our plan is to leave first thing in the morning and misdirect Philippe and the others. We hope we can confuse them. One more thing: my wife is showing up tomorrow to check on me and determine if I have another life, or try to figure out if Erick is my boyfriend and lover. She's gone through some of my things at home and found Erick's address in an old Rolodex. By the time she arrives at his apartment, we'll be in flight to Spain. Erick's neighbor will handle her arrival and let her into his place. Okay, here comes our salads."

During dinner, Nina shared several more thoughts about the diary and the next day's trip. "I believe the initial translation of the diary into English by the old, retired Interpol agent had several errors. I went over those things again and have come up with a few changes."

"Like what?"

"Let me pull out my notes. First, some abbreviations by the author for both nouns and verbs were misinterpreted. I believe KvR's penmanship had something to do with the mistranslation. Several words now make more sense than in the first translation Bronn attempted. Next, KvR was probably Lutheran. He might have thought he was in a Moorish or Muslim mosque. Since many Catholic churches in southern Spain were originally Moorish mosques, I suspect that may have confused him, and you can see he tried correcting himself in his notes. Third, in the initial German-to-English translation, Bronn wrote 'KvR planned to put the paintings in a Muslim.' His use of the word 'Muslim' seemed wrong. However, I reread KvR's German handwriting and believe he meant to say he intended to wrap the paintings in *muslin*—with an 'i-n'—cloth and hide them in a Muslim—with an 'i-m'—mosque. KvR simply wrote some of these words incorrectly, and Bronn's translation didn't catch it. KvR could have been tired or confused, or both, or on methamphetamine called Pervitin, commonly used by the German military.

"Several original mosques that now are Catholic churches are on our list of targets. Also, palaces, commonly called alcázars, have chapels inside and are worth looking into. For example, while in Granada I plan to visit the Alhambra. It's a magnificent Moorish palace and the last stronghold of the Muslim kings of Granada. Brian, in Cordoba you should visit the Alcázar of the Christian Monarchs—the primary residence of Isabella I of Castile and Ferdinand II of Aragon. Next, visit the Great Mosque of Córdoba. It's known locally as the Mezquita and its now attached to the Cathedral of Córdoba. I hear it's one of the most beautiful religious buildings in the world because of the mosque and colorful arches inside. It was built in 785 by the Moors and controlled by them until it became a Catholic church in 1236.

"Next KvR writes in the diary: 'Finally complete. The art is safe and hidden. Ceiling repaired. Eliminated all workers. No record of location, except this diary and these words as a clue: Look up! Der Führer checkmates Franco in the very colorful arch. The Spanish had the right idea with the Alhambra Decree by chasing all Jews from Spain in 1492.'

"I believe in this passage, KvR delivered the goods to the hiding place and then killed the workers. His 'checkmate' reference is a key clue. In my opinion, it may pinpoint the location of the paintings in a uniquely painted or decorated arch in a building or in a ceiling. KvR talked about playing chess with a commander the night before they went into the battlefield in an earlier entry. He undoubtedly liked chess. I'm imagining he visualized a board in the ceiling. Perhaps the ceiling of the place where the two paintings are hidden looks like a chess board. You know—lots of squares. Brian, this entry could lead us exactly to where the paintings are.

"I believe the next note is a key to the city where he's located. KvR writes, 'Now I'm headed to see what the Romans built.' This puts him in Córdoba. During the Muslim control of that city, the original Roman Bridge was reconstructed. There's also a recently discovered amphitheater. It may be the largest in Europe—next to the Roman Coliseum."

"*Brava*, young lady! Your effort to reassess the translation, make better sense of his words, and pick up those details is great detective work and problem solving. Is there anything else?"

"Well, yes, one more thing. My head's still spinning about Paolo Luzzi. My gut tells me he's dangerous like an iceberg—much more of his troublesome nature is hidden below the surface than we can see. He can do nothing but cause us problems the rest of this investigation."

The discussion and her words dampened the mood among the three. When they finished eating, Erick drove Nina home while Brian walked back to Erick's by himself. Along the way, he wondered what the next few days would bring, whether his search would continue beyond the stolen paintings, and if he'd be reunited with his birth mother, Katrina.

CHAPTER FIFTEEN

Day One and Grace Arrives

The next morning, the three took a taxi to Amsterdam's Schiphol airport, bought tickets, and compared notes one final time before leaving. All agreed to follow Nina's plan to investigate the biggest churches, former mosques, and alcazars. For Day One, Nina was flying to Málaga, renting a car, and driving to Granada. Erick would fly to Seville and begin his inspections there. Brian would fly to Córdoba, the city with the highest-priority targets. They agreed to call each other every six hours and meet on Day Two in Córdoba. Erick took the task of calling Mueller with their collective updates. The spring weather in southern Spain was perfect for the trip.

***

Grace couldn't sleep on the overnight flight. First, the flight had been delayed unexpectedly. Then she mistakenly took the wrong medication. When the plane finally landed, she was held up at baggage claim when it was discovered one of her three bags never arrived. After dealing with the paperwork, she hailed a cab and headed to the address identified in Brian's old Rolodex as Erick's place. Emotionally exhausted and anxious, she wondered whether her impetuous decision to travel to Amsterdam made any sense, and it suddenly struck her for the first time that Erick's address in the old Rolodex might not be current. Nevertheless, she was determined to see for herself what was going on in Amsterdam.

The cab ride wasn't long. When she arrived, she asked the driver to wait, then stepped from the vehicle and knocked on the front door.

A moment later the door opened, and a beautiful young woman greeted her. "Good morning! You must be Brian's wife, Grace. I'm Solmaz, Erick's neighbor. You can call me Solie."

Grace looked around uncertainly. "Uh, well, yes. Hello."

"Don't worry, you're at the right place. I'm here to let you into Erick's apartment, where Brian is staying. Can I help you with your bags?"

"Sure. Where is Brian? Isn't he here?"

"No. Brian said to let you know they went to Spain to search for some art. Erick said they'd be back next week."

Grace motioned to the cab driver, who brought her two bags to the door. Her third bag was sitting, partially destroyed, in lost and found at Newark Airport. Flustered over Brian's secret life and anxious about her flight, she'd left her third piece of luggage sitting curbside near the airport's front door entrance. The unattended and unmarked bag caused a huge response by the local bomb squad, which delayed all departing flights for two hours.

"Here, let me grab those for you. Let's go inside. You can freshen up and I'll make you a cup of tea."

"Did you say, 'look *at* art' or 'look *for* art?'"

"Erick said, 'look *for* art.'"

Grace, still unsure what was happening, attempted to brush off her tiredness, went inside to freshen up, and returned to the kitchen table. Curious about Solie, she asked a pointed question.

"So, Miss Solmaz, how well do you know Brian?"

"Well, I know he comes and stays here occasionally and works with Erick. We've spoken occasionally. Brian tells me you've been married a long time. He says pleasant things about you."

Grace's defensive attitude softened, and she took a liking to Solie after realizing she couldn't be the woman Brian was interested in. "My husband will be the death of me! He's always leaving me to go somewhere to do his art-history thing. I'm convinced he has another life, and maybe another wife here in Amsterdam or perhaps elsewhere in Europe. He's here so often. It's been even more often in recent years. And frankly, I'm surprised he came here so soon after his mother's death and burial just days ago. And then the bombshell hit!"

"Oh my! Mrs. O'Sullivan, what was that?"

"Solmaz, please call me Grace."

"Certainly, please call me Solie."

"Well, after they buried Brian's mother, he and his sisters returned to their mother's house and began going through her hope chest. When they got to the bottom, they couldn't believe what was in it." With that, Grace embarked on a thirty-minute rant, unloading the entire Katrina-letters story on Solie, who patiently absorbed it all.

One block away, Philippe pulled up a white van and stepped into the back, where surveillance equipment could listen to the voice-listening devices and monitor movement of the GPS devices. He expected Erick and Brian would make their moves in the apartment and then leave. Instead, in a daring move, Erick had placed the GPS and listening devices he'd found in an envelope outside the front door earlier that morning as they left for the airport. Normal pick up by the local postal worker was sometime between 8 and 9 AM. Erick addressed the envelope to the attention of Senior Director Pieter Van Deusen, Wilhelm Mueller's supervisor at Interpol headquarters in The Hague.

When Erick scanned the apartment the second time, he collected the devices on the table but stopped short of conducting a complete sweep. As a result, he missed one voice-listening device Philippe had planted in the light fixture centered directly over the kitchen table.

So, when the two women sat for tea and Grace began to speak, her voice triggered an automatic recording system. Philippe sat up and readjusted his headphones to listen. Her constant chatter kept the recording machine going and it took a few minutes before Philippe understood one of the women had to be Agent O'Sullivan's wife.

Philippe listened closely, taking copious handwritten notes as the conversation continued. Grace's description of what was found in the deceased mother's hope chest astonished him. But when she began describing what was revealed in a letter found inside the Bible, the details fully grasped his attention. He found Grace's explanation of the story about Katrina and her relationship with Karl von Richter, the SS soldier, so extraordinary that for a few minutes he lost the purpose of his surveillance task.

Eventually, Grace's full thirty minutes of non-stop chatter turned into a bitter rant against her husband and his constant trips to Europe. Engrossed in her monologue, Philippe was both surprised and delighted with the details of what she disclosed. Feeling proud of his surveillance mission, he knew the voice recording and his notes would interest his uncle.

Just then, he noticed the GPS devices moving.

They were already a tenth of a mile away. Having recorded enough information, he quickly started the van and followed the signals. After swiftly catching up to a small white van, Philippe stayed about one hundred yards behind it. The movement slowed, stopped and became intermittent every few hundred feet.

Ten minutes later, the movement completely stopped. As he drove closer for a firsthand look, Philippe found himself at the rear of the local post office building. Realizing he'd been tricked, he turned his van around and headed toward the Interpol offices to update his uncle.

His uncle was in a meeting with Van Deusen, so he shared the story with Ursula, crowing over the value of capturing O'Sullivan's wife's rant. When Wilhelm returned, Philippe read from his notes and explained in detail how Agent Brian O'Sullivan had this seemingly odd connection to a woman named Katrina, and a German SS soldier named von Richter.

***

Early that same morning, Luzzi and Gozzo, using old-fashioned surveillance methods, followed the trio to the airport. Using their Interpol badges, they learned from the ticket agent where they were headed. The two decided to split up: Luzzi would follow O'Sullivan to Córdoba and Gozzo would follow Schmidt to Seville. They weren't concerned with Nina's flight to Málaga, and they had no way of knowing her plans drive to Granada and then Córdoba to meet up with the others.

After hour-long flights, Erick, Brian and Nina each arrived in their target cities. Hiding in plain sight, Gozzo and Luzzi flew on the same planes as Erick and Brian. Minutes after arrival, Brian was on his way to pick up his rental car. A hundred yards behind him, Paolo's cell phone rang.

"*Pronto!*"

"Paolo?"

"Ah, Director! *Come stai?*"

"*Bene.* Paolo, I have some news for you. My nephew had technical difficulties this morning and he lost the trail of O'Sullivan and Schmidt, but we have new information about O'Sullivan."

"Ah, you don't need to worry Director. We are, how do you say, old-fashioned investigators and are on their trail right now in southern Spain. I'm following the Americano. Gozzo is following Schmidt."

"Terrific! Stay on them, Paolo. Let me tell you what we learned this morning."

"Not now, Director. I am busy getting a rental car. We will talk to-night."

"Wait! Paolo, this is important. You need to hear it before I let you go."

"Okay, what do you have?"

"Agent O'Sullivan's wife flew to Amsterdam to find her husband."

Paolo gave an indignant sniff. "Why should I care about that?"

"This morning Philippe recorded a lengthy conversation in Schmidt's apartment between O'Sullivan's wife and a neighbor. She revealed Agent O'Sullivan was adopted after a woman gave him up as an infant. He was sent from Italy to America."

"Director, why are you telling me this? How does this involve me?"

"O'Sullivan's wife talked about letters recently found in a hope chest. O'Sullivan's wife said his birth mother was a woman named Katrina. She sent several letters revealing her own background and noting his real father was a malicious and brutal SS officer in the war."

"O'Sullivan's wife said the letters say Katrina's boyfriend, whom she had loved and moved to Germany for, returned to the house one night, high on methamphetamines called Pervitin, and he raped her. This Katrina woman said the rapist's name was Karl von Richter."

"Hmm. Interesting. Let me understand what you're saying. The stolen paintings referenced in the diary—the ones we are looking for—were planted by the SS solider named KvR. The KvR diary references a 'Katrina' several times. And O'Sullivan's wife says he was born to a woman named Katrina after claiming to be raped by an SS soldier. Do I have this right?"

"Yes."

"Director, are you saying Agent Brian O'Sullivan is Katrina Luciano's son?"

"Exactly. From the voice recording Philippe played for me, O'Sullivan's wife's explanations to the neighbor made it clear that letters left in an old German Bible with a family tree titled The von Richter Family and discov-ered days ago by O'Sullivan, imply precisely that mother-son relationship."

"Director, if you're right, O'Sullivan's head must be spinning right now and his concern to recover hidden paintings is no longer a priority. He's got to be more interested in finding his mother."

"Yes. And if he finds Katrina before your birthday, you know what that means, right?"

"Yes, Director. I understand your thinking, but I never like when you reach into my private life. We'll speak later. Let me process what you have told me. *Ciao!*"

"Remember, Paolo, right now you need to find the paintings. And when they're recovered, the money from selling one of the paintings can be shared just between you and me. We don't need Antonio involved in this. He and the others can be discarded. Good-bye, Paolo."

The information about Brian O'Sullivan was a gut punch to Paolo and had him suddenly feeling uncomfortable and concerned. His sixty-fifth birthday was in a few days and O'Sullivan had suddenly become a problem he needed to resolve.

Paolo was signing the paperwork for his rental—a smaller, less conspicuous white SEAT Ibiza—when he noticed Brian's red SEAT Leon rental leaving the lot. He scribbled part of the plate number, hurried to his car, and followed at a good distance, still thinking about the Director's revelation. Suddenly, finding the two paintings wasn't as important as it had been only an hour earlier.

CHAPTER SIXTEEN

Followed in Seville

I n the Seville airport, a similar scenario took place with Erick getting his car and Antonio following at a cautious distance. Antonio checked his phone and retrieved a voice message from the Director wishing him good luck.

After a short drive into the city, Erick arrived at the first church on Nina's list: the Cathedral de Seville. Nina provided extra notes about the site's history alongside each target location. The huge church was originally ordered to be built as a mosque in 1172 by caliph Abu Ya`qub Yusef. It was dedicated in 1182 and completed in 1198. Like other mosques in Andalusia, the building and the adjoining Alcázar Palace was Christianized in 1248 when the Moors were pushed south into Africa by Spanish Christians.

Erick went to the rectory's office and introduced himself to the priest as an Interpol agent. He was given permission to walk around the grounds and through the interior of the mosque-turned-church. He wanted to observe the layout and create a mindset as if he were an SS officer in the middle of World War II carrying two paintings with the purpose of hiding them. Antonio parked across the busy street and watched Erick walk the exterior of the property. He was certain he knew what Erick was thinking as he moved about.

After his walk of the perimeter, Erick headed inside and when he finished, returned outside with a priest. As he waved his arms, pointing to distinct architectural elements, he was undoubtedly talking about how grand the building was. Antonio knew if something had been discovered, Erick's body language would have been upbeat as he exited. But that wasn't the case. After about five minutes, Erick and the priest shook hands and Erick returned to his car thinking about the design. *The Cathedral de Seville is a beautiful and classically designed gothic church with flying buttress wings, but it's not where the art pieces are hidden.* He was off to his next location.

***

After arriving on time in Málaga, Nina rented a car and used a paper map to find her way to Antequera to inspect the Alcazaba. Along the way, she made a side trip and drove through the nearby Torcal de Antequera to see its unusual landform. She stopped three times, taking in the amazing sight. A local road sign identified the area as the largest karst landscape in Europe, having been under water millions of years earlier. After spending about twenty minutes, she continued on to Antequera, arriving about 11. As she hadn't had breakfast, she stopped for a quick lunch.

After Nina finished her salad, she crossed the street to her first stop: the Alcazaba. She spent forty-five minutes walking through its many halls and rooms, admiring the beautiful Arabic and Moorish architecture. But not seeing any indication of newer mortar or construction where KvR might have hidden art, she returned to her car. It was almost 1 PM as she left for Granada. The drive would take only 90 minutes. Her plan was to spend the balance of the afternoon walking through the Alhambra and the Granada Cathedral, stay the night in a local hotel, and leave the next morning to catch up with Brian in Córdoba.

On the way, Nina grew tired from having been up so early that morning. She found the heat of the day oppressive. She stopped at a service station in Loja for an iced coffee. Her first few sips provided no relief, so she decided to nap in the car with the windows open under a shade tree. She thought about Brian as she dozed off and had a very pleasant dream. She was comfortable in his arms and was kissing him passionately. Her heartbeat raced in her sleep.

The blaring horn from a truck passing the little service station and cantina jolted her from sleep. She was startled and the dream flew away. But she knew something had made her feel good. Her brief stop had become a forty-minute nap. It took a few seconds to recall her day's objective. The ice in the coffee had melted but the remaining watered-down coffee with milk and shot of vanilla syrup still tasted good. Now feeling refreshed, Nina consulted her map and drove away, briefly thinking about the missing art, but pondering Brian's circumstances with his wife, and what might become of his search for his mother.

This whole situation is a complicated puzzle. First, I don't like Luzzi. He's bad news. KvR was bad news, too. Implementing Hitler's Final Solution against the Jews was horrible. I wonder who Ruth was? KvR mentions her several times with simple, short memories. Perhaps she was a young lover of his, but no doubt his focus was Katrina. He implies he wants to spend more time with her, but each time he does, he ends the entry by refocusing on his commitment to the SS.

And poor Brian. What he's been through! Finding out he was given up, sent to America, and adopted. Gosh! And the string of numbers Brian mentioned written on Katrina's final note. Perhaps it's the combination to a lock, or a safe, or something else holding valuables. But what? And where? It's all so complicated. I need to figure this out. And what's with his wife? Why do you stay with someone for so long when it's just not working!

Then her thoughts focused only on Brian. She realized she was becoming more attracted to him, and then images from her dream returned. It seemed so real. It made her want him more.

Nina was only ten miles from Granada when her rental car jerked and slowed down. Seemingly out of gas, it rolled down a small hill. She steered it onto the side of the highway for the last hundred feet as it slowly came to a stop.

Oh my God! Now what do I do?

She teared up momentarily, then composed herself and wiped her eyes. She got out of her car and opened the hood but had no idea what she was looking at. A few minutes later, two young men stopped to help. She explained what seemed to be the problem. One fellow jumped in the car and turned the key while the other stood next to her.

They heard the engine turning but not firing. "*Señora, no gasolina.*"

"Oh, but I must. I just rented the car, and the gasoline gauge says it's almost full."

"Ah! *Si. Pero la gasolina… no esta en el motor.* Uh, *la bomba por la gasolina es decompuesto.* Uh, how you say, gasoline pump no work?"

"*Señora,* come with us. *Yo soy Miguel. Mi hermano es Julio.* We are nice. We bring you to your house."

They seemed sincere and, having no alternative, Nina left the rental car at the roadside, got in their car, stuffing herself into the tiny back seat with her heavy carry-on bag.

She called Erick.

He sounded startled to hear from her so soon. "Nina, you sound a bit rattled."

She explained her situation, adding, "I'm changing today's objective in Granada because of this delay, and because I slept earlier. I'll go to the Alhambra first when I arrive and inspect it until it's dark outside. Tomorrow morning, I'll visit the Cathedral de Granada and catch a late morning train to meet Brian in Córdoba around noon. That'll give us plenty of time to inspect the Mezquita tomorrow afternoon."

"Taking the train is a good alternative," Erick suggested. "I'll be finished here in two hours. I'll call BJ to let him know what happened to your car and your change of arrival time in Córdoba."

Feeling better about her change of plans, Nina relaxed. The car ride with Miguel and Julio took twenty minutes.

Upon arriving at the majestic Alhambra Palace Hotel, where she planned to stay the night, Julio turned to her. "Ah, we are here, *señora!*"

Miguel lifted her bag from the back seat and rolled his eyes, surprised by its weight. He handed it to the hotel porter, and they smiled at Nina as she walked from the car.

"*Adios, señora!*"

"*Adios and muchas gracias, mi nuevo amigos!*"

They looked each other and sighed. "Ah! Julio, look at her! She is such an attractive woman. Her beauty stirs me deeply and makes me wonder."

"Miguel, how will you ever complete your schooling at the seminary with thoughts like that? Unless our pope can convince the old conservative Italian cardinals to remember the Apostles were married, the chance of a priest being allowed to marry in our Roman Catholic Church is hopeless in our lifetime. You are out of luck."

"I know. I love Jesus and want to serve him, but my desire is to make love to such a beautiful woman like that lady. I admit it remains a problem for me."

"Miguel, Mama committed you to God when you were born. Now you must enter the priesthood to fulfill her promise to God."

"I know. I know. You tell me this all the time. Why don't you be a good brother and go instead of me."

"Never."

CHAPTER SEVENTEEN

Day One – Late Afternoon

The Alhambra Palace Hotel lobby was bright from the afternoon sun coming through tall windows. Nina admired the decorative tile floor as she approached the ornate front desk. Given a magnetic-style electronic key, she rode the elevator to the fourth floor. Inside her room, she immediately charged her phone, then called the rental company to explain how the car had stalled. She gave them the road marker and said the key was under the front mat.

Her next call was to Brian. "Hi, it's me."

"Hi Nina. How's your day going? Did you get to the Alcazaba? Are you in Granada now?"

"Well, yes… and yes. I went through the Alcazaba in Antequera earlier today and found nothing. I just checked into the hotel and will head to the Alhambra in a few minutes."

"Nina, you sound tired."

"I am. It's the heat. I even napped briefly on my way here. Did Erick call you?"

"No."

She explained the fuel pump failure and how she got a ride into Granada. "I'll take a train to Córdoba tomorrow. The mid-morning train arrives at noon. Is that good for you?"

"Sure. I'll be at the station waiting for you."

"Thanks. Just talking to you makes me feel better. What did you accomplish today?"

"I followed your list. I inspected the Mudejar Chapel of San Bartolomé and the Synagogue of Córdoba. I saw no signs of the old arches being disturbed by any recent construction in either location. I'm on my way to the hotel now. I'm thinking of a salad for supper and a good night's sleep."

"After I walk through the Alhambra, I'll return and take a nice bath."

"Sounds good. We all were up early. It's been a long day and tomorrow will be another busy day. Last night at dinner you said the Mezquita was your number-one target. I'm looking forward to doing that inspection with you."

"Same here. Given its interior architecture and the clues left by KvR, I'm betting we'll find something there. Pleasant dreams, Brian."

"Have a good sleep, Nina."

Minutes later, Brian parked a few spaces from the hotel's colorful entry canopy. The late afternoon sun was beginning to set behind distant mountains to the west. He checked in and a hotel porter brought his bag upstairs. Brian used the restroom off the lobby and headed to the dining room.

At that same moment, Paolo, who'd been trailing Brian all day entered the hotel and headed across the lobby to check in. He suddenly saw Brian who was heading directly toward him. They were only two seconds from bumping into each other when Paolo turned and looked away to hide his face. Brian walked right past him, less than three feet away, and continued to the dining room.

Paolo held back a moment and then approached the front desk. He pulled out his credit card and flashed his Interpol badge. Placing a U.S. twenty-dollar bill on the counter, he asked the desk clerk for information. "My good friend, Brian O'Sullivan, arrived in the last fifteen minutes. Can you tell me his room number please?"

"One moment. Yes. Mr. O'Sullivan's in Room 302. Shall I call him for you? I can put the call on the house phone over there."

"*No, grazie.* We have a meeting first thing in the morning, and I want to be able to bang on his door if he's late."

"Here's your key. You're in Room 402, the room directly above his. Good evening, Mr. Luzzi."

"*Si. Buona notte.*"

Brian sat and scanned the menu. He asked for a glass of local red wine. The waiter suggested a local red blended Cuvée made with Tempranillo, Mazuelo, Graciano, and Garnacha. He totally enjoyed the full-bodied flavor of the wine and was enjoying his salad when his cell phone rang.

"BJ, how are you making out?"

"Hi, Erick. I found nothing of interest today, as we all expected. Nina arrives tomorrow, and we'll head over to the Mezquita. We'll see you late tomorrow for dinner, right?"

"Yes. I called an old friend when I arrived this morning and am seeing him tonight. We grew up together. He has a wonderful wife and two young children. He invited me to stay over."

"Good for you. Have you checked in with Wilhelm?"

"Yes. For some reason he seemed surprised to hear from me. I gave him the rundown and explained you and Nina would be working together tomorrow and I'd join you tomorrow night. Did you speak with Nina yet? She had an issue with her rental car."

"Yes. Initially she was all upset at first but sounded decidedly better after we talked. Have a good evening."

"You too, Brian."

After supper, Brian took a brief stroll around the hotel grounds. He then returned to his room and read Katrina's letters, her extra pages with the sad and horrific details, and the other letters she sent to Sheila. He wiped away a few tears. He read them twice more, each time trying to observe something different about her. He paid attention to the words she used in each sentence, as well as her penmanship. How she formed the shapes and loops of her letters above and below the lines showed she was a passionate woman. *Gosh, is there any chance she's still alive?*

Two hours later, thinking Brian was settled in his room for the night, Paolo headed down to the hotel bar. He sat at the far end and lit a cigarette.

"Sir?"

"Campari. No ice."

Reflecting on his director's earlier comments, Paolo's mind drifted to his own family's circumstances long ago—when he was a youngster.

Papa's passing made things difficult but when Mamma died, life became impossible, and everything changed. Nonna and I had nothing. I remember the first time I was caught stealing bread. But I had to continue to steal to bring home food. Then the lady came to visit Mamma. I took her to Mamma and Papa's grave. She saw we had nothing. She was kind and took us into their home. But after Nonna died, life in their house became unbearable. I hated her husband and the pious way he tried to punish me, always making me kneel and pray the rosary. I hated every inch of him. And I didn't want to be adopted. I didn't belong to them. I wasn't their property. Changing my name back to Luzzi felt good.

And then I fixed him good… the big boss… the wine-business owner. I made sure he'd never enjoy the fruits of his efforts. Ha! It was even easier than I expected. All these years the sale of the stupid business paid an allowance, but it's never been enough. I've had plenty of escapades along the way, thanks to Old Man Mueller to support my lifestyle. And in a few days, when I turn sixty-five, I become eligible to inherit all the money Luca left in escrow. It's rightfully mine because I've cared for her all these years.

But now, could what Wilhelm said be true? Is it possible this O'Sullivan character is Katrina's real son? Could he be the other rightful heir to their business fortune sitting in escrow? Fate is playing a cruel game! Whether it's true or not, I'll stop O'Sullivan the same way I stopped Luca. But first, we'll play the art-discovery game tomorrow. In the morning, I'll call Mueller and find out the latest information he has for me.

Paolo took a last swallow of Campari and headed to his room. He set his alarm to wake him early, making sure he could track Brian's activities in the morning.

Upstairs, Brian climbed onto the bed, lay atop the covers, and closed his eyes. The ceiling fan spun slowly above him. He was exhausted, but his mind remained active, thinking through a dozen things. After ten minutes, he got out of bed, sat at the desk, and began writing a list of events in his life.

Growing up in Astoria
Moving to Staten Island
College
My doctorate
Dad's passing
Mom's accident
The hope chest and discovering the Bible
Katrina's letter and the more detailed pages
The Luciano Wine Export Company's business address on the two pages of Katrina's addendum pages.

He started a new list, going further back in time and inserting more milestones and people.

Being given up by Katrina

Meeting the lady with the blue eyes

Meeting Grace at McSorley's

Our disappointment of not being able to have children

My professorship

Being recruited to Interpol

Keeping the secret from Grace all these years

My retirement

Erick

This trip

Nina

Wilhelm

Paolo

Antonio

The Luciano Wine Company.

Oh, yes, the code! The code on Katrina's addendum. Let me add that. What is the code for?

Placing those thoughts on the list, Brian felt free to sleep and get much-needed rest. But he woke several times during the night, each time warm and uncomfortable. Then, just before dawn, his deepest subconscious thoughts and concerns coalesced into a dream.

He found himself in a room with dark wooden walls like those in a cabin. He witnessed Karl's drunkenness and his brutality. Seeing Katrina's horrific rape, he tried to help her but felt bound and motionless. He yelled, but his sound was silent. His dream then moved him to the comfort of being in his mother's arms. He could see her face, and then her blue eyes. They teared up as she lifted him. Then he saw the face of an old man and he heard her words, "Please take care of my child."

Brian suddenly woke, startled at recalling her exact words echoing so clearly and from so long ago. He bunched his pillows and fell back to sleep.

CHAPTER EIGHTEEN

Day Two – Followed in Córdoba

The next morning, Brian woke feeling tired. He shaved and showered, thinking about his day's itinerary.

My first stop, the Alcazar of the Christian Monarchs, will take most of the morning. Then I pick up Nina at the train station at noon. A quick lunch, and we'll head to the Mosque Cathedral of Córdoba, commonly known as the Mezquita. I think we'll find the two paintings we're looking for, but it won't be easy, given its interior design.

The phone rang as he stepped from the shower. It was room service, apologizing. "The chef never showed this morning, so we can't provide a robust breakfast service to your room."

So, Brian dressed and headed downstairs for toast and coffee.

On the far side of the dining room, Paolo sat in a dark corner, peering over the local Spanish newspaper. He spotted Brian arriving.

Ah, Katrina's son. I recall the conversation when she first told me about her baby boy, and how I suddenly felt so awkward. I felt like a replacement. It made me angry. But Katrina will soon die. The millions put in escrow at the sale of Luca's business will be mine in a few days. I can finally quit this stupid Interpol job and live my life as I see fit. I will have the houses in Sorrento and Capri, and the villa in Malta where Katrina now lives, all to myself.

Today and tomorrow will be interesting. Brian won't be happy when I'm done with him. It will be sudden and quick. On the other hand, maybe I'll let him suffer a while for not visiting his mother sooner.

Brian brought his bag downstairs, ate breakfast, and headed outside. Paolo watched him walk to his rental car and drive away. He followed behind by twenty seconds.

From his study of Mudejar art history on the Iberian Peninsula, Brian knew the immense Alcazar of the Christian Monarchs complex was a

Visigothic fortress in medieval times. Moors eventually captured Córdoba, and the Caliphate updated the Alcazar during the 1100s and early 1200s. Christian forces recaptured Córdoba in 1236 and in 1328 the building was again updated as a Christian church. In 1492 Queen Isabella, sitting in the Alcazar's upper corner room, gave Christopher Columbus the approval to find a new trade route to India by sailing west on behalf of Spain.

Having been here years earlier Brian again took the opportunity to admire the magnificent gardens and courtyards before going inside. He spent three hours walking the interior and inspecting walls and arches before concluding KvR hadn't hidden the art in this building. He saw he had thirty minutes to pick up Nina at noon.

Paolo followed Brian from a good distance and concluded his brisk pace through the interior implied the paintings were elsewhere. He followed Brian toward the exit. Brian walked halfway around the building's exterior before returning to the car.

While exiting the Alcazar of Christian Monarchs, Brian noticed a small white car he'd seen parked at the hotel earlier that morning parked at the hotel. That same car seemed to be following him at a good distance. To confirm his suspicions, Brian began driving in a rectangle around several streets, all unnecessary turns. The white car followed.

Meanwhile, in the other car, Paolo spoke aloud to his ghost passenger.

"Ha! He is lost! He is driving around in a big square! *Stupido!*"

Recognizing he was being trailed, Brian made a final turn and headed for the train station. Nina's train was due in five minutes. *I'm guessing it's Paolo following me. I should call Erick and let him know what's happening here. He might also be in the same situation but not be aware of it yet.*

He parked at the station and called his Interpol partner.

"Erick."

"Good morning, BJ! How's the weather where you are?"

"Never mind the weather, Erick. We have a problem."

"Has Nina not arrived?"

"Her train should be here in two minutes. Our problem is more serious."

"What's happening?"

"I'm being followed."

"Really?"

"Yes. I made several driving maneuvers this morning that made no sense and the car continued to follow me. In fact, the same car has just parked at the far end of the parking lot here at the train station. I'm not sure who it is, but I'm guessing it's one of the Italian agents we met at headquarters. I'm concerned. If Luzzi is following me, Gozzo is no doubt following you. Watch for him. When Nina arrives, we'll grab a coffee and head over to the Mezquita. Despite being followed, we still have to find the missing art."

"Thanks for the heads up. Obviously, winning a few extra months' pay isn't their only goal. I can't help but suspect the Director has something to do with this. If they find the art, those two might be up to the old tricks they were suspected of with Klaus. Do you have a handgun with you?"

"Me? Handgun? Of course not! I inspect and validate art. Erick, you're freaking me out!"

"BJ, these two paintings are unbelievably valuable. You know as well as I do, they could be worth over thirty million U.S. dollars. I told you rumors imply our Director's father may still be alive. I'd say Wilhelm, his old man and those two are scheming to defraud the Agency. So, listen closely. If you spot a location where the art may be hidden, be nonchalant. Don't bring attention to yourselves. Act as if nothing has been found. I'll see you this evening and we can discuss the situation further. If I find I'm being followed, I'll fix it. Call me if anything else happens. Good luck on your search with Nina."

"Erick. Should I go to a gun store?"

"No."

"Well, I'm thinking maybe I should. Hey, Erick, I see the train pulling in. We can chat later."

"Remember to act nonchalant so he doesn't get any idea where the paintings are if you spot the hiding location. I'll see you both at the hotel tonight."

As Brian hung up, he saw Nina stepping down from the train and making her way along the platform. A moment later she exited the small station building's front door.

He got out to greet her. "Hi Nina, how was the ride?"

"Not all that great. The back-and-forth rocking on those old, uneven tracks almost made me seasick. And we're a little late because the train stopped halfway here. We heard someone saying *'Vacas! Vacas y un grande toro!'* They were saying cows and a large bull were on the tracks ahead of us. The conductor was very blunt saying, 'if it were just one, the train would have kept going. But when there are many, we must stop or it's a terrible mess.' Anyway, I'm here now and delighted to see you."

"I'm happy to see you, too." Brian bent to get her bag. "Here, let me get that... Oh, goodness! What do you have in this, young lady? Uh, never mind, I shouldn't be asking a question like that." He hefted the bag and lugged it to the car.

As he tossed the bag into the trunk, she gave him a kiss. "Thanks so much for picking me up, Brian! You're looking good today. Was the hotel nice? Did you have a nice sleep? How about the Alcazar of Christian Monarchs? How did that go? I'm sorry to barrage you with so many questions at once. But it's so nice to see you."

"Before I answer all those questions, have you eaten anything this morning?"

"Not really. I had a black coffee and an almond biscotti on the train."

"Then let's grab a bite. There's a little café nearby. And we need to chat about something that's come up."

"Sure, Brian. Is it about your wife arriving in Amsterdam?"

He shook his head. "I'll tell you once we're seated."

Keeping his eyes wide open, he scanned the area for the little white car. He spotted it about seventy-five yards away. A man stood beside it, smoking a cigarette, but it was too far to see his face. They got in his rental car, and he drove completely around the block, returning to the same spot where he'd parked.

"Did you forget something?"

"No. We're here, Nina. The coffee shop's right over there. Let's go quickly."

"Really, Brian? We could have walked. What's going on?"

"We need to hurry."

He got out of the car, slammed his door, and grabbing her arm, whooshed her across the street to the café in a slight run. Once inside, he spotted a table at the rear. Still holding her arm, they headed briskly to the back of the café. He positioned himself with his back up against the back wall, where he could see the entrance and the café's front window.

"Brian, what's going on? What was the drive around the block about? And why did we just run from the car?"

As she spoke, a man's silhouette moved past the café's wide plate-glass window. Brian immediately focused on the door as it opened. As he suspected, it was Paolo Luzzi. Just then, the waiter came to the table, blocking Brian's view.

"*Señor y señora, buenos días.*"

Brian leaned to the side, then scooched his chair over a bit, staring frontward as Nina replied to the waiter.

"*Dos café negro, por favor. Y pan tostado con mantequilla. Gracias, señor.*"

As soon as the waiter left, she asked, "Brian, what are you staring at?"

"We have a problem. I thought I was being followed yesterday but wasn't sure. This morning, on the way here to the train station, I confirmed that by making a few unnecessary turns and the same white car stayed with me. I called Erick and told him Paolo's tailing me, and to be on the lookout because Antonio might be following him."

"Are you sure?"

He gave a grim nod. "Luzzi just walked into this café. Look. He's sitting up front, looking out the window with his back to us. Remember the other night when we went to dinner, we said we found the GPS and voice recording devices? We know they were planted to enable them to follow us. We got rid of them, but now it seems we're being surveilled in person. I suspect they're keeping an eye on us, letting us do all the work."

"Maybe it's just a coincidence? After all, they're also trying to find the art."

"No, Nina. Luzzi wouldn't have driven in a big square if he weren't following me. Here's my concern: Once we find the art, it could be stolen from us, and we become expendable."

"What do you mean, expendable? All that happens is they win the prize. Right?"

"Maybe not. Erick told me two Interpol agents assigned to Wilhelm's father went missing. Wilhelm must be scheming with Luzzi and Gozzo to benefit from the art hidden by KvR."

"Brian, you're scaring me."

"I'm uncomfortable about this, too. Erick gets here tonight. He suggested we explore the Mezquita today, as planned. It's likely Luzzi will follow us. If we find the paintings' hiding location, we need to be quiet and pretend we didn't see where they're stashed. We'll act like we're still looking and later, when we eat dinner with Erick, we'll devise our extraction plan to retrieve the art."

Brian paused a moment, as if to catch his breath.

"Are you okay?"

"I'm all right but my heart's beating very fast. It should calm down in a few minutes. Frankly, Nina, I'm feeling a bit overwhelmed. There's something else at play here I can't put my finger on."

"It's gotten complicated," she agreed. "And now you have Grace to deal with, as well. I can't believe she had the nerve to follow you to Amsterdam. Is your marriage a happy marriage?"

Brian shrugged. "No marriage is perfect. Grace has her difficult moments. Maybe more than most women, and in the last few years, perhaps even more. She's been depressed. But let's not talk about her right now. We have bigger concerns to deal with … and I'm curious as to what you learned about the Luciano Wine Export Company and what Luzzi has to do with that."

Nina looked at him as he spoke and, despite the dangerous circumstances, she couldn't help wondering what it'd be like to be with him.

"*Señor, señora, tu café negros con tostadas.*"

"Brian, I care a lot for you. I'd like to… I mean maybe can we—"

"Nina, right now we have the project. And with these guys following us, we might be in danger. We both need to stay focused on finding the art. But I understand how you feel. I really do."

He glanced up front. Paolo was still holding up a newspaper. In a low voice, Brian continued whispering how they'd map and inspect the interior of the Mezquita. They speculated about how they might extract the paintings and conceal them from Paolo if they managed to find them. Both concluded Erick's help would be necessary.

Brian's phone rang suddenly, and the ringing caught Paolo's attention. He peaked around his newspaper. Nina could see him turn and look as Brian ducked his head, answering in a muffled voice.

"BJ, you're right," Erick told him, forgoing the pleasantries. "I spotted Gozzo following me a little while ago. He can follow me all he wants. I'm going to do my job, investigating the churches."

"How's that going?"

"Yesterday I visited the Cathedral De Seville and the Iglesia de Santa María la Blanca. I visited and stayed with my friend and his family last night. This morning I've already been to the Basílica De La Macarena, the Church of Santa Caridad and the Capilla de San José. All are beautiful and ornate. I inspected the interiors. Not one of them has the type of arches KvR describes we're looking for. I'll leave early today. Gozzo's presence is annoying. I have a mind to confront him if he gets too close."

"Don't do that. We need you here in Córdoba. We're headed to the Mezquita now. It should take us three hours to inspect the interior. Nina's convinced it's where KvR hid the art. If we find what we are looking for, we'll leave and return to the hotel to develop an extraction plan based on what we see.. I've been inside there before. The arches are very high so we will need and ladder and your help. We can discuss the details tonight. But I'm concerned. I'm getting strong feeling our lives may be at risk. You'll be here by six, right?"

"Correct. I have one more church to check out. I'll leave Seville by four thirty and should get there just before dinnertime. Good luck this afternoon!"

"Thanks, Erick. Watch your back."

"Don't worry about me."

Brian closed his flip phone. Paolo raised his newspaper.

"Nina, let's slip out through the kitchen. We'll leave my car where I parked it for now and get a cab to the Mezquita. Let me know when you're ready."

"Let me finish this slice of toast and we can go. Wow! I feel like I'm in a spy movie."

His expression turned grim again. "It's not a movie. This is the real thing, Nina. We need to be quick."

As she took a last bite, he put a twenty-dollar bill on the table, and whisked her out through hanging pots and pans, bumping into a chef along the way. Outside, they ran down a long alley putting them far from the front door. Still holding her hand, they turned left past a smelly Dumpster, causing two rats to scatter. They turned right, reaching the street behind the restaurant and jumped into a parked cab.

"*Hola, señor!*"

"Mezquita, por favor!"

"Si, señor."

"Brian, now my heart is pounding!"

Nina sat next to him in the back seat, clutching arm. She nervously looked up at him. Brian looked back at her and smiled. *Why am I thinking in this crazy situation that she has beautiful eyes?*

CHAPTER NINETEEN

The Mezquita

The ride to the Mezquita took three minutes. Built as a mosque, the imposing structure now housed a Catholic church. Amid its nineteen aisles stood ornately designed double-tiered columns supporting a flat ceiling beneath a flat roof. Brian took the brief time to remind her what they would see inside.

"Nina, the building has a huge space originally designed to allow Muslims to worship and was also used for teaching and preaching. I first visited here with Grace years ago, for our tenth wedding anniversary. I had a meeting in Barcelona, and we headed over here to Córdoba because of a recommendation from a colleague. I started counting the columns and couldn't believe there were hundreds, all made from granite, marble, onyx, and other stone. The tops of the columns were originally a Roman design, but when a Sultan expanded the building, Moorish column tops called capitals were used. There are so many it's been described as a 'forest of columns.'

"Based on KvR's diary and his references to 'those columns,' you're right in saying this is the most likely place for the art to be hidden. But with so many columns, we'll have our work cut out for us. We might only see a patch of disturbed mortar. The paint color at the top of the columns or on the ceiling will differ, so we need to look carefully."

"I had studied about this place and I'm so excited to be here and see it in person. But Brian... so many columns!"

"That's why we now need to think like KvR. Remember your comment about a chess move putting the king in check?"

She nodded. "Yes. It was a note in his diary."

"Well, that notation was a hint to himself, or perhaps to another, as to where the paintings are. We must think of the spaces between the columns as squares on a chessboard. Using that approach, we'll cut our search time."

Nina gave an emphatic nod. "I think your idea is exactly right."

"Just wait 'til you get inside. My idea's only a start. With a total of eight hundred fifty-six columns holding a flat roof, the ceiling spaces equal almost fourteen chess boards!"

As they reached the old mosque, Nina checked to see if they were being followed. The white car Brian described earlier was nowhere in sight.

"I have money for the driver." Nina handed the cab driver cash and they hurried to the front door of the Mezquita.

Once inside, it took a moment for Nina's eyes adjust to the darkness. She was awestruck, peering through the endless array of colorful columns. For the first time, she had a full sense of the size and scope of the challenge.

"Oh my God, Brian! Finding an arch with slight discoloration from work done in the mid-nineteen forties to hide paintings will not be an easy task. The paintings are likely rolled up inside muslin cloth so the disturbance might only be one to two feet in diameter."

Brian walked ahead, again recalling his visit here with Grace, and her exact words saying, 'I don't like it here,' and 'Why would someone build such a place?' But now, Nina stood beside him and, in stark contrast, expressed excitement and complete awe at the fantastic Moorish design. He so appreciated her love for art and, in this case, the artful and decorative construction. He then thought about Nina's earlier question that he cut short. *Where was she going with her words earlier? Maybe it's the soft lighting in here, but she's suddenly attractive. What is wrong with me? We're in the middle of a crazy — and dangerous — situation and I'm thinking things I shouldn't about a much younger woman who's not my wife!*

"Brian, this pamphlet shows the layout and outline of the building. Let's use this information to spread out and examine the different arches."

"I'd rather we stick closer together. It won't be long before Paolo shows up. I don't want him to separate the two of us."

Nina retrieved her notes from the diary. She looked up the reference to the chess board, citing where the "checkmate" takes place. Using a pen on the pamphlet, she divided the space among the columns into multiple chess boards. "How's this look?"

"It's a start. Let's scan the perimeter first. Remember what I said earlier. We should see some minor difference in the color of the wood or painted plaster or molding along the edge of an arch."

"It won't be easy in this lighting. Our eyes need to adjust."

"A checkmate usually happens in the last two rows of a chess board. We should go down two rows at a time, side by side."

Following Brian's suggestion, Nina moved to the next row and walked parallel with him, gazing up at the ceiling. The colorful stone columns and decorative red-and-white arches amazed her. Brian kept pace with her one row away.

She remained amazed at the colorful stone columns and red and white arches.

Five minutes later, Paolo Luzzi arrived outside. From reading the diary, he'd also concluded the Mezquita was a likely place for the paintings to be hidden. He entered the front and scanned the huge area. He found the area very dark and full of flickering shadows from the hanging candles. He took a full minute to let his older eyes adjust. The light was barely enough to see fifty feet ahead. Another twenty seconds passed and with his eyes now adjusted to the dark he spotted Nina and Brian some thirty yards ahead of him.

He watched them methodically pace the interior's perimeter for almost an hour. They occasionally would skip several aisles and continue walking side by side again. He silently wondered at their odd movements. Thirty yards away, Paolo slowly followed them, hiding behind one column and then another, and another. His neck ached from constantly looking up at the ceiling.

Then she saw it!

"Brian! Brian! Over here! I found it! It's over here!" Nina's excited voice echoed loudly through the former mosque's cavernous space.

Darn it! I told her to be quiet if she saw anything! Her voice could raise the dead!

Hearing Nina's apparent discovery, Paolo edged closer in a squat, peering from behind a column.

Brian, lagging behind quickly hurried to her location. "Nina, quiet! First, this is a church. Worse, someone might be spying on us."

"Sorry, Brian. Look up. Right there! Can you see it?"

"Uh, not yet."

She moved closely beside him and pointed.

"Now I'm seeing what you mean, but Nina, you must keep your voice low."

"Look at what I drew on the brochure. If you take a chessboard and lay the white square in the lower right corner, and imagine we're standing on the chessboard, this space is where a king is often trapped on the last row. It follows the 'checkmate' hint KvR gave in the diary. He obviously knew how to play."

"Good find, Nina. I know you're excited but keep your voice down. Let's continue to go around a bit more as we planned. Later tonight, we can discuss what we've found with Erick."

"I'm sorry I got so excited. It's just so *obvious*. The paint colors are a bit different. Can you see the red is slightly different from the other arches? The wooden trim isn't sealed with shellac – there's no shine. Nor is the wood stained properly. It was done poorly."

"Well, right now, poorly is good, since it allowed you to notice the difference in the finish even in low light. Now let's move on and keep walking as if we're still trying to find the spot. Paolo could be here someplace, watching us."

The two continued on, pretending to be scanning the ceiling. They eventually made their way to the front of the Muslim prayer area and toward the Catholic church. Paolo watched and waited at a distance. He remained still for a few minutes and when they were far enough away, he moved to where she'd gotten excited and spoke so loudly. He looked up and noticed the same decorative variations she had indicated. He smiled, impressed with the young woman's acuity in finding the probable hiding place.

Nina and Brian were much further away now. They entered the church and were getting ready to find the sacristan. He had already begun thinking about how to proceed and access the ceiling.

"When Erick arrives later, we'll explain what we found. We'll return in the morning to remove the art. I'll find the sacristan or the pastor now, explain who we are and what we're doing, and let him know we'll need a ladder tomorrow morning. Then we can head back to wait for Erick."

Brian saw a sign identifying where the office was located. Upon entering, he learned the elderly pastor was taking his siesta, and it would be about thirty minutes before he would wake. Understanding the circumstances, the office assistant said she would alert the sacristan and agreed to allow them to return in the morning, providing they completed their extraction before the 9 AM Mass, to eliminate any noise in the prayer area and the church. With that condition agreed upon, they took a cab back to the café across from the train station, got into his rental car and headed back to the hotel.

"We sure worked well together today."

"We sure did, Nina. Your logic and spatial skills came in handy. Nice work—although you needed to be quiet. During dinner with Erick, we can discuss our plan to remove the ceiling panel that appears to be hiding the art. The office assistant said their sacristan would bring a ladder by seven. It shouldn't take long to get the paintings. We should be good after that. Then you and Erick can return to Amsterdam with the paintings. I'd like to look at the last bit of paperwork about the sale of Luciano Wine Exports Company to Global Wines and Spirits. Maybe if I follow the money trail, I'll uncover exactly what happened to Luca and Katrina."

CHAPTER TWENTY

Day Two – Late Afternoon

Two hours away in Seville, not yet aware of Nina and Brian's find, Erick completed his last inspection. The Alcázar of Seville was a royal palace built by Peter of Castile after the conquest of the Abbadid Mosque. Magnificent in its design and construction, it also lacked any noticeable work or modifications near any arches.

Finished for the day, he headed back to the car, planning to call the Director and leave for Córdoba. Twice during this inspection, he'd spotted Antonio. Erick wanted to confront him but knew a fistfight could be nasty, and Brian and Nina needed him tomorrow in Córdoba. He thought he might mention to the Director that Antonio was following him but decided against it.

As he walked up to the rental car, he discovered it had a flat tire. Shaking his head in frustration at the inconvenience, he grabbed his key, popped open the trunk and pulled out the spare tire. As he leaned forward to grab the jack, Erick felt a sudden jolt in his back. The unbearable, searing pain lasted only a moment. He fell forward, his torso conveniently slumping into the trunk.

Antonio smiled. The silencer had effectively muffled his handgun. He reached for the car keys still in Erick's hand. Then, grabbing his lower legs, he lifted Erick's body the rest of the way into the trunk. Antonio shoved the jack to the side next to Erick's body and slammed the trunk.

From behind a nearby tree, Juan saw it all and approached Antonio.

"*Ah, Antonio*. It is good to meet you in person. I heard from Wilhelm yesterday and he explained everything. We spoke again this morning and he told me where to find you. I have been watching you both from a distance and I will take the keys and take over from here. You are free now to go meet Paolo in Córdoba."

"*Grazie*, Juan! I know your father. He has been a fixer for many years for Klaus, and now you are helping as well. *Bravo!* I was told you might come by at some point to help Paolo and me."

"Yes. I will finish changing the flat tire, then dispose of this car and your friend."

"I'm planning my next vacation in your hometown of Málaga. Will I see you there?"

"I don't think so."

"Too bad. Here, take this envelope for your troubles, Juan."

"*Muchas gracias!* Your generosity is unnecessary. It will go to my daughter's school fund."

Antonio handed him an envelope thick with cash then walked to his rental car parked nearby. He got in and when he turned the ignition key, the explosion blew out nearby windows. Within seconds, a raging inferno engulfed the car. The fire was so fierce Juan raised his hand to shield his eyes. He squinted and looked closely at the burning car. He could barely make out Antonio's desperately writhing figure inside as the car's paint bubbled and peeled away from the metal.

Quickly changing the tire, Juan put the jack and flat into the backseat, and drove Erick's rental toward Málaga. On his way south, he pulled over alongside a large old tree, opened the trunk, and removed Erick's body. He dragged it to the back of the tree, and then kicking it several times, rolled the body down an incline into a ditch. As Juan drove away, he called Wilhelm and left a brief message. "It's all done, as you requested. Regards to your father Klaus."

Juan looked at his watch. If he hurried, he'd be home just in time for his daughter's seventeenth birthday party.

***

In Córdoba, Brian and Nina returned to the hotel and arrived just as the lobby's antique grandfather clock chimed five.

"Nina, while you check in, I try calling Erick."

He dialed. The call went straight to voicemail. He tried again a minute later, with the same result.

Brian frowned. *Maybe his battery died. He's done that before, and he told me at the airport he forgot his spare battery. It's late but let me try calling the Director. Even if he's in on this scheme, we need to report.*

He punched in the sequence of numbers for Interpol and then Wilhelm's extension number.

"Yes."

"Director, it's Agent O'Sullivan. We're finishing up in Córdoba and will continue tomorrow. Has Erick called you with today's report?"

"No, he's not called in yet. I've been expecting to hear from one of you before I left my office this afternoon."

"I've been trying to reach him but haven't been able to."

"I'm told Schmidt is a capable agent, but I understand he's gay. Maybe he met someone or went to see one of his gay friends. How was your day, O'Sullivan?"

"We're making progress, Director. Nina's joined me here in Córdoba, and we've eliminated a few places where the art pieces might have been hidden. But we both believe we're close to finding them."

"Great. Let me know as soon as you come across anything."

"Will do, and if Erick calls you, please have him call us. Oh, one last thing Director: Erick's private life is his own business. He's never been one to let his personal life interfere with his work. I couldn't just let your comment slip by without addressing it."

An uncomfortable pause stretched across the phone line. Brian somehow knew Wilhelm would dislike being put in his place.

"Call me tomorrow with any news, O'Sullivan," he said, his tone curt. "Good evening."

Nina finished checking in then looked around and found him in the corner of the lobby. She went and sat next to him, listening as he concluded the call. She noted his worried expression as he flipped his phone shut and peered into the distance, appearing to be lost in a dozen different thoughts.

"I'm concerned. Erick may show up later and simply tell us his phone battery died, but my gut instinct tells me something's wrong. He said he'd leave early; he should be here by now. Knowing Erick, he'd have called one of us to say he'd been delayed."

"Relax, Brian. I'm sure he's fine. Turn your thoughts to what we've accomplished today! Finding the hiding spot in the Mezquita is an *enormous* success for our team."

"You're right. It was a great find. Tomorrow we'll gather what was hidden and be eligible for our reward. But for now, it's time for a little celebration dinner. There's a great little place around the corner. I ate there years ago. You'll like it. Erick should get here soon. I'll leave a message for him at the front desk to join us when he arrives. Let's meet back down here in fifteen minutes."

Nina nodded. She stood and stretched. Then raising her arms, she removed a hair clip, let her hair swing loose, and ran her fingers through it.

Taken by her attractive and shapely body Brian mused that it'd been a long while since he'd appreciated an attractive young woman. He thought about her as they went to their respective rooms to freshen up.

Nina put on a little makeup and a bit of expensive perfume; it was the first time she'd worn it in Brian's presence.

When they returned to the lobby, they left the name of the restaurant at the front desk for Erick.

The restaurant was tiny, its entrance indistinct, and Brian walked past it by a few steps. Realizing his mistake, he took Nina's hand and turned back to the almost-hidden doorway. The inside was dark but decorated festively, with colorful candles atop each table. The menu was robust, and they dined on fresh fish brought to the restaurant earlier that day from the coast. Although white wine would have been appropriate, Brian selected a bottle of estate-grown Tempranillo. The wine loosened their tongues, and their attraction grew as they laughed at one another's old college stories. Crushed San Marzano plum tomatoes, basil, lemon zest and capers covered their freshly caught baked-cod dinners. Long-grain wild rice and sautéed baby spinach accompanied it. Smartly, they left room for dessert: sweet peach torte, dark-roast espresso, and Sambuca Black. As good as the meal – and the company – had been, Brian still waited for Erick to walk through the door.

Throughout the meal and afterward, Brian and Nina never stopped chatting. Each admired each other's work skills, and they filled each other with positive affirmations. A joyful spark rose between the two. Neither wanted it to end as they walked back to their hotel.

Nina, now completely obsessed with Brian, invited him back to her room. He didn't turn her down. Within minutes they were undressing each other and quickly in bed.

It had been years since Brian had felt this surge of deep feelings. He and Nina spent the balance of the evening – and well into the early-morning hours – satisfying each other. Brian was surprised at how aggressive she was as she made love. They finally fell asleep, satisfied and holding each other close.

Shortly before dawn, a disturbing dream woke Brian: a dream of Grace telling him to stay home. He lay awake, pondering her words. A moment later, he felt Nina's warm breast against his chest, and her leg across his thigh. *She feels so good. It's been so long. What do I do?*

CHAPTER TWENTY-ONE

Day Three – Morning in Córdoba

A ray of morning sunshine peeked between the window drapes, waking Nina. She found her leg straddling his and his arm across her chest. She smiled. Last night's time with Brian was so much more satisfying than she had ever imagined it could be. She gently moved his arm and slipped from the warmth of the comfortable bed.

After showering, she decided to wake him before dressing. She leaned over the bed and awakened him with a kiss. "Good morning, handsome."

He smiled. He reached up to stroke her cheek, then caressed her breast. "Good morning, beautiful. You were great. Thank you. You made me feel alive again. I'll head back to my room and meet you in the lobby in twenty minutes. We have a date at the Mezquita at seven with the priest and his sacristan."

"Great. It'll give me time to dry my hair." She smiled and arched her back slightly, watching him admire her still-naked form. "You are wonderful and amazing, Brian. Thank you."

She returned to the bathroom to dress. He slipped his pants on and returned to Room 302, shoes and shirt in hand.

As soon as Brian entered his room, he immediately checked his cell phone. He'd left it charging since they left for dinner. *Gosh. No voice messages, not even a text from Erick. That's not good.* He tried calling him again, without success.

He showered quickly, dressed, and went down to the lobby. He asked the front-desk clerk if Erick Schmidt had checked in last night. Upon learning he had not, Brian was even more concerned. *Our plan to remove the hidden art requires Erick's help.*

Moments later, Nina arrived downstairs beaming. Then she noticed Brian's long face.

"Erick never checked in last night. I'm really worried."

"I'll send him a text. If his phone was dead, he should have charged it by now. I'll let him know to come straight to the Mezquita."

"Good. Hurry. We need to leave right now. Text him from the car."

She texted him but got no response. Arriving a few minutes before seven, the sacristan and the old priest greeted them. Brian had requested a stepladder, a hammer, and a large screwdriver for this morning's project; all were there for them to use.

Brian carried the ladder and they searched for the location where Nina had discovered the arch's flawed repainting and refinishing. It took several minutes of walking among the maze of hundreds of columns before they finally arrived at the spot in the ceiling.

As they approached the space, they saw plaster dust, chips of painted plaster chopped at and pried away from the decorative arches, all laying with pieces of wood scattered across the floor. They looked up and saw part of the ceiling and a small section of one arch pulled down.

"Oh, God, no! Brian, they've been here already!"

Brian surveyed the scene in dismay. He wasn't entirely surprised. He knew they'd been followed yesterday. And Nina's loud outburst no doubt tipped them off to the exact location. Brian turned to the priest. "Father, here's my business card. Please let me know what it costs to repair the damage and I'll send the funds to you, along with some extra money for the inconvenience we've caused. Nina, we're done here. We need to leave." His tone indicated no room for discussion.

Brian took her hand and escorted her to the door. Once outside, he turned to her. "Now I'm certain something bad has happened to Erick. I fear our lives are in danger, as well. We need to accept that Paolo and Antonio have recovered the two hidden art pieces. The size of the opening probably accommodated two large rolled-up paintings."

Tears filled her eyes. "It's all my fault, Brian! I'm so sorry. He must have been watching and I gave it away, being so loud."

"Take it easy, Nina. We'll figure out what we can do."

"Oh, Brian, I'm really so sorry! What are we going to do?"

"First, now I believe Wilhelm, Paolo, and Antonio are in cahoots. They'll call Wilhelm sometime this morning and let him know they've found the paintings. My guess is one will be recovered 'officially' and brought back to headquarters, and the Director will get a star inside the Interpol hierarchy. The second painting will be sold for a profit, with the money split among the three of them.

"Next, if something bad has happened to Erick, and I think it has, Antonio's responsible. Third, and I've thought this through since waking this morning, Antonio could be at risk, too. Being younger than Paolo, he might not have the same relationship with Wilhelm's father, Klaus. His being out of the picture would allow the money from the sale of a single painting only to be split between Wilhelm and Paolo. My next concern is they could still kill you and me."

"Oh my God! But why would we be at risk? They have the painting. Shouldn't they leave us alone now?"

"Yes and no. They might see us as being able to expose their game. I'm going to be proactive and call Wilhelm and Van Deusen right now and let them both know the team of Paolo and Antonio beat us to the painting and congratulate them. I think acknowledging their win in front of Van Deusen positions Wilhelm differently in the caper."

"Will you say painting or paintings?"

"I'll just say 'painting.' We have no evidence right now that it's two, except for the notes inside KvR's diary and the diameter of the hole in the arch. If it's two paintings, it leaves them room to steal one, not worrying that you and I know both paintings were recovered."

"I see where you're going with your thinking to call Van Deusen. Then what?"

"Here's the rest of my idea. I'll call Kristofer Bronn, the art and antiques dealer in Leipzig who initially purchased the diary. He's a retired Interpol agent. I'll let him know a painting stolen by the SS in Paris may soon be on the black market. I'll suggest he call Wilhelm and say something like, 'I'm an old friend of your father. One of my wealthy customers approached me a month ago looking to invest in a painting worth up to ten million dollars. I've put out feelers but have had no success yet. If you hear of any paintings, let me know.' With that call, I believe Wilhelm's greed could trigger a follow-up sequence we can use to our advantage."

Nina gave a pensive nod. "That's interesting and certainly possible."

"If both paintings *were* found, Paolo and Wilhelm could arrange to sell the second one to the imaginary investor through Bronn."

"I see. That will expose Wilhelm and Paolo as the art thieves they've been all these years."

"Exactly."

"What becomes of Paolo and Antonio?"

"If something bad happened to Erick, Antonio's on the hook. But as I said earlier, Antonio may not survive this greedy escapade. With him out of the way, it leaves a fifty-fifty split between Paolo and Wilhelm."

"Brian, what do you mean about Antonio not surviving? Aren't he and Paolo close friends?"

"Taking control of one or both paintings stolen from the Lieberman family in Paris is a huge multi-million-dollar caper. Antonio is expendable. You and I are expendable. But if we openly acknowledge losing the race to find the art, it may improve our chances to get out of this mess alive. As I said earlier, I need to speak right away with Wilhelm and his superior.

"If there *are* two paintings, and if Paolo controls both, he may manage the sale of both for his own gain. This would create a good bit of conflict with Wilhelm"

"Oh my God! Brian, you're frightening me."

"I'm nervous about all of this, too, Nina. The best thing we can do now is speak to several people at headquarters about losing the race to find the art. But we mustn't mention we believe two paintings were recovered. Now, as I say this, I'm thinking Kristofer Bronn should also call Paolo to make him aware of his imaginary investor. That would whet his appetite to hold the paintings."

As they drove to the hotel in Brian's rental, Nina expected they'd get their bags, check out, and she'd catch an afternoon flight back to Amsterdam. Along the way, she reflected on the situation they were in. Then her thoughts shifted to last night. She smiled. *It was so nice. I think I love him.*

"Brian, I wish you could stay and live in Amsterdam. You would be happy, perhaps much happier than you've been in a long time. I hope I made you happy last night... you certainly made me feel good."

He looked at her, smiled and took her hand. But he remained silent on the ten-minute drive. His thoughts moved from Paolo and Wilhelm and the stolen art to Paolo's possible connection with the Luciano Wine Export company. As they arrived at the hotel, he parked, shut off the ignition, and finally spoke.

"Nina, it was awesome to be with you last night. I had a terrific time, and I haven't felt like that in years. I was disappointed at the Mezquita this morning, but on the way here, I've changed my mind about a few things. You and I will remain here tonight, and we'll fly out in the morning. But instead of going back to Amsterdam, I'd like you to come with me to Rome. You can be an immense help researching what's happened to the Luciano Wine Export Company and figuring how Paolo Luzzi really fits into this labyrinth. You can begin this afternoon at the hotel by following up on your research in Amsterdam. I've got a few calls to make. Then I'll email Grace, saying I'll be gone another week. And I'll email Erick and ask him to send a note to Solie, thanking her for spending time with Grace."

"What about Erick? Is he okay?"

"With any luck, we'll hear from him soon and he'll tell us a crazy story about where he's been. Meantime, I still fear something bad has happened to him."

"Brian, I promise you I'll find out more about Luca Luciano and his company. I'll also look more into Paolo Luzzi's past. Maybe I can find out what's become of Katrina. And I've come up with an idea, too. I'll make a list of every bank in Rome and determine if any have a lengthy six-digit code to open their safe-deposit boxes."

Brian nodded his approval. "Interesting. You're always thinking."

The two went up to their separate rooms, disappointed about the end of their search for the art. But now they began preparing for the next search, the search for Brian's mother.

CHAPTER TWENTY-TWO

Day Three – Afternoon Phone Calls

Brian made his first call to Wilhelm and congratulated Luzzi and Gozzo for their detective work and getting to the painting first. He mentioned his plan to submit his Interpol retirement papers.

The news O'Sullivan would soon be out of the picture pleased Wilhelm and made him reconsider eliminating him.

Brian then called and left a voice message with Wilhelm's boss, Pieter Van Deusen. "Pieter, Nina von Scholz identified the art's possible location in the Mezquita in Córdoba yesterday afternoon. When we returned this morning to remove it, we discovered part of the ceiling and the top of a decorative arch had already been removed. The opening was large enough to hide one or two paintings, but at the moment we have no evidence any paintings were discovered. A full written report explaining what happened will follow."

Brian then wrote what had happened, including being followed, sealed, and addressed the envelope, and brought it downstairs to the clerk at the front desk. *"Hola."*

"Hola, señor."

"This letter… it must be mailed today. *Comprende usted?"*

"Sí, señor. Yo comprendo. Mail today."

"Here. For you. Twenty American dollars. *Comprende?"*

"Sí, señor! Muchas gracias!"

Upon returning to his room, Brian's next call was to Kristofer Bronn. As he was dialing, a knock came at his door. He put down his cell phone and went to answer the door.

A smile broke across his face. "Nina! I've got a few more calls to make and a couple of things to finish up. Can you come back in half an hour?"

"Sure. Want me to bring you anything? Maybe a drink?"

"Just bring some ice and whatever you'd like to drink. I have a small flask of scotch."

She reached up and gave him a peck on the cheek. "Be back in thirty."

He dialed again and as the call went through, he heard the distinctive ringing of the Siemens central office in Leipzig.

"*Guten tag!*"

"Hello. Is this Kristofer Bronn?"

"*Yah!* It is Kristofer. Who is dis calling me, and how can I help you?"

"My name is Brian O'Sullivan. I'm an Interpol agent from the United States, and an Interpol partner of Erick Schmidt. We research historical art and look for lost or stolen art. Erick asked me to work with him on the SS soldier's diary brought to you by the German woman whose mother passed away.

"Yah. I know Erick. How can I help?"

"I'll explain more but it's best you call me back from a phone line outside your shop or home. When you get to the other phone, text me at the number you see on your Caller ID. I'll call you back."

"Yah. I see the number. It's amazing what these phone systems do now. I will call you. Ten minutes, yah. Give me ten minutes and I will text you from my new cell phone."

At that same moment, at the Interpol headquarters in The Hague, a young clerk was alerted automatically to activity on the traced phone line. As the recording machine started, he listened to the call placed to the antique shop. He wrote notes and headed upstairs.

"Sir, we have a hit on the line you asked us to monitor in Leipzig. Just now, I heard a call from a man who called himself Brian O'Sullivan to the art dealer Kristofer Bronn at his shop. O'Sullivan anticipated the line was being monitored and asked Bronn to call back from another undisclosed location."

"Interesting. Thank you, Johan. Excellent work. Continue to monitor that line for the next two weeks."

Wilhelm buzzed his secretary. "Ursula, get Paolo Luzzi on the line. It's urgent."

"Yes, Director."

***

Ten minutes later, Bronn texted Brian with the number to safely reach him, and Brian called back.

"Kristofer, it's Agent Brian O'Sullivan again. I need a few minutes of your time to explain what's happening."

"*Yah*. Go ahead, Agent."

Brian reviewed the past few days' occurrences, the apparent discovery made in the Mezquita, and that Wilhelm Mueller had sent a second team of agents, two Italians, to also search for the hidden paintings. He concluded by telling Kristofer although his team discovered the paintings' location first, the Italian duo had extracted them overnight and took credit.

"*Yah*. Agent Brian, I have some advice. Watch out for *die Müllers. Der* father, Klaus, is treacherous. And *der* son, whom I hear is now a rising star in headquarters, is no doubt corrupt like his crooked papa. And two Italians! *Yah,* I bet one hundred Euros it's Luzzi and Gozzo. Am I right?"

"Yes."

"Yah. See. Now you owe me one hundred Euros! No. No. Only my silly joke. Those two agents are crooks and partners with *der* big crook, Klaus Mueller."

"Erick told me about how Klaus had been suspected of stealing and selling stolen art found in the nineteen seventies, eighties and nineties. Erick also said Wilhelm may be engaged in the same illegal art theft activities.

"We believe Luzzi has found – and now has control of – both paintings mentioned in the diary, and he may be returning to Amsterdam with them. We believe one may be officially recovered with Interpol's blessing, and the other will become available for sale. There also exists the possibility both may be sold, either by Wilhelm Mueller or Paolo Luzzi."

"Yah. I know Luzzi. He's been a crooked agent for years. He was *der* young agent working with Klaus years ago. He participated in Klaus' shenanigans but *die zwei* were too slippery. We could never find any evidence against either of *dem*. There's no doubt Luzzi helped move *der* stolen paintings. We just don't know where *dey* went. Some agents believed *dey* disappeared into private collections. One agent – a disgruntled Lutheran – had a silly idea. Yah, he said *der* Catholic Church was buying them with all their money!"

"Kristofer, I have a plan to expose these thieves. It involves using these newly discovered paintings. I need you to make two phone calls. One will be to Wilhelm. You will say: 'I have a Russian investor looking for a painting by a classic artist and he is willing to spend up to ten million American dollars. I have been working on this customer's request for over two months. If you come across anything, let me know and a connection could be made for the sale to take place with a deposit made through a Zurich bank.'"

"*Yah. Dis* is a good story, Agent O'Sullivan. A good plan, a clever idea! *Yah*, I see what you are doing."

"I'd also like you to send a text to Paolo Luzzi."

"*Yah*. I can do *das. Dis* is good. Give me *der* number. What do I say in *der* text?"

Brian read off Paolo's cell number, obtained by Nina before leaving from recent HQ files. "Tell Luzzi the same thing you tell Wilhelm Mueller in your call."

"*Yah!* Very good, Agent Brian! When should I make der call and send der text message?"

"Tomorrow morning would be good for making the call and sending the text. I'll text you again, at this number, in two days. There's a strong chance your shop's phone is tapped, or a listening device has been planted near you. When you get my text, find a secluded place outdoors and call me back."

"*Yah*. I say again, *dis* all is a very good plan. But you must be careful. *Die Mü*llers murder people and make people disappear. *Yah, dis* is interesting for me. *Danke*, Agent Brian."

"*Bitte schön*, Kristofer."

As they hung up, a soft knock came at the hotel room's door. When Brian opened it, he found Nina holding an ice bucket in one hand, a bottle of sangria tucked under her other arm.

"Come in! Put those down over there. I've made a few calls. Let me tell you about them."

They chatted over one drink, then another. They called room service and ordered an early dinner. They chatted non-stop through dinner, laughing often. They spent the rest of the evening together, forgetting about the world outside the room. Nina, awash with intense emotions, felt convinced she'd finally found the right person for her. She eventually fell asleep with her head on his shoulder, her warm naked body against his.

Tired as he was, Brian remained awake, first wondering about Erick and then his thoughts returning to Grace. *What happened to our marriage? She was so lively and fun when we first married. Her depression in this past decade has made life together difficult. Why aren't her meds working? Is there something deeper? Is our marriage even worth saving?*

CHAPTER TWENTY-THREE

Day Four Morning – Headed to Rome

Morning arrived and Brian woke moments before his alarm went off. The room was dark and outside a heavy rain made the morning bleak. He swung back the dark burgundy curtain to get light into the room, and the motion reminded him of sweeping a matador's muleta in front of a bull. He turned and looked back at the bed. *She is so sweet.* He covered her shoulders with the sheet, then showered. She awakened as he dressed.

"Good morning, Brian."

"Good morning, young lady. How are you feeling after all that sangria?"

"I'm fine." She paused a moment. "And you were absolutely wonderful."

"As are you. Our plane leaves at ten. But we have time for breakfast. I'm heading down now to get a bite and read the paper. There's lots to accomplish today, and no time to waste. I'll see you downstairs."

She watched him leave then turned back toward her pillow and hugged it. She imagined what it might be like to be with him all the time. Feeling warm inside, she closed her eyes.

The ringing of the phone startled her.

"Nina! Where are you? I left the room thirty minutes ago."

"Oh no! I'm so sorry! I must have fallen back to sleep. I'll be down in ten."

Brian was well into an English edition of the morning paper when the waiter came by again.

"*Señor*, another American coffee?"

"*Sí, por favor.* And I'll have slightly charred toast with fig jam and orange juice."

"Si, señor."

He finished the newspaper, and then opened his laptop. Using the hotel's Wi-Fi, he checked his email. Most were worthless and he deleted them. Then he noticed Grace's email. He knew it was waiting there for him, just like many other times he traveled, and he knew it wouldn't be pleasant to read. His finger hovered over the "Open" button for a few seconds before he hit it.

She began her note to him by immediately ranting about not being able to get through to his cell phone, about his career being more important than their marriage, about his lack of attentiveness when he was home, and about his avoidance of doing more things with her. But that outburst was just the beginning of her tirade.

I can tell you're purposely holding off retirement. You could very well have retired five or six years ago. You just don't want to be with me. You need to be honest, Brian. Something is going on. It's like you have another life—a life that's more important to you than being with me.

To make matters worse, even though Solie now has that stupid cat, I'm still sneezing, and my eyes are all red and tearing from its dander still all over this apartment.

She made it clear she wasn't happy. In Brian's mind, Grace had not been happy anytime in the last ten to fifteen years. When he looked back and began figuring out when her unhappiness had increased, he realized it had been more like twenty years. He decided to write back.

Hi Grace, I read your note. Your cell phone isn't set up for international calls so email is the best way we can communicate at the moment. Our research assignment in southern Spain is complicated and I've been extremely busy. Erick is missing, and we're worried about him. Unexpectedly, I now must travel to Rome. It may be another full week before I return to Amsterdam. I hope the accommodations at Erick's place are okay, aside from the cat dander. If you need to go to a hotel, just go ahead and do so. There are several highly rated ones nearby. I hope you're spending pleasant time with Solie. She's a nice young woman and a good neighbor to Erick. I suggest you take a *daily walk around Vondelpark if you haven't done so already. A day trip to the Anne Frank House and the other two museums at the end of Vondelpark will fill your time. Ask Solie to take you to Zaanse Schans to see the windmills. It's a beautiful place, Grace. Go shopping for some clothes or take Solie out to dinner. And please stop at a phone store to set up an international plan so I can call you.*

He ended his note by saying he'd be flying today and wouldn't be available to respond to any e-mails for another few days. He paused, and then added additional information.

I have some things to go over with you when I return to Amsterdam. Some personal information I've had to withhold from you for a long time. But I hope after this week's project, I can share with you all that's been going on.

While I'm in Rome, I'll be checking on my birth mother's husband's wine-export business, the Luciano Wine Export Company. I need to find out when it was sold, who was on the board at the time, and who received the proceeds. I also want to research that code my birth mother left on those other pages she wrote. Goodbye for now. See you at home in New Jersey. - Brian

Immediately after Brian hit "Send," he realized he should have worded his message differently. From what he'd said, she would no doubt imagine the worst – like a long-running affair with another woman.

In Amsterdam, Grace was playing online Solitaire and waiting for Solie to come over for tea and breakfast, when Brian's email arrived. She immediately read his note and frowned when she read he'd be further delayed by his trip to Rome to research the Luciano business. *Here he goes again, suddenly and without any prior warning, off on his next adventure, finding places to go and things to do without me. I'll tell Solie how Brian's avoiding me yet again. This time with a trip to Rome in search of his birth mother, who was probably dead and buried twenty years ago.*

Nina finally arrived in the hotel dining room, her hair still wet. Brian closed his laptop. He ordered tea and toast for her, and he reviewed the day's itinerary as she ate. A few minutes later she ran upstairs, grabbed her heavy bag, and they were off to the airport. They arrived with plenty of time to spare for the one-stop flight to Rome's Fiumicino Airport.

Brian got through security and the metal detectors without incident, but Nina got pulled aside when the detector sounded. Scanned head to toe by the security woman, she grew embarrassed when it became evident the underwire in her bra had triggered the overly sensitive machine's alarm. Brian enjoyed a hearty laugh at her expense.

Once the anxiety of a bumpy takeoff and strong turbulence as they rose through heavy rain clouds subsided, Brian opened up to the crossword puzzle in the morning paper. Nina shut her eyes and leaned against his shoulder. Halfway into the puzzle, he closed his eyes and leaned toward Nina. The fragrance of her hair and perfume made him recall last night.

Minutes later, Brian listened carefully as the pilot announced the weather conditions in Barcelona were quickly worsening with tall thunder clouds producing hail. The one stop and change of planes suddenly became questionable. Another few minutes passed when the captain announced the stubborn storm was sitting over Barcelona, and they were diverting to the nearby Girona Airport. He apologized and said ground transportation would bring passengers and their luggage to Barcelona for connecting flights. Brian knew traveling by bus to the next airport would result in their missing the connection to Rome. But he was with Nina, so it seemed fine. The later flight to Rome meant they'd arrive around 1, still early enough to get a few things accomplished that afternoon.

***

Earlier that same rainy morning in Córdoba, Paolo Luzzi drove to the airport with the two paintings, planning to catch a direct flight to Amsterdam. While waiting to board, he called Wilhelm.

"It's Luzzi. I have the two paintings and am heading back to Amsterdam now."

"Good. Juan the Fixer called me late yesterday. He saw Antonio shoot Erick and push his body in the car trunk. Juan then dumped the body into a wooded area along a road south of Córdoba on his way home to Málaga."

"And Antonio?"

"As planned, Juan took care of him. He rigged Antonio's rental car to blow up on ignition. The body was incinerated. My father blessed the idea and said it was a good decision to reduce the shares in our little business caper to a fifty-fifty split. It's just you and me now. When you return, bring me both paintings right away. I'll need to declare one as 'found' because that idiot O'Sullivan called headquarters to congratulate you on the discovery and for winning the bonus pay. We won't mention the second painting. If we have some luck, we might be able to sell it quickly and split the proceeds.

"My father tells me you're a day or two away from your birthday and about to receive funds left in the trust fund from the sale of the wine-export company. Now I must share with you some more information."

"What's that?"

"My nephew, Philippe, still has a recording device planted in Erick Schmidt's apartment."

"And?"

"He overheard another conversation minutes ago. Agent O'Sullivan is heading to Rome. The woman believed to be Brian's wife was telling another woman that O'Sullivan just emailed her. She said, 'My husband's going there to investigate the Luciano Wine Export Company.' His wife then began ranting about her displeasure with him.

"Now, I don't know the smallest details of your family business, Paolo. But we now know from two days ago, when Philippe recorded O'Sullivan's wife the first time, a connection exists between O'Sullivan and Katrina Luciano, the woman who adopted you. When I spoke to my father, he verified this as true. He said you are due to receive proceeds from the sale of the Luciano Wine Export Company. So, Paolo, it now looks like this: if Brian O'Sullivan arrives in Rome and unravels his childhood and your connection to the Luciano Wine Export Company, your pot of gold gets split in two.

"My father also indicated the circumstances surrounding Luca's sudden death could easily be opened again. So, my advice to you? Drop the two paintings here with me, fly to Rome and find O'Sullivan, then eliminate him to keep him from discovering anything that could affect the money Luca Luciano put in escrow for you. Do you hear me, Paolo? Eliminate him as soon as possible. Your upcoming windfall from the Luciano family fortune is huge. It's worth far more than either of those two paintings. So be smart. Don't worry about splitting half the money from one painting worth ten million dollars when fifty million is sitting waiting if you don't have to split it with O'Sullivan."

"*Grazie,* Wilhelm. That's useful information and I get your point. I might change my plans as to where I go first. Let me think things over."

"Now don't suddenly get stupid, Paolo. Bring both paintings to me here at The Hague. Or, if you need to make a connection, I can meet you in Amsterdam at Schiphol, and you can fly on to Rome. Let me show Van Deusen you found one painting, and I'll oversee the sale of the other one. I'm sure we can sell it quickly. Let me repeat: Fly here, drop the painting, then eliminate O'Sullivan."

"*Buona giornata,* Wilhelm."

Paolo hung up, suddenly angry. He resented Wilhelm's telling him what to do regarding his personal business. It seemed Wilhelm and Klaus knew too much about his family business—forgetting that years ago he'd told Klaus more than he should have. Learning Brian was headed to Rome to investigate the sale of Luciano Wine Exports reconfirmed his conclusion that Brian was Katrina's natural son.

Lucky for me this cranky Grace woman complains about her idiot husband and inadvertently revealed his location. Her problems will soon be over and O'Sullivan's life will soon be ended.

Paolo paused. *Should I bring the paintings to Amsterdam? No. Fuck Wilhelm. I'll cut him out. Maybe I'll sell one and share the money with Klaus and I'll keep the other at my home in Malta. I trusted Klaus for years, but his son behaves like a hungry snake. He's probably thinking of some other angle to screw me right now. I'm better off without him. I'm close to my big payday, so I finally can leave Interpol. As for O'Sullivan, I'm not willing to share my rightful family fortune with him. I've waited so many years for this! I'm the one who put up with all the garbage from 'Holier Than Thou Luca' all those years. I'll head to Rome. . I'll find him and put an end to his life – just like I did with Luca.*

CHAPTER TWENTY-FOUR

Luca Luciano and Katrina Amorino

In June 1944, after the Americans and their allies liberated Rome, it was time for the Vatican to rebuild the Catholic Church hierarchy in Italy. Besides looking for new young, newly ordained priests to assign to parishes, Pope Pius XII asked Giovanni Cardinal di Botticino to focus on reconstructing damaged churches from Rome as far south as the provinces of Calabria and Basilicata. Cardinal di Botticino, whose family owned a stone quarry fabricating columns and ornate statuary, was quite popular in the Vatican. The di Botticino family not only sourced the stone material for churches in Italy, France, Germany, and even Poland, but they provided considerable financing.

As Giovanni began to search through the resumes provided to him, he came across one from a young, recently ordained priest, Luca Luciano. In the years prior to his ordination, Luca had spent time in the Jewish Ghetto in Rome, helping Jews. Luca even became involved in assisting Monsignor Hugh O'Flaherty in hiding Jews and American soldiers from the Nazis within Rome.

Cardinal DiBotticino called Luca in for an interview. He found the bright young man, and lover of the arts, to be from a family also involved in finances, with an extremely strict father. In fact, as punishment for an early indiscretion, Luca was sent to the Capuchin Crypt for a year. There with the friars he studied Latin, French, and German before he entered the priesthood. Cardinal DiBotticino understood the young man well and selected him as the new pastor of the Holy Angels Church in Bernalda, Italy.

The young priest nervously accepted his assignment and upon his arrival, he determined his four main tasks as fulfilling his parishioners' spiritual needs, repairing the parish's run-down buildings and property, renewing parishioners' interest in church activities, and caring for the spiritual needs of forty contemplative nuns residing in the cloistered convent attached to the church.

Father Luciano embraced the challenge but felt unprepared and unworthy of his assignment. Over the next six months, his confidence grew. He frequently engaged with the sisters during their confessions and met with a group of younger sisters in small meetings to discuss religious topics. He found them much more spiritually mature than many of the priests he knew at the Vatican during his training and time there.

But in the last month of 1944 and into the spring of 1945, during discussions with the Mother Superior, he revealed his concern for one of the sisters—a novice who had not yet taken her final vows. Luca explained how her emotions varied substantially during several conversations. The Mother Superior expressed similar concerns, suggesting the postulant might not have a true calling to the sisterhood. She told Luca she'd received a note from Cardinal DiBotticino on Katrina's arrival almost two years earlier, indicating the young woman might not have a true calling to religious life. He went on to say she was fleeing a "terrible situation" and suggested Mother Superior not permit her to profess her final vows hastily.

Mother Superior encouraged Father Luca to help Katrina decide whether her presence in the convent was a true commitment or perhaps an impetuous decision to atone for past mistakes.

In spending time with the young sister, Father Luca recognized his own spiritual challenges. As the youngest in a large family, he'd entered the seminary at the insistence of his father as punishment—not as the result of being called spiritually. Over time, Father Luca and the postulant became attracted to each other. It wasn't long before Luca felt he was falling in love with Katrina Amorino, the beautiful blue-eyed woman conflicted about her desire to become a nun.

One spring morning, having had little sleep because of caring for an elderly nun overnight, Katrina broke down in the confessional booth. She shared with Luca the details of her impetuous decisions. As her story unfolded, her sobbing grew uncontrollable.

Shocked at hearing her painful tale, Luca pulled back the confessional curtain, and embraced Katrina, who was shaking and crying aloud in her state of exhaustion. In his brief moments of embracing and consoling her, Luca decided he wanted to care for Katrina the rest of his life. His own doubts about lacking a true calling into the religious life were confirmed. From that day, he and Katrina discussed how to respectfully transition their lives. It wasn't long before they acknowledged a mutual attraction and candidly discussed the possibility of being together at some point in the future.

Only weeks later, in May 1945, Karl von Richter, the man with whom Katrina had been briefly enamored before he joined Germany's SS, and who had brutally raped her a year and a half earlier, arrived at the convent in Bernalda, looking for her and their child. Von Richter, under cover of deceit, tricked a nun and entered the convent. Once inside, he followed the small nun, and quickly found his way to the Mother Superior's office. There, by chance, stood Father Luciano and postulant Katrina Amorino.

A verbal confrontation ensued. Katrina told Karl off, face to face, fueled by courage and emotional fury as she recalled his brutality. Katrina handled the dangerous situation using powerful and truthful statements that served as gut punches severely damaging his ego. In response, Karl wielded his SS Luger pistol, demanding their child be brought forward from his hiding place.

When Katrina proved resolutely defiant, Karl threatened to kill the nuns one by one if she didn't reveal their son's whereabouts. As Karl pulled her into the foyer, Katrina admitted giving up their infant son for adoption. She explained Karl's uncle, Bishop Giovanni DiBotticino, had sent the child to America.

Karl refused to accept her explanation. Even more upset, von Richter continued to threaten Katrina with his gun. Outside the front door, Father Luca was preparing to enter, pistol in hand, to defend the woman with whom he had fallen in love.

Then, suddenly, a shot rang out. A muffled thump sounded in the foyer as Karl's body fell to the floor, dead.

Off to the side, amid a puff of gunpowder smoke that hung in the air, stood Sister Carmella, the petite nun and convent's greeter. Having hidden in a nearby coat closet, when it became apparent Katrina's life – and those of other sisters – had been threatened, she inched open the door, rested her single-barrel shotgun against a hinge, and pulled the trigger. She put an end to the SS monster who had directed and participated in the deaths of thousands of Jews in death camps across Germany.

Father Luca came running inside, fearing the worst. He saw Karl on the floor in a pool of blood. Sister Carmella's action left everyone in a state of shock! Several nuns ran to the foyer after hearing the gunshot.

Mother Superior, a distant cousin to Katrina, did her best to calm everyone. Minutes later, U.S. soldiers stationed in Bernalda arrived. The soldiers confirmed it likely had been Karl von Richter who had, the previous day, shot to death his uncle Cardinal DiBotticino and another priest at the Vatican.

Katrina and Luca soon left their positions as postulant and parish priest in the fall of 1945. In early 1946, with the war over and traveling safer, Katrina traveled to Lecco, where she learned of her parents' deaths in the malicious firebombing of her father's bakery. She had often thought about what would have happened had she and her son stayed with them. Seeing the destruction made her realize she might have died while helping her father in the bakery.

Luca and Katrina married in May 1946. Soon afterward, Luca presented his business plan to his two oldest brothers, Stefano and Dominic, both of whom shared responsibilities for the Luciano family's banking and investment business. Pleased with the outline of his intentions, both expected he would use family finances to provide the capital needed for the expansive growth he projected. They waited for the request to make an investment, but Luca proceeded on his own.

Luca's idea of exporting wine began shortly after his leaving the priesthood. While visiting a friend at the Vatican, he cut a deal to provide all the churches in southern Italy a low-cost blended red table wine to be used during Mass. Within a year's time, he also began selling Amarone della Valpolicella, Chianti, and other hearty Tuscan wines.

In 1947, Luca established his wine-exporting business. He struck deals with dozens of grape-growers and winemakers by providing financing and helping them set up bottling facilities in Cortona and Arezzo in Tuscany, southward all the way to Basilicata, and to Reggio at the tip of Calabria. He approached selling with a cheerful and strong personal effort. Luca was convinced the post-war years offered many opportunities for Italians to export their products—especially wines—throughout Europe, to the United States, and as far away as South Africa and South America.

Over the next two years, sales more than quadrupled. Projections based on his research, coupled with newly signed contracts, suggested huge growth. Luca passionately believed the pace of growth in the 1950s in the U.S. market would be almost insatiable.

Luca sometimes reflected on his initial success, kneeling bedside during his morning prayers. At those times, he'd remember a particular moment that made him smile.

The day Karl was shot was the turning point in our lives! Afterward, we sat in Mother Superior's office, reviewing the harrowing day's horrible events. Sister Bianca washed Karl's blood-stained clothes and brought up his duffel bag. We were all shocked by its contents – all those diamonds stolen from Hitler… and Eva Braun's jewelry! Then Mother Superior brought in a bottle of Amarone della Valpolicella and opened it with that tarnished old brass-handled corkscrew from her desk drawer. That day changed my life – and Katrina's – completely.

As the closest thing to Karl's only surviving family, Katrina gained possession of Karl's vehicle and everything in it – including the duffel bag and all its contents.

As Luca's business grew, Katrina began accompanying him on business trips. In 1951 she traveled with him to New York City. While visiting the O'Sullivans, they met the child she'd given up for adoption. The couple who adopted Bruno, renaming him Brian, were loving and kind. But seeing him broke Katrina's heart and left her empty.

In 1953, when Luca traveled to Verano to negotiate a deal. Katrina spent a day catching up with a friend from nursing school. She headed for the last known address of Sophia Luzzi, near the western shore of Lake

Garlate, south of Lake Lecco. She found Sophia's elderly mother struggling to make ends meet while caring for her orphaned grandson. A month later, after talking it over with Luca, Katrina sent for both to come and live with them at their home in Positano.

CHAPTER TWENTY-FIVE

Arriving at Ciampino Airport

Heavy rains across the Mediterranean were common, but the day's excessively long, stormy weather front extended from Spain clear across to Italy. Unusually tall thunderclouds produced large hail and intense winds and made the plane rise and fall several times in the extreme turbulence. Through it, Nina gripped Brian's hand, painfully mashing his middle and pinky fingers against his wedding band. When they finally landed at Rome's smaller Ciampino Airport, she made her way slowly from the jetway to the baggage area, where she sipped a bottle of ginger ale while Brian waited for their luggage. The baggage from the small flight emptied quickly.

"I have both our bags, Nina. How are you feeling now?"

"Thanks for suggesting the ginger ale. I'm already feeling much better. Gosh. I've never had that happen before."

Brian shrugged. "Bad weather happens. I remember a trip from Dallas to Seattle in severe weather. We bounced so badly, I thought the wings of the airplane would eventually snap off."

"Brian, where's the hotel information where you suggested we stay tonight?"

"Across from the Trevi Fountain. We'll get a cab and talk on the way. Trying to talk on the plane obviously wasn't a good idea. You were as pale as a ghost the whole way!"

She gave him a small smile, still not feeling well enough to laugh.

Outside the airport, a young cab driver saw Nina holding Brian's arm to steady herself. He ran up to meet them. Believing the two visitors were American, he tried his best English.

"Ah, let me take those bags from you. Ah! Your young wife is beautiful! But is she okay?"

"*Grazie.* The turbulent flight from Spain has made her feel sick."

"Yes. We also had terrible storms here in Rome this morning. It should be nice later with a beautiful sunset."

"We're headed to the Hotel Fontana, right across from the Trevi Fountain."

"*Si! Certo!* Uh, certainly. It will take twenty-five minutes, maybe less if I hurry for you."

The cabbie threw Brian's bag into the trunk, then used both hands to lift Nina's. Minutes after they drove away, the lane-to-lane jostling of the fast-moving cab made Nina queasy.

"Brian, tell him to stop! Please stop the car!" Before Brian could speak, she shouted, "*Signore, ferma l'auto, signore, adesso fermati!*"

At her direction, the cabbie hit the brakes, jerking the car to a stop.

Yanking open the door, Nina leaned out and threw up in the street. Doubled over and heaving, she groaned as her stomach churned in protest.

When at last she straightened up and shut the car door, Brian offered her a couple of paper napkins he had stashed from breakfast.

She accepted them gratefully and dabbed the side of her mouth. "Oh, my goodness. I'm so embarrassed!"

"Not to worry, Nina. My dad used to go deep-sea fishing with his fireman buddies a dock in Great Kills Harbor years ago, near where I grew up. He took me once. Throwing up on deck spoiled all the fun. I knew early on I'd never be a sailor. And you didn't see it, but I had that paper bag right next to me on the plane. It was ready for either one of us!"

Brian gave the cabbie a nod, and they continued. After slowly making their way through the narrow streets to the hotel, the cabbie jumped out and brought their bags inside to the lobby. Brian tipped him generously.

Brian checked them into their rooms while Nina immediately freshened up in the restroom. She emerged with a modest smile and her coloring not as pale.

"We're on the third floor, at opposite ends. Let's take a break, relax, and meet back down here in forty-five minutes. It's still early enough to do some research today. I've asked them to bring sparkling water, a lemon, an orange, and a small knife to your room. If you thinly cut the peel and put the lemon zest and orange zest into the sparkling water, drinking it will help you feel better."

"That sounds good, Brian. Thank you."

Nina accompanied the porter who brought her bag upstairs. Before going upstairs himself, Brian stepped outside. Tourists returned to the area as the clouds cleared. The stormy weather had been so unusual for Rome at this time of the year.

He walked to the far end of the Trevi Fountain and peered through the growing crowd to determine whether they'd been followed. His stomach was tense. The turbulent flight through storm clouds had been uncomfortable, but concern over what had happened in Córdoba dominated his thoughts and proved even more unsettling. He mulled over the events of the past few days and decided trying to find his mother would be far more complicated than first imagined. He couldn't put his finger on it yet, but he sensed his search in the next 24 to 48 hours would present intrigue and deception!

Brian scanned the area in front of the fountain again. Satisfied they weren't followed, he returned to the hotel and headed to his room. He tried calling Grace at Erick's apartment. When she didn't pick up, he sent an email saying he was in Rome, staying at the hotel across from the Trevi Fountain where they'd once stayed years ago. After sending his email, he lay down for a moment and fell sound asleep.

An hour passed when he awoke to knocking on the door.

"Brian, it's Nina. Are you okay?"

He looked at his watch, surprised at the time. It took a moment to reassemble his thoughts. Another dream had invaded his shallow sleep. It surfaced more deep feelings and concerns over his marriage. Unlike so many dreams that wisp away on waking, this one stayed with him. It was clear, taking him back to when he suggested to Grace they adopt, and her refusal. In his dream he relived how upset she'd been.

Rubbing his sleepy eyes, he opened the door.

"Oh, I woke you. I'm sorry. I waited downstairs for fifteen minutes. I figured you might be busy, but I also know you wanted to get started searching. We still have about three hours."

"It's okay." He shook his head. "I had this dream..."

"Something good I hope."

"Just the opposite, but no worries. Thanks for coming to get me. What do you have planned?"

"I've created two lists. One is a list of prominent banks likely to have large vaults with safe-deposit boxes. The other list has three places where information about Italian companies might be located. I'll start by visiting banks to see if the code Katrina gave you matches any vault or safe-deposit box numbers. Meanwhile, you can search the details of what happened to the Luciano Wine Export Company. The banks close at four. Let's meet back here at four thirty."

"Good planning, Nina." As they returned to the lobby and went their separate ways, both wondered what their search would lead to next.

CHAPTER TWENTY-SIX

The Next Search Begins

Nina's list included some of Rome's oldest and most prestigious banks. She imagined Luca Luciano, having grown up in Rome before entering the priesthood, might be attracted to such an institution.

What she didn't know was the Luciano family were wealthy investors, and Luca's two eldest brothers, Dominic and Stefano, were majority stockholders of one of the banks she'd listed. There, at the bank owned by the Luciano family, Luca secured a safe-deposit box years earlier, in 1952, filling it with the diamonds and jewelry Katrina found in Karl's duffel bag, and later adding legal documents.

Her search began in mid-afternoon. The proximity of the banks allowed her to visit five in two hours' time. Her search method was smart. At each one, she said she needed to secure a safe-deposit box for securities left by her father, a multi-millionaire in the Netherlands, and would ask to see the deposit-box area. As she was being shown the area, she would joke with the banker, saying she often forgets where she puts things and ask how they located boxes on the card she would sign.

Approaching 3:45 and having entered the sixth bank – the last on her list – Nina finally found what she was looking for. The numbers Katrina had written – 10-28-14-16-18-0 – were initially believed to be a date, a code, or a combination lock of some kind. But at the sixth-largest family-owned bank in Rome, she found the safe-deposit box locations had a particular sequence matching the numbers Katrina wrote. Here, the boxes were identified by section, column, and row or level. The card the banker carried showed her how to find the section, column, and row for each box. The next three digits represented the combination for the lock on the face of the door to access the individual box.

She asked the lady assisting her, "So, if I had a box that was in Aisle Ten and Column Twenty-eight, would the next numbers be the level of the box?"

"*Sì.* Please permit me to show you an example. Aisle Ten is just ahead. Now, in this aisle, we go to Column Twenty-eight. It's easy to find. See? The next number is the horizontal level. We begin at the bottom with Level One and going up toward the ceiling. Here we have twenty levels. A ladder would be required to access all rows above Level Eight. Since you're a petite woman, you might want your safe-deposit box no higher than Level Five or Six. We have several available at that level." The lady paused. "Permit me to explain there is one exception. The boxes on the bottom level, Level One, are large and deep. They are used more as temporary or permanent storage lockers by our customers. They use keys and not combination locks. The regular safe-deposit boxes sit behind a small door with a built-in combination lock using three numbers. The combination can be changed when you first secure the box, or at any time thereafter."

"Thank you so much for the explanation. It looks very secure here. I'll need to speak to my uncle, who's in town. He has a safe-deposit box here already. I will be back tomorrow with him."

Brian will be so pleased. I wonder what's inside the box. Maybe it's another letter or more papers. Maybe it has something to do with their wedding papers? Or maybe some stock certificates are inside?

The bank was closing as she was leaving. Thrilled with her find, Nina was floating two inches above the ground. Suddenly her stomach growled, and she looked at her watch; it was 4 PM

No wonder I'm hungry; I haven't eaten since breakfast… and what a crazy plane ride that was.

While she searched the banks, Brian searched business records at the European Business Registry Association.

In 1993, the responsibility for keeping the Italian Business Register nationwide was assigned to individual regions' chambers of commerce. They managed data through a wholly self-owned consortium called InfoCamere. Its registry held information on more than six million companies in the Italian Business Register. Of those, 1,200,000 were limited companies, some one million others were partnerships, and more than 3,700,000 companies were owned by individuals.

Brian was surprised at how well organized they were. Nevertheless, his search proved challenging and a woman at the front desk, seeing him fumbling through file after file, offered assistance.

"*Ciao!* You say the company was owned by Luca Luciano?"

"Yes. The company's name was the Luciano Wine Exporting Company."

"Do you know when the company was incorporated?"

"Sometime in nineteen forty-six or forty-seven."

"We have all the older information stored on microfiche. Let's walk over to those cabinets. Anything saved before nineteen sixty-four is in there. Let's see. Do you know the exact date of incorporation?"

"No. But if you can, you might start in the second half of nineteen forty-seven."

The woman turned on the reader, skillfully loaded the microfiche film, and scanned decades-old documents. A minute passed before she spoke.

"*Signore*, it seems this is your lucky day. I've found it already. On Thursday, July 3, 1947, Luca Luciano filed to set up the Luciano Wine Export Company. He was the principal stockholder, and it looks like Katrina Luciano was a stockholder. There were two more stockholders: Dominic Luciano and Stefano Luciano. Both were named as directors and only had ten shares each, which is insignificant. Is there something else you need or want to know?"

"Can you tell me if there are any other events in the company history? For example, can you tell me if the company was sold? And if so, when was it sold, and to whom? And did anything else happen?"

"There's nothing else on the microfiche. Let's go back over to the other area. If anything happened after nineteen sixty-four, we could search for it on the computer."

"Look after nineteen sixty-four."

"Okay. I'm making the entry for the search query. Just a minute. The computers are slow today. It's so nice outside now. Earlier today was so frightening with all that thunder and lightning. And we had hail. Such weather it's very unusual for *Roma*. Okay. Here we go. *Si*. I have it.

"The information you asked for. The activity in the file for the Luciano Wine Export Company. It's right here. It begins with a person named Paolo Luciano being added to the Board. Next, it looks like this Paolo Luciano legally changed his name to Paolo Luzzi-Luciano. Oh my. This is interesting."

"What's that?"

"It seems the company was sold. This says it was bought by Global Wines and Spirits, Inc. Proceeds of the sale were directed to be put in escrow by order of the court. According to these notes, the majority owner Luca Luciano died. Oh, my goodness! Look at the date! Luca Luciano died a day before the deal to be acquired was finalized. According to this, his death left his widow as in charge since she then became the majority stock holder. She ended up as ninety-nine percent owner when he died."

"What about Paolo Luzzi-Luciano? Is there anything in those files that says what happened to him?"

"It says here the company was sold for fifty-three million U.S. dollars. Oh! It appears the two simple stockholders on the Board of Luciano Wine Export Company, Stefano Luciano, and Dominic Luciano, directed the proceeds be deposited in the bank where Luca is—or I should say *was*—a board member. Hmm! Look at this. The bank is privately held entirely by the Luciano family. Amazing! Would you like a printout of all this information?"

"Absolutely. Thank you."

"Mr. O'Sullivan, it's not my place to ask, but how do you know about this company?"

"Katrina Luciano is my mother."

"Oh, my goodness! I thought you were an American."

"I am. Please, can you do one more thing? Can you tell me the names of the Luciano family members who work at that bank today? And the positions they hold?"

"Sure. Give me a few moments to pull it up. Wait. Ah, here it is. Dominic Luciano, Junior, is now president of the bank, and Stefano Luciano, Junior, is the executive vice president. Both live in Rome and own most of the outstanding shares of stock. This says Dominic is a wealthy philanthropist with close ties to the Vatican. He is an art collector and consults to the Vatican to help it manage its investments.

"It also says here, 'the Luciano family has donated many art pieces over the years to the Vatican's huge art collection.' Maria Luciano is the treasurer and secretary of the company. It says she is a large stockholder, Stefano's sister, and never married."

"Interesting. Thank you. Yes, I'll take a copy of everything you've found for me. Uh, one more thing. The bank owned by the Lucianos, where is it located?"

The woman jotted down the address. Brian left with his head swirling, wondering what the Luciano fortune was all about. He looked at his watch; it was 3:58. He hailed a cab and headed straight to the nearby Luciano bank.

Two minutes later, Nina was exiting the bank's front door with a satisfied smile on her face.

As his cab slowed to a stop, he saw a woman coming down the front steps and then laughed aloud.

"Brian, I can't believe it's you! How did you know where to find me?"

"It's a long story – and a coincidence."

"Well, it's four and the bank just closed."

"That's okay, I have some interesting information to share."

"So do I! You won't believe what I discovered just now!"

"Let me guess: the safe-deposit boxes inside this bank conform to the numbers left by Katrina."

"Gosh! How'd you know?"

"The Luciano family owns the bank."

"Oh my God! What a coincidence. Uh, Brian, I'm hungry. Can we have an early dinner? We can sit and chat."

Outside Rome at the Ciampino airport, a small plane whose arrival had been delayed several hours finally touched down at 4:08. Moments later, Paolo exited the jetway and called the Director.

"Wilhelm, I've come directly to Rome. I have both paintings in a locker here at the airport. I have longtime friends in Rome who move art pieces. I'll check to see if they're interested in one or both paintings. I've also had a call from an art dealer I knew years ago. He left a message saying someone he knows is looking to invest in art. Maybe I can let them bid?"

"Listen, Paolo, I have more news for you. O'Sullivan's wife has been blabbing again to the neighbor in Erick's kitchen. She's saying O'Sullivan is in Rome. Philippe got a hit on O'Sullivan's credit card. He's staying across from the Trevi Fountain at the Hotel Fontana. It's fortuitous that you're in

Rome. You may be able to sell one of the paintings and eliminate O'Sullivan at the same time. I heard through the grapevine you've ordered a yacht from a dealer in Naples. You'll soon be rich, my friend! Maybe when we're done with this profitable endeavor, you can invite me to your home in Malta."

"I know the hotel. And yes, it's good that I'm here. But Wilhelm, you should mind your own business and not stick your nose in my personal affairs."

"Paolo, while you're my employee, I need to know what you're up to. If you need a hand dealing with O'Sullivan, I can send Philippe to Rome tonight."

"That's not necessary. I'll put an end to O'Sullivan myself. I'll call you tomorrow."

Paolo hung up, now even more annoyed at his boss.

Wilhelm, still holding his phone, called his nephew. "Philippe, I want you to catch the next flight to Rome. I want you there late this afternoon, absolutely by tonight."

"But I have tickets for the game..."

"I don't care about your tickets for any game. I want you checked in at the Hotel Fontana tonight across from the Trevi Fountain. It's where you said O'Sullivan checked in earlier today. I'll reserve you a room and pay for it from here. I'll let them know about your late arrival. Take as much cash as you can. Call me tomorrow morning at eight. I'll have another important task for you then. If you succeed, I'll promote you within the organization. Don't forget to have one of the clerks in your group take over listening in on Schmidt's kitchen and we'll maintain monitoring the line in Leipzig. Fortunately for us and for Luzzi, O'Sullivan's wife is a real complainer."

"Thank you for your confidence in me, Uncle. I'm sorry about mentioning the game. I'll call you in the morning."

Brian and Nina returned to the hotel, changed, and headed to dinner. The restaurant, within walking distance, was one Brian had been to previously. The sun was setting as they arrived. A few of the day's storm clouds remained far off in the distance, reflecting the sunshine in pink, gray, and burgundy.

At dinner, Brian recounted what he had learned about the Luciano Wine Exporting Company. He filled in some of the empty spots in the information about the Luciano's Nina had gathered earlier. Most important-ly, the printed information he read aloud to Nina seemed to indicate Paolo Luzzi may soon be eligible for all the money left from the sale of the wine export business.

"Do you think Luca had set up the trust account because of tension between him and Paolo?"

Brian nodded. "I'm sure of it. One other thing. Having read the dozen pages she printed, there's a strong chance I may be entitled to half the money left in escrow. But first, I'll have to prove I'm Katrina's son."

"Oh my God, Brian. You're rich!"

"Hold your horses, Nina. This situation has become volatile. We've had two guys stalking us. Erick's missing. The paintings are missing. We know Wilhelm, Paolo, Antonio and maybe Philippe are in cahoots. And, if he's still alive, I bet Wilhelm's father Klaus is involved, coaching his son, and manipulating all of this like a marionettist."

"So, what do we do now?"

"Well, first, I made a huge mistake by using my Interpol-issued credit card when I checked us in. Wilhelm probably knows I'm here; that means Paolo knows I'm here, too. But I don't think you're on their radar yet."

"Brian, you're scaring me again!"

"Let's finish dinner, check out and find another hotel to stay in for tonight. We'll go to the bank first thing tomorrow to open the safe-deposit box and see what's inside. Once that's done, we can leave Rome."

"And go where?"

He shook his head. "Honestly, I don't know yet. Let's see what we find waiting for us in the safety deposit box at the bank, then decide. How much cash do you have?"

"A couple hundred U.S. dollars."

"Careful. You don't want to burn through your cash too fast."

He asked for the check and paid with cash. As they left, he briefly reminisced about being at the restaurant a dozen years ago with Grace, then going back to the Fontana with her.

Those were good days. We were close. Why did things change so much?

Arriving back at the hotel, they each went to their rooms and packed their belongings. Downstairs Brian apologized to the desk clerk, saying an emergency required them to return to the airport. Pulling their luggage, they left the Fontana. Brian, turning toward the right, took Nina's free hand.

"I know of another place within walking distance. Let's see if they have space for us."

"Can we call?"

"No. Knowing I might be worth twenty million, I suddenly fear I'm being hunted. We need to go dark – and stay dark – for now."

"Well then, hold on a moment."

Then looking around, Nina pulled him into a deserted alleyway. She stopped and reached into her purse – which could easily be mistaken for a small duffel bag.

"Here. I've realized if Paolo finds you, he might kill you. I bought this earlier today before I went to the banks." She thrust a small pistol into his hands. "Careful. It's loaded. It's got a safety you need to release. Here's an extra magazine. It's loaded, too. And here are some extra rounds. *That's* why I'm down to two hundred."

Brian was stunned. "Nina! I don't know what to say."

"Perhaps a thank you is in order. You're an agent, so you can carry concealed."

He leaned and kissed her on the cheek. "Historians and art experts don't *ever* carry," he reminded her.

"Perhaps not. But right now, you need to."

They continued down the block, their luggage bumping along the stone street. Ten minutes later, the fourth place they tried had a vacancy, but it was one room with one double bed on the second floor. Brian paid for the room in cash, then lugged Nina's heavy bag up the stairs while she carried his. Little was said as they changed. They climbed into bed and spooned. Nina fell asleep quickly, but Brian remained awake. Feeling her warmth, he thought about their night in Spain. He wanted to wake her, but the moment passed, and he fell asleep holding her close.

Blocks away, Paolo found his way to the Fontana and checked in. He scanned the register, saw Brian's name, and noted the room number. He asked for a nearby room and began to plan how to end Brian's life. It would be easy. Being an Interpol agent gave him special carry privileges, including having a silencer. He'd wait until a few hours after midnight and then strike. He set his alarm and fell sound asleep.

An hour later, Philippe landed in Rome. He caught a cab to the Fontana, checked in and, by chance, was given Brian's room. Paolo woke two minutes before his alarm was set to go off. He made his way down the hall, quietly picked the lock, and entered the room. He heard the sleeping man's soft breathing. Making his way over to the bed, he put the gun to the side of the man's head and whispered, "You should have visited your mother twenty years ago. She's cried for you all these years." Then he pulled the trigger.

He unscrewed the silencer, wiped the gun's handle, and placed it in the man's hand, making it appear to be a suicide. Paolo, whose eyes were now accustomed to the darkened room, suddenly recognized Philippe and realized his mistake.

CHAPTER TWENTY-SEVEN

The Safe Deposit Box

The next morning, Brian woke and showered while Nina remained asleep. While he dressed, a siren wailed outside. Looking out the window, he watched as a police car sped toward the Trevi Fountain area. He checked his watch. 7:15. *Hmm, it's awfully early for the police to be in such a hurry.* He turned back toward the bed and gazed at Nina.

She is so pretty, and I so enjoy her company. I'm feeling like I need to spend more time with her. But not now. I need to learn what's in the safe-deposit box this morning and see where it leads me. I hope there's information about Katrina's whereabouts. If there is, I need to find her. Please God, let her still be alive.

"Wake up, sleepy girl; we have a lot to do this morning – and no time to waste!"

"Good morning, Brian. You look wide awake. Why don't you come back to bed?"

"Your suggestion is tempting, Nina, but we need to get to the bank as soon as it opens and see what's in that safe-deposit box. Maybe we'll have time for each other tonight."

"I'd like that. I so enjoyed our night in Spain."

When they were ready to leave the hotel, Brian gave the clerk five U.S. dollars to hold their bags behind the desk. They grabbed coffee and anise biscotti from the hotel's breakfast buffet, then headed out. Brian and Nina arrived at the bank's front door five minutes before its scheduled 9:00 opening.

"Are you nervous?"

"Yes," he admitted. "Finding her letters, especially the one with the code has brought me to this very moment. Thanks for your efforts in finding the bank. And Nina, I wanted you last night. And I was sincere this morning about wanting to be with you this evening."

"I can't wait. You need to relax. What you've gone through in the last two weeks can't be easy."

"I'm still nervous about Paolo. There's no doubt in my mind he's trying to find me. The information about Luca's company from those old files was revealing. Hopefully, the safe-deposit box will reveal even more."

"Brian, do you have the gun on you?"

"Yes."

"Good. Here comes the woman to unlock the door."

"*Buon giorno!*"

"*Buon giorno. Signora, lei parla inglese?*"

"*Si.* I mean yes."

"We'd like to open a safe-deposit box this morning."

"Ah yes. Come with me. Is this your uncle? The one you mentioned yesterday?"

"Yes. He wants to access his box this morning before I open an account for my own safe-deposit box."

"Wonderful. Come right in and please have a seat. I'll be with you in a minute. *Cappucino?*"

"No, thank you. We're all set," Nina replied with a smile. "But can you please show me to the restroom?"

"Certainly. Come right this way."

When Nina returned, another woman came and greeted them. "*Buon giorno.* Do you have a box number for me to bring you to?"

"Yes, it's in Aisle Ten, Column Twenty-eight, and Level Fourteen."

"Very good. We'll need a ladder. Come with me, it's down this way."

They walked by several aisles before reaching Aisle Ten. The middle-aged woman helping them went to another aisle to get a small ladder.

"*Ecco.* Uh, here. Please be careful."

"Uncle, do you want me to open it for you?"

"I'd appreciate that."

Nina climbed up to Level 14 and turned the dial of the combination lock: 16 right, 18 left, then back to 0. The lock didn't open.

"Nina, be sure to spin the dial a few times and start over."

"I'm sorry, Uncle."

She tried again, doing what he said. The combination worked. The lock released and the small door swung open. She pulled on the small handle of the long grey metal box. It was five inches tall by eight inches wide and about twenty-four inches long.

"*Signora*, please be careful. Let me help you bring it down. I'll bring you both to the table over there. When you're finished, come to the front desk and I'll help you return the box and close the front door. There's a small clip to twist to open the top."

They walked to the table and sat side by side as the lady returned to her desk.

"Brian, are you ready?"

"I am, and I'm nervous. Here goes."

He lifted the top of the box. Inside was a letter sitting on top. Below the letter was a small green velvet bag, several gold bracelets, and four wedding rings. Nina watched Brian stare, frozen, at the contents, and not moving an inch. She then leaned forward and reached for the letter and handed it to him. Brian began to read it softly aloud.

My Dear Brian,

The items in this safe-deposit box were in your father Karl von Richter's possession when he came to the convent in Bernalda looking for me and you.

He never said how he came across these things. But in our last few minutes together, he said he had 'plenty of money to start a new life together.' He wanted to know where you were. He wanted to have you back in his life. Your presence might have changed him. I have come to believe that perhaps he may have been remorseful toward the end. But in those last minutes in the convent's foyer, Karl's temper and angry disposition made him extremely hostile. Hitler's Nazi ideas, enforced by Himmler's SS leadership and Joseph Goebbels' fake news and lies, misled hundreds of thousands of young German men. He fell into a trap, believing them and their wicked ways.

I want you to have these things. Your father was no doubt a senior person in the SS at the end of his career. I believe he was with Adolf Hitler at the Fuhrer's Bunker at the end of Hitler's life, because of escape plans and maps found in his car, and taken by the U.S. Army personnel after Karl's death.

Selling these items should give you plenty of money to enjoy your life and take care of your own children for many years to come. God bless you, my son.

Your loving mother,
Katrina Amorino-Luciano

PS: I'm still so sorry I gave you up for adoption so quickly. It pains me every day.

Brian folded the letter and picked up one of the gold bracelets. Examining it, he noticed the inscription inside, then handed it to Nina. "Take a look at this."

"Oh my God! Brian! The German words translate to:

To My Dear Eva, Together, forever.
Your loving husband, Adolf XO April 28, 1945.'"

The other bracelets bore no inscriptions. Also among the items were two plain gold wedding bands and two rings with diamonds.

Nina picked up the green velvet bag and as she pulled open the gold drawstring, she heard a strange sound. She tilted the bag and out rolled a handful of dingy-looking rocks. She counted them. Twenty-four in all. She recognized the rocks as uncut diamonds.

A small note, folded several times, was stuck inside the bag. She pulled it out and handed it to Brian.

It was Katrina's handwriting and he read it aloud.

Dear Son,

When the bracelets and diamonds were found in your father Karl's duffel bag, there were thirty-two diamonds in this pouch. I gave Luca three diamonds, which he sold, using the proceeds as capital to start his wine export business. I recently gave him five more to use as capital to expand his business. This enabled us to move to Naples and Luca to acquire larger warehouse space to hold the wine he exports. Luca is a fine man, a good husband, and an honest businessman. Maybe you will find these items as your 50th birthday gift, as I suggested to your adoptive mother.

PS: We've also recently bought a lovely vacation home in Malta, overlooking the sea. Perhaps you can visit us there. Use the money wisely. God bless you.

Your loving mother,

Katrina

"Brian, you were supposed to get all this years ago," Nina exclaimed. "It seems your adoptive mother hid that letter in the Bible in the bottom of her hope chest, not knowing what Katrina intended you to have. Worse, Katrina may have been waiting for you to visit her these past twenty years. Oh, Brian, how sad! God only knows if she's still alive now."

"This is all unbelievable. I hope Mom simply forgot. She was terribly depressed after Dad died. We need to leave, Nina. Pack everything up and let's get out of here. Paolo's likely looking for me."

"Brian, you didn't read what's in this other envelope beneath everything else." She opened it to find several pages typed on thin, legal-size paper. An attorney's name, address, and phone number in Positano were imprinted on the letterhead and on the envelope. "Let me read it to you."

To Whom It May Concern – This document updates my final Will and Testament:

Attached are the signed deeds to the houses in Sorrento and Capri belonging to me, Luca Luciano, and my beloved spouse, Katrina Amorino-Luciano. They shall be given to Brian O'Sullivan, Katrina Amorino-Luciano's son, free and clear of any taxes.

Attached is a copy of the final papers regarding the sale of the Luciano Wine Export Company, its warehouses in Italy and overseas, and all other assets to Global Wines and Spirits, Inc. in the amount of 53 million U.S. dollars. In addition to the sale price, Global Wines and Spirits, Inc. agrees to pay all taxes due from the sale to the various governments where the assets are located.

Attached is the signed paperwork directing one million U.S. dollars from the sale of the company to be placed into an account in the Luciano family bank to provide a regular monthly stipend to Paolo Luzzi-Luciano.

Attached is the signed paperwork directing six million U.S. dollars from the sale of the company to be placed into an account in the Luciano family bank to provide a regular monthly stipend to me and/or Katrina Amorino-Luciano.

Attached is the signed paperwork directing the balance of the money from the sale of the company to be placed in an escrow account in the Luciano family bank in the event of my premature death.

5a) Forty-five (45) percent of the money in the escrow account, plus earned interest, shall be disbursed to our legally adopted son, Paolo Luzzi-Luciano, on his 65th birthday. If Paolo Luzzi is deceased, his share shall go to Brian O'Sullivan, Katrina Amorino-Luciano's son, on his 65th birthday.

5b) Forty-five (45) percent of the money in the escrow account, plus earned interest, shall be given to Katrina Amorino-Luciano's son, Bruno Amorino, who was adopted and sent to the United States and raised in Queens, New York, and Staten Island, New York, as Brian O'Sullivan. The money shall be released to Brian O'Sullivan on his 50th birthday. If Brian O'Sullivan is deceased, his share shall go to Paolo Luzzi-Luciano on his 65th birthday.

5c) Seven (7) percent of the money shall be given to the Vatican for the sole use of supporting Catholic churches located south of Naples.

5d) Three (3) percent of the money shall be given directly to the Church of The Holy Angels in Bernalda, Basilicata, in support of the parish convent and church building maintenance program, to update the church interior and the convent chapel, and to construct a new residence for the parish priest.

Signed this day, May 20, 1972

Luca Luciano

Luca Luciano

Witnessed by:

Dominic Luciano

Dominic Luciano

Witnessed by:

Stefano Luciano

Stefano Luciano

Prepared by:

Giuseppe Fellini   Fellini and Fellini, Attorneys at Law, Positano

CHAPTER TWENTY-EIGHT

Paolo Shows Up

Stunned by the contents of the safe-deposit box, Brian and Nina sat speechless for a few moments.

"Wow! Brian! I don't know what to say after reading this and seeing all these things."

"Nina, pack it all up. Quickly!"

"Why are you in such a hurry all of a sudden?"

"I can see the front door from this angle. Guess who just walked in."

Nina paled. "Oh my God! No!"

"Paolo's heading into one of the offices up front. Ask the woman to come back here right now. We need to get out of here fast, but we can't let him see us leave."

"Brian, there's no way we're getting out that door without being seen. Here, take the letters and hide in the men's room. I'll dump everything else in my purse."

"Okay. But watch to see if he heads back this way. He knows you by sight."

"Go now, Brian. Hurry."

As Brian sprang from his seat and rushed into the men's room, Nina waved to signal the woman, who immediately returned with the stepladder to place the emptied box back into its open slot on Level 14. The woman then closed the door and spun the dial on the combination lock.

Nina saw Paolo and another man leaving the front office and headed their way. She excused herself hastily and darted toward the restrooms.

She opened the men's room door. "Brian, not in here. Come with me. We both should hide in the ladies' room. Hurry."

Saying nothing, he quickly followed her.

"We'll need to stay here a few minutes. I'll keep the door locked. Just be quiet."

"Jesus, Mary, and St. Joseph! This is crazy," he said in a low whisper.

"Shhh! Quiet! He's right outside."

Bending down, she peeked through an air vent at the bottom of the ladies' room door. Two pairs of men's legs were right outside. She held a finger to her lips and looked again. Moving to the far end of the ladies' room, away from the door, Nina whispered, "They're at a table right across from us. I think he's signing papers. He might have a copy of the same document we just read drawn up by the attorney in Positano. If you show up, his fortune is cut in half. But if you're gone, he's home free and all the money is his. He'll get the houses in Sorrento and Capri and have enough money from your share to live a lavish life style."

"Nina, let's just be quiet and wait." *I can't believe what's happening. All those things Katrina saved for me and the money that's due me! And here I am hiding for my life in a women's bathroom.*

Five minutes passed. It seemed like an hour. They heard noises as if the seats were moving against the floor.

"Sounds like they're leaving," Nina whispered.

She peeked out again. Paolo and the other man were gone.

Nina stood, unlocked the door, and seeing no one, told him it was safe to come out. With all the goods in her oversized purse, and the letters in his pocket, they headed to the door.

As they approached the front door, the woman she'd met with the day before hurried to catch up with them. "*Uno momento! Signora,* yesterday you said you needed your uncle's approval. Are you now ready to secure a safe-deposit box?"

"Yes, but unfortunately, we have an appointment in ten minutes. I'll be back after that."

The two office name plates on the left caught Brian's eye as they hurried to the exit. Nina led the way out and, ensuring they didn't see Paolo, they walked two blocks back to the hotel, retrieved their luggage, and hailed a cab. As they were getting into the cab, she asked, "Where do we go from here?"

"Ciampino airport! Nina, we're headed to find my mother."

She looked baffled. "Headed where?"

CHAPTER TWENTY-NINE

Wilhelm's Call

O n the way to Rome's smaller airport, the cabbie mentioned an overnight shooting at Hotel Fontana.

Brian and Nina shook their heads in disbelief, curious about the circumstances and details. Nina's mind flashed to the papers in Brian's jacket pocket. "Brian, did you see who witnessed the attorney's document in the sale of the wine export company?"

Brian nodded. "Luca's two brothers. In yesterday's microfiche search, they were identified as majority stockholders and directors of the Luciano family-owned bank. Luca died two days before the final sale and closing, so a few things probably happened.

"First, Paolo probably didn't know Luca changed his will and planned for the money from the sale to go into escrow in case of his own death. The two probably weren't on good terms with each other. Even though Paolo was technically an officer of the company, he had no controlling interest. Frankly, given Luca's sudden death, I'd wager Paolo had something to do with it, believing he'd gain immediate control of the proceeds from the sale. But he was outsmarted by Luca or by Luca's lawyer who authored the papers.

"Next, regarding the money deposited into the Luciano's family bank… I bet the amount of money in the escrow account from the sale of the business is no different today than when it was deposited. With Luca dead, his brothers had free use of the compounded interest all these years, wrongly filling their pockets. Which leads me to the third point. Did you see the nameplates on the two offices out front as we were leaving?

"One said 'Dominic, Jr.' and the other said 'Stefano, Jr.' They must be the sons who now run the bank. It also means they're Paolo's cousins by his adoption. His visit there today seemed quick, as if it were a familiar or regular stop to say hello. They must give Paolo his monthly allowance."

"Brian, when I peeked from the bathroom vent, Paolo was signing something. Maybe it had something to do with the money and his sixty-fifth birthday. I wonder if his birthday is coming soon?"

"Maybe. But after reading that document, my showing up is dangerous to my health."

"But with what was found in the safety deposit box, Brian, I think you have enough evidence now to make a claim against the escrow account."

Just then, Brian's phone rang. Curious as to who was calling, Nina leaned in closer to listen.

"O'Sullivan, it's Wilhelm. Where are you?"

"Why do you ask?"

"The young man you met in my office, Philippe, was killed last night at the Hotel Fontana. I was told you checked into the Fontana yesterday afternoon using a credit card. O'Sullivan, Philippe was my nephew. Are you responsible for his death?"

"That's a hell of a question! I checked out at 6:30 last night, four hours after I checked in. I never saw Philippe. What is going on? Erick's missing. Antonio was following him, and Paolo was following me. And why in God's name did Philippe follow me to my hotel? This art-recovery mission was completed. I even called and acknowledged the other team beat us. But now things have suddenly become very ugly."

"Listen. Luzzi and I just spoke. Yes, he told me he recovered two paintings in Córdoba and has them in a locker at the Ciampino airport. He was supposed to bring them to Amsterdam. I need you to go to the Ciampino airport and keep an eye on the lockers. Look for Luzzi and see if he picks up any packages. Do not confront him. Avoid contact. Just report back to me what you see. Can I count on you to do this?"

"Well, Wilhelm, things have become quite curious and, to be honest, I'm not exactly sure which side you're on here. Have you heard from Erick at all?"

"O'Sullivan, just listen to me and do what I say! You don't want anything to happen to Grace, now, do you?

"Grace? What does Grace have to do with any of this?"

"Her trip to Amsterdam and her stay at Erick's has been frustrating for her, but she's been safe so far. I expect you don't want that to change. Right? So, I strongly suggest you do as I say. Find Paolo. If he picks up the paintings, follow him. Call me in the morning. I want those paintings back here in my office in The Hague." Wilhelm slammed down his phone ending the call.

Brian shook his head and gritted his teeth in frustration. His face reddened as his blood pressure rose.

Nina, seeing — and frightened by — his reaction, grabbed his arm. "I couldn't hear most of that. What did Wilhelm say that's upset you so?"

"We need to stop and find a quiet place to sit for a few minutes. I need to calm down before I have a stroke. I don't know how, but Wilhelm knows Grace is at Erick's. My heart is racing."

Nina asked the cabbie to stop at the next café. "*Signore,* keep the meter running. We'll return shortly."

Once inside, Nina ordered two sparkling waters while Brian closed his eyes and took a few deep breaths. Then he recapped with her what Wilhelm said, including the veiled threat to Grace.

Noticeably upset, Nina teared up. He took her hand, holding it gently. "Don't worry. It'll all somehow work out. Right now, we need to calmly think this through this confusion. It's our move and we have an advantage. We have the goods Katrina left for me, we have the legal documents, and we know those paintings are in a locker at the airport. By now Erick's friend, Kristofer Bronn, should have called both Wilhelm and Paolo saying he has a buyer wanting to spend ten million U.S. dollars. That should create tension between them. Maybe that's why Wilhelm called me. He must be motivated to get the paintings back. Let's see what piece moves next on this figurative chess board."

Nina heaved a relieved sigh. "Thank you, Brian. I feel more confident, knowing you can figure out a strategy for us."

"Before we leave here, I have to call Grace. She needs to leave Erick's place immediately. "Grace is somehow at risk. I thought Erick made a clean sweep of his apartment. They must be listening to her conversations with Solie."

Brian made the call but got no answer. He tried a second time. Still no answer. He became genuinely concerned when the voicemail didn't pick up.

He thought to call Solie but didn't have her number.

Feeling better, they left the café, and they back into the cab. Initially quiet on the ride, Brian cycled through a multitude of thoughts like a chess expert facing a tough opponent.

"Paolo may have expected to get a big payday with the company's sale but was thwarted by the will Luca's attorney drew up. Perhaps Luca told him, or he somehow got wind of the new will and he got angry. I'm now convinced Paolo caused Luca's death. Since then, Paolo's love of money has led him to become involved in art thefts, beginning with Klaus Mueller years ago, and now in this deal with Wilhelm. Our best next step is to find Paolo and watch what he does."

They arrived at the Ciampino Airport, exited the cab, and headed to the area with dozens of lockers of all sizes.

"Stay near this column and keep an eye on this area, Nina. I'm headed over to the other side where there are more lockers. If you see Paolo, call me right away."

Half an hour passed without any sightings. Then Nina spotted Paolo walking with another man. When she called Brian, he casually approached her, with his own luggage. She watched, partially hidden by a column.

"He's over there. They arrived together and are chatting."

"That's Stefano Luciano."

"How do you know?"

"He was sitting in the bank's front office as we left."

"Well, why is he here?"

"No clue. This has gotten way more convoluted than I first thought. When I was searching for paperwork on Luca's export business, the woman helping me mentioned Stefano and his brother Dominic are philanthropists. They have an extensive family art collection and claim special ties to the Vatican."

"Brian, look! Paolo's pulling a colorful canvas bag out of the locker! He's giving it to Stefano!"

"Hang on, Nina. Don't get ahead of yourself. Let's see what happens next."

Their voices echoed across the hard terrazzo floor as Stefano offered thanks to Paolo.

"*Ciao, Paolo, multo bene! Arrivederci e' grazie!*"

Paolo gave Stefano a hug and headed toward the ticketing counter.

"Nina, we need to split up. You follow Stefano. I'll follow Paolo. Let's see where they go."

"And our luggage?"

"I'll stow them in a locker and follow Paolo. Just get going. Call me when you see what Stefano does with the canvas bag. Quick. Don't lose him."

CHAPTER THIRTY

Following Paolo and Stefano

B rian stashed their bags in a large locker and hurried to keep up with Paolo. Remaining at a distance, he had a full view of Paolo as he purchased a ticket. Once Paolo had moved far enough away, Brian flashed his Interpol credentials and learned Paolo had purchased two tickets to Reggio, Calabria's Aeroporto dello Stretto. The next flight headed to Reggio would leave in two hours. Tasked by Wilhelm to find and follow Paolo, Brian bought one ticket with his company credit card, and a second one with cash. Wilhelm had not mentioned Nina, and Brian wanted to keep her out of Wilhelm's mind.

Brian kept a careful eye on Paolo as he made his way down the concourse to a bar, sat at a tall table, and ordered a drink. Within ten minutes, Paolo had begun checking his watch. He stood and paced across the bar's entrance several times. A tall, long-haired woman in a tight leather skirt, revealing top, and high heels approached him. She kissed him and they disappeared into the bar.

Meanwhile, Nina hailed a cab and followed Stefano Luciano in his red Maserati. Anxious, she was convinced she'd selected the slowest cab driver in all of Rome.

"Quickly, quickly! Catch up to the red car!" she urged.

She eventually noticed familiar locations along the road and realized Stefano was headed back to the bank. As the cab arrived, she saw Stefano's car parked out front. He returned to the car, opened the trunk, and grabbed the big colorful embroidered canvas bag and carried it into the bank. Once he was inside, Nina tossed the cabbie money to cover the tab and hopped out. Entering the bank, she scanned the premises for Stefano.

Suddenly she felt a touch on her arm.

"*Ah, signorina*, I'm so glad you have returned. Shall we open the deposit box now?"

"Uh, yes. Yes, let's do that."

She followed the persistent woman to the rear where the safe-deposit boxes were located. She sat and went along with the process of signing papers. Off to the side, twenty feet away, she spotted Stefano opening an exceptionally large deposit box on the lowest level – the ones more like lockers. Then he stood and walked past her. Not wanting him to see her face, Nina ducked down, pretending to fix her shoe. She watched him return to his office. Minutes later, he returned, crouched down, and shoved a large canvas bag inside the box. He shut the door and locked it with a key.

I guess that's the bag with the paintings. I need to go over there to see the column and section where they're hidden.

"*Signorina*, your paper work is complete. Thank you. Now do you have something to put into the safe deposit box?"

"Yes. I certainly do."

"Come with me. Here is your box. I've selected a lower level for your convenience. I'll step aside to the next aisle and let you put your things in. Remember, you can set the lock combination yourself."

"Thank you."

Nina slipped the diamonds and jewelry from her oversized purse into the safe-deposit box. *All these things will be safe in here. I'll set the combination lock to 16, 18, 0. That number is etched in both our brains. There. Now let me spin the dial. Done. Okay, here she comes.*

"*Ciao? Senora?*"

"*Finito.* I'm all set. It's closed."

"*Ah, molto bene. Por favore*, uh, please, come to the front and I'll take your payment for the first six months."

"Yes. I just need to use the ladies' room first."

"*Certo!* Uh, certainly, I'll meet you up front."

Perfect. I can check the exact location of the low-level locker where Stefano placed the bag with the art. Hmm. Here we are. I'm guessing the large, embroidered bag must be 36 to 45 inches long. That width could hold the two stolen paintings we were looking for. Let me go up front now.

Two minutes later, she made her payment at a teller's window up front. Nina was anxious to leave, and on her way to the bank's front door, she saw

Stefano shut off his office light. She turned away, hoping not to be seen by him. Just then, the woman, two steps behind, called out, *"Signora,* you dropped your receipt."

"Oh! *Grazie."*

Nina turned to exit, but a step away from the front door, the woman again called out loudly.

"Stefano, questa e' Nina von Scholz. She has just opened a new safe-deposit box."

"Ah, grazie, signorina."

"Prego, signore. I need to run! *Ciao!"*

Frightened by the impromptu face-to-face meeting, Nina faced forward and walked straight into the heavy glass door. Mortified, she pasted on a smile, then opened the door and left. Outside, she hailed an empty cab stopping for a traffic light. Grabbing the door handle, she jumped in, shouting, *"Aeroporto! Ciampino aeroporto!* Quickly!"

Inside, Stefano commented, *"Maria, la signorina,* she is very pretty."

"Yes, and her uncle has an account here, as well."

"Oh? What is his name?"

"He was here earlier today. His name is B.J. O'Sullivan. I haven't had time to tell you this, but he opened one of the oldest boxes we have. It hadn't been opened in forty years. I checked the records after he left."

"Oh, really? Do you remember the location of the box?"

"Yes. It was ten, twenty-eight, fourteen."

"No. That's impossible."

"Yes. Aisle Ten, Column Twenty-eight, and Level Fourteen. I'm certain of it."

"It can't be. Show me."

She walked to the back with Stefano, stopping at Aisle 10. She walked down a few feet and pointed to Column 28.

"There. Yes, right up there, in Level 14."

"You're certain you saw him open the box on level 14?"

"Yes. Well, she opened it. Then I stepped away and saw her slide the box out. They were alone for about ten minutes. Then they returned the box to its space and closed the door. But I don't recall seeing her spin the combination lock."

"Maria, get the ladder. Maybe it's still open."

When the woman returned with the ladder, Stefano motioned for her to climb up. "You go."

"The door, it's still open," she called back down. "Here, let me slide this box out."

Maria climbed back down the ladder, the long box under one arm. "Stefano, you open it."

Stefano carried it to the table and raised the lid. "It's empty! Maria, do you know where Dominic is right now?"

"No."

"Find him. Now! Tell him we have a problem, then get Paolo on the phone for me."

"Of course. What's going on?"

"I'll tell you when Dominic gets here. Well, I'll tell you now. Uncle Dominic and my father left a note for us to keep an eye on this specific safe-deposit box. They said Luca's wife, Katrina, was in here a few times, back when Uncle Luca was starting his business. They thought he had some things hidden inside, but out of respect, they never tried to break into the box. But they insisted if someone came in and opened that box, we needed to make a note of who it was."

Maria returned to her office, called Dominic, and left him a voice message for him to call Stefano immediately. When she called Paolo, the call went straight to voicemail. She left him a similar message.

At Ciampino Airport, Paolo was sipping his fourth glass of Cinzano dry vermouth. He was telling Elena about his recent purchase: a 77-foot-long yacht with forward and aft master bedrooms with their own bathrooms; two smaller rooms, each with a bathroom all on the lower level; a full living room; dining room and galley on the main deck; and a fancy wooden bar, a barbecue grill and a 14-foot runabout on the top deck. It also has every modern electronic feature available.

"How are you suddenly so rich?" Elena asked.

"I've invested well, and I'll be retiring in the next two weeks. I set this up a week ago as my birthday neared. Last night I reserved a slip at the *Porto de Reggio Marina* for my yacht for tonight.

"My childhood friend, the salesman who sold me the yacht, already has brought the boat from Naples to Reggio. I wanted him to test my new yacht on the run from Naples down the coast to Reggio. I'm flying down to Calabria in an hour. From Reggio, we'll cruise to the harbor in Siracusa, Sicily. Once in Siracusa, my friend will depart, and I'll captain the boat the rest of the way to Malta. I have a beautiful home on the south side of the island, overlooking the Mediterranean."

He paused and looked at her. Then he reached out and touched her.

"Elena, I'd like you to spend the next two weeks with me. Please, join me. Maybe we can be together even longer."

She was smitten by his offer, and duly impressed. "Paolo, I'd love to join you, but I'll need to go home and pack. When are you leaving?"

"In an hour. Don't pack. Stay here now and fly with me to Reggio. You can get all the clothing you want in Siracusa on our way to Malta. Here. Look. I already have your ticket to accompany me to Reggio."

"Oh, Paolo. This sounds wonderful! So, does this mean you and I will finally be spending a lot more time together?"

"If things go as planned, maybe we'll be spending years together."

"Paolo, I've wanted to be your woman for a long time. You're such a wonderful man."

"Another drink?"

"Of course! Especially if I don't have to go home to pack."

He waved to the bartender, who then brought another round. Elena clinked her glass of dry vermouth with his. Leaning over, she ran her hand along his upper thigh and then, stroking his crotch, gave him a huge kiss.

As they sat enjoying their dry vermouth, off in the distance a cell phone rang.

"Nina, where are you?"

"I'm on my way back to the airport. I just accidentally met Stefano Luciano at the bank, and it's made me nervous wreck."

"How did that happen?"

"Well, first I saw where the paintings are stashed on the lower level. Then that pesky woman asked me to open a new safe-deposit box. It occurred to me it'd probably be best to put the diamonds and jewelry in it. I should be there in ten minutes."

"I'm in the back, off to one side, about a hundred feet from the bar, behind one of those kiosks where they hawk sunglasses. Avoid the bar.

Paolo's sitting there with a woman. They're looking quite cozy. They need to get a room. She's been pawing him and he's getting overly friendly. That's been going on almost the entire time they've been having cocktails."

Nina's cab was pulling up outside the airport when Paolo's cell phone rang. He stood and walked away from his girlfriend.

"Paolo, I need you to bring those paintings back to our offices in The Hague."

"Wilhelm, I've decided it's not going to happen your way. I have a local buyer in Rome who just two hours ago offered me three million U.S. dollars for each one."

"Paolo, I've negotiated a deal with an antiques dealer who has a wealthy investor in Switzerland with ten million U.S. dollars to spend. They're offering up to five million U.S. dollars for each painting if those turn out to be the same ones taken from the Lieberman family in Paris. Listen, we can do this. We can say you only found one painting and then it was stolen. We can blame O'Sullivan by saying he lost it. No one knows you found both paintings. The deal in Switzerland gives us both more money."

Paolo remained silent while Wilhelm began to sputter.

"Goddamn it, Paolo. Listen to me! I didn't want to tell you this, but my father is fifty-fifty on my share of the deal. He's paid attention to all your moves so far. He's telling me to be patient with you, saying, 'Paolo's a good guy and will come around.' So, Paolo, I need you back here in The Hague with those two paintings tomorrow, so I can close the deal in Switzerland. Don't be stupid. You'll need the extra money just for the diesel fuel for that new boat of yours."

"Fuck you, Wilhelm. I'm controlling this deal now. I'm the one who's selling the paintings, and when I get the money, I'll send your father half. If he wants to give you a piece of the pie, so be it. But I hope you fucking choke on your tiny slice."

Paolo snapped his flip phone shut and shoved it back into his pocket. Pausing to collect himself, he took a deep breath, put a smile on his face and returned to Elena. *My deal with Stefano is already completed—and the art is already delivered and sitting securely in their bank.*

During his visit earlier that day, Stefano told Paolo the Luciano family would buy both paintings for five million U.S. dollars. Stefano promised

Paolo he and Dominic would donate one to the Vatican—making him feel good—as if he was self-absolving his sinfulness. It was the same deal Paolo and his uncles Stefano and Dominic, had cut many years earlier, and then carried on with their sons, his cousins. This practice was how the Luciano family had grown their personal net worth and their incredible art holdings over the past three decades.

In this caper, Luciano family money purchased both stolen paintings. Then, according to the instructions from Paolo, one million U.S. dollars would be wired to Klaus Mueller's Swiss account, and four million U.S. dollars would be wired to the Naples yacht company. That would pay off the balance due on the deposit. Paolo was riding high.

Paolo's birthday was now only a day away, and so was his inheritance. Earlier today, when Paolo was at the bank, Stefano had him sign a loan against his upcoming inheritance. The loan would allow Paolo to complete the purchase of the $14 million yacht. A cashier's check was cut and dated for the day after Paolo's birthday, to be hand delivered to the Naples yacht company. But unbeknownst to Paolo, Dominic and Stefano Luciano shared a thirty-year secret they'd never let their adopted cousin in on.

CHAPTER THIRTY-ONE

The Next Calls

Nina was just greeting Brian when his phone rang.

"O'Sullivan, it's Wilhelm. Have you located Paolo yet?"

"What's in it for me if I have?"

"I didn't expect a response like that from you, O'Sullivan. There's something in it for you if you find Luzzi and bring those paintings to me. Let me go over a few things. First, your partner Erick is dead; Antonio shot him in Spain. Second, Antonio is dead, as well. Paolo made that call. Perhaps this shocks you—but maybe it'll give you an incentive to avenge Erick's death. So, pay close attention to what I'm about to ask you to do.

"Luzzi is on the run; he's purchased two tickets to Reggio. He's also negotiated the purchase of a multimillion-dollar yacht in Naples. It just docked in Reggio today, where he'll pick it up later tonight. He's planning to stop in Siracusa and continue to his home in Malta. Besides buying the yacht, he's treating himself to a huge birthday party tomorrow at his home. It's at the villa where his elderly mother lives."

Brian sat up, suddenly interested in what Wilhelm had said. He ran his hand through his hair, mulling over his response. "Wilhelm, never mind the others right now. Be specific about what's in it for me if I help you retrieve the art and pay Paolo back for Erick's murder."

"I can offer you two million U.S. dollars for the return of both paintings. It would be put in an account on a Dutch-controlled Caribbean Island for you."

"Make it three million, and you give me your word not a hair on Grace's head will be harmed."

"Of course. We can do that. So, you have access to the paintings?"

"I know where Paolo is, and where the paintings are currently hidden. I'll text you the address where the paintings are at six tomorrow morning.

You'll need the support of the local police in Rome, as well as two clean Interpol agents. When you have the warrant in place from the judge, call me, and I'll give you a Swiss account number. After I get word the money's been deposited, I'll provide details on where to find the paintings. Plan on retrieving the art at nine AM."

"Very good. So, they are being held in a bank?"

"Yes. But that's all I'll say for now."

"O'Sullivan, I'm surprised by your position on this. You're smarter than I thought. You'll be happy with your decision on turning over the paintings. Oh, one other thing. These deaths are an example of Luzzi's complete disregard for people who get in his way. He's been like this for years. Few knew he was the prime suspect in his stepfather's death. But now he's going rogue. His sixty-fifth birthday is a day away. He's been planning to inherit a huge sum of money."

Brian's brain twisted at Wilhelm's mention of Paolo as a suspect in Luca's death.

"O'Sullivan, here's a final warning: Your life is in danger. Luzzi is on to you. He knows who you are, and that you're claiming to be related to Katrina Luciano. He wants you dead. He'll kill you as soon as he finds you, and apparently his pot of gold will be twice as big with you out of the way. I'll set in motion the steps to retrieve the art in the morning. As for trying to find this woman, Katrina, you'll need some luck. The villa where she lives is not easily accessed, and it has an armed guard."

Wilhelm hung up and immediately called his secretary into his office. "Ursula, get me a ticket on the next plane to Rome. If there's nothing before eight tonight, call operations and have them roll out a plane for me."

"Yes, Wilhelm, I'll get right on it."

"And do we have anyone else in Amsterdam right now?"

"Yes. Johan Voorst lives in Haarlem. He's just returned from a project in Brazil."

"Give him a call. Have him go over to Schmidt's apartment and detain the woman there. Her name is Grace O'Sullivan. She's an American. Have him plant some drugs in the apartment and get the local police involved. They should hold her for the next several days in the local jail under suspicion of bringing drugs into the Netherlands. And see that her cell phone is confiscated."

"How soon do you want this done?"

"Have him go in tonight, and have them pick her up before six AM tomorrow. She's older and will be disoriented by an early-morning raid."

Brian stood and wiped sweat from his forehead.

Nina saw he looked distressed. "Who was that?"

"Wilhelm, again. He just shared a lot with me. Circumstances are becoming more dangerous by the hour. Tell me, did you see the art physically being put into a safe-deposit box at the bank?"

"Yes."

"You're absolutely sure?"

"It was the same embroidered bag Paolo took from the locker and handed to Stefano. And I saw Stefano push it into the locker."

"Locker?"

"Well, you know. It's that bottom row, the first level with all the smaller boxes above."

"And you memorized the location number?"

"Yes."

"Good. In the morning I'll need to call Wilhelm and give him the location of the paintings being held in the bank. Next, Luzzi is flying to Reggio this afternoon. He's buying, or just bought a large yacht in Naples. He's taking delivery in Reggio where he'll be boarding and taking the yacht to Siracusa and then Malta. And Nina, get this: Wilhelm just said Luzzi's mother—*my* mother—is alive and living in Malta. In an oceanside villa."

"Oh my God, Brian, my head is spinning. The last several hours of my life are no different than living in an intense chapter of a novel! What do we do now?"

"Give me ten minutes to think things through, and then let me make a few calls. Darn. My phone battery just died."

CHAPTER THIRTY-TWO

Close Call

As Brian and Nina searched for an outlet to charge his phone, Paolo and the woman grabbed their jackets and prepared to leave the bar area. Nina pulled Brian back to hide with her behind the kiosk with the sunglasses. Paolo and his woman casually stopped to try on sunglasses.

Eventually, they left without making a purchase, proceeding hand in hand down the concourse. They stopped at Gate 11. Brian and Nina let out deep breaths and shook their heads. Releasing the tension, they both broke into smiles. They headed over to the bar and sat. Brian plugged his phone into a nearby outlet.

"I have a few calls to make once my phone recharges. Right now, I need to return to the ticket counter. Earlier, while you followed Stefano, I got two tickets to fly to Reggio, but I'm going to trade them for two tickets to Catania, Sicily, the airport closest to Siracusa. Wilhelm said Paolo's getting his new yacht in Reggio, stopping in Siracusa, and going on to Malta where he's throwing himself a birthday party.

"My old friend Massimo taught art history at NYU in Greenwich Village. He retired several years back and bought a home in Costa Bianca. It's on the south side of Siracusa. He was the commodore of a yacht club, and he's wanted me to visit. I'm certain we can stay with him. He can arrange our transport to Malta by boat. I'll call and let him know we'll be arriving late tonight."

"Shouldn't we just fly to Malta?"

"We don't want any of the locals seeing us arriving at the airport there. Paolo has lots of shady friends, and we don't want our arrival announced to him. We'll go to Sicily first. As soon as my battery's charged, I'll call Kristofer Bronn. I need his help to set up an account for me in a Swiss bank this afternoon. And there's one more call I need to make."

"What's that?"

"Wilhelm said Paolo's birthday is tomorrow. Based on what those papers said, I need to let the Luciano family bank know I'm alive, and I intend to make a claim on the funds deposited there for me."

"Why don't you just go there now, while we're here in Rome?"

"Going to the bank might be dangerous for me right now. I'm going to call the law firm on the pages in the legal document outlining Luca's wishes. I'll tell them who I am and let them explain to the bank I'm alive and well. Do you recall the name of the law firm?"

She shook her head. "I put everything I had into the new safe-deposit box, except one of the uncut diamonds and a gold bracelet. But the letters from Katrina and the document you're referring to with the attorney's name... those should still be in your pocket."

"Gosh, Nina, thanks for remembering." He sighed as he pulled the papers from his pocket. "It's okay. Maybe it's the pressure we're under."

He went to the ticket counter and exchanged the tickets. By the time he returned, his phone battery showed it was charged enough, so he called Grace's number, hoping she'd set it up on an international plan. The call went unanswered again; this time he left a message.

"Grace, it's Brian. Listen closely. I can't go into details right now, but your life is in danger. This is not a joke. You must leave Erick's house immediately and go to a hotel tonight—*any* hotel. Pay cash. In the morning, take the first flight to Cork, Ireland. Pay cash for your ticket at the airport. In Cork, pay cash to rent a car and drive to Kinsale. Stay at the Friar's Lodge on Friars Street. We've stayed there before, years ago. Say you're Professor O'Sullivan's wife when you check in and they'll give you the educational discount. You'll be safe there. Don't use your credit card. Pay cash when you check in. Grace, do not, I repeat, *do not* discuss what I'm asking you to do with Erick's neighbor Solmaz. Just gather your things as soon as you hear this message, and leave. Get a room tonight, and fly tomorrow morning. I'll try to reach you again later but expect a call from me tomorrow night and I'll explain more."

His next call was to Kristofer Bronn. When it went to voicemail, he left a simple message.

"Hello Kristofer. It's Agent Brian O'Sullivan again. I need your help setting up a bank account by tomorrow morning. You know where to set it up. Go to a park and call me from your cell phone when it's completed."

Moments later in Leipzig, Kristofer returned from a visit to the local bakery and saw his cell phone's message light flashing. He listened, then called his nephew in Zurich who worked for a Swiss bank and asked him to set up an account. The nephew promptly complied. In less than ten minutes, he texted his uncle back to let him know it was done. Kristofer in turn texted Brian.

Nina was handing Brian a bowl of minestrone when his cell phone beeped. Kristofer's incoming text read: "Acct # 011-448-5587-727-4566-53 Credit Suisse."

Brian was relieved to see the account was set up, but, with much on their minds, the two were quiet. Nina only half finished her chicken pesto panini. She doodled on the paper placemat, imagining what life might be like with Brian if they survived this ordeal. She moved her plate, with the half-eaten sandwich, toward Brian. A few more minutes of silent doodling passed. Brian looked at his phone.

"Darn. This charger isn't working! My phone isn't charging."

"Well, of course not, silly. Your plug's fallen out of the wall."

"Geesh!"

He plugged it back in and took a short walk toward Gate 11. Still some distance away, he saw Paolo and the woman sitting and waiting for their plane to leave. They were chatting, and then Paolo stood and began walking toward him. Brian turned and hurried back to the bar.

"He's on his way back. We need to move. Quick, over there near that column. It'll block his view."

Paolo returned to the bar and ordered two more dry vermouths. The bartender put them in plastic cups and waived payment. As he departed, Nina sneezed. Paolo turned but didn't see anyone and returned to the gate.

"My God, Nina! That was close. I've never heard you sneeze like that!"

"It's dusty over here."

"My darn heart's pounding again like I'm running a race."

"You need to relax. Tonight, when we get to your friend's place, I'll help you with that."

CHAPTER THIRTY-THREE

Massimo and Giuseppe

Brian's phone, now recharged to 39 percent, allowed him to make two more calls. The first was to his friend in Sicily. "Massimo! It's your old Greenwich Village drinking buddy, Brian O'Sullivan."

"Brian! I can't believe you're calling me! It's been too many years! How are you?"

"I'm fine, Massimo. I trust you are well. How is Pierre Louie?"

"Pierre Louie and I are no longer a couple. Please. Just leave it at that. It's too painful for me to recount what happened."

"Very sorry to hear that, Massimo."

"We had a wonderful life. I'm still upset and bitter. But enough of that What can I do for you, Brian?"

"I have a favor to ask."

"Anything for you, my friend. By the way, how is Gracie? Ha! That hot redhead of yours has always been a challenge! Is she still so demanding? I'm laughing as I ask."

"She's okay. Listen, Massimo, right now I'm in Rome, at the Ciampino airport. I'm flying to Catania within the hour. Would you mind if I stay at your place tonight?"

"Not at all! It'll be like old times! Is Gracie with you?"

"Actually, I have a business associate with me."

"Terrific, bring him along. Is he good looking? I have some good American bourbon here called Pappy's. A friend in Kentucky sent me a bottle a few months ago. Good old Hank says it's quite a sought-after commodity. Maybe we can trash the bottle like we used to in the old days."

"That was a long time ago, my friend, back in that bar on Bleecker Street and MacDougal, first semester at NYU. Thanks, Massimo. I knew I could count on you. See you late tonight."

"The lights in front will go on automatically as you approach the house. My doorbell has a camera—you'll show up on my TV set as you walk to the door. Have a safe trip."

Nina gave Brian the phone number for his next call: the Fellini and Fellini law firm in Positano. A woman answered, but her English was poor, so Brian handed Nina the phone. Their brief conversation allowed the legal assistant to understand the purpose of the call. She assured Nina a principal in the firm would call back within a few minutes.

The return call came quickly.

"*Pronto.*"

"*Pronto, signori! Lei parla inglese?*"

"*Si,* I speak English. My assistant gave me insight into your call. I remember Luca Luciano. What do you need from me?"

"*Signori, un momento...*" she handed the phone to Brian and whispered, "He speaks English... go ahead."

The weak, barely audible voice on the line was attorney Giuseppe Fellini, an elderly gent, once a close friend of Luca Luciano. They knew each other seventy years earlier as seminarians. Giuseppe left the seminary after three months. He went on to study law, then joined the family law firm. Luca knew he could trust Giuseppe and the Fellini family for legal guidance when his export business began to grow.

"*Signori,* many years ago you had a client, Luca Luciano. You created a document for him at the time he was selling his company, Luciano Wine Exports. It included Luca's personal will and instructions regarding the disposition of the income from the sale of his company. The document specified money from the sale of the company be deposited in a bank in Rome and set aside as monthly income for Luca and his wife and their adopted son Paolo Luzzi-Luciano. A considerable sum of money was set aside to become available for their adopted son, Paolo, and for Katrina's son, Brian O'Sullivan, when they attained certain ages."

"Yes. I remember all of that. How can I help you?"

"*Signori,* I am Brian O'Sullivan, the son of Luca's wife, Katrina. I was sent to the United States as an infant, adopted, and raised in Staten Island, New York. Recently, my adoptive mother passed away. My sisters and I found letters addressed to me, hidden in her hope chest, inside an old German Bible. The letters were from Katrina."

"Mr. O'Sullivan. Let me ask you a few questions. Do you know the name of your birth father?"

"Karl von Richter."

"And his profession?"

"He was a German SS soldier."

"Before that?"

"Katrina wrote that Karl worked with his father, Otto, in a foundry in Ravensburg, making parts for German tanks before World War II. Their family home was in Friedrichshafen on Lake Constance. Karl's house was in a tiny hamlet called Langenargen."

"Very good. One more thing. Katrina Luciano told me she left a message for you on a letter in the form of a code."

"Yes, it's 10, 28. Uh. I'm not going to repeat the rest of it."

"That's okay. I know the code. Have you figured out what the code is about?"

"Yes."

"Can you tell me what it's for?"

"I can, but I don't want to."

"Young man, it has to do with a bank. I knew Katrina well. She told me she put some things in a safe-deposit box intended for just you, and not to be shared with her adopted son, Paolo."

"Yes. I've been to the bank and found what was being held inside. It's how I knew to call your law firm."

"Okay, I am confident you are her son. Can you come to my office in Positano to sign some documents?"

"I'm currently at the Ciampino airport outside Rome, flying to Sicily late this afternoon."

"*Perfecto.* My youngest son, who now runs our law firm, has an office just outside Ciampino, on the way to Castel Gandolfo. Can you see him before you leave?"

"I can do that."

"I'll call him now and tell him to expect you within the hour. Young man, I'm glad you have found these things while Katrina is still alive. Like me, she is old now, and failing. I was the executor of Luca's will and visited

Katrina once a year after he passed away. Then my wife died unexpectedly while my two sons were still young. Katrina and I became close, and we enjoyed each other's company. We began spending more time together and even vacationed together twice. She liked to ski, but I only watched. She told me stories about her decision to go to Germany and her time as a nurse. She was crushed when she learned about Karl's being involved in constructing death camps. She even told me about the night he hurt her and how he traumatized her so terribly.

"As much as we loved each other, becoming a couple was impossible. She simply could not get past her youthful sorrows. It was incredibly sad for me. She is so beautiful, her blue eyes so striking. She remains in my mind as if she were sitting here with me.

"You are a good son to finally return. Your presence will make her happy and you will warm her heart. Now, I have said more than was necessary."

"*Signore, grazie* for your kind words. I deeply regret not knowing anything about her until just last week, when my adoptive mother passed away. Since then, sudden circumstances aligned with my learning about my birth parents. Worse, having just read the papers in the safe-deposit box, I can see why Paolo is upset that I have suddenly appeared and may spoil his big payday."

"Yes. You must be very cautious. Paolo was a troubled child… and is now an evil man. He caused Luca and Katrina constant troubles while he was growing up. He avoided being jailed as an adolescent because Luca would go to the police station and explain Paolo's ill-fated childhood. And then look what happened. I must say I always wondered why Luca died so unexpectedly."

Giuseppe paused to reflect, and his thoughts drifted. There was silence on his end of the line.

"*Signore? Signore Fellini?*"

"*Si.* Uh, yes. I'm sorry. My old memories just took me away. What is your plan after this?"

"I plan to go to Malta and introduce myself to Katrina, thank her for my life, and apologize for not knowing about her sooner."

"Here's what I suggest. Go to my son, Fausto, and sign the papers. That will give you access to claim—and enable you to withdraw—what was left for you by Luca and Katrina. My son can withdraw the money for you, if that's more convenient. But do not keep it in the Lucianos' bank any longer."

"*Signore Fellini,* I have a Swiss account."

"*Buono.* Give it to my son when you meet. He will create a demand note for the bank and will see that your money is electronically transferred. I will call Fausto now, so the papers are ready for you to sign when you arrive. He will give you Katrina's address. But, young man, be cautious. The house where she lives overlooks the ocean. It is protected by two guards living in a small guest house beside the front entrance gate. Paolo has anticipated your arrival for years! He wants no part of you, and will make you disappear if he gets the chance. If you want to see your mother, you must devise a way to get past them.

"Also, you cannot trust *anyone* in Malta. They would make Paolo mayor if they could. He throws lavish parties every few years for his own birthday. I was there once with Katrina. My memory is old, but his birthday is soon. Check with Fausto when you sign the papers."

"*Grazie, signore,* for your wise counsel. I'll head to your son's office now. May I give Katrina your regards?"

"*Si.* Please send her my love and say I am too old to travel. Tell her I so enjoyed our visits together. And if you can find a red rose, bring it to her for me."

"Of course. *Ciao, signore.*"

Old Giuseppe wiped a tear from his cheek when they hung up, then he called his son.

Brian turned to Nina, who sat anxiously beside him listening to his side of the conversation.

"Thank God she's alive. I have to sign several papers to make a claim on the money left in escrow. The law firm has an office nearby. They'll execute the claim and wire the money to the Swiss bank account for me. I'll return in an hour. We'll fly to Sicily, drive to Massimo's home, and spend the night there. We'll need to figure out a way to get to Malta, then approach Katrina's house safely, because Paolo has it guarded. Massimo will help me figure how to get there."

"Please be careful, Brian!"

"You be careful, too! Don't let Paolo see you. He and the woman should be catching their plane soon. But he may return before they leave, for another drink or two."

Hustling through the airport's front door, Brian hailed the nearest taxi. He gave the address for the nearby law office of Fellini and Fellini run by Giuseppe's youngest son, Fausto. He arrived in fifteen minutes later and introduced himself. As he waited for the paperwork to be completed, he tried Grace one more time. Again, it rolled into voicemail without ringing. *She should have upgraded her phone service. Something must be wrong if she's not picking up any of my calls.* Just then his battery died again.

CHAPTER THIRTY-FOUR

Sign the Papers

Nina doodled while drinking an espresso and nibbling a pistachio biscotti. Her phone charged nearby. She picked up her bag to move it onto the seat next to her and saw a cell phone sitting there on the seat. She picked it up and looked at its tiny screen. Two incoming calls were highlighted. One said, "Wilhelm – new boss" and the second said, "Stefano Luciano – bank."

She immediately realized Paolo had mistakenly left his phone on the seat. Looking up just in time, she saw him approaching the bar. She quickly gave the cell phone to the bartender and ran to the ladies' room.

Paolo approached, planning to order more drinks.

The bartender laughed as he called out to him. "Hey, are you missing something?"

He checked his pockets and smiled. "Yes. I turn sixty-five tomorrow and my memory is already betraying me!"

The bartender showed him the phone.

"Ah, yes! That's mine! I'll take two more drinks. Make them doubles and 'to go.' "

Peeking from the ladies' room, Nina watched the bartender hand Paolo the phone and two drinks. She watched him walk down the concourse and sit next to the woman. Feeling the coast was clear, she reclaimed her seat near the bar and resumed doodling, still hoping to think of a plan to access Katrina's house.

A few minutes later, a brewing commotion near Gate 11 caught her attention. The terrazzo floors and ceramic-tile walls echoed a pair of loud voices two hundred feet from her position. The two men began shouting. Taking a closer look, she saw Stefano and Paolo, face to face, yelling at each other, arms flailing, and fingers jabbing into the other's chest. She wondered if a fist fight was next.

After several minutes of yelling, they calmed down, but the final hand gestures and Stefano's stalking retreat revealed Paolo as the clear winner. Nina wondered what had happened and concluded it must have been about her and Brian's visit to the bank. Their accessing the old safe-deposit box must not have gone unnoticed. A nervous flutter over the confrontation unsettled her insides, but just then, an announcement came over the public-address system, and she saw Paolo and the woman move to board the plane. Stefano passed her on his way out. Nina took a deep, cleansing breath and continued doodling and daydreaming.

Brian returned nearly an hour later. He sat and smiled. He looked relieved.

"The papers are signed. My portion of the money, which was due to be given to me when I turned fifty, will be in my Swiss bank account first thing tomorrow. I also have the exact address of my birth mother's home.

"I was told two beautiful and well-kept villas are in my name here in Italy. One in Sorrento, the other in Capri. The third home… well, that's a longer story. For now, I'll just say it's located on Lake Constance in Friedrichshafen, Germany. Katrina left a note with the attorney's office years ago about the lake house being a two-hundred-year-old family heirloom."

"Who's looking after these properties?"

"One of the Fellini grandsons left the law firm and established a property-management company fifteen years ago. He assumed control of the houses in Sorrento and Capri, fixed them up, and has kept them rented full time to vacationers all these years. The revenue has created a tidy sum in an account in my name. The young Fellini pays himself a fair management fee, and occasionally borrows from the principal to purchase and rent more property. In our discussion, his father, Fausto, suggested when this is all settled, I should head to Capri for a few days. Nina, maybe we can do that when this all ends. It'll be a huge relief for both of us."

"Did you say a house on Lake Constance in Friedrichshafen, Germany?"

"Yes. But it's a long story. But briefly, the attorney gave me a copy of a document he received from Katrina. The house is currently occupied by the pastor of a local Lutheran church there in Friedrichshafen. The church pays the rent, and the rent money goes into the fund managed by the young Fellini grandson."

"That's interesting. My parents came from that area. Hey, have you heard from Grace?"

"No. I never reached her."

"Did you call the hotel in Kinsale, Ireland, where you told her to go?"

"I did just before my phone died. She hasn't made a reservation yet."

"What do you think has become of her?"

"I don't know."

"By the way, while you were gone, I found Paolo's phone. He'd left it on that seat, where you're sitting. I opened it and saw he had two calls, one from Wilhelm and one from Stefano. I gave the phone to the bartender. Paolo came back, got two drinks and his phone. Right after that, Stefano showed up at the gate. They were arguing.

"There's got to be something bad going on right now between Paolo and Stefano. I've concluded both art pieces are being sold. And Wilhelm must be pretty upset with Paolo for not returning the art to him. I'm guessing that's what Wilhelm was calling about."

"Nina, Paolo doesn't care at all about Wilhelm right now. During my visit with Fausto Fellini, he confirmed Paolo's sixty-fifth birthday is tomorrow. So, Paolo will be legally entitled to his share of the money from the sale of Luca's business."

"During his visit to the bank, when I peeked out the ladies' room door vent and he was signing papers, maybe it was for more than just turning over the paintings. Can the bank just give all the money to him?"

"I asked the lawyer the same question. Fausto said, 'No.' Those same papers must be signed by Paolo at the law firm and only then can his firm tell the bank to legally release the money from the escrow account. He needs to do what I just did earlier with Fausto—who, by the way, told me he hasn't heard from Paolo, nor from anyone at the Luciano family bank."

"Ah! Maybe that was part of their loud, angry conversation earlier. Maybe Stefano told Paolo that he, Paolo, needs to sign the proper legal papers for the bank to release the funds in his trust account. During the loudest part of the argument, it looked like Paolo was going to hit Stefano."

"You're probably right. I'm guessing that's what Stefano told Paolo."

"By the way, I know a way to get past the guards at the house."

"How?"

"I'll tell you on our way to your friend's house."

CHAPTER THIRTY-FIVE

The Yacht

During Paolo and Elena's flight to Reggio, she spoke about their future together while he thought about his new yacht, his party and all the money he was about to get from the trust fund.

Upon arriving, they took a taxi to the marina. Paolo called his friend on his way to make sure he'd be there at the yacht and meet them as planned.

The taxi slowed as it neared the marina, then made the last turn. The moment had come. For many years Paolo's big dream was to have a large yacht. His birthday was tomorrow, and he was about to treat himself with his dream yacht. He told himself the snafu regarding the release of his money from the Luciano family bank was a mere wrinkle. He had ended his argument with Stefano by telling him, "Your fucking life depends on completing any papers that are needed. Forge anything that needs my signature." In his mind, all the obstacles had been removed.

As they pulled up to the marina, Paolo saw his childhood friend, and cohort in adolescent crime, already there to greet him. They greeted each other and hugged like long-lost brothers.

"Paolo! It's been too long. Look at you! You're all grey, like an old man!"

"*Ciao*, my friend. You're grey, too! It must be thirty years! How can that be?" Paolo pulled Elena forward. "Gianni, meet my Elena. She is my woman and will be with me going forward."

Gianni gently took her hand and kissed it. "*Signora*. The pleasure is mine. It's so nice to meet you."

"Elena, Gianni is my oldest friend. We were like brothers as boys, always running wild and always in trouble! We haven't seen each other often enough over the years. But now I am about to retire, and my hope is that we will get to spend more time together.

"Gianni, remember, my plan is for all of us to stay aboard the yacht tonight, here in the marina, and we sail to Siracusa in the morning."

Paolo reached to the bottom of his duffel bag. He searched for a moment and then pulled out a roll of cash, which he handed to Elena. "Put this in your purse before I forget. Buy whatever clothing you want when we arrive in Siracusa tomorrow."

She took the money and whispered a few words in his ear that promised him a very pleasant evening. He smiled.

"Come aboard and let me show you around your new toy."

Paolo was taken by the yacht's size as they boarded. He felt intimidated, almost frightened. They removed their shoes and toured the main deck in stocking feet. Gianni showed off the living room, dining room, back deck, and a small office.

"*Mamma mia!* I made my reservation to buy this boat from you over a year ago. I'd forgotten how big it is!"

"My friend, I see a worried face as you look around your yacht. I already have a solution to ease your worries. Follow me up to the captain's seat."

Elena gave Paolo a big kiss as they began climbing the stairway. As they reached the next landing, a tall, handsome, smiling young man in a white captain's uniform greeted them.

"Here is the answer so you will not need to ever worry about sailing on this boat. My friend, Vittorio, will accompany us on the trip to Siracusa and on to Malta. He has a captain's license and much experience sailing between here and Sicily, Mykonos, Santorini, Capri, Ischia, and Malta. Infer no pressure in my saying this, but you might want to employ him for the next several months, especially if you plan to sail this yacht from Malta."

Paolo nodded in approval. "Always thinking, Gianni. That's a good recommendation."

Vittorio simply smiled.

"Gianni, remind me where the bar is. I want to have a drink and discuss a few things. Vittorio, if you're as good as my friend claims, I trust you've stocked the bar with plenty of Campari and dry Cinzano."

"*Certo!*"

Paolo turned to Elena. "Gianni and I need some time alone. Vittorio, show her back down to the master suite. Relax, my love. I'll be down later, and you can make good on your promise."

The two old friends moved to the bar, and as expected, it was fully stocked, thanks to Vittorio's anticipating the arrival of the yacht's new owner. The small ice machine, with the capacity to keep up with a small on-board party, worked perfectly. Soft background music featuring songs by old Italian tenors played from the speakers located throughout the yacht. Gianni poured the drinks, and they clinked their glasses.

Paolo said, "To mischievous old times… and to a few mischievous new times in the days ahead."

"Paolo, how in Heaven's name can you afford this boat on the salary of an Interpol agent?"

Paolo laughed, saying he'd explain shortly. As the drinks flowed, he talked about his years in Interpol focusing on recovering lost art. He then explained about his recruitment to Interpol years earlier. He opened up and described how his former boss would sometimes steal some of the newly recovered art and re-sell it. He told how he became part of small part of the ring and set aside his share of money from each caper. He mentioned his new boss in the agency wanted to engage in the same illegal activity and had recently offered him a piece of the action.

Gianni listened closely, growing envious. He had moved from small crimes in Naples as a teenager to becoming a yacht salesman in his mid-twenties. During those early years, he worked as a gigolo, dating and servicing wealthy single women, and widows who owned yachts. He eventually married a much older woman, an heiress to a mid-west American manufacturing company. It was a sweet living arrangement in a magnificent villa on the Amalfi coast. His arrangement with her lasted for almost seven years, until she caught him in bed with the two housekeepers. Brashly, he invited his wife to join them, but she walked away, taking with her the keys to the Lamborghini she'd bought for him. Gianni soon found another wealthy widow, but it lasted for only a year before he was again kicked out for similar indiscretions. Despite his inappropriate failings, his flirtatious and extroverted manner kept him number one in the yachting-sales game in the Bay of Naples, and he earned him fine commissions every year. His reputation and lifestyle were the envy of many men in the area.

The alcohol flowed freely and Paolo eventually grumbled about how Luca's wine business had grown beyond expectations to become an international success.

"He was always so goddamn righteous. Always giving me a tough time while I was growing up. His company reached new sales levels when he began selling more and more to America. He eventually cut a deal to sell his wine-export company to a global distribution company for fifty-three million U.S. dollars. I couldn't believe it! Then I found out even though I served on his board of directors, the bastard was cutting me out of a chunk of money from the sale. Instead, he set me up on a monthly allowance, while putting nearly fifty million in escrow. I hated him for that. So I made sure he'd never enjoy any money from the big sale. I got even for how he treated me. It was easy. No one ever suspected my method—the chemistry was virtually undetectable. He was a prime candidate to die from a heart attack, with all the pressure of selling the company. And that's how it looked. And now, my good friend, all that money will be released to me tomorrow, on my sixty-fifth birthday."

"Incredible, Paolo. Unbelievable."

"Now listen. There's one more thing I need to tell you, and here's where I need your help. I recently found my adoptive mother's son. Yes, Katrina had a bastard kid before she met Luca. I was reminded this afternoon by one of my cousins at the bank, this guy – who's a perfect stranger to me and never visited Katrina in his life – is somehow entitled to half of the money left by Luca in the escrow account—but only if he's alive. So, Gianni, have another drink and let me tell you what I have in mind…"

Paolo slowly laid out his plan, hoping to engage his friend's assistance.

"Gianni, I throw a huge birthday party for myself every five years, using Katrina's allowance money from the sale of the business. All the important people in Malta come and show me respect, like I was their capo. Many even bring sizeable gifts and pledge themselves to me. For this year, I've made calls and wired money ahead, and once again have made all the arrangements for a spectacular birthday party at my house in Malta tomorrow night. I have at least three hundred people coming.

"But back to my problem. I've been told Katrina's bastard son has only become aware in the last two days of his mother's being alive and her presence in Malta. I'm certain he'll try to see her as soon as he can. He's already been to the bank where Luca's millions are held. He's a very bad man and is already trying to steal all my money. He's even accessed a safe-deposit box in the family bank for the first time in forty years. Only God knows what this thieving bastard is up to.

"So, my friend, instead of your leaving me in Siracusa tomorrow and flying back to Naples as first planned, I want you to come to Malta and attend my birthday party. We'll stop in Siracusa to pick up some friends, let Elena buy some fancy clothing, and refuel. Then we'll sail together to Malta. Before we arrive, people will already be cooking and setting up for the event. I haven't told Elena about the party, because I want to surprise her with the festivities. And if she performs in bed tonight on the yacht as I expect, I'll surprise her by announcing our engagement in front of everyone at the party.

"So, Gianni, can I count on your help to knock this guy off if he shows up? I promise to put one million U.S. dollars in your pocket if you help eliminate this bastard. Are you in?"

"Of course, Paolo! Count me in! I'm so glad we've gotten back together after so many years. Now, I'm off to bed. I didn't tell you, but I invited along a wealthy woman whom I intend to enjoy tonight. She should have arrived by now and been brought downstairs by the captain."

CHAPTER THIRTY-SIX

The Lawyer Visits the Bank

Brian checked his watch. The flight to Catania, the airport closest to Siracusa, would leave in twenty minutes. Seeing it was time to go to the gate, he unplugged the phone from its charger and retrieved their luggage from the nearby locker. Nina gathered her things and glanced again at her doodles.

Luggage in hand, they proceeded down the concourse in silence. She wondered what would become of her and Brian. He wondered about meeting his mother and about not being able to reach Grace. Then Giuseppe Fellini's warning echoed in his mind: "Paolo wants no part of you. He will make you disappear if he gets the chance." Then he recalled his own words to Nina that they had the advantage and needed to out-think Paolo.

***

In Rome, a transaction needed to be placed before the bank closed for the day. Fausto, knowing the importance, sped his modest Fiat to the Luciano family bank. He arrived ten minutes before closing and went inside.

"*Ciao, signora.* Is Stefano or Dominic in?"

"Stefano left earlier. He should be back soon. Dominic is at the Vatican, meeting with Monsignor Borrelli."

"I have papers for a wire transfer. It needs to be done before you close."

"Let me look at what you have."

He presented the demand note and showed the woman the papers and signatures.

"Oh, goodness! I'm not sure we can get that done."

"Signora, this is a legal document. By law the transfer *must* be completed today! You have five minutes to make it happen."

"Let me make a call. I'll be right back."

The woman placed several fruitless calls. She felt sick to her stomach as she recognized the significance of the desired transaction and her inability to reach either man.

She returned to her office, where Brian's lawyer sat patiently. "Sir, I'm unable to reach either of the senior executives. I'm sorry, but this transaction will need to wait until morning."

"I'm sorry, but this transaction is a demand note. The appropriate papers have been signed by the client whose money this is, and it must be paid upon presentation of the note. You now have two minutes left to complete the transfer of his money. And before this charade goes any further, I happen to know you're not a powerless lackey. I've checked the records. Even though you're sitting at this desk as if you were an assistant, I know your name is Maria. You are on the bank's board of directors, and you have full authority to complete the transaction. Isn't that right, *Signora Luciano*?"

Discovered, the woman had no choice other than compliance.

"Let me have the papers. I'll need to make copies, and I'll be right back."

"If you don't mind, I'll walk with you as you make the copies and execute the transfer."

***

The flight to Catania would be short. Brian asked to sit on the right side of the airplane. Flying across the Strait of Messina and down the coast of Sicily would give him a bird's-eye view of Mount Etna. The eleven-thousand-foot volcano was a glorious sight as they flew by with the sun setting far in the background. His memory flashed to a view of the fourteen-thousand-foot Mount Rainier on his first flight into Seattle. He turned to Nina. She was napping. *I'm so glad she's here with me. She's so beautiful.*

The planed landed with a hard jerk like a Navy pilot planting his tail hook on an aircraft carrier's deck. At ground level, the sun had already set, and it was getting dark. Brian used Nina's personal credit card to rent a car. They loaded the luggage into the small trunk, and they headed to Massimo's seaside home. The drive was about an hour long but being unfamiliar with the roads, he expected it might take longer.

"Brian, let me tell you my idea to get past the guards and into your mother's house."

"What's that?"

"Maybe we can pose as a doctor and nurse. You can be a cardiologist who has 'arrived because of a call you received.' It should get us past the guards."

"Sounds plausible. You'd look good in a nurse's outfit."

"Brian!"

***

Dominic Luciano was delivering a piece of art to the museum's director, Monsignor Giorgio Borrelli at the Vatican. It was a recently completed work by Agostino and would be another donation by the Luciano family to the massive art collection in the Pinacoteca.

"It's good to see you again, Dominic. Your family has been so wonderfully generous to us over the years. As with all the other paintings you've donated, we'll hold this in silence for the next five years. Then it will become eligible for placement within the gallery."

Then he lied to the priest even further with a fictitious story behind the gift. "Monsignor, this is one of two recently found paintings we've purchased. They were among a dozen paintings the Nazis confiscated in Paris as their soldiers marched up the Avenue des Champs-Élysées. The Nazis moved them into hiding during the war. We've already confirmed the entire family who owned this painting perished. Look closely at the signature of the artist. One of his paintings sold last year for just over twenty million U.S. dollars in a New York City auction. In five years, the value of this piece will double; in ten, it could double again. As in the past, Monsignor, we feel it is appropriate—and our duty—to donate to Holy Mother Church one of the two paintings we've just acquired."

"Dominic, the Luciano family has been so generous. I knew your father briefly and have been told many wonderful things about your uncle, Luca, who served as a priest in southern Italy during the war. God bless you, my son. Give my regards to your cousin Stefano and to Maria. I'll have the next Mass offered by our Holy Father celebrated in your family's name."

Dominic gave a slight bowed and left. On the way to his car, he opened his phone and saw four calls made by Maria. He quickly dialed her number.

"Maria, what's going on? Why all the calls?"

"Dominic, you need to come back right away. A demand note was just placed by an attorney to transfer money from our bank."

"So?"

"Hurry back. It's the amount being withdrawn. We can discuss it when you arrive."

"Where is Stefano?"

"He went to see Paolo at the airport today."

"About?"

"Paolo's birthday is tomorrow."

"We know that. We have a plan in place to deal with him."

"Well, Paolo called Stefano earlier and told him to wire a check to a yacht company to pay for the balance of a boat he bought. Then Paolo said, 'Don't forget to release all the money tomorrow.' Stefano told him papers need to be signed by a lawyer in order to release the money. Paolo got all upset, saying he has no time to do paperwork with attorneys.

"So, Stefano went to see him at the airport just before his flight to Reggio. At the airport, Paolo insisted Stefano transfer all his money out of the old trust account into an account he has sole access to. Stefano said they got into a shouting match."

Dominic scowled. The money in question was sufficient to meet the institution's on-hand capital requirements. To lose it would be disastrous. "Maria, you know we don't want to give Paolo all that money. We need to stick to our plan to give him a larger monthly allowance. He can pay for the boat over time."

"That's what Stefano went to talk to him about. But Dominic, that's only half the story."

"What do you mean?"

"Those calls I made to you earlier. I was calling to say an attorney came in late this afternoon with a demand note to withdraw the other half—well, forty-five percent—of Uncle Luca's money. It's almost twenty million U.S. dollars!"

"Who was the attorney? And who, in God's name, was *that* for?"

"Fausto Fellini. He's with the firm Uncle Luca used for his will. The withdrawal was for Luca's wife's son, Brian O'Sullivan. Apparently, he's alive and proved his identity to the lawyer."

"What do you mean 'the withdrawal *was* for'?"

"Well, you weren't here, and I couldn't reach you or Stefano by phone. I wired the money twenty minutes ago from our bank to a Swiss bank."

"Dear Mother of God! Maria, with that withdrawal, our bank may have an insufficient loan-to-deposit ratio. Damn it! I'll need to go to the monsignor and get back some of the paintings we've donated and sell them to make up the difference."

"But Dominic, those paintings that you donate—aren't they the worthless copies Old Man Agostino paints in the attic over your garage? And I thought the originals you bought from Paolo were in our homes."

In truth, for years the Luciano family had been buying paintings worth millions and donating meticulously rendered copies—copies admittedly worth hundreds of thousands of U.S. dollars—to the Church, while claiming millions in charitable tax deductions.

"Yes, we own all the originals and they're all worth millions," he said, growing exasperated. "But Agostino's copies have real value because they're so good they pass for originals. And we've only given Agostino's fakes to the Vatican. For thirty years our fathers passed those copies along to the Vatican, and neither Monsignor Borrelli nor his predecessor has ever noticed. We've just continued the practice."

"Dominic, the auditors are due in two weeks. We're headed for trouble unless we sell some original paintings from our private collections and deposit the cash in our bank—and fast! If we don't sell enough, we'll need to do some short-term borrowing to fix the depletion of capital from today's withdrawal. Oh, and one final thing about Paolo: It's been five years since his last birthday bash and he's throwing another one tomorrow in Malta. Stefano mentioned it. I'm just reminding you Paolo asked you and Stefano to go. I think he wants to show off his new yacht."

Dominic ran a hand through his hair. "Okay. I'll straighten a few things out with Paolo and hold off on giving him his money, but I don't yet know what we're going to do about replacing the money you sent to Switzerland."

"It's obvious now. The three of us need to sell several pieces of our art. I'll talk to Agostino later. He might guide you as to which paintings should be released from our collection. I'd guess the two new paintings from Paolo stolen by the Nazis will bring a decent price on the black market. The three of us should talk tonight and decide what to do."

CHAPTER THIRTY-SEVEN

Arriving at Massimo's

The drive between the Catania airport and Massimo's was faster than Brian expected, and he found the house easily. As he pulled into the driveway, the exterior spotlights came on. He opened the car door and stretched his legs while Nina pulled their bags from the trunk.

"Leave the luggage for a minute and come with me."

They approached the front door and knocked.

A cute, long-haired dachshund showed its face in the door's glass side-light as the foyer light inside flicked on and the ornately carved wooden door opened.

"Brian, my friend! How are you! And, oh my, who do we have here?"

"Hello Massimo! Let me introduce you to my coworker, Nina von Scholz."

"The pleasure is mine, miss. Come in, come in. It's so good to meet you."

"Nina, go on in. I'll get the luggage."

She followed Massimo in. The open floor plan made the home feel spacious. One wall was all glass windows from floor to ceiling, but it was pitch black outside. In the open kitchen, Massimo had already prepared a magnificent charcuterie board for snacking.

"Come sit here, miss. You and Brian might be hungry. There's young Gouda cheese, provolone, capicola, sweet soppressata, and pepper tarallini. And Brian, look at this loaf of crusty bread. It's the same as we used to get at Zito's Bakery on Carmine Street, off Bleecker. And I've decanted a hearty Super Tuscan red an hour ago for you. This will make your hunger disappear in no time!"

"Thank you, Massimo. You're still tops in my book."

"The spare bedrooms are upstairs. Bring your things upstairs and get settled, then come back down and tell me what brings you to my humble abode!"

Upstairs, Brian hesitated for a moment, then opted to put Nina's heavy bag and his own in separate bedrooms. He rejoined them downstairs and sat next to Nina at the kitchen's island. After Brian's toast to old friendships, they began drinking the Super Tuscan. Their three huge goblets emptied the bottle on the first pour. Massimo had uncorked a second bottle earlier, allowing it to breath. As he declared the vintage and pedigree of the next bottle, Nina was captivated and in awe, but Brian's mind drifted. He peered through the glass wall into the darkness of the ocean. Turning to Nina, he smiled, took a deep breath, and let it out slowly. She smiled back and put her hand on his knee. Massimo noticed their unspoken exchange.

Brian complimented his friend on how beautiful his house was and proceeded to unravel the story of his search. He began by explaining his role in Interpol and detailing the events of the last two weeks.

"I'm searching for my birth mother and suddenly I've become a multi-millionaire involved in a dangerous escapade, chasing an art thief and murderer, and at risk to be eliminated. My once-simple search is suddenly rife with intrigue and deception."

Massimo expressed sadness at hearing of Brian's mother's death, and astonishment at the rest of his story. Having been at the Mezquita years earlier, he appreciated and understood Brian's search in the picturesque interior. But news of the thievery and Erick's death proved upsetting. It wasn't long before he opened a third bottle of wine and cut more soppressata and crusty bread. Brian was well into the wine when the deeper truths of his life and his search emerged.

"Frankly, Massimo, this last week is taking an emotional toll on me. I'm a wreck. Nina is a clever work partner, and I'm fortunate. She's comforted me through this if you know what I mean. Unfortunately, Grace and I have been at odds for the last fifteen years. At times, she's been cranky and explosive. Home just doesn't feel like home anymore. I feel like I'm walking on eggshells all the time. I see it more when we leave my sisters' houses. They've been blessed with children. We never had any children, and I think that's the root cause of her being so moody and emotional.

"At her insistence, I retired from teaching at the university a year ago, but my work with Interpol all these years, supporting efforts to recover lost art, has been exciting and, frankly, I don't want to stop. Work has become my escape. And now, to make matters worse, Grace is missing. She decided to follow me to Amsterdam, believing I have a secret family somewhere in Europe. I haven't been able to reach her for two days. I have no idea what's happened. I'm worried about her."

Brian put his hands to his forehead and rested his elbows against the island where they sat. He was exhausted both emotionally and physically. The three sat in silence for a few moments when the clock on the mantel chimed.

Nina stood. "Brian, it's late. I'll help Massimo straighten up here. You need to go lie down."

He gave her a kiss on the cheek, hugged Massimo, and headed upstairs.

Nina picked up the tiny plates and charcuterie board and placed them in the sink.

"Thank you for letting us stay here tonight. I'm sure he'll be fine in the morning."

She outlined the rest of Brian's search, explaining the villa was oceanside, and Katrina was over 90 years old, and her idea to disguise themselves as a doctor and nurse to get past the guards at the front gate. But she mentioned her deep concern over the lawyer's warning.

Massimo took it all in and shared what he knew, explaining how he thought he might help. The conversation lasted another half hour. They ended up with a plan to run by Brian in the morning.

At last, Nina bade Massimo goodnight. Finding Brian asleep atop the sheets, she removed his shoes, socks and pants, and rolled him under the sheets. Then she stripped off her clothes and climbed in beside him.

CHAPTER THIRTY-EIGHT

Late That Night

On board the yacht, Paolo was enjoying the late evening with Elena. They had been together occasionally, but over the years Paolo was always restless, never wanting to settle down. Now with his fortune about to arrive, he decided to speak to Elena about living together in Malta, traveling on the yacht, and maybe even marry. While Vittorio served a magnificent dinner for the two, Elena basked in the low light of the dining room. Paolo's words seemed prepared and he seemed to struggle for eloquence. But she believed he was sincere. She enjoyed the attention. After the late dinner, they headed back to the master bedroom suite. Her bedtime ritual only took ten minutes, but when she came from the bathroom unclothed, Paolo was snoring. *He will have to wait until tomorrow.*

In another bedroom, Gianni's date was a no-show, and his plans for a wild evening with his latest woman never materialized. He wondered about tomorrow. Paolo's offer to help eliminate the fellow named O'Sullivan was attractive. He began to think about his recent circumstances. *Maybe this encounter with my old friend will change my fortune.*

The captain checked on tomorrow's weather and reviewed the electronic gauges and settings. He had spoken earlier to Tony, the first mate, and everything was in order. He retreated to his quarters and was reading when he received his final text message of the day. He acknowledged it in a simple response: "Yes."

***

Wilhelm arrived in Rome on a company plane late that night, far later than he originally expected. He found his way to the small hotel where his nephew was shot to death the night before. Staying next to the Fountain put him in a central location where he could easily head toward any bank in the morning.

His plan was to meet two Interpol agents at 7. The one flying in from Brussels was already in Rome; the other was an Italian agent already living in Rome. Ursula made the calls and arranged for the police in Rome to secure and deliver a search warrant to Wilhelm early the next morning. He'd have them put the address on the warrant once Brian gave him the specific bank address—which would happen only after the money Wilhelm promised was in Brian's Swiss account. Accustomed to managing situations and being the one to string people along, Wilhelm was annoyed having to meet Brian's demands.

By the time he arrived at the hotel, he had a severe migraine from over thinking everything. He asked for a 5:50 AM wake-up call and set the alarm on his small travel clock for the same time. Lying on the bed, reviewing circumstances and ensuring he hadn't missed anything for the morning, he became chilled and felt a fever coming on. Shivering, he got under the covers to stay warm and finally fell asleep.

During the night, he had a dream. His parents and sister were in the kitchen. In a fit of anger, Klaus turned on his wife, yelled and struck her. His sister ran from the house. Frightened, young Wilhelm called out to her, but she didn't look back. As he called out again, he woke up. The fever had broken, and he found his pajamas soaked and the bedsheets sweaty. He wondered whether that was only a dream or a deeply repressed memory of something that might actually have happened. He stripped off his clothes, moved to the dry side of the wide bed, and fell asleep again.

CHAPTER THIRTY-NINE

Early the Next Morning

Wilhelm woke and looked at his watch. It was only 5:15 but he got out of bed and showered. He thought about the morning's wire transfer of the money to Brian's Swiss account, getting the address of the bank for the warrant and securing the paintings. Then he recalled it was Paolo's birthday today. *Hmm. Maybe I'll attend his party after I recover the paintings at the bank. I don't need an invitation.*

Two miles away, in an ultra-posh Rome suburb, Stefano and Dominic were up earlier than usual, to meet for breakfast at 6:15 and to discuss alternatives to their dilemma.

"Goddamn that Paolo. I never liked him. He's been a pain in the ass all these years, coming in, always checking on his stupid allowance or borrowing against it. No one can blame Uncle Luca for the issues those two had with each other. Paolo's always been a problem for everyone, and always, it seems, at the most inconvenient times."

"Yes, like right now!"

"On the other hand, he's made our family rich from all those paintings."

"Actually, it was our fathers who made our family rich with their scheme using Agostino's masterful copies and hanging out a carrot for Paolo. Our make-believe donations and tax deductions still look legitimate. I think the old priest, Monsignor Gaeta, the curator before Monsignor Borrelli, knew or suspected what was going on, but he was handed some spending money to remain silent and keep accepting those paintings into the collection."

Stefano showed Dominic the invitation to Paolo's birthday party in Malta.

"Maybe we should both go?" he suggested.

"Why not? We can fly out later and be there before dark."

"Let's do it."

"Stefano, I picked up the paintings from the bank on my way here. They're in my trunk. I'll bring them to Agostino later this morning.

***

In the Siracusa seaside suburb, Brian woke as light coming through the window brightened the room. He looked at his watch. It was exactly 6:30. He stretched, then turned to the side, and felt Nina next to him. She was warm. Her skin was soft. It felt good and aroused him. He rolled onto his side and kissed her forehead. His kiss woke her from her sleepy imagination and her dream vanished.

Nina gave him a warm hug and a gentle push, landing him on his back. Then she rolled over on top of him, sitting on his thighs. They spent the next twenty minutes playing and enjoying each other. His age was of no consequence as they made love. She helped him perform as if he were thirty years younger, and he made her feel like a woman.

"Brian, I don't want this to ever stop."

"I know. Our time together has been so good."

They lay there another ten minutes, coming down from the intense moments they had just shared.

"I smell coffee."

"Yes, Massimo's up and, knowing my old friend, I'm certain we'll find an assortment of pastries filled with almond paste, powder-covered sfogliatelle, coconut biscotti, and prosciutto on sliced melon, all arranged perfectly on his dining-room table. Oh, and I wouldn't be surprised if he's also squeezed some fresh orange juice for us."

"You told me on the way here Massimo had a partner for many years. But he didn't mention anything last night about his breakup."

"Having a relationship end is never easy, and I imagine at his age it's even harder. Sadly, it's where Grace and I are right now. Our marriage is teetering badly. I've tried for years but just can't shake her from her frequent bouts of depression. She's miserable. I often feel it's my fault but then sometimes I'm not sure."

"Her erratic moods must be a burden for both of you," Nina commented. "Neither of you deserves to be sad in this chapter of your life. I

188

believe we should love the people we are with and be grateful we have them in our lives. Isn't that how a marriage should be?"

"Life isn't that simple, Nina. Sometimes unexpected things happen along the way and the circumstances that follow can have a lasting effect. People carry those effects with them, either intentionally or not. Often it becomes a huge burden, and changes their outlook from being happy, bright, and cheerful to being sad, moody, and depressed. Whatever the root cause of the sadness, it's hard to overcome because you usually can't go back and correct some of life's mistakes."

He looked at his watch. It was nearly 7.

"I need to make a call and send a text before we go downstairs."

Brian peered out the window and made the call to the Swiss bank's automated system to see if the money from Wilhelm had arrived in his account. He entered the password on the phone, then entered the account number. The automated system spoke robotically, citing the new deposit.

"Your account's last deposit made earlier today was three million U.S. dollars."

For added assurance, he punched in more numbers to request an account balance. The robotic response made him smile.

"Your account's current balance is twenty-three million four hundred thirty-two U.S. dollars."

Brian texted Wilhelm the name of the bank, and identified the first level of large safe-deposit boxes where both paintings could be found. He hit Send and turned back to Nina. "I'm all set. We can go downstairs."

She put on a pair of light blue silk pajamas, and they headed down to the kitchen.

"Ah! Good morning! I'm so glad you are here, Brian. How are you feeling this morning? The strong wine hit you hard last night."

"We're good, my friend. The best part is that Nina is helping me get through a lot of crazy stuff right now."

Brian put his arm around Nina, gave her a squeeze and a peck on the cheek. She did likewise, putting her arm around his waist, kissing him and then rested her head against his shoulder.

"Well, I can see in both your eyes how much you care for each other."

Massimo poured a round of coffee as they all stood at the kitchen island. Nina excused herself and ran back upstairs.

"Brian, last time I saw you, we had a long talk," Massimo said.

Brian nodded, recalling the encounter.

"Honestly, I wondered then if you'd stay with Grace. Nina seems to be a new bright spot in your life."

"Nina's been a breath of fresh air for me, aside from being a terrific investigator in our unit," Brian agreed. "And this job of chasing down art has proved to be a good distraction all these years. It certainly gave me an outlet from the house. Nina has been a breath of fresh air for me besides being a terrific investigator in our unit at work."

Nina returned to the kitchen. "Massimo and I spoke after you went to bed last night, Brian. We've got a plan to go over with you."

"You know I'm the commodore of the local yacht club. But what you don't know is I've recently received an application from Paolo Luzzi to join our club. In the envelope along with the application, I received notification about his sixty-fifth birthday party. It starts at one this afternoon and goes on until midnight. I had planned on going and made arrangements two days ago with a local friend who delivers wine and produce to Malta. On my invitation is a handwritten note. It says, 'Accommodations in the city will be tight. Those with yachts are asked to sleep on board overnight.' Perhaps since I am the yacht club's commodore, he actually sent four invitations."

A slow smile spread across Brian's face. "Interesting. I knew something would work out for me to find her."

"Here's another fact, my friend. I met Paolo Luzzi ten years ago at a party here in Siracusa. We were introduced by an older fellow with Interpol, who was probably ten years older than me. Luzzi might not remember me. He's an interesting character. He has quite a following of a certain type of people in Malta and even here in Sicily, if you know what I mean. Everything your lawyer told you about him is true. If you want to see and speak to your mother, and more importantly, if you want to survive to enjoy your new-found millions, you'll need to stay close with me. Given your situation, I think we should go together. I have a woman friend who can join us and we can pretend to be two couples entering the party."

"It seems like you have all the answers to a mighty complicated situation."

"Your arrival here has been fortunate, and of course I'm here to help. Now sit and enjoy some prosciutto and ripe melon. And these almond pastries are just like the ones we used to get in that bakery right across from Our Lady of Pompeii and John's Pizzeria.

"We'll need to leave here around eleven. Our sailing time won't be too long, but we don't want to be the first showing up at the party. I've already called my friend at the yacht club to confirm we're definitely taking the trip to Malta today and will be staying overnight. We should go to the club and board around ten thirty. I mentioned my friend makes the trip to Malta every other day, bringing products to the island. We'll be well cared for on our journey there. In the meantime, enjoy your breakfast and the beautiful view you couldn't see last night in the dark."

"Thanks, Massimo. By the way, what exactly happened between you and Pierre Louie?"

"It's not pleasant to recall what happened. He took a trip to Manhattan. He said it was for his mother's seventy-fifth birthday. While he was there, I got a call from a friend saying he saw Pierre Louie with his old boyfriend, Raymond, who lived on Christopher Street in the Village. When he got back, we had a devastating argument. He walked out and I never heard from him again. I still don't fully understand why he strayed. I gave him everything he wanted. He had a sports car, even a generous clothing and jewelry allowance. I loved him, and he said he loved me. His leaving was so unexpected! That was three years ago. A year ago, I got word from a friend on Charles Street that Pierre Louie died of AIDS." He paused, overcome by a swell of emotion. "I'm still heartbroken. Can we please change the subject?"

Just then, a knock came at the door. The housekeeper entered.

"Assunta, these are my friends. Can you just clean down here this morning? Then please come back around ten and bring your brother. We need him to return the rental car that's outside."

Nina smiled and put her hand on Brian's thigh.

"Okay, you two, let's enjoy our breakfast. From what you both told me last night, we have an interesting day and evening ahead."

***

It was 7 AM in Amsterdam and Grace was startled awake by a loud knock at the front door to Erick's apartment. She put on her robe and slippers and went to peer through a tiny window in the door. She was surprised to see a female police officer. Thinking something could be wrong with Brian, she unlatched the lock.

The policewoman rushed in, along with three male officers.

Horrified by their rude entry, Grace exclaimed, "My God, what are you doing, barging in here like this? What's going on?"

"Are you Grace O'Sullivan?"

"Yes."

"We have reason to believe you have illegal drugs here in this house."

"What are you talking about? That's preposterous! I'm just waiting for my husband to return from a business trip. This isn't even my apartment. It belongs to my husband's friend."

One of the three policemen returned quickly from the guest bedroom.

"Captain, here it is. It was inside in her bedroom."

"What was in my bedroom?"

"Grace O'Sullivan, we have laws in this country you have failed to observe. You are under arrest for the possession of illegal drugs. The Dutch Code of Criminal Procedure says you have the right to remain silent until you are interrogated. Thereafter, any statement you make must be made freely, but you are not obliged to answer the interrogator."

"Wait! What is going on?! Goddamn it. I'm not guilty of anything other than being pissed at my husband – and now I'm pissed at all of you, whoever you are, for breaking in like this," she said with indignant bluster. "You've got a lot of nerve coming in here like this. Now get the hell out of this apartment. Get out this instant! Get out!"

"Grace O'Sullivan, you will be coming with us. Olga, please cuff the lady, get her some clothing and a coat for her to wear to the police station."

"You've got to be kidding. Is this some kind of sick joke? Okay. It's a joke." She yanked her arm free from the policewoman's grasp. "Goddamn it, get your hands off me! Leave me alone! I haven't done anything wrong. I just came here to find my husband. Please, leave me alone. Oh my God, I've seen this kind of thing on TV. You must be in the wrong house! Yes, that's it. You've got the wrong house. I didn't do anything wrong. Goddamn it, Brian. This is all your fault."

Grace began crying when the female officer brought clothes out to her, placed the handcuffs on her, and put her coat on her shoulders. They walked her to a police car. People out walking their dogs stopped to watch from the other side of the street. Solie, who'd seen the police cars' flashing lights through her front window, stepped onto the porch in time to Grace being walked to the police car.

***

It was 6:56 AM in Rome and Wilhelm anxiously awaited Brian's text identifying where the paintings were stashed. A minute later the text message arrived with the details. Wilhelm smiled and spoke aloud to himself, "Of course! I should have known they're sitting in the Luciano family bank. Damn. That bit of info just cost me three million dollars. I'm glad Father's not looking over my shoulder on this."

At 7, the two Interpol agents arrived at his hotel. Wilhelm gave them the bank's address and told the local Italian agent to call the local police and get the bank's address added to the search warrant. He then explained his plan to rush the bank as it opened and search the premises.

As he was finishing with them, another text arrived. "Dutch police have Grace O'Sullivan in custody." He was pleased to see his additional leverage over Brian in place, although the paintings would be his in another two hours' time when they get into the bank.

An hour later the local police arrived. The search warrant was updated and Wilhelm briefed them on the plan to enter the bank. They left the hotel, positioning themselves at the staging point two blocks from the bank. They waited in their cars as 9:00 approached. Finally, the time came. Wilhelm gave the 'go' signal, directing his agents and the local police to pull out. His grey rental car followed. Within 30 seconds, eight police cars – sirens blaring and lights flashing – pulled up to the Luciano bank.

Already inside, Maria was unlocking the front door when the swarm of police cars arrived. Wilhelm quickly led the charge of a dozen men, running up the front steps, fully prepared to assault the front door. Although he could see her through the thick glass, he disregarded Maria's presence and shoved the door open, pushing it against her, pinning her between the heavy glass door and the wall.

She instinctively pushed back, gasping in fright. "*Signore!* What is this?"

"Let us in!"

"What is this onslaught about? Aren't you the police?"

"Yes, and we have a search warrant."

"For what, may I ask?"

"For stolen art."

"We have no art here except for what is on the walls."

Stefano was pulling up outside just at that moment. Seeing all the police cars and flashing lights, he panicked. He saw the group heading up the steps, pushing through the front door. He dialed his cousin. "Dominic, pick up," he shouted impatiently as the phone rang. "Pick up the damn phone!"

"Ah! Good morning, Stefano. Are you ready to party later today?"

"Dominic, we have a serious problem. A bunch of police cars are outside the front door of our bank. I don't know what's happening. I saw Maria opening the door and they all rushed inside."

"It's got to be the damn paintings. That bastard Paolo. He set us up and ratted us out. Fuck him!"

"What should I do?"

"Just walk inside calmly, as if nothing is happening. They can look all they want. We're in the clear and we have nothing to worry about. I told you, I pulled the paintings out early this morning on the way to our breakfast meeting."

"Jesus Christ! I forgot you said that!"

"Those two original paintings Paolo found in Spain at the Mezquita – the ones he brought to the bank – are in the trunk of my car right now. I told Paolo we'd buy both and donate one to the Vatican to make him feel better. It's what we've been telling him the past fifteen years. So I brought one of Agostino's copies – the one he finished six months ago to the monsignor. No one can match his skills, and the Vatican loves his paintings; they think they're originals worth millions. Stefano, now get inside and tell Maria to keep her trap shut."

"Okay. I just parked and I'm about to go inside."

"Well, hurry up and get in there to help Maria. Give me an hour. I'll bring these two paintings to my house and give them to Agostino. He'll love seeing the Matisse, and he'll adore the Renoir."

"Okay. Just get back here as soon as you can, Dominic. This all makes me nervous."

"I can't wait to get my hands on that bastard. He must have done this on purpose when he got my text saying we couldn't transfer the money Uncle Luca left him. But revenge is sweet. I'll get him back even if I have to bash a hole in his damn yacht."

"Be careful, we need to think things through before we make any moves."

"Stefano, enough chatter. Just go help Maria. She's got to be a wreck. I'll see you after I drop off the paintings."

Inside, the Interpol team demanded Maria direct them to the largest safe-deposit boxes. As she walked to the rear of the bank, she began crying. Intent on finding the paintings, Wilhelm demanded each first-level box be opened, one by one.

"*Signora*, give me the keys to open all these large boxes."

She returned to her office. Her hand shook as she reached for the keys in her desk drawer. She returned and reluctantly handed them to the agent to whom Wilhelm was speaking.

As they were about to start unlocking the large boxes, Stefano attempted to enter the bank, but was stopped at the front door.

"I'm an owner of the bank. Let me in."

Getting a nod from his supervisor, the police officer stationed there let him in. Stefano strode to where the safe-deposit boxes were located, and asked a police officer, "Who is in charge?"

Then seeing his sister, he pulled her to his side and whispered, "Don't say anything. And relax, because there's nothing here. Dominic removed the paintings early this morning. They're in his car and they'll find nothing here. They'll be on their way soon."

Distraught with unbearable tension, Maria wept against her brother's shoulder while holding his arm tightly.

Stefano asked again, this time shouting in anger, "Who's in charge here? What's happening? Do you have a search warrant?"

Wilhelm stepped forward. "I'm in charge. My name is Wilhelm Mueller. I'm with Interpol and we're searching for stolen art. We were told two paintings are being stored in your bank, in a lower-level safe-deposit box. Here's the search warrant."

"Well, Herr Mueller, you won't find anything like that here, and you're upsetting my sister."

"We'll be done in a few minutes. We were told the art was placed in a large, lower-level box. And young man, I am not a German. This is an official Interpol investigation."

"Well, your men are rude, behaving like the Gestapo. You can search all you want. There's nothing here."

The Interpol agents supporting Wilhelm searched another ten minutes. Finding nothing, they turned to Wilhelm with shrugged shoulders and facial expressions that said, *What next?*

They all huddled, spoke briefly, then left the bank. Outside, the Interpol agents released the local police from their support role while Wilhelm placed a call to his assistant.

"Ursula, get me on the next flight from Ciampino to Malta."

"Sir, a flight leaves at ten thirty this morning and puts you in Malta by eleven twenty. If you hurry, you can catch it."

"Book it."

That damn O'Sullivan. What's he up to in all of this? He just beat me for three million, but I have his wife as leverage, and I'll be able to get it all back.

***

In Reggio it was 9 AM and Vittorio had the cappuccino machine waiting for the first guest to arrive in the galley. He'd prepared a special breakfast of scrambled eggs with bits of porcino, pancetta, grated mozzarella, grated Pecorino cheese, and cracked pepper all poured over small cubes of Italian bread. It would go in the oven once a few more guests arrived on the main deck.

"*Buon giorno, Vittorio!*"

"*Buon giorno, Signore Luzzi.*"

"Please, call me Paolo. Vittorio, did you know today is a special day for me?"

"No. Why is that?"

"Today is my birthday and, according to many, today I am officially an old man. But my gorgeous and aggressive woman is keeping me young and alive!"

"Ha! You're a lucky man! What time do you want to be in Malta?"

"Well, Elena's showering now, and will go shopping this morning. Gianni told me yesterday if we leave at eleven, we should arrive in Malta by seven this evening, when the birthday festivities are in full swing."

"While you were sleeping last night, we quietly left Reggio and I've brought us to Siracusa. Elena will find a greater variety of stores here, and we're that much closer to Malta. If we leave at eleven and cruise gently, we can get to Grand Harbour by four. I've already reserved a slip in the Vittoriosa Yacht Marina with access to transportation in Valletta to your home. You just gained three extra hours to enjoy your party!"

"*Magnifico! Bravo*, Vittorio. And I see you can cook. *Bellissimo*, young man."

"Paolo, one more thing. You have a note this morning from the commodore of the yacht club where we docked earlier."

"Open it and tell me what he says."

"It says, 'Greetings and welcome! Your application and deposit to the Vecchio Siracusa Yacht Club have been received. The board has met and accepted your application. You are now eligible for all the rights and privileges of full membership. As a personal gift from me, I have approved your taking two hundred fifty gallons of diesel fuel from our club's filling station onto your vessel at no charge.' I'll pump the fuel he offered before we leave; it'll top us off perfectly."

"Good idea. What's the commodore's name?"

"His name is Massimo. Massimo Marini."

"Yes. I sent an invitation to my birthday party along with my application to the yacht club. Did he say anything about that in the note?"

"No."

"Maybe he'll come, and I'll get to meet him. Repositioning us overnight was a clever idea. Excellent work, Vittorio."

Minutes later, Elena entered the dining room. "Paolo, darling, Vittorio just told me we're in Siracusa, where the shopping is plentiful. I'm skipping breakfast and heading to the stores now. I should be back in a few hours."

"Be back by ten forty-five. We leave at eleven. I'll leave without you if you are not here."

"You wouldn't dare."

"Try me. Several women in Malta are awaiting my return."

CHAPTER FORTY

Leaving Siracusa

This morning seemed different for Brian and Nina. It felt like all the pressure they'd been under had suddenly evaporated. After breakfast, they returned upstairs and lost track of time, enjoying one another in bed. Basking dreamily in the afterglow of their lovemaking, they fell asleep, arms and legs wrapped entwined together.

Downstairs, Massimo was moving several cases of wine that were just delivered. He stored the bottles in the huge eight-foot wooden rack spanning the entire width of the wall. While picking up the next bottle, his cell phone's ringtone distracted him. He reached for the phone with the bottle still in his hand, inadvertently hitting the rack. The bottle fell hard, smashing against the marble tile floor.

The loud crash and Massimo's subsequent string of cursing awakened Nina. She sat up, noticed the time and gave Brian a gentle shove. Now pressed for time, she jumped in the large shower. A moment later, he joined her.

"Last night was great... and this morning. I've not felt like this in years—maybe not in decades."

She rubbed her soapy breasts against him. "My pleasure. Truly my pleasure. You are terrific, Brian."

After drying off, Nina finished packing and then dried her hair. She thought about their morning. *I can only hope it somehow continues.*

Brian looked at his watch. "Don't be too long up here." He picked up his bag and went downstairs. Nina finished with her hair and then stashed half of her things in a smaller bag Massimo loaned her for the short trip to the party.

Brian heard Massimo giving instructions to the housekeeper, who had just returned with her brother.

"I dropped a bottle of wine inside and made a mess. I did my best to pick up the glass and clean the floor, but please go over it. We all will be back tomorrow, or at least I will. Here's some cash and a list of items to pick up for our return. Oh, and please have your brother return the rental car out front to the airport. The papers are in the glove compartment."

Now noticing his friend, Massimo said, "Ah, Brian! We'll head over to the yacht club in my car. I've asked the housekeeper to have her brother return your rental car. I'll drive you both back to Catania when we return here tomorrow or maybe you'll just fly from Malta at a later date if you find your mother."

The Vecchio Siracusa Yacht Club a mere ten-minute drive away. Massimo's call to the boat's captain three days earlier had prepared him for today's trip. Now with Brian and Nina's arrival, they'd be using his extra tickets. The boat on which they would travel was used both for pleasure excursions as well as for the captain's small business, delivering certain commercial products to Malta. He told Massimo in a brief call this morning he'd just been asked to bring a variety of fresh vegetables, mushrooms, and six cases of expensive wine for a restaurant on the island. He indicated everything was already on board, the sea was calm, and the trip should be quite pleasant.

Nina changed her mind about using a smaller bag, and so Brian heaved her heavy bag and his bag into the back of Massimo's white 2010 Mercedes G-Class SUV.

"Have you taken this on a safari yet?" Brian asked, impressed with the opulent vehicle.

"Ha! I wish! I did well, flipping some art pieces I picked up at bargain prices in Greenwich Village years ago. The work, by a young artist who made his debut in the annual open-air art show along Sixth Avenue, turned out to be a big hit in Madison Avenue corporate offices and among the Upper West Side's jet set. I knew him because he was taking classes at NYU. We occasionally saw each other in Washington Square Park. We got to know each other as friends. He was gay, much younger, and careless— with too many men. Regrettably, he contracted AIDS." Massimo sighed.

"I learned he was dying and went to New York to visit him. It was incredibly sad, seeing him so ill. He gave me six of his paintings while I was there. Quite good for a young artist. I held on to them for the memory.

One day I learned prices on his paintings had skyrocketed in several high-end Manhattan auction houses. I soon found myself sitting on several million dollars' worth of his art.

"I sold just one of his paintings to buy this house. It left me enough cash to buy this car two years ago. His name was Cole, but he went by Argyle and signed his paintings just that way: 'Argyle.' Okay. Enough sad memories for now. *Andiamo tutti!*"

Gosh, it kills me to think of that kid. "Nina, can you spare a tissue?"

They left the Punta Castelluccio neighborhood on Via del Faro Massolivieri and Via La Maddalena and then headed along Via Lido Sacramento to Via Elorina. Three minutes and a quick turn later, they were on Via Malta, headed to the Ponte Santa Lucia. On the other side of the bridge, several yachts were docked along the bulkhead. Unknown to Brian and Massimo, Paolo's new yacht sat two slips away from their ride to Malta.

Massimo had made two calls along the way and when they pulled up, two young men and the boat's captain greeted them. As introductions were made, one young man carried their luggage on board while the other parked Massimo's car in the hotel lot across the street in a space reserved for the yacht club's commodore. A minute later Massimo's impromptu party date crossed the street. She carried a small pink handbag.

"Isabella! How are you, my dear friend?"

"Frankly, my dear Massimo, I'm still stunned by your call. I never thought I'd be going to a fancy party in Malta with my favorite handsome gay friend."

"Oh, my goodness, Isabella! You never hold back your thoughts or opinions. It's why I love who you are! And dear woman, you look absolutely sparkling today!"

"And do tell me… who is this attractive couple?"

"Meet Brian and Nina. Brian is an old friend who's visiting. Nina is his colleague. I've invited them both to join us at the party."

"Very nice. Young lady, your colleague is gorgeous. You'd better hope I don't steal him on our trip!"

Her forward comment caught Nina by surprise. *No way I'll let that happen!*

"Nina, don't be surprised by anything Isabella says," Massimo said. "She was born without a filter. Whatever thought pops into her head arrives on her lips a moment later."

"Massimo, this party is going to be fun! You old dog, you do look unusually attractive today!"

The captain, hearing a break in the chatter, announced they'd be leaving in a minute. He had committed to get the goods to the restaurants and was anxious to leave on schedule. He knew what he was delivering was for a massive birthday party being catered by the restaurant. Last night's late update on the number of guests caused the owner to panic and order more food and more high-end wine.

He gave the signal and the ropes holding the yacht in place were thrown back onto the bulkhead. The horn blasted as the yacht drifted from the dock. Brian, Nina, Massimo, and Isabella were under way.

Three hundred feet further down the same bulkhead, Elena climbed out of the taxi with ten bags of clothing in hand and called for help. Vittorio responded first, grabbing several bags and assisting her up the gangway stairs and onto the yacht. Paolo watched from an upper deck, laughing as she fumbled her way aboard. Vittorio returned to the helm and started the engines once she was settled in the huge master bedroom. Tony loosened lines and prepared to toss them onto the pier.

Suddenly the departure of Paolo's yacht was delayed when Elena panicked, realizing she'd misplaced her small purse.

"Stop the boat. We can't leave yet! My pocketbook is missing!"

Watching from the cabin doorway, Paolo laughed again when she found the missing purse buried under the paper wrappings of her voluminous purchases. He shouted up to Vittorio, saying he was clear to leave. Moments later, the horn sounded, and they sailed away from the Vecchio Siracusa Yacht Club. Paolo's brand-new yacht was on a direct course to Malta, about three minutes behind Brian's ride.

Gianni, Paolo, and Elena went up on deck to watch the Siracusa skyline and harbor gradually disappear. Vittorio handed control of the yacht to Tony and went below to send a status update: "Departed Siracusa."

As both yachts left the harbor, a small, twelve-seat airplane flew high overhead. On board, Wilhelm Mueller sipped vodka as he worked a crossword puzzle, still recovering from a fruitless morning. At 11:10, the plane leaned slightly to the right for a course correction. Gazing down from the window Wilhelm saw the beautiful blue water below and two yachts, one seemingly following the other, just leaving the Siracusa harbor. He sipped his vodka and checked his watch. *I'll be in Malta in plenty of time for Paolo's birthday party. I look forward to confronting him in person about his disgraceful actions and contemptable attitude. Father won't be happy.*

CHAPTER FORTY-ONE

To Malta

Brian and Nina lounged on the back deck, enjoying the scene departing Siracusa. The 143-nautical mile trip aboard the 45-foot Sargo would take just over five hours at an efficient cruising speed, allowing them to arrive in the Port of Valletta around 5 PM.

Massimo and Isabella enjoyed the departure as well, and then headed below deck to one of the three bedrooms. She had heard enough topside and probed Massimo for a full update on his other two guests.

Brian and Nina began discussing their strategy for entering the party. He acknowledged the good fortune of Massimo's receiving a formal invitation for four attendees. They talked about the house, wishing they had a bird's-eye view of its layout on the property. Nina went to the captain, asking if he had internet access on the boat.

"No, but if you hurry, you can still get a cell phone signal from several nearby towers as we pass along the shoreline."

Nina plugged a cord into her cell phone and then into her laptop's USB port and in no time was up and running. She fired up a new app called Sky Vision and asked Brian for the address Fausto Fellini had given him. She entered it, and in a flash, the image on the laptop was as if she were flying over Katrina's home.

"Look, Brian. Here's where your mother lives."

"Your use of technology amazes me! How do you even know about these things?"

Moving closer to Nina, Brian saw the house adjacent to the ocean and the walls around its perimeter. They also saw a fair-sized guard house at the front gate, the one Giuseppe Fellini warned about.

Nina pointed to the property's exceptionally large side yard.

"I bet that's where the party will be. With any luck, we'll be able to just walk in."

"I suppose so, especially if Massimo and Isabella lead the way. He has such a huge presence."

"Did you see that dress she's wearing?"

"I'm not really into fashion, Nina, but I'm sure she'd stand out at any party."

"The colorful orange, pink, and rose-colored flowers are flashy, and those colors are a terrific contrast against her dark tan."

"Never mind the colors. The low-cut top, her lack of a bra and that thigh-high slit will draw the most looks!"

"Brian!" She socked him in the arm.

"What? You just asked me if I saw the dress… and I did."

Just then the signal dropped, and the screen froze.

"Damn!" Nina scowled. "I need to find the bathroom. I'm nervous — and whenever I get nervous, I get queasy."

'It's down below where the bedrooms are."

Brian mulled over a range of scenarios while Nina scuttled below.

We enter the party, staying right behind Massimo and Isabella. We scope out the house. Maybe take a walk around it and look for a room on the south side overlooking the ocean. That could be where Katrina spends her days. Or maybe we each grab a tray with empty glasses or empty hors d'oeuvre dishes and follow a server into the kitchen. Then we walk through the house—we can say we're looking for the bathroom.

What if he comes up behind me with a gun in his pocket, poking in my ribs? There'll be too many guests for him to do anything in front of everyone. But maybe he'll direct me to a dark area. Maybe the quiet side of the house where we are alone. He'll either shoot me with a silencer and dump me behind a bush, or he'll take me to see Katrina. That's it. He'll let me see her, then when we leave her, he'll kill me.

Maybe this trip to Malta is a huge mistake. Perhaps Nina and I should stay on the boat and go back to Siracusa. We can stay at Massimo's house. Maybe I should have waited until after his birthday and he was off the island. Or maybe I should've watched more movies and read more Ian Fleming novels because right now, I'm feeling ill-prepared for this nerve-racking drama. The next twelve hours will—

Brian's thoughts scattered as he heard more of Massimo and Isabella's laughter below deck, their boisterous laughing fueled by cocktails Massimo had brought along.

Nina returned from below, smiling coyly. "Brian, we have another couple of hours before we arrive. Would you like to go downstairs?"

"Yes, but not right now. We need to come up with a firm plan. Then we need to let Massimo know what we want to accomplish. I'm hoping he isn't too inebriated by the time we get there."

"Sorry. I was just thinking about you and our time this morning."

He stood and gave her a big hug and a passionate kiss.

Returning to the main deck, Isabella exclaimed, "Look at you two! You still have a couple of hours if you want to get it on before we land."

Nina and Brian smiled, as Isabella continued up the stairs to join the captain.

When she was gone, Nina said, "Okay, back to business. I might have an idea for when we land."

"What are you thinking?"

"Massimo and Isabella will attract a lot of attention. People will be looking at the bigger-than-life Massimo and will hear his loud belly laugh. Then they'll notice her and see she's bouncing around. No one will notice us if we stay about six feet behind them, hiding in plain sight. If we stand apart and back to back, we can scan the area until we find Paolo. When we spot him, we spy on him until he's occupied. Then we find Katrina."

Brian nodded. "Good thinking. That's close to what I was thinking."

"Really? Now the art-history teacher's thinking like Sherlock! By the way, have you called Grace today?"

"I tried this morning just before we left Massimo's house. Still no answer. It went straight to voicemail."

"You may need to get the Dutch police in Amsterdam involved."

"That occurred to me, too."

"Of course it did, Sherlock."

The combination of warm late-afternoon sunshine and the cool ocean breeze felt invigorating.

Nina donned a jacket and snuggled close to Brian. She slid an arm around his waist and turned to him.

"A lot will happen in the next few hours, but I need to share something with you. A year ago, when I joined the art-research team with you and Erick, and we first started working together, I thought you were just a nice, older guy. As our working relationship grew closer, our age difference disappeared for me. You're very handsome, and kind, and I'm highly attracted to you."

As she paused a moment, tears filled her eyes. "I'm falling in love with you, Brian, and I want to spend all my time with you. I don't know what else to say."

"I know how you're feeling, Nina, because I'm feeling the same way. You're beautiful, bright, and always upbeat. It's such a respite from my ordinary life, and I so enjoy your company. Our relationship's become complicated. When this adventure is over, we'll need to talk. But for now, let's head downstairs."

CHAPTER FORTY-TWO

Arriving in Malta

Approaching Malta, the captain checked the GPS for their exact position. He called the restaurant on his satellite phone, saying his ETA was fifteen minutes. Massimo checked with the captain for an assurance he'd keep the boat there overnight. He responded saying it would be available for the two couples to sleep on board and he'd sleep in the third room once all the products stored in there were unloaded.

The captain switched the ship's radio dial and called the local dockmaster as he maneuvered into the small harbor. Two minutes later he eased off the engines and let the vessel coast toward the bulkhead. He reversed the engine briefly and the boat came to a stop. Lines wrapped tightly around the boat's cleats were thrown onto the bulkhead. Two dockworkers pulled the boat in, tied it up, and extended the gangplank.

Brian watched intently, admiring the captain's skill. Memories of growing up in Staten Island and watching the ferry dock in Manhattan flashed through his mind. Occasionally, high winds and the water's current made docking a challenge. In contrast, this was gentle and precise.

The captain shut down the pair of diesel engines and gave the okay to leave the boat. Massimo had changed into a blue-and-white seersucker suit with a wide yellow bowtie. Isabella, still decked out in her eye-catching dress, now sported a multitude of bangle bracelets and extra-large hoop earrings. She immediately drew wolf whistles from the dock hands. She expected it and loved it. Massimo led them across the gangway and down onto the pier.

Nina dressed conservatively in loose white slacks and a thin navy blouse with light-blue embroidered flowers—the same outfit she'd worn in southern Spain. Brian wore light-grey pants and a burgundy Izod golf shirt.

Nina carried Brian's bag and he hers. Beneath two changes of clothing and a long-sleeved sweater she'd stowed her own loaded .22 she'd never told Brian about, a spare clip, and two boxes of small-caliber bullets.

Brian's bag held a spare pair of pants, a navy shirt, a spare magazine, and a small box of bullets. He tucked his Interpol badge and identification card in his wallet. Before stepping onto the gangway, he tightened his belt a notch, ensuring the holster with the small handgun Nina bought him sat snug against his waist.

Word of the big party had spread through the city and a half dozen taxis were lined up at the dock for the guests arriving in their yachts. The four of them climbed into two taxis and left for the party. Brian and Nina held hands in the back seat.

"You're going to see your real mother in a few hours."

"If I survive Paolo and his party."

"Brian, we've got a plan. It'll work out fine. Our story needs to have a nice ending, then you can write a book about it someday."

"Stories don't always have happy endings."

"Just keep your chin up. You got this."

"We'll see."

The ride took about fifteen minutes. When they arrived, the house appeared larger than any of them expected. Massimo had paid and tipped both drivers before leaving the dock. As the cabs drove away, the four exchanged their final thoughts before entering the party through the guarded gate.

"Massimo, please remember why we're here. It's a special moment for Brian," Nina cautioned.

Isabella responded in her trademark brash manner. "Listen honey, I'm here for a fantastic time while you two do your thing! Now keep those pretty eyes of yours open and watch me and old Massy in action. We'll be drinking our share and have people laughing while you two sleuths move around, seeing what you need to see, and doing what you need to do. Okay old man, let's get inside and have some fun!"

She grabbed Massimo's arm and swaggered forward, leading them toward the gate. She waved the four invitations as they passed the guards. After entering a large courtyard, they were directed along a slate path. A hundred feet along, they came to the side of the house and made a turn into the side yard where a huge tent as colorful as Isabella's dress covered half the yard. Brian commented to Nina that it looked like a carnival tent.

"It might as well be," she replied. "This seems like it's going to be a huge circus!"

Under the shade of the tent stood a half dozen tables virtually groaning under the weight of an amazing array of food. Two tables held various northern Italian mild and strong hard cheeses, fresh mozzarella, burrata, and sliced, crusty brick-oven bread. Deep-dish pizza rustica sat alongside sliced sweet and hot soppressata, prosciutto, Genoa salami, sweet dried sausage, and smoked ham. Another table held giardiniera, sweet peppers, pitted Kalamata and green olives, cantaloupe and honeydew melon, peeled orange sections, dried and fresh figs, and fresh juicy grapes just flown in from South Africa. One table displayed enormous shrimp, clams on the half shell and thinly sliced raw tuna on ice. Another table offered skewers of fried clams, calamari, oysters, scungilli, polpo, and grill-seared tuna. One more table held fried melanzana, baked lasagna, and broccoli di rapa drenched in oil and large pieces of garlic.

Fully stocked bars at each of the four corners of the tent featured bottles of a Super Tuscan wine called Marchesi Antinori Tignanello Toscana 1971, and a locally grown Grenache blend. Both Greco di Tufo and Fiano di Avellino waited on ice, for those who preferred white. Each bar already had a line of guests waiting to be served. Few weddings offered such a diverse and generous display.

The partygoers who arrived early had already been drinking freely for up to four hours. Loud and almost shouting, they tried to get their voices heard over the six-piece band and two singers providing American-style music from the 1970s. More people arrived in taxis and cars. The large, already-boisterous crowd was growing. Paolo's birthday feast was already a hit.

Brian and Nina stayed behind Massimo and his date for the first ten minutes. Then, feeling safe, they gradually began walking around the perimeter of the large yard. The two then broke ranks, but kept within fifteen feet of each other. Neither spotted Paolo, so Nina decided to walk up to a handsome young waiter pouring iced water for guests.

"*Acqua, signora?*"

"Please. *Grazie*. Do you live here in Malta?"

"*Si.*"

"Nearby?"

"*Si*, uh, yes, near the harbor."

"Do you know where Paolo is? I've been looking for the birthday boy. I haven't seen him yet."

"Fifteen minutes. He is coming in fifteen minutes. He's just arrived in his new yacht. The last time he was here, he told me I could take a ride on it when he gets it."

"How lovely! Paolo told me he wanted me to meet his elderly mother."

"Oh. Uh, she's not here right now. They moved her next door, where it would be quieter."

"Oh, yes. That's right. I remember him saying that to me. She's in that house over there, right?"

"No, she's in the other one, over there on the other side."

"Say, you're a handsome kid. Do you have a girlfriend?"

"No. I'm only fifteen, but I wish I did."

Nina smiled. His age didn't surprise her. Rather, he had just served her purpose. She thanked him with a peck on the cheek. He smiled and blushed.

She turned around to tell Brian what she'd learned, but he was gone. She scanned the crowd. *Gosh, how could he vanish so quickly?*

In the harbor, Paolo's new yacht had just docked. Tied up appropriately, the gangway was set in place. Vittorio gave word it was safe to leave. Eager to join the party, Paolo and Elena moved to the edge of the gangway. Carrying a small clutch for her makeup and a sweater to stay warm after sundown, she held Paolo's hand as they made their way to the pier. With his free hand, Paolo checked for his gun and its silencer. Both sat in the deep pocket of his loose trousers. Feeling ready, he led her off his yacht with a wave of thanks to Vittorio and Tony.

Gianni stopped before the gangway and spoke briefly with Vittorio before stepping onto the pier. As Paolo approached the first waiting cab, Gianni called out loudly to him. "I've just invited Vittorio and Tony to the party. They deserve some fun tonight. They're bringing the two maids."

Paolo gave him a nod and shut the cab's door.

Vittorio made a call. "He's just left for the party. He'll be there in about fifteen minutes. Everything is as we discussed. We'll arrive a few minutes after Paolo."

Gianni passed the next cab waiting in line and walked two blocks to a waiting car. Vittorio and the first mate grabbed a few things, left the yacht, and approached the car where Gianni waited. A moment later, the three of them and the two maids were headed to Paolo's grand party.

Nina nervously scanned the side yard again.

Brian suddenly stood beside her. "Looking for someone?"

"Damn! Where were you a moment ago?"

"A woman behind that table bumped into me and knocked a glass out of my hand. I bent over to pick it up. Did you miss me?"

"You nearly gave me a heart attack. Let me tell you what I was just told by a young waiter. Your mother is in the house next door. Now, don't move! Just wait here, and for heaven's sake, please don't disappear again!"

She found Massimo and told him what she'd learned, saying she and Brian were going to take a walk next door.

When she returned, less than a minute later, Brian grabbed her arm and pulled her into the early evening shadows.

"What?"

"Turn around. Look behind us at the far end of the tent."

"What?"

"He's here, standing with a drink in his hand, next to a vivacious blonde."

"Paolo?"

"No. Wilhelm!"

"Oh, my God! What in heaven's name is he doing here?"

"I have no idea."

"Let me think. Wilhelm's presence can only mean one thing: Something's gone wrong. I bet he never got the paintings! Gosh, Brian, that means he's got three million reasons to be here to find you, because he thinks you screwed him. And I'm sure he's pissed at Paolo for not bringing the paintings to The Hague. He's got to be completely besides himself."

"Let's hurry next door. We can't let him see us now."

Brian and Nina began walking away. They approached the front gate. He told the guard she wasn't feeling good and needed fresh air and a short walk. Less than ten feet from having passed the guard, Nina heard a car pull up behind them. Turning her head slightly, she spotted Paolo and a woman exiting the cab. She shoved Brian in the back, hurrying him along, further away from the party.

"What's that about?"

"Just keep walking. They just arrived."

"Who?"

"Paolo and the woman from the airport."

Brian hurried along the property's eight-foot-tall security wall. Thirty feet farther away, they turned and watched Paolo greet several other invited guests. Guests already inside surged out through the gate to greet the guest of honor. Moments later the inebriated mob wildly cheered his presence. "Paolo, Paolo, Paolo!"

Nina shook her head. "If they only knew. From the looks of things, he'll be tied up with his guests for a while. While he's occupied, let's go find your mother."

"Which way?"

She pointed to a house about a hundred yards away. "That house, way over there is the house 'next door' the young waiter pointed to when we spoke."

"Okay, let's do this."

CHAPTER FORTY-THREE

The House Next Door

It was dark when they reached the house next door. They looked around and, seeing no one nearby, made their way to the front porch. Crouching down and peering through the front window, they saw a white-haired woman in a chair, reading a book. Nina motioned for them to go to a side window for a better view.

A few more feet along, when they looked again, they saw the woman was in a white uniform and appeared to be a nurse. Nina motioned again to continue to the rear of the house. They were walking through the garden when Brian stepped on a small branch and broke it. The loud snap startled them. They stood motionless for a minute. Then, assured it was safe to move, they tiptoed a few feet further along when they came upon two tall windows side by side. It took a moment for their eyes to adjust as they crouched and peered into the darkness inside. They could barely see someone lying in bed, sleeping, but the person's back was toward them.

"Do you think that's her?"

"Probably."

"What should we do?"

Brian's phone rang. He answered in a whisper. "Hello?"

"Hello, Agent Brian, it's Kristofer Bronn."

"Kristofer, why are you calling me?"

Nina put her finger to her lips. "Shh!" Motioning with one hand, she suggested he move away from the house.

"Brian, I'm calling to tell you there are some things in motion you need to know about. But before I begin, I understand you are in Malta right now and at the party. Is that correct?"

"Yes. How do you know?"

"That's not important now. Listen carefully, here's what you need to know…"

Brian listened intently, amazed at what Kristofer was saying.

"Thank you, Kristofer, thank you very much. I owe you. I may even owe you my life."

He ended the call and crept back to Nina to share what Kristofer had told him.

"Oh my God! Brian, we just need to stop right now, and not go inside. Let's head back to the party and lie low. We need to wait and see what unfolds."

On their way back to the party and as they walked through the gated entry, Nina spotted Massimo and Isabella laughing with a small crowd surrounding them. It was like they were king and queen, holding court. Brian and Nina made their way along the outer edge of the tent, knowing they were safer in the shadows.

Nina squeezed Brian's hand. "Look. That's Stefano Luciano over there at the bar."

She nudged Brian and pointed. "I bet the other guy is Dominic."

A moment later, grey-haired Paolo, the cousin by adoption, approached his cousins, flanked by two muscular men. Both wore dark suits, black ties and stood with their arms folded. In less than a minute, the conversation became loud. Before another minute passed, Paolo was poking his fingers in his cousins' chests and then their faces. The heated debate grew even louder. Meanwhile, Nina noticed Wilhelm hiding in the shadow only ten feet from the three arguing cousins.

"Brian, look who's standing near them. Wilhelm's leaning in with a hand cuffed to his ear. It looks like he's trying to block out the music and listen to what they're saying."

Brian felt a tap on his shoulder. He jumped in surprise, and as he reacted, Nina reached for the handgun Brian didn't know about.

"Agent O'Sullivan?"

"Yes. Who are you?"

CHAPTER FORTY-FOUR

Strangers

S hocked by the two strangers who'd emerged from the dark, Nina reached under her blousy top to the waist of her pants and pulled the gun from its tiny holster. Keeping it hidden, she maintained her aim, prepared to shoot through her loose sweater.

"We with Interpol. Come with us now and we'll explain. Hurry."

Brian seemed open to the suggestion, but Nina wasn't buying it. She kept her pistol aimed at the taller of the two.

"Come with us?"

The men persuaded Brian and Nina to follow them to the end of the yard, then led them down a dark trail. They heard sea waves lapping at the shore. The taller man spoke as they reached a sandy patch by the water.

"My name is Vittorio Petrullo. This is my partner, Tony Massa. We're undercover agents operating from Milan for the past fifteen years." They showed their badges. "Several weeks ago, immediately after Kristofer Bronn came across the Nazi soldier's diary, he contacted Pieter Van Deusen. The Chief Director listened to what Bronn had to say and the information initiated our investigation."

"Bronn just called me. He mentioned the investigation but said nothing about either of you or your being here."

"Agent O'Sullivan, allow me to explain. Years ago, Bronn undertook an unsuccessful effort to expose a small ring of thieves working within Interpol who illegally enriched themselves with stolen art pieces, including paintings, statues, ancient Egyptian and even Iraqi artifacts stolen by Nazi Germany and Axis forces during World War II.

"Wilhelm Mueller's father, Klaus, was thought to be the ringleader, but that was never proven. Across two decades, our agents Luzzi and Gozzo supported Klaus' illegal activities. Klaus went underground after retiring, but we now have evidence, dug up by Kristofer, that as his son rose within the ranks, Klaus remained involved, coaching Wilhelm in several recent discoveries and a theft. When these questionable activities resumed, Pieter Van Deusen became suspicious and he called in Kristofer Bronn, seeking his background knowledge and insights to old patterns revealed in several incidents. There is no doubt Klaus Mueller's style was at work once again, according to Bronn.

"So, when the young German woman randomly visited Kristofer with the diary, he read it carefully, then called Erick. Bronn felt the hidden art mentioned in the diary could draw Klaus Mueller's unlawful activities back into the open and his son would steer the illegal escapade. Bronn convinced Erick Schmidt that the activities of Wilhelm and Klaus Mueller, Luzzi, and Gozzo might finally be exposed if the KvR diary case could be played properly.

"Kristofer and Erick went above Wilhelm and contacted our Chief Director Pieter Van Deusen about the diary days before they told Wilhelm Mueller about it. Kristofer explained how he envisioned the thieves might be caught. He told Van Deusen the operation to capture the thieves would be risky, and the team would need additional support from outside the art unit. We were called in a full week before your activity began in Andalusia. Unfortunately, your team's excellent research and speedy actions didn't enable us to reach you before you flew to Andalusia.

"Our internal investigation was revealing, right from the start. We followed the money in Luzzi's account. Besides a modest monthly allowance, we saw enormous deposits made by the Luciano Bank of Rome. We traced the dates of those deposits and found they aligned with dates several paintings were either stolen or recorded as missing. We concluded Stefano Luciano, Sr. and Dominic Luciano, Sr. purchased numerous paintings stolen by their nephew, Paolo Luzzi, beginning more than twenty-five years ago. That practice of illegally purchasing paintings continued by their two sons with similar names in the last decade.

"During our investigation, we also discovered the Vatican has unknowingly been the recipient of both stolen art and reproductions in the form of donations by the Luciano family. In fact, only three days ago we informed Monsignor Borrelli in charge of the Vatican art collection, what might be happening now and what likely happened in the past. He agreed to go along with our guidance, and purposely accepted a painting donated by Dominic Luciano, Jr. yesterday morning. We've asked the monsignor to make a list of all paintings donated by the Luciano family since day one. We're planning to raid the houses of Dominic, Jr., Stefano, Jr., and Stefano's sister Maria, as this case nears its culmination.

"Agent O'Sullivan, coincidental to all these events, the letter you wrote in Spain to Pieter van Deusen arrived on his desk a few days ago. It confirmed Kristofer's suspicions, identified your dire circumstances, and helped us quickly set up this sting by leveraging Luzzi's old childhood friend who sold him the yacht.

"All of this brings us to this evening. This sixty-fifth birthday feast Paolo arranged is conveniently drawing several of these guilty individuals into a small space, where we expect to collar them. Our plan is to make all the arrests within the next hour. But there's still danger ahead. We've just seen tempers flare between the Lucianos and Paolo. We've been proactively in touch with Fausto Fellini, ensuring his law firm is unavailable to certify paperwork for Paolo to withdraw his millions.

"Next, we know you had three million dollars belonging to Klaus Mueller deposited by Wilhelm in a Swiss bank under your name, thanks to Kristofer Bronn and his nephew's assistance. While Wilhelm was tapping the phones of others, we were tapping his. We know he threatened you about Grace's well-being. But now he can't be happy about his father's millions landing in your Swiss account and not recovering any paintings. So, you're at risk this evening if he sees you before we can arrest him.

"There are a few more things I must mention. First, in my undercover role, I piloted Paolo's new yacht from Naples to Reggio, then to Siracusa last night and here this afternoon. My first mate, Agent Tony Massa, and I were tracking Paolo as part of a different internal investigation a month before the diary was discovered. Several emails he sent discussing his yacht purchase were flagged and brought to our attention. In another email Paolo reached out to his childhood friend Gianni, the salesman of record for the yacht's sale in Naples. We've targeted Gianni for his lifelong history of indiscretions and mistakes. His most recent arrest by the Naples police came only three weeks ago. We're taking full advantage of this most recent arrest and are leveraging him as an informant here by forcing him to roll over on Paolo. His alternative is ten years in jail and an end to his playboy lifestyle. As a result, Gianni had no choice but to introduce me as the captain of the yacht and Tony as the first mate. The two women who accompanied us on the yacht as cleaning women are also agents. They're here tonight as our girlfriends, but Donna and Corina are trained agents working the sting.

"Next, in a rare coincidence in the context of this investigation, you've found information in the diary about your birth parents. From research of German war records completed yesterday in headquarters, we have confirmed him to be Karl von Richter.

"We know you've come here looking for your mother, but she's not next door. Two Interpol agents, a licensed cardiologist and a nurse, moved her at three today from the house next door to one further down the street, for her safety. You'll have a chance to see her in the morning. Our nurse is next door; we're hoping to prevent random visitors from going in. We had eyes on you when you were peeking into the front bedroom. The body you think you saw is just some pillows.

"There's more. Wilhelm arranged to have your wife arrested and jailed on false charges. We'd been surveilling Wilhelm and his nephew Philippe's activities. We're aware of the messages Philippe sent Wilhelm after he broke into Erick's apartment. And we knew Wilhelm ordered your wife to be held by Dutch police. Grace is in jail right now. She's terribly upset, but she's safe. And while it's been uncomfortable for her, we needed to let this all play out. Grace will be freed in the morning and returned to Erick's apartment. Late this afternoon we spoke with Erick's neighbor to let her know the arrest was a terrible mistake, but nothing else about the investigation. We'll have someone from our staff in The Hague go to Erick's house tomorrow and be there when Grace arrives, to explain what's happened. We hope she'll understand. But from what I'm told, she might not.

"Two more things. Paolo attempted to kill you in the hotel in Rome, but he shot Wilhelm's nephew instead. Erick was a good team partner to both of you and we're sorry about losing track of him in Seville. Our wire taps indicate he was killed, but we haven't been able to confirm his death, nor discover the whereabouts of his body.

"Now, we need a few minutes to refocus on the rest of this evening. Here is our action plan for when we return to the party."

Vittorio meticulously laid out the next steps the four of them would take. As he ended the instructions, he reiterated he and Tony along with female agents Corina and Donna, were present at the party; a nurse was in the empty house, and a doctor was staying in the house at the end of the street with Katrina.

Tony added a new young agent named Marcello who was in Malta, had been called in to assist with tonight's operation.

"Okay. Let's get back to the party before we're missed. I'll return first. Our first target is Wilhelm. I'll have Corina approach him. She's exceptionally beautiful and will make him think of other things as she approaches him. Tony and I will approach Wilhelm from the side. Marcello and Donna will cuff him and hustle him out to an unmarked van. The local police have been excluded from this operation because of potential leaks. They've been instructed to come at nine to discuss an event scheduled for tomorrow. They're completely unaware of our activity tonight.

"Brian and Nina, once Wilhelm is arrested, you'll move into the shadows in the side yard and wait there for five minutes. Locate the Lucianos and maneuver close to them while remaining in the shadows. Nina, your target is Stefano. You should come out of the shadows and smile at him."

He may recognize you from your brief visit to the bank, but he won't place you right away. When he realizes where he saw you, he will likely ask what you're doing here. Take his arm, tell him you have a secret. Separate him from Dominic by taking him to the side of the tent and bringing him into the dark. Tony will be waiting for you.

"We'll cuff him and take him to the van," Vittorio concluded.

"Brian, you need to approach Dominic differently. Bring an extra drink with you. He's a scotch drinker like you. Begin your conversation saying, 'It was for a woman, but she's... hey, aren't you Paolo's cousin Dominic?' Wait for his response. Then mention you are an art-history professor. Let five seconds go by, then be blunt and say, "By the way..." Then tell him your full name and say, "Hey, thanks for all the money your cousin Maria wired to Switzerland for me yesterday." Then add, "And by the way, I'll be suing your bank for all the compounded interest on my principal you never paid."

Brian exclaimed, "That's brilliant!"

"He's a big guy and he might just have a heart attack when he hears you say that. We'll have another agent come up behind him right when you deliver your final bombshell and cuff him. He'll be the third person sent to the van."

After listening to the action plans, Nina asked, "How about Paolo? What's your plan to deal him?"

<u>CHAPTER FORTY-FIVE</u>

Gathering of Thieves

They took up their positions and within minutes, the plan began unfolding precisely as Vittorio had orchestrated.

As Wilhelm was being cuffed, he angrily sputtered, "Do you know who I am?" His unruly objections went unheard because of the loud music. He was shuffled away in the dark, and the few who noticed his unwilling departure didn't care.

Nina played her role like a seasoned actress, giving Stefano a tantalizing come-hither smile. He responded as expected to her good looks. She raised a hand and curled her pointer finger, as if pulling him toward her on an imaginary string.

"Hey there, beautiful. Haven't I seen you somewhere before? Wait... The bank! You opened a safe-deposit box at our bank yesterday! What the hell are you doing here?"

"Come with me handsome," she breathed in his ear, "and I'll share my secret with you."

He was captivated. Her red lipstick and intoxicating perfume were such strong attractions, Stefano was ready to accompany her anywhere. He followed her into the shadows, eager to get to the bottom of the mystery. Nina pulled him along. He went along willingly, anticipating a wonderful ending to this impromptu adventure. His heart beat faster as they headed further into the darkness.

She turned and flashed a bewitching smile. "Let me hold your drink a moment."

His expression indicated question, but he didn't hesitate to hand over his half-full glass.

Within seconds, two agents had slapped steel cuffs around his wrists.

"Wait! What's going on? Who are you? What's this all about?"

Nina smiled. "Funny you should ask. It's a little about stolen art, a little about your phony art donations to the Vatican, and a whole lot about your uncle Luca's money." She shook her head. "Tsk, tsk, tsk. I'm so disappointed, Stefano. You're not nearly as bright as you are good looking!"

By the far corner of the tent, near another bar, Brian cleverly moved toward Dominic, who'd been scanning the inside of the tent for his cousin.

Brian inched up to him. "Wow! Old Paolo sure knows how to throw one heck of a party!"

"*Ah, Americano!* What brings you to Malta to celebrate his birthday?"

"I'm an art-history professor. My expertise is searching, finding, and validating lost or stolen art. You'd be amazed what technology can do these days. Did you know x-rays can see through the top layer of paint and see other paintings underneath? And these new machines easily spot copies by distinguishing brush techniques not noticeable to the eye."

"Yes, that's interesting."

"The other thing bringing me here today is my family."

"Oh? How so?"

"I'm Katrina Luciano's son—the guy who withdrew forty million U.S. dollars from your bank yesterday. Be honest. How's that make you feel?"

Shocked and livid, Dominic reacted with a roundhouse right to Brian's face. Still spry and possessing excellent reflexes, Brian ducked, then returned with a right of his own to Dominic's large belly and then a left hook to the temple. Dominic went down hard and rolled over. Surprised at his own reaction, Brian looked down at his victim. The agent backing up Brian immediately slapped handcuffs on Dominic's wrists while he was on the ground, then struggled to help the heavyweight to his feet.

"Wow! Agent O'Sullivan, are you okay?" Agent Donna asked. "I saw the whole thing! Your one-two punch was amazing! Uh, sir, you're looking kind of pale."

"I'm a little dizzy but I should be better in a minute. Let me sit down. I think I might throw up."

Nina standing only a few feet away, brought a folding chair and a glass of sparkling water while Vittorio and Tony muscled Dominic into the van being watched by Marcello. Then the two agents returned.

"Agent O'Sullivan, we have a problem. Paolo is gone. Marcello, our junior agent's primary objective was to keep his eyes on Paolo but lost him while we were getting the Luciano cousins into the van. We've lost track of him only for the moment, but I had put a tracking device in his clothing while we were on the yacht. Marcello's going to the van now for a piece of radio equipment to enable us to locate him. He'll be back in a minute."

Nina looked worried. "This isn't good, Brian. He could be targeting us right now."

Ten minutes earlier Paolo had walked through the crowd, on his way over to speak to his cousins again, to discuss retrieving his millions from their bank. Still twenty feet away, he watched a woman approach Stefano, speak briefly, and disappear into the dark with him.

Then, peering through the crowd of revelers, he noticed Brian. He took several steps toward him, but realized he was approaching Dominic. He stopped to observe their interaction. He smirked when he saw Dominic take a swing at Brian and miss, and Brian counter, landing two quick punches, putting his cousin on the ground. To his great surprise, his yacht's captain and first mate helped Dominic up and put him in handcuffs. When the attractive young woman he'd seen moments earlier with Stefano stood beside Brian, Paolo remembered who she was. Then seeing all four huddled in conversation and he realized Vittorio and Tony had to be Interpol plants. He watched at a safe distance as Dominic was brought to the van.

I've been set up. Wilhelm must be behind all this. I've waited years for this birthday and my party was supposed to be a generous celebration for my friends, but Wilhelm and this O'Sullivan character have made a mockery of it! He needs to be eliminated, then all the money will be mine. How do I do this and get away? I must hide, but first I need to get more ammunition and a few more clips.

Paolo ducked his head and crouched down. Staying low in the crowd, he made his way to the side of his house and darted inside, where he was greeted by a few people preparing to set out desserts. While retrieving the ammo, he realized he might not see Katrina again for a while. Deciding to pay his respects, he left through the back door and walked about three hundred feet in darkness toward the house next door, where she was to be moved earlier in the day. He thought about what was happening. He knew the timing would be critical in his next moves. Growing angrier with every step, he finally arrived at the next-door neighbor's house.

CHAPTER FORTY-SIX

Locating Paolo

Marcello ran to the van and opened the storage compartment. He began searching each of the bags and realized he'd neglected to bring the GPS locator. He returned to Vittorio and the others, head down, confessing his mistake. Vittorio was angry.

"I understand this isn't the first time you have screwed up," Vittorio told him, unleashing his anger. "That new phone of yours and those new games you play on it have been a huge distraction to your performance as an agent. You'll be on written notice when we return."

As the six agents reviewed their predicament, Nina said she and Brian would check on Katrina. She suggested Vittorio touch base with the nurse next door while Tony, Donna, and Corina remain at the party and continue searching for Paolo. Marcello, already back at the van, should stay there with the handcuffed trio.

"Vittorio, which house is Katrina in?" Brian asked.

"The last house on this road. The doctor is there."

"Why is that?"

"We didn't want to upset you. As we planned to put our people in place, we learned Katrina had a minor stroke a few days ago. We wanted her far away from the noise, but not so far as to alert Paolo."

The party was in full swing with the musicians now playing American pop music. The food consumption had slowed, but the wine was still flowing. The waiters commented to one another, saying, "This is the best party in Malta in years!"

***

Paolo with inside and retrieved his additional ammunition. Then he went next door to the neighbor's house to check on Katrina. He slipped in through the back door. A small light was on in the front room, and he headed down the hallway. Reaching the entrance to the living room, he saw a nurse in uniform seated in a wingback chair. She was asleep, a book open on her lap. He turned and approached the first-floor master bedroom. Keeping the other lights off, he let his eyes grow accustomed to the darkness. He scanned the room and saw Katrina sleeping. Something was wrong, though. Her wheelchair was missing. Paolo went to the bed and laid a hand on her frail body. He quickly realized the supposed figure was just pillows. He returned to the front room, pulled his gun, and pushed the nurse's shoulder. Startled, the woman woke to a gun pointing in her face.

"Where is she? Where is Katrina?"

"I-I can't say."

"You'll tell me right now, or else."

"Please, don't hurt me. She's at the end of this street, in the last house."

"Let's go."

He pulled her up by her wrist and walked her to the rear door. Stepping outside, he practically dragged the old woman down the porch steps. "Where is she? Which way? Show me!"

She pointed. "It's... it's the last house in that direction. Please, please don't hurt me. I'm just a nurse."

Realizing the old nurse would be a drag, and having no regard for her life, Paolo shoved the gun in her ribs and pulled the trigger. His silencer muffled the shot. All the revelry next door would have drowned out the sound anyway. The small old woman fell to the ground. He bent down and rolled her body into the bushes.

I have no time to play their little game. Today is for me.

Walking quickly along the common path through the back yards, he'd gone another three hundred feet before he arrived at the home where Katrina was sleeping. He peered in the window. A doctor sat at a table, sipping a cup of espresso. Paolo opened the door and entered.

"Can I help you?"

"Yes. I'm Katrina's son. Can you tell me where my mother is?"

"She's inside. She's asleep right now."

"Why is she here and not at the other house?"

"She's had a mild stroke. She seems to be doing better now."

"When?"

"Two days ago. She needs complete quiet. We decided late this afternoon to move her once again from your neighbor's house to avoid all the noise and music from the party. If you come back in the morning, she should be able to speak with you."

"Why did you put pillows in the bed at the other house?"

"The stroke paralyzed one side of her body. She's been resting up against those while lying down."

Accepting the explanation, Paolo left the house. While hurrying back to his party through the rear yards, he now focused on just two things: killing Brian and getting off the island. He remembered the fellow called Massimo, with whom he spoke earlier, was the commodore of the Vecchio Siracusa Yacht Club. *Surely, he can captain my yacht.* He came through the side gate and entered the yard, staying in the dark shadows, and searched for Massimo in the crowd.

It was approaching 9 PM. The crowd was drinking heavily, and it was time for the caterer to bring the desserts and the birthday cake to the main table. The restaurant owner catering the party sent his 15-year-old waiter nephew to find Paolo and bring him to the center of the tent. The main food tables were cleared, and a variety of sweets were placed on it. Locally made tiramisu cakes were placed in the center with almond-paste croissants, coconut biscotti, fig-filled butter cookies, and two varieties of cannoli that caught everyone's attention. The bartenders filled another table with small shot glasses of white and black Sambuca, Amaretto, and Galliano.

Paolo spotted Massimo with Isabella. He walked up, took his arm, and brought him off to the side. Isabella took the opportunity to explore the table with the liquors.

"My friend, something has come up and I need to leave the island. I want you to captain my new yacht."

"Oh goodness! I would like to do that, but rumor has it your yacht is much bigger than I can manage alone. We'll need help."

Paolo pulled his gun and stuck it in Massimo's belly. "I'm sure the commodore will oversee my big yacht just fine. We need to leave now."

They headed toward the east side gate, avoiding the front gate where agents Corina and Donna stood. Massimo wondered how to extricate himself from this unexpected situation. His conversation with Brian last night alerted him to Paolo's dangerous character. He saw Isabella returning from the dessert table and shouted, "I'll be right there, sweetheart!"

As several nearby women turned to look at him, he pulled free from Paolo's clutch and ran to the sweets table.

Paolo moved away in the opposite direction, frustrated by Massimo's maneuver. Just then, the young waiter sent to retrieve Paolo for the cake cutting, ran up and tugged at his arm.

Paolo, gun still in hand, instinctively turned and shot the teen in the chest.

Several people nearby caught a glimpse of the muzzle's flash and witnessed the handsome youngster's fall to the ground. A collective gasp rang out among the small radius of people.

Recognizing his mistake, Paolo ran through the side gate into the darkness. *When I find him, I'll kill him.*

CHAPTER FORTY-SEVEN

Paolo Finds His Cousins

A small group surrounded the teenager's dead body, unintentionally hiding the horrific scene at the yard's east gate. Someone ran to the front gate to tell one of the house guards what had happened. Agent Donna immediately went to the boy on the ground and sent Corina to find Tony.

The large crowd, ignorant of the shooting, surged toward the dessert tables. The band's music continued, seemingly even louder. Massimo, still shaking from his harrowing incident with Paolo, remained at the center tables with all the food. He cautiously looked for Brian, hoping not to be grabbed again.

Unaware of the shooting, Vittorio and Tony went to check on the nurse. Upon entering the house, they called out to her but got no response.

"She should be here."

"Look, the book she was reading is on the ground. Something's wrong."

"Check the other rooms. I'll check outside."

Alert to possible danger, Vittorio drew his gun as he walked around the outside of the house. It took only a minute before he stumbled over the dead nurse, whose feet were sticking out from under the bushes. He called Tony.

"This murder was senseless. I scheduled the local police to come here soon. I'll ask them to pick up Mueller and the two Luciano cousins. We'll need more help."

Vittorio's cell phone rang.

"A young waiter's been shot," Donna reported. "He's lying dead on the side yard."

He and Tony left the nurse's body and headed back.

***

Meanwhile, Brian walked with Nina to the last house on the street, where Katrina was sleeping, unaware of the two shootings. He was particularly concerned for his mother's health, given her recent stroke. The two reached the last house and approached the front door. He knocked.

A moment later, the doctor came to the door. "Yes?"

"Is Katrina Luciano here?"

"Who are you?

"I'm her son."

"Really? If that's so, your brother was just here minutes ago."

Nina grabbed Brian's arm. "Oh my God, Brian, he's here someplace."

"He left ten minutes ago. You must have passed him on the street."

"Is Katrina all right, doctor? I was told she had a stroke."

"I was with her late this afternoon. She experienced what we call a TIA. She seems to be doing well. Her speech was unaffected, and we spoke earlier. Of course, at her age she needs a wheelchair and a nursing assistant. Please tell them to send the nurse back down here to help me when she wakes."

Brian's cell phone rang.

"Brian, it's Vittorio, where are you?"

"We're at the house with Katrina."

"There've been two shootings. The nurse at the neighbor's house and a young waiter who was working the party are both dead. The local police are due here in a few minutes and Paolo's still in the wind. You need to watch for him. We're not sure what he'll do next."

***

Paolo hid in the dark, collecting his thoughts, then returned to the edge of the side yard. He saw eight people gathered around the boy's body on the ground, and two hundred others shoving and elbowing each other for position around the dessert tables. He shook his head, feeling a twinge of guilt. He knew the young boy. Then he noticed an unmarked van on the road nearby, and a young man standing alongside it focused entirely on his cell phone.

Paolo walked up to him. "Where's Agent Vittorio?"

The young man scarcely looked up from his phone. "Uh, he's coming back to check on the boy who was just shot."

"Open the door and let me see the prisoners."

Now Marcello looked up, studying the other man's face. "Hey. Aren't you—"

Paolo took the shot, and Marcello fell to the ground, his phone still grasped in his hand. The game prompting him for his next move.

Paolo bent down, grabbed his keys, and opened the van's back door. It took a moment for the three sitting inside in darkness to see who it was. Paolo looked at Wilhelm and sneered. Then, cursing, he shot the Director in the chest. Stefano and Dominic, recoiled in fear at their adopted cousin's rage.

"Now do you two finally understand? I want my money and I want it now."

"Paolo, we can't help you if we're dead. We'll move all your money in the morning, but we need to get out of here."

"Get up off your asses. Let's go."

He opened their handcuffs and walked them two hundred feet to the parking attendant. Paolo gave the man 20 Euros and pointed to a car. The three jumped in and escaped down the road into the darkness.

Moments later, three local police cars passed by Paolo and the Lucianos and arrived at the front gate of the house. The chief of police got out and introduced himself to Vittorio, who explained two shootings had just taken place. He first showed them the body of the boy. He and Tony then took the officers to the house next door to see the dead nurse.

The chief immediately radioed for the coroner and additional assistance. Vittorio then brought him in through the front gate onto the street and headed to the van to show him the prisoners he was to pick up. As they approached, they noticed another body on the ground. Stepping closer, Vittorio recognized Marcello gripping his cell phone, its speaker still loudly asking for the next move. At the rear of the van, they opened the door. Wilhelm Mueller, still handcuffed, lay dead on the van's floor, but the Lucianos were missing. Vittorio called Brian.

"Besides the young waiter and the nurse, it looks like Paolo's killed Marcello and Wilhelm, and taken both Luciano cousins from the van. You should return right now. The police are here, and a few people are leaving the party because of their presence. I'll need your help going through this mess with the local police. They'll have a lot of questions for us. We can assume Paolo and the others are on the run and will try to leave Malta. Get back to the yard pronto. I'll ask the police chief to halt any outgoing flights and position some of his men by the docks to keep an eye for them if they try to escape by boat."

When he hung up, Brian explained to Nina what had just happened. She broke into tears

Brian's nerves were on edge and his eyes filled up too. "We need to go back. We're probably safe the rest of the night. Vittorio said Paolo left with Stefano and Dominic, and they'll probably try to flee the island tonight."

On the way to the marina, Paolo thought about his best way off the island. As he drove, he realized there was no way he could use the yacht to escape. Besides, he still wanted to kill Brian. He slowed the car and turned down a side road. Coming to a stop, he turned off the ignition.

"Get out. One of you is going to call Maria right now and tell her to go to the bank and send the money to my account."

"Paolo, that's not going to work. She'll know something's wrong and she won't do it."

"Get her on the phone. If she's not willing to go to the bank, one of you will die. That might change her mind."

"Paolo, you're not being reasonable. What's wrong with you?"

He took his gun and shot at the ground between Dominic's legs.

"What's wrong you ask? What's wrong is that I've had enough of you two all these goddamn years."

"Okay, okay. Enough, enough! Stefano, give me your phone. My battery's dead."

"Here."

Dominic made the call. It rang five times before being picked up.

Maria, woken by the phone call, looked at the Caller ID.

"Jesus Christ, Stefano! What in God's name are you calling me for? You know I go to bed early. Are you crazy?"

"Maria, it's Dominic. Don't ask questions, just do as I say. Go to the bank. Send Paolo's money to the account we just created for him so he can retrieve it himself."

"Oh my God. Something's wrong. Is he there with you now?"

"Yes, and just do as I say."

"You mean the account that's set up so he can do withdrawals without your approval?"

"Yes. Just do it now."

"Okay, give me twenty minutes to get dressed and drive to the bank."

"Call me back on Stefano's phone when it's done. I'll expect a call back within forty minutes."

Paolo grabbed the phone. "Maria, do what your cousin Dominic says, or I'll fucking shoot him. I've had enough of you goddamn Lucianos."

"I will, I will. Just give me time to get to the bank and make the transfer."

Now satisfied Maria would do what she was told, Paolo hung up. Eyeing them in contempt, he reached into his ugly soul. "I know you both have hated me all my life. And you both know I've always hated you. I hated Luca, I hated both your fathers, and I've hated both of you and your fancy bank. Fuck you both."

Aiming the gun, he pulled the trigger, shooting Dominic in the chest.

"No, no Paolo, don't kill me. You need me. There's a lot more money you don't know about. A whole lot more. We have dozens of old paintings. I can get them for you when I get back. You can have them all."

"No worries, cousin. I'll get everything I want from Maria when I get back."

He raised the gun and pointed. Stefano turned and began to run. Paolo aimed and shot him in the back.

Damn these two. Born into privilege. Never struggled and never hungry a day in their lives. Fuck them.

He bent over the body and picked up Stefano's phone. Little battery power remained. Back in the car, he tried plugging the connector into the end of the cell phone, but it didn't fit. Frustrated, he cursed and threw the phone out the window then turned on the ignition and headed back to his party. *I'll find that bastard.*

When Paolo approached his mother's villa minutes later, the flashing lights of a half dozen police cars and several ambulances greeted him. Everyone was leaving. He parked the car, retrieved a new magazine from his pocket and shoved it into the handle of his gun. Then he filled the empty magazine with the extra rounds in his pocket.

As he stepped from the car, the young parking attendant approached him. "Hey mister, I'm sure glad you're back. The guy who owns that car is really angry."

He ignored the kid and stalked toward the east wall. A few people he'd been with earlier in the evening saw him and waved goodbye. Upon reaching the wall, he walked another twenty yards, staying hidden in its dark shadow. Reaching the east side gate, he paused and peered in. Thirty feet inside the gate he saw Brian, Nina, Vittorio, and Tony speaking with the local police chief, no doubt reviewing the evening's sequence of events.

I need to separate him from the group. His search will have been fruitless. He'll never see her or talk to her. No mother, no money, nothing. Just a last breath and… and then the emptiness.

From a distance, Paolo's girlfriend Elena who traveled there with him today, saw him just outside the side gate. Walking along the wall she reached the open gate. Taking one more step, she moved in front of him and began yelling in his face.

"Damn you, Paolo! Where in God's name have you been? Do you have any idea what's happened here? You invited me here and when we arrive you dump me. I've been looking all around for you for the last hour. I'm such a fool! I thought you might have proposed to me tonight. You've always been a big question mark in my mind. I thought we were past that yesterday with your sweet talking at the airport, then this morning in bed, and again before we arrived here today. But you've gone and messed everything up tonight. Between your disappearing and these killings, I'm an absolute wreck! Even Vittorio's looking for you. He's right over there with Tony. I'm done here, and I'm done with you. I'm leaving now and I'm going to ask Vittorio or Tony to take me back to the yacht."

He grabbed her by the arm. "No. You're staying right here with me."

"Paolo! You're hurting me. Let go of my arm. Paolo! Let go!"

He spun her around and put his other hand over her mouth. "Shh! Be quiet, bitch."

Upset, she bit down hard on his fingers, drawing blood. He pulled back from the sudden pain and lost his grip her arm. She ran from the gate to Vittorio, blood coming from her mouth.

Nina spotted her running towards them first. "Brian, it's the woman we saw at the airport."

"Vittorio, help me! It's Paolo! He's at the gate! Please help me!"

Vittorio ran to her, and as her words sank in, he ran past her. Tony instinctively followed. Nina went to the woman, who tripped and fell to the ground. Nina offered her hand to help her up. Elena's knees and the palms of both hands were bleeding from the rough stone walkway she landed on. Paolo's blood was still in and around her mouth.

"Are you okay?"

She shook her head. "I don't know. Paolo's not the same man I came here with today. I don't know what's happened or what's wrong with him."

"Was he just there at the gate?"

"Yes. I bit his hand and got away. He was hurting me."

Tony pulled his gun and rounded the corner, entering the pitch-black darkness behind the wall. His eyes still not fully adjusted, he took three steps and immediately tripped over Vittorio's body, lying dead on the ground. Alarmed, he jumped up and ran back through the gate's opening to Brian and Nina.

"Vittorio's on the ground. I think he's dead. Paolo's become a killing machine. We need to stop him before we become his next victims. I'll be right back. I dropped my gun when I fell."

Tony returned to the gate and cautiously peeked around the corner. Letting his eyes adjust to the darkness, he saw his gun just ahead of Vittorio. He walked past Vittorio's body and bent to retrieve it when the near-silent shot came. Tony felt the sudden sting in his chest and took his last breath.

CHAPTER FORTY-EIGHT

The Confrontation

Brian and Nina watched the police chief solicit several men to retrieve Vittorio's body, still unaware of Tony's demise. Nina began wondering why it was taking so long for Tony to get his gun. She walked to the gate and before stepping into the darkness she saw Tony's feet right near the opening.

She screamed. "Oh my God! Tony's dead, too!"

Brian and the police chief ran to the gate and saw Tony's body slumped on top of Vittorio.

"Nina, pull yourself together. We've got to find Paolo. He can't be far."

The police chief spoke. "Agent O'Sullivan, we have more police and another ambulance on the way, but it'll be a few hours before the coroner arrives. Please be patient with us. But what on earth is happening here? You said this Paolo is an Interpol agent. Why's he doing all this killing?"

"It's a long story and we don't have time to go through it now, Chief." He pointed to Donna and Corina. "The two women behind us are Interpol agents. They're at your service right now.

The party was almost over. A few people were leaving, but a large group, unaware of the night's horrific events, remained around the table with the Sambuca and Limoncello. They all assumed the police had arrived to end the noisy party but didn't care.

Brian turned to Nina. "Paolo's obviously not leaving Malta any time soon. But I have an idea where he is. Come with me."

"Where are we going?"

"I'm certain he's gone back to the house where my mother's being kept. And I'm sure he's waiting there for me."

"Oh my God. I think I'm going to throw up."

"Go over there. Here's my handkerchief."

Nina's mind was spinning. Then she got sick.

A minute later, she returned to Brian. "I feel better now. I'm sorry."

"Good. Let's go. Here's what I'm thinking we need to do…"

The two walked down the dark street toward the house where the doctor was minding Katrina while the police chief remained at the scene asking Donna and Corina for assistance. They saw a light on in the kitchen where the doctor had been sitting. Moving closer, Brian put a finger to his lips, cautioning Nina not to make a sound.

"Come stand next to me and look," he whispered. "Can you see what I'm seeing?"

"Oh my God. Paolo's putting tape over the doctor's mouth."

"I'm guessing his hands and feet are already taped. Watch. He'll shut off the kitchen light next."

As Brian finished speaking, the room went dark.

"How did you know he'd do that?"

"He's drawing us in to him. We need to split up and be at an angle, so we don't accidentally shoot each other."

"Okay."

"Can you still see him in the dark kitchen?"

"Not yet. Oh wait. Now I can barely see him."

"Keep your eye on him and move closer, but only inches at a time. Remember to hold your gun with two hands – with both thumbs on the same side of the grip – and keep your eyes open if you pull the trigger. I'm going around to the side."

"Oh my God, please be careful."

Brian left Nina and slowly inched his way to the side of the house.

Inside, Paolo finished binding the doctor with tape, then left the room and went to check on Katrina. She was sound asleep. *She's old now and doesn't have much longer to live. Everything will be easier with her dead and buried. I'm certain with everything that's happened tonight O'Sullivan will come snooping here again soon. I'll be waiting, and he'll never know what hit him. Maybe I can take Katrina out permanently and blame him. Yes, that's what I'll do.*

Paolo knew Brian would return because the doctor, only a few minutes ago, foolishly made the same remark to Paolo about seeing his brother earlier.

Outside, the full moon shone intermittently at first, then began shining brightly as a sudden strong breeze pushed all the clouds away. The palm fronds moved wildly back and forth, and the moonshine cast shadows through the tall windows.

Hearing the wind and seeing all the motion outside, Paolo prepared himself for Brian's entrance by moving to a corner of the kitchen. He sat in a chair, his back against the cabinets, giving him a full view of what was ahead. The doctor, sitting in the center of the room grew anxious and struggled to undo the tape binding his hands, ankles, and mouth.

At the side of the house, Brian had an unobstructed view of the doctor peering through a window. Edging over, he could see Paolo sitting, holding a handgun. On the other side of the house, Nina lost her view of Paolo when he moved himself against the cabinets. She crept closer and, seeing an open door to her side, took a huge risk and entered the house. She fully expected to have a good angle to shoot Paolo.

Brian moved a few feet again as the strengthening breeze churned the palms trees. Just then, a large frond fell at his feet, giving him an idea. But he'd need Nina's help. He went back to where he'd left her. She was gone. He returned to his last vantage point and looked inside again. Paolo now had his gun pointed at Nina standing in the doorway. Her hands and arms were up, above her shoulders. Brian's was shocked seeing her caught and facing a gun. His heart sank.

Paolo believed the attractive female agent was an important card to win the 'Kill O'Sullivan' game, and figured it'd be just a matter of minutes before Brian would attempt to rescue his young damsel in distress. Holding the gun to her chest, he pushed her with his free hand, telling her to stand next to the doctor. He ordered her to get down on her knees in front of the doctor and put her hands behind her back. Walking behind her, Paolo bound her wrists with tape, then put tape across her mouth. He looked at her for a moment, admiring her shapely figure and unbuttoned her blouse. Then he pulled it down her arms to the back of her hands.

"*Ah, signorina,* you're very pretty and have a beautiful body! Will your Romeo come to rescue you? He never came to see his mother. So why should he care about you? He's just a make-believe agent. He has no courage. Pretty lady, as I look at you, I see you are much more attractive than I realized. Let me take a closer look at how beautiful you are."

He stepped behind her and, reaching down, unhooked her bra.

"*Bellissima!* You are so beautiful! Let me see—"

Suddenly the hard end of a large palm frond crashed through the window only three feet away from Paolo. The shattered window showered Nina, the doctor, and Paolo with long, sharp slivers of glass. Paolo turned and shot several times through the window. He heard no response but a moment later, he felt a small, warm trickle down the side of his neck. He reached to his ear lobe, then lowered his hand. His fingers discovered a piece of the shattered glass stuck in the side of his neck.

Moments later and farther from where the doctor and Nina huddled together, a second frond crashed through another window, again spraying glass chards about the room. Paolo took several more shots at the waving shadows. This time voice from outside called out.

"It's over, Paolo."

"No. The killing game is still on, and you, the bastard son is about to lose your most important piece."

He lifted Nina up by pulling on her taped wrists. Standing beside her, Paolo raised his gun, aimed at her, and instead shot the doctor. Nina screamed loudly as the doctor slumped forward in his chair.

"How do you like that move? She's next. But before I kill her and then you, let me ask you a question. Why did you take so long to visit your mother? You're a very cruel bastard son to let her worry about you all these years. You never called. You never wrote, and you made her cry. Yet she always talked about you, and she always worried about you. I never meant anything to her. And I hated Luca. You deserve nothing of Luca's. He was nothing to you."

Paolo raised his gun again. As he moved to point it to Nina's head, he felt dizzy. Blood loss from his carotid artery pierced by the glass in his neck was quickly deprived his brain of oxygen. It made all his movements feel as if they were in slow motion. Extremely woozy, Paolo felt the room spinning as he struggled to pull the trigger. *What's happening to me?*

Just then, the trigger was pulled. A shot resounded, hitting its mark.

Fortunately, it was Brian's perfect shot, taken from the dark through the broken window.

Paolo collapsed against Nina and the dead doctor. Already near the floor, Nina was shoved hard against a fragment of splintered glass. In less than a second, it sliced her upper thigh like a butcher's sharp knife. The wound was deep and immediately bled badly.

Brian hurried through the door, and while crunching across the shards of glass, pulled Paolo off Nina. Then he noticed Nina's serious injury. Fearing the possibility of her femoral artery's being cut, he immediately took off his belt, put it around her upper thigh and pulled it as tight as he could, allowing it to function as a simple tourniquet. He helped Nina up, sat her in a chair, pulled the tape off her mouth, unwound the duct tape that bound her hands, and helped her put her bra and blouse back on.

"Nina, here. It looks like whatever glass cut you is out but put this dishtowel directly on your wound and press hard. I need to get you to an ambulance right away."

Brian saw a wheelchair at the end of the kitchen. He lifted Nina into it and wheeled her outside and up the street. He was pushing her up a small hill and his heart was racing.

"Hang in there Nina. We're almost there. The ambulance is just ahead."

"Brian, I'm feeling dizzy. I think I'm going to pass—"

CHAPTER FORTY-NINE

CHAPTER FORTY-NINE

Grace's Call

Brian was struggling and out of breath by the time he reached the ambulance sitting in front of the gate to the birthday party. The EMTs lifted Nina inside and quickly assessed the two-inch gash in her thigh. They replaced Brian's belt with a proper tourniquet, commenting how his swift application of the makeshift tourniquet likely saved her life.

As they worked on Nina, Brian's phone rang. He pulled the phone from his pocket and saw the Caller ID showed the number from Erick's apartment.

"Brian? It's Grace. Where are you?"

"Grace! Thank God! I'm in Malta. How are you?"

"I'm okay. I was just freed from jail an hour ago. What are you doing in Malta?"

"It's a long story. My mother is alive and living here. I'll get to see her tomorrow morning."

"When they released me, they told me my arrest was a mistake. They found drugs in your co-worker's apartment. The authorities thought I brought them into the country. It's really made me angry. How did you find your mother? Are you alone or are you with someone?"

"It's a long story. I have a few things to explain."

"You sure as hell do. I spent a whole day in jail because of your stupid friend Erick. He's the one who called the day your mother was buried, right?"

"Yes. Grace. Erick is—"

"I don't care about your damn friend. Brian, you're with someone, right? Who are you with? Are you with a woman? Of course. That's it. You're with a woman. And that story about finding your mother is just a bullshit story."

"Grace, I just told you, it's a long story. Look, it's late. It'll be much better if we discuss this tomorrow."

"Brian, I don't need to wait until tomorrow. I've had plenty of time to think things over while I was sitting in jail. I don't want to hear your 'it's a long story' crap. I'm not happy with our marriage. I think you have kept secrets from me all these years. And now I'm thinking we need to part, and each go our separate ways. You can do whatever you want from now on."

"Grace, we can discuss this tomorrow, after you've had a good night's sleep. Tomorrow I'll get to meet my birth mother, Katrina. I plan to spend a few days with her. She's in her nineties and recently had a mild stroke. She's not able to walk, and I don't know if she'll even remember me."

"So, you're not coming back to Amsterdam in the next two days. Is that what you're telling me?"

"Grace, please take a deep breath. Listen to me closely and try to understand. I'm meeting my birth mother tomorrow. She's had a stroke. If she knows who I am, I want to be with her. It'll be three or four days before I get back to Amsterdam. Will you stay until I return?"

"Well, I should have figured you always do exactly what you want, without ever considering anybody else's needs. And this time is no different. No, Brian, I won't stay here. I'm flying back to New Jersey tomorrow. I'm extremely disappointed in you. When I get back, I'll be hiring an attorney. Here's some news for you: While I was sitting in jail, I decided to file for a divorce. I just can't deal with you and your being away so often anymore. At first, it was the art exhibits, but then these trips of yours became too frequent. I started doing research and there weren't any art shows when you said there were. But you'd leave anyway and disappear to Europe. And now you've done it again. For God's sake Brian, I'm not even sure right now you've truly found your mother. I don't know how to believe you anymore. You're probably at a nice house overlooking a nice beach and fucking some attractive young woman who'd be your daughter's age if we had children." She bitterly spat out her last words.

"Grace, don't talk like that."

"Don't say another word, Brian. I'm hanging up. I'll be heading back to New Jersey in case you ever decide to return."

"Grace, we need to—"

The line went dead.

Brian was lost in his thoughts mulling over Grace's announcement when the police chief approached.

"Agent O'Sullivan, we have several more hours' work here tonight. You should get some rest."

Before he could respond, the ambulance driver called to Brian standing at the rear of the ambulance. "*Signore*, we are about to bring the young woman to the hospital. If you are coming, jump in. She's your daughter, yes?"

Ignoring the question, he grabbed the bar and stepped onto the vehicle's back bumper. He carefully moved next to the stretcher. As he sat, Nina looked up. Their eyes met.

He took her hand, and leaning forward, kissed her cheek.

"You'll be fine, Nina. You'll be fine. Just rest."

After the ride to the emergency room, Brian decided it was best to sleep there at the hospital. Nina was taken into surgery shortly after midnight. As the doctor stitched her thigh muscle, he commented to the surgical team how close the gash was to her femoral artery.

CHAPTER FIFTY

The Next Morning

Early the next morning, Massimo and Isabella awakened. They laughed hysterically at finding themselves in bed together, naked. Surprised by his own behavior, Massimo gave Isabela a squeeze and then headed to the boat's tiny shower. When he finished, he dressed and made a call.

It rang while Brian dozed in a lounge chair at the foot of Nina's hospital bed.

"Brian, buddy, it's Massimo. Isabella and I made our way back to the boat last night and got up a short time ago. The captain says we need to leave as soon as you return. Things got a little crazy at the party last night and Isabella and I left early. Where are you?"

"My friend, you missed a lot by leaving early. Paolo's dead. Two agents who met us at the house are dead. three other people died, and I'm at the hospital with Nina."

"My God! What happened, Brian?"

"Paolo lost control and started shooting people left and right. He cornered Nina and almost killed her. I ended up shooting him. She was injured when a piece of glass slashed her thigh. She needed surgery overnight. She should be okay, but it'll be two days before she can travel. Her leg needs to remain elevated. I'm hoping to meet my mother this morning, and I'll stay with her at least 'til Nina can leave the hospital. We had planned to head back to your place for a few days, but now we'll probably fly straight to Amsterdam."

"I can't believe all that happened after we left. I'm sorry we left you like that."

"No worries. Thanks again for all your help, Massimo. You're a special friend. We can't let time go by like this again. Let's agree to stay in touch."

"Brian, I must tell you about last night. Paolo grabbed me late in the evening and wanted me to pilot his yacht. He had a gun. I pulled myself away from him and ran to the middle of the tent. I didn't see you, so I grabbed Isabella, got a cab, and came back to the boat. I felt bad leaving then; now I feel absolutely awful. Well, my friend, I'm glad to hear you are okay and Nina will be okay.

"On an interesting note, my boat ride back to Siracusa today will be more interesting than I ever imagined. Isabella and I had a wild time in bed last night!"

Brian's eyes felt like they were going to pop out of his head. "Well, hey, good luck with your new lifestyle, Massimo. Isabella seems like the type who can keep you on your toes and make you a happy guy. I'll try to make it back to your place soon. Maybe you'd be willing to sell me one of Argyle's paintings. Goodbye, my friend. God bless."

At 11 AM, Nina finally woke. Her leg felt sore and uncomfortable.

"Good morning! The doctor was in a while ago to check on you. He used dissolving stitches; they'll make your leg a little uncomfortable for a few days. But you were really lucky, Nina; another half inch and you could have bled to death. You'll need a couple of days to rest with your leg up."

"Thank you for your quick thinking last night, Brian. You saved my life. I was so scared! I can't believe Paolo shot the doctor while he was right next to me. I thought I was going to die next."

"Do you recall the ambulance ride to the hospital?"

She shook her head. "No."

"Do you remember what you asked me?"

"No. Should I?"

Brian smiled. "I'll tell you later. Right now, knowing you're okay, I'm headed to see Katrina. A policemen dropped off our clothing bags from the boat this morning. Yours is over there in the corner on the floor."

Nina's latest dose of IV pain medicine had begun working. She vaguely heard what he said but closed her eyes and nodded off again. Brian kissed her cheek, checked with the nurse and left.

CHAPTER FIFTY-ONE

Visiting Katrina

Outside the hospital, Brian hailed a cab and gave the cabbie the villa's address. His thoughts were completely focused on seeing Katrina. His mind flashed back to seeing the lady with the deep blue eyes during her visit to Astoria when he was a child. He remembered how striking she looked, and how seeing her somehow stirred him inside.

Upon arriving at the villa, workmen were taking down the tent. Others removed tables, chairs, and the staging used by the band. Several police cars remained on the scene. Yellow crime-scene tape surrounded the locations where the bodies were found, including the nurse's body under the bushes on the side of Katrina's neighbor's house. Brian saw the police chief he'd met last night. Then he saw the two other Interpol agents, Donna Padula and Corina Varrichio. Both were struggling to remain awake on little sleep. Corina approached and greeted him.

"Agent O'Sullivan, we didn't meet formally last night. My name is Agent Varrichio. Let me brief you on the status. Everything here is under control. Pieter Van Deusen is flying here today to inspect the site and accompany Wilhelm's body to Amsterdam this evening. Early this morning, someone found two dead bodies not far from here while walking their dogs. They turned out to be Stefano and Dominic Luciano. The police recovered a cell phone near one of the bodies. A voice message left on the phone said, 'Stefano, I'm so sorry but something went wrong, and I couldn't complete the money transfer. I'll try again but it's like the system is locked up. I'll try again in the morning.'

"Several Interpol agents were sent to the Luciano family bank first thing this morning. They identified Maria Luciano, a sister of one of the two men, as a bank officer and took her into custody. She asked for a deal of some kind, then directed agents to a hidden attic in the wing of her cousin Dominic's house. Agents found an old artist living in a well-lighted room. It was essentially a full apartment and art studio. They found over a hundred paintings. Some were hung on walls, others propped on easels. Some were rolled up in muslin cloth. Maria said the two paintings just recovered in Spain at the Mezquita would be among them. The old artist, Agostino, in his eighties, pointed to two rolled-up canvasses, saying Dominic had just dropped them off early yesterday morning. He told the agents not to unroll the paintings until they were properly prepared. Whatever that means.

"As part of her plea deal, Maria explained to the agents that her brother and cousin would buy valuable paintings recovered by their cousin, Paolo Luzzi-Luciano, and have Agostino make copies. Then they would donate the copies while taking the tax write-off for the donation. They accumulated dozens of genuine paintings, worth hundreds of millions of dollars. Maria said Paolo never knew copies were being made. She added the Vatican's collection has at least nineteen copies painted by old Agostino. She also said this was a practice begun many years ago by her father, Stefano, Sr., and her uncle, Dominic, Sr.

"As a result of what has happened with Paolo, Dominic, Stefano, and Maria Luciano, the case of the missing paintings stolen by the Gestapo and hidden by KvR is now closed. Now we have enough evidence to go after Klaus Mueller, who – together with Paolo and Antonio – stole paintings for many years as part of a grand scheme. We've also been on the phone this morning with Kristofer Bronn. We've told him of our success here, and that we have a half dozen agents headed to Klaus Mueller's home. Kristofer is thrilled with the outcome of the operation. We told him you were at the hospital with Agent von Scholz. He sends his sincere regards and congratulations for your outstanding work as an Interpol agent, and says he'll be in touch with you later today."

"Terrific work, Agent Varrichio. You and the Agent Padula should go get some sleep now. I'll be here at the house for the next few days."

"Agent O'Sullivan, there are two more things."

"What's that?"

"First, an Interpol informant, Gianni Giordano, was found dead during the police department sweep of this property early this morning. His body was found in the backyard. The coroner has already determined he was shot with the same caliber round found in the other bodies. When we began our investigation, we contacted the police in Naples and asked about the man who sold the yacht to Paolo. The police knew who Gianni was. We leveraged him and used him in our setup. That enabled us to introduce agents Vittorio Petrullo and Tony Massa as the captain and first mate to pilot the new yacht here from Naples. Gianni's role supporting Interpol's sting efforts in this case would lessen or possibly eliminate his last sentence. Agent Donna Padula and I posed as Vittorio and Tony's girlfriends, but we were also to be hired on as cleaning women on the new yacht."

Brian nodded. "Vittorio told us some of this last night, but not about Gianni Giordano."

"The second thing I must tell you is your wife was released from the local jail in Amsterdam late last night."

"Yes, she called just as I was heading to the hospital with Agent von Scholz."

"I've also been told to inform you a decision was made to accept your paperwork to retire from Interpol. It is effective June eighteenth, less than ninety days from now. Since your retirement is officially approved, and you'll have no more cases to work on, HR has decided to share the news of your retirement from Interpol with your wife. The wire taps revealed the excessive stress she's been under, and they were hoping to alleviate some of her anxiety. Unfortunately, she'd already left. The next-door neighbor came over and said she had left early for the airport."

Brian frowned and rubbed his forehead. "I see. Well, okay. Now what can you tell me about Katrina? Is she back here at this house or is she still down the street?"

"She was moved back here an hour ago. The chief of police was helpful once he understood the circumstances of her health. She is awake and she's saying she's 'waiting for her son's arrival, since it's his birthday.' We think she's confused. Aren't you her son?"

"Yes, I'm her son but it's complicated. Does she know what went on here last night?"

"She knows it was Paolo's sixty-fifth birthday, but we don't think she knows about the party, or the murders, or that you're here. The police chief sent for a cardiologist earlier after learning she had suffered a mild stroke the other day. He was with her for an hour. He just left. He said she's doing well, and he'll be back tonight. A nurse is with her now. She's the regular nurse who is here all the time, but she wasn't here yesterday."

"Thank you. That was all very thorough. Now go get Agent Padula, head inside and find a place to sleep."

"Yes, Agent O'Sullivan. Thank you."

Brian strode toward the door of the house, suddenly anxious. *Dear God... how do I greet her? What do I say?*

CHAPTER FIFTY-TWO

Grace Heads Home

Determined to catch the first morning flight back to Newark, Grace had her suitcase packed before 7. She was waiting outside the apartment for a car to Schiphol Airport when Solie saw her.

"Grace, I just got a call from someone who knows Brian and Erick. They told me you got back late last night. What happened? Where'd you go? How are you?"

"Well, I'm sure as hell not happy. I was in jail! Then they said it was all a big mistake. I can't wait to get out of here and go home. Brian and I are through. I've had it with him, and I've decided to leave him."

"Oh my! I'm so sorry to hear that. When I got a call telling me you were here, I was also told someone from Interpol would be coming to see you. Have they called yet?"

"Interpol? Why Interpol?"

"Uh, yes. Maybe they'll tell you when they get here."

"I already shut my ringer off and I'm not taking calls from anyone. I'm fed up with all of this and I'm going home. My coming here in the first place was a huge waste of my time."

"Grace, Erick once shared something with me I haven't told you in our conversations, but it might be time for you to know."

"What's that?"

"Erick and your husband have known each other twenty years and been partners just over ten years."

"Oh my God! My husband's gay? How did I miss that? That *really* does it for us."

"No, no! Well, Erick is gay, but not Brian. They're Interpol agents. Your husband and Erick are assigned to an elite group in Interpol who search for and recover lost art."

"Well. Brian's never said anything about that to me. So, this Erick guy is feeding you a bunch of garbage. Maybe he wants to look important to you. I need to catch a flight, Solie. You've been so nice, but everything else here has been crazy. The car's pulling up. I need to run."

"Before you leave, Grace, let me show you this. Here's my badge."

"Oh, good God, you're with the C. . ."

"Yes. I'm stationed here in Amsterdam. I report to a place near Washington, D.C. Your husband's role in Interpol is legitimate and he is excellent at his profession."

"Well, he's managed to keep it a secret from me all these years."

"As he has been required to. Let me give you a bit of advice. You'd do well to wait for the person from Interpol to arrive and listen to what they have to say."

The horn honked, and the cab driver got out.

"I really must leave, Solie. This is all unbelievable. I'm guessing you must be one of the women he's been with. How do I know that badge is real? Maybe you're in on this stunt. I don't know what to believe anymore."

Grace huffed and grumbled as she moved her two oversized suitcases. The cheerful driver helped her with the luggage, loading everything in the trunk.

Unfortunately for the cabbie, he got an earful on the way to the airport. Grace told him how dangerous it was walking through Vondelpark and around Amsterdam because of the bicycle traffic. He smiled and nodded, agreeing with everything she complained about.

On the flight back to Newark, Grace thought about what Solie had said about Brian's being an agent. It was hard to believe. Then she thought about what her life would be like without him. Her thoughts flipped back and forth between pros and cons. But she needed a third column to list all the complaints and annoyances of their life together.

I've had enough of him. He gets in my way and it's annoying. I don't like it when he just sits and reads all day. I hate when he's in the basement, tinkering. But it lets me do my own thing and shop with my friends. I've told him to retire, but if he does, he'll just go golfing all the time to get out of the house and away from me. I want the freedom to decide what I want to do at any time, on any given day, but when he wakes up, he always wants an itinerary for the day, listed hour by hour. He's so ridiculous.

I'm fed up with his crazy interest in World War II, the Nazis, and all the art stuff. But his interest lets me watch my own TV shows on our other set. We truly live separate lives and can go for hours – even days – not seeing each other inside our own house. Our house is too big, but maybe it's good it's so big, so I don't have to be bothered by him. There's nothing left—no emotion, no warmth, no comforting sex. That fire died out years ago. Our marriage is just a pile of ashes now. It's clear I can do without him.

She imagined the process of visiting the lawyer and demanding what she believed would rightfully be hers. She knew the exact amount in Brian's 401k, and her own work over the years had contributed to their nest egg. She absolutely wanted half of his, and to keep her own. Then she thought about the house, believing it should be hers as well.

What's this big secret? What's he been hiding? Is it a woman? He's over in Europe so much. But my own secret—dear God, it's bothered me for years. I never told Brian. How could I? Nor did I tell him all the fertility doctors I visited, without his knowledge, agreed why I couldn't conceive. Maybe if we'd been able to have children, we'd have more in common with each other, like his sisters and their husbands. The last doctor said my inability to have children is likely why I'm so depressed. But I can never share my secret with him. God, I'm feeling so old. Everything is exhausting.

An hour into the flight, Grace ordered a glass of wine, then another, and then a third. Her thoughts drifted back to sophomore year of college, several years before she met Brian. Her first semester at St. John's University had ended and she went home to Bay Ridge. A girlfriend called to say her friend's parents were looking at property in Naples, Florida, and she was having a party. She was told Collin might show. Word about the party spread like wildfire and before long, a hundred friends had crowded into the house. Everyone was drinking heavily, and all the bedrooms quickly became occupied.

After Grace's old boyfriend arrived, it was less than an hour before she and Collin took their turn in an empty bedroom. In their brief time together in bed he became aggressive—beyond her expectations. But it was Collin. And too intoxicated to care, neither considered protection. Eleven weeks passed when Grace visited a private clinic without her parents' knowledge. But the abortion didn't go as expected. Damage to her insides affected her physically and emotionally, and she missed the last few weeks of the spring semester. She had no way of knowing at the time that one wild, carefree night would have such heartbreaking repercussions and even prevent her from ever conceiving or being able to carrying a fetus to full term in her scarred uterus.

A few years later, she and Brian met at McSorley's and married soon afterward. A dozen years into their marriage, Grace realized her efforts to get pregnant in the prior six years were futile. Several *in vitro* procedures, attempted at great cost, failed. Their hopes of having children and a robust family life were shattered. Crushed by sadness, she chose to not tell Brian of her botched abortion before their marriage.

Then as the years passed, she feared telling Brian the truth would destroy their marriage. But what she didn't expect was her growing depression, the ongoing guilt, and eventually erratic mood swings. Over the last fifteen years her relationship with Brian had diminished and now it had reached its end. Grace suffered greatly for her mistake, and she had never forgiven herself for her carelessness. It became a shroud of regret laid over her marriage.

CHAPTER FIFTY-THREE

Brian Meets Katrina

Brian knocked on the door and was greeted by the nurse who regularly took care of Katrina.

"*Buon giorno, signora.* Is Katrina awake?"

"*Si.*"

The young nurse then tried her best to speak English. "The room with the sunshine. She waits for her son."

"*Grazie.*"

"Uh… uh… and you, who are you?"

"*Io sono,* Brian. *Il figlio di Katrina.* The son who she sent away to be adopted."

"*Ah! Gesu Christo!* I know of you! *Uno momento,* uh, one minute please."

Then, running down the hallway, she shouted "*Lui e' qui!* He is here!" before disappearing into the spacious sunroom.

Brian waited several minutes, then slowly approached the door at the end of the hallway from which he heard pleasant music. At the doorway, he looked inside and smiled. The room was much larger than he expected. Short palms trees, hanging vines and tall plants dominated one end of an atrium-like enclosure. Colorful flowering plants, large leaf philodendron and showy orchids surrounded the perimeter. Small colorful birds cheerfully chirped and moved about freely in an atrium cage fifteen feet high. In front were tall floor-to-ceiling windows.

Katrina sat in a chair facing the ocean. Her long, salt-and-pepper hair was brushed back and held in place with two ornate cloisonné hair clips. Her TIA stroke had only affected her right arm.

She turned and looked up as Brian approached. "Is that you? Brian, is it really you?"

"Yes."

Both immediately teared up.

"Oh, dear Lord. Thank you for having him finally come to visit me. I've been so sad, for so many years. You need to know how sorry I am for what I did. Giving you up as a baby is the biggest mistake of my entire life. Forgive me. Please forgive me, my precious son."

He went to her chair, knelt on one knee, then hugged and kissed her. "What happened is in the past. Today is our present and today is our gift."

"Oh, my dear son. I can't believe you're here with me. Oh my God, how I've missed you."

After a bout of tears and sniffling, they wiped their eyes and for the first time looked more closely at each other. Brian felt overwhelmed by her deep-blue eyes, her lovely face and her creamy complexion.

Katrina was startled. She had remembered baby Bruno, but now she looked at a grown man. She quietly studied his features and good looks. "Brian, you are quite handsome. You look exactly like my father, Dino Amorino."

"I'm so sorry for not visiting you sooner. Sheila died two weeks ago. After her burial, my sisters and I were going through her hope chest. We found an old German Bible and a mandolin. Inside the Bible were the letters you wrote revealing I was adopted. Neither my three sisters nor I ever knew. We opened the letters and read them. I can't begin to imagine how difficult your life in Germany was. And then your life in the convent. I read how you and Luca met and fell in love. I'm so glad you had such a wonderful life partner."

"Luca left me much too soon. I miss him so. He understood my deep sorrow for my hasty decision to have sent you away. Luca's kind words were my only comfort. Later my attempt to raise the son of a childhood friend became a sad burden for us. It placed unnecessary strain on Luca – which he didn't deserve. It was my fault again. I believe the stress of the business and his conflict with our adopted son broke his heart. Do you know about Paolo? He should be coming here for his birthday."

"Yes. We met under a strange coincidence, but it's a long story and not for right now."

"Brian, please tell me you're happily married and have lots of children."

Her words cut him deeply. He shook his head. "We never had children. We tried for years, but my wife was never able to get pregnant. I often suggested adoption, but she was never open to the idea. As you know, adoption or fostering a child isn't easy. But on a positive note, Joe and Sheila, who raised me, were wonderful parents. They loved me no differently than my three sisters."

"I remember my brief visit to your home just before Easter in 1951. You were headed to a Cub Scout meeting with a small wooden car in your hand. Your twin sisters were also running off to a meeting after school. Your mother had an infant staying nearby at her mother's house.

"Brian, I don't know how to express my apologies to you. I was so self-centered at the time. It was all about me. I was driven, competitive, and impulsive. My work as a nurse and my career were paramount. My first mistake was wanting to go to live with Karl in Germany. I foolishly ignored my father's warning about Germany's going to war. My second mistake was to not return to Italy right away. He'd just left for the army and SS Officer training. I had no idea what that was, but when he didn't return right away, my gut told me something was wrong. Still, my ego and my competitive nature made me believe I was better than the other nurses at the hospital in Friedrichshafen. The administrator, a gentleman named Kirk von Scholz, took me under his wing and I became the nursing administrator and made very good money. I was also helping Karl's mother but then I watched Valentina's life with her husband, Otto, become a mess.

"It was a terrible time in Germany and Italy. I naïvely hoped Karl would return home after a short while and we'd have a happy life. But the Nazis were barbaric, their actions horrific. Hitler, Himmler, and Goebbels corrupted the souls of so many German men. Just imagine the right wing Nazi propaganda turning all those good Lutheran and Catholic men into monsters who would commit acts of genocide against Jews and others. The atrocities we began hearing were unthinkable and unbearable, and Karl was in it deeply as an SS officer.

"My third mistake was giving you up for adoption. We needed to leave Germany and I didn't know how I'd provide for you when I returned home to Lecco. I gave you up to the Church and left home yet again. It was too hasty a decision.

"My next mistake was thinking life in a convent could erase my sins. But my time cloistered in solitude and prayer only made me focus more on my mistakes. I was still crushed by the thought of my baby not being with me. Then I was blessed with Luca coming into my life. He helped me through my worst days. He was kind and understood me. We fell in love. We tried to have children, but it never happened again for me. Then, he had some promising ideas. He worked hard and was blessed with success.

"Brian, did you understand the code I left for you in one of my letters?"

"I read your letters over and over, and I knew it had to mean something, but I couldn't figure out what. A bright young woman I work with unraveled your code. Just days ago in Rome, I found the safe-deposit box at the Luciano family bank. Its contents are amazing!"

"And did you follow up with Giuseppe Fellini? He's such a beautiful man."

"Yes. After I researched the Luciano Wine Exporting Company and learned about Luca's business, I saw Luca's will on the attorney's stationery in the safe-deposit box. I called and spoke with Giuseppe on the telephone. I worked in person with his son, Fausto. Giuseppe sends his love. He also wanted me to bring you a red rose. He says he misses you and regrets he is too old to travel to see you. He has taken care of several legal matters for me in the past few days. Mother, you and Luca have been so generous to me. I don't know how to thank you."

"Oh, my dear son, it's the least we could do."

"My plan is to stay here with you for a few days. The young associate who unraveled the code was injured yesterday and is recovering in the hospital. I'll introduce you when she's released. Then I'll head back to Amsterdam to finish some business and return home to the United States."

"That's a good plan. But you didn't answer my question about being happily married."

"We were happily married for many years, but in the last decade, my wife has become very depressed. I believe she remains upset we could never have children. She enjoyed our nieces and nephews as they grew up, but was unable to conceive, and her emotions changed. Eventually her patience with my sisters' children disappeared. It seems her patience for me has disappeared as well.

"My work at a university was intense as a department chair. I traveled to Europe twice a year. Then my overseas trips became more frequent. I was recruited by Interpol and was busy all the time. She felt neglected."

Katrina nodded her understanding. "She needs more time with you. Isn't that Interpol thing the same as Paolo's work?"

"Yes."

"Where is Paolo? The party for his birthday... is it tomorrow? He should be here soon."

Before he could answer, the nurse came into the room. "*Signore* Brian, there are people here to see you."

"Me?"

"Yes. The people are from Interpol."

"Excuse me, Mother. I need to step outside."

CHAPTER FIFTY-FOUR

Van Deusen Arrives

The young nurse pointed to the hallway. Brian got up and kissed his mother. The nurse fluffed up Katrina's pillow for her nap and followed Brian to the foyer. Waiting there were Pieter Van Deusen, Wilhelm's superior, and the two female agents. Apparently, Van Deusen had come to review the murders and accompany Wilhelm's body back to Amsterdam.

"Agent O'Sullivan, I'm glad to see you are still with us. Last night was a horrific evening, leaving too many dead. We needlessly lost the doctor and nurse assigned to the case. Vittorio Petrullo leaves a young wife pregnant with their first child. Tony Massa leaves behind a wife and three teenagers. The young waiter died for no other reason than Paolo's carelessness.

"And the Luciano cousins, Dominic and Stefano, led lives of deception and crime. Stefano's sister, Maria, is in custody, although she's guided us to a treasure trove of stolen art. I've already visited the morgue, where they're readying Wilhelm's body for my return flight to Schiphol. Paolo's childhood friend, Gianni Giordano, was found dead this morning. We suspect Paolo shot him after discovering Vittorio and Tony were agents and he felt betrayed.

"Two other people must be accounted for. First is your partner, Erick Schmidt. We believe he was shot and killed in or near Seville, but we haven't recovered his body. He remains missing. I'm sorry for your team's loss. He was a good man and a good partner to you. Second is Nina von Scholz, whom I understand is recovering from a severe leg injury. She is an excellent researcher and will be promoted for her role in supporting your and Erick's efforts to break up this ring of thieves. And Brian, I understand you not only found your birth mother in all of this—but I've also received word on my way here you are now a wealthy man and will soon retire from Interpol.

"Now, that said, I learned some disturbing news on the way here. With the evidence we gathered during this case, the extensive internal wiretapping we put in place, and Kristofer Bronn's reports from years ago, we've been able to piece together a complete case with enough evidence to arrest and convict Klaus Mueller. Regrettably, although he was under surveillance, Klaus wasn't at his home in Mallorca late yesterday when we went to pick him up."

"Do you know where he might be? Or how he got away?"

"The agents who entered his home discovered a trap door in the basement that opens into a tunnel leading away from the house. He somehow got wind we'd be taking him down and escaped. We recognize this case is not yet over and has one more important piece to be resolved, which is Klaus Mueller's capture and imprisonment.

"Like you, Brian, Klaus is an agile seventy-one-year-old. The agents who surveilled him say he's active and in reasonable shape, bicycling daily on the roads near his house. Of concern now is Mueller's long history of vengefulness. He will go to great lengths to get even with those who cross him, or those who he believes have harmed him or his family. We now know Klaus and Paolo had a good relationship for years—perhaps he considered Paolo like a younger brother or even a son. From our profiles of Paolo, we know he found taking risks fun, and Klaus took full advantage of his inclination to do so.

"Now, with Paolo and Wilhelm dead, Klaus is likely to look at you as the root cause of his little empire's fall. And of course, we can't overlook the issue of Wilhelm's sending you three million dollars for information to retrieve the paintings at the bank. Our initial research at headquarters shows the money Wilhelm wired you came from his father's account. So, Brian, I'm reminding you you're still an Interpol agent and Klaus, or someone he pays will come looking for you.

Brian took it all in, then asked an obvious question.

"Tell me again where Klaus Mueller lives."

"He's living in a house in Mallorca in a small community called El Tore, on *Avinguda de la Mar*, southwest of Palma. Like this house, the back of Mueller's place overlooks the Mediterranean. Its hillside position makes a backdoor tunnel very convenient. We're not exactly sure when he might have left the house, or even if he's left the island.

"Finally, from the wiretaps, we sent one of our teams to Málaga to pick up a fellow called Juan De León—whom we know killed Antonio in a car blast. But he's missing too. Intel obtained from the wiretaps of conversations between Wilhelm and Juan revealed Klaus' long friendship with Juan's father, Carlos. Juan picked up where Carlos left off, as the fixer for the Muellers' various crimes. Our immediate guess is Klaus and Juan may be on their way here and ... "

The doorbell rang. The nurse, listening to Pieter's recap, responded and went hurried to answer it. A moment later, her footsteps stopped outside.

"*Buon giorno, signora. Brian O'Sullivan e' qui?*"

"*Uno momento.*"

The nurse walked to the room off the foyer where Brian and Pieter and the other two agents were meeting. She apologized for interrupting and awkwardly tried to explain that a young woman on crutches was outside asking for Brian.

Suddenly understanding the meaning of her gesture to show crutches, Brian ran to the front door and found Nina standing just inside the threshold.

"My God, Nina! What in heaven's name are you doing here? Here, let me help you. We have an important guest inside. But before I take you in, why are you here? The doctor told me only early this morning that you needed two days of bedrest before you could leave the hospital."

"I know. The nurses at the hospital all heard about the big party last night and were surprised to learn I was there. I showed them my badge and convinced them I was needed back here. I also told a little lie, saying I'd return to the hospital later. But I'm hoping I can recover here with you. Do you mind?"

"Well, maybe," he replied with a grin, "but first, let's go inside and get you seated with your leg up."

Inside, Pieter and the other agents greeted Nina warmly, and asked how she was.

"I need to limit my movements and rest with my leg up for the next few days. The doctor said Brian's quick action, using his belt as a tourniquet, saved my life."

"You've arrived at an interesting point in our conversation," Brian told her. "Pieter was just relating some disturbing information." He explained about Klaus and Juan De León. Pieter then added a few more disturbing facts about Klaus.

"Oh my God, Brian! I thought this was over, but now it looks like Pieter has presented another few chapters for us to deal with. So, besides seeing your mother this morning after seventy-plus years, you must now deal with two more assassins. And, oh yeah, everything going on back in New Jersey."

Brian grimaced. "I can't think about anything Stateside 'til I know those two are in custody and you and I are safe. Pieter and the two agents were just about finished before you arrived. They'll be leaving shortly."

"Well, Pieter, what are you going to do, now that you know they might be coming after Brian?"

Van Deusen shook his head. "Nothing else, Nina. Once we're finished here, we head back to the airport."

Brian turned to Pieter. "So, based on our conversation, two new agents will arrive late today to replace agents Varrichio and Padula, and they'll stay here overnight. Is that right?"

He nodded. "They'll be here at five PM, and two more will arrive in the morning. By tomorrow, this place will be surrounded. The first two agents will be in hiding; the other two are snipers equipped with night scopes. We hope to lure both men into the open and trap them here."

"And you want me to stay and wait for them. In other words, I'm the bait?"

"As we see it, that's the only way we can lure them out into the open."

"Brian, I'll stay and recover here, so you can count on my help, too."

"Well, Pieter, remember Nina and I are art experts, not marksmen. Our jobs have been investigative. We're not experienced at bringing down gun-carrying killers."

"Brian, you both were trained in the use of handguns, and it's your sworn duty now to help us finish this case."

Nina turned to Brian. "Looks like we need to hunker down and make a plan that makes us feel safe – and protects your mother."

"Nina, I think you should return to the hospital."

"No. I'm staying here."

Brian turned to Pieter.

"Well, I must admit your plan to use us as bait makes me nervous. Frankly, Pieter, with Paolo's longstanding connections in the local police here in Malta, I'd guess one or more of them are within reach of Klaus Mueller's influence."

"Good point, Brian. You'll need to prepare for what happens next. We need to leave. Nina, congratulations on your work to retrieve the art, and my best to you for a speedy recovery. Make sure you keep that leg up. Good day."

They watched Pieter and the others leave. Then Brian helped Nina negotiate her way down the hallway to the atrium, to meet his mother. When they got there, they found her sleeping.

Brian suggested they go to a nearby room where Nina could rest on a couch and get her leg up again.

As she sat, Brian leaned to give her a kiss. "Nina, I'm so glad you're okay. I was really upset last night when I saw you were hurt." He paused. "We have a lot to talk about."

Nina gave him a weary smile. "I know. I've been thinking about a lot since last night. But I'm tired and need to close my eyes now for a bit."

CHAPTER FIFTY-FIVE

Later That Afternoon

Nina fell asleep quickly—evidence she needed the rest after her injury. Meanwhile Brian returned to the atrium and spent an hour with Katrina, reminiscing about his childhood in Astoria and Staten Island and reviewing for her his educational and business experiences. She cried often. She was so proud of him.

"Brian, maybe giving you up for adoption was the right thing. I haven't told you this, but after I left the convent and returned with Luca to my parents' apartment in Lecco, I learned the building where my dad had his bakery was firebombed by Nazis. I'd worked with him in the bakery's kitchen a few nights, making dough for bread and pastries while you slept in a tiny bassinette nearby. Had I stayed and continued bringing you to work with me, we both might have died with him. I can only hope in God's infinite knowledge and mercy, He took us away from that terrible moment."

"Mother, what's important is we're together. I need to head inside to check on my associate. She left the hospital and she'll be recuperating here a few nights. I found a room in the back where she can stay. She's been napping there the last... gosh, it's been almost two hours. Close your eyes and rest. I'll be back in thirty minutes. I'll fluff the pillow before I leave, like the nurse does for you."

She patted his hand. "Thank you, Brian. You are a very sweet and kind man."

As he walked away, Katrina murmured, "Where's my nurse? And where is Paolo? Isn't it his birthday tomorrow? He said he'd come see me."

Brian headed to the room across from the atrium.

Nina was just waking. "Are the other two agents here yet?"

"No. It's just four. I haven't heard the doorbell yet and besides, if they were here, they'd surely have announced themselves to us."

"We need to plan how to defend ourselves tonight if Klaus and the other one come looking for you."

"Yes, we also have a few things we need to discuss. But those should wait until this case is resolved."

"I'm willing to wait," she assured him. "Well… no. I need to get this out in the open with you. I'll get right to the point. I've fallen in love with you. I know you're older and I know you're married. But I've fallen for you for so many different reasons. You're such a wonderful man. I just want to be with you all the time. I don't know how else to explain it."

"Nina, I get it. You're bright, fun, warm, and loving. You've reawakened my heart and rekindled my deepest emotions. Spending time with you is comfortable, and our conversations are always in sync, whether we are working or relaxing. We listen to each other and, most importantly, process what we hear before replying. You're incredibly positive and refreshing. You're a terrific and energetic lover, and I've thoroughly enjoyed our time together. So please know I've got strong, heartfelt feelings for you, as well.

"But here's my problem. Over the last dozen years, and especially in the last three, life with Grace has been a struggle. She's on new medication for depression. In the beginning, when she first showed signs of being depressed, the meds the doctor prescribed helped. But over time, and despite increased dosages and trying several new types of drugs, her depression has grown worse. I've tried many times to be upbeat and suggest we go places or do things—all to try to have fun together. For example, we used to visit my sisters and go places with them and their children, but all that has stopped. She no longer wanted to be around the family, and she'd tell me she found the youngsters 'annoying.'

"It's become a tough predicament. She's angry at me for not being home more, but she stays alone and acts indifferent to my presence when I *am* there. It's as if she's already checked out of our marriage. There's nothing happening between us. Her fiery nature, which used to make her lots of fun, has been extinguished—except for when she has something to complain about—which seems to be all the time lately. It makes me sad and it's why I enjoy my time in Europe. The camaraderie with you and Erick has been a huge lift to my spirits. And Nina, I've fallen in love with you, as well.

"But Grace and I are married, and I feel obliged to go back to New Jersey. I need to spend more time with her and dig deeper, with the hope of helping her resolve her depression. For years, I've felt something must be at its core."

Nina was about to respond when something caught her attention. She cocked her head to listen more closely.

"Brian, did you hear that?"

"No."

"It sounded like a door opening. What time did Pieter say the agents are coming?"

"At five."

"Oh God, there it is again. Brian, where's the gun I gave you?"

"It's inside."

She groaned. "Mine is in my bag on the porch, where the cab driver dropped it."

This time Brian heard the noise.

"Stay here, I'll be right back. Maybe it's just the nurse or the house-keeper at the back door."

He headed to another room where his bag was. The handgun was buried under his shaving kit and clothing. He reached for the pistol, wondering for the first time whether a small-caliber bullet would stop a large person coming at him. He grabbed the gun and the extra magazine, silently praying the next set of agents would arrive sooner than scheduled.

As he returned, Nina was moving her leg off the couch. He sat next to her and ensured the magazine was loaded.

"I need my gun, too. It's in the bottom of the bag outside. Please hurry."

He found the gun where she said it would be. He handed it to her and said, "My mother's been inside the atrium. Let me check on her."

Brian left the room and headed to the atrium. Katrina was gone. He went back to the hallway to find the nurse, hoping she was returning Katrina to her bedroom in the other wing of the house. He heard what sounded like murmuring. He reached a point in the hallway where the voices echoed off the tile floor and archway. Crouching, he peeked around the corner.

The nurse held the handles of Katrina's wheelchair. Two men stood beside her. He assumed the older, grey-haired man was Klaus, and the taller, muscular bald one was the "fixer" called Juan. The two followed the nurse and Katrina into what he guessed was Katrina's bedroom.

He returned to Nina. "They're here!"

"Oh good. I'm relieved."

"No! Not the Interpol agents. It's Klaus and his fixer. We need to get to the atrium. I think it's our safest place to hide."

He helped Nina up and they moved about ten feet across the hallway to the atrium.

"Look, over there. We need to position ourselves among the trees and get down on the ground among all the greenery."

"Oh my God, Brian, my leg hurts."

"Shh! Give me your crutches. I'll put them on the floor behind everything. Now get down on the floor. Lie flat and be still. I'll place these leafy philodendrons in front of you."

She did as Brian suggested.

"Good. You're hidden. I'll stay down here and pull a few of these taller broad-leaf plants around me. When they come in, I'll let them have it."

"Brian, my leg really hurts."

"Shh!"

Nina shut her eyes and grimaced as pain shot along her thigh.

Five feet away, Brian crouched, pointing his gun toward the doorway. His irregularly fast heartbeat, once diagnosed as atrial fibrillation, quickened. Suddenly feeling dizzy, he blinked as his vision grew faint and foggy. The room swirled and Brian passed out flat on the floor behind the plants, dropping his gun on the floor.

CHAPTER FIFTY-SIX

Two Intruders

Six feet away from Brian, Nina opened her eyes when she heard a noise. She watched in horror as Brian keeled over and collapsed to the floor – as if in slow motion.

Oh my God! What's wrong with him?

She did her best to stay hidden as she crept toward him. He was unconscious. She grabbed his gun, then heard conversation just outside the atrium room. It was getting closer. She could hear Katrina's nurse talking as she appeared at the doorway. "The two of them were just in the room over there across the hall. I have no idea where they went. Let's go in here, into the atrium."

Nina watched as the nurse stepped into the room. It seemed as if she was giving the two a guided tour.

Then a man spoke. "Wow! This room is huge! I'll stay here for a minute and check out the alcove over there. Klaus, go with the nurse to check the other rooms."

"You need to be quick," the nurse cautioned. "The Interpol boss said more agents would be here around five. You only have half an hour, or you'll have to come back in the dark."

"I hate the dark, Klaus. We're getting this done now."

Klaus and the nurse, Paolo's *puttana*, moved down the hallway, checking the other rooms, while Juan entered the atrium. He scanned the perimeter of the room and made his way along the flowering plants, admiring the assortment of colorful flowers. Afternoon sunlight glistened through the tall windows. He thought of the greenery surrounding his Málaga home as he took in the beautiful view of the ocean. He moved another few feet closer to the plantings. Catching a glimpse of something among the plants on the floor, he leaned in to take a closer look.

Smiling, he raised his gun. As he aimed, Nina pointed back and closed her eyes.

Suddenly a six-foot section of the atrium's glass wall shattered from the bullet and Juan collapsed to the floor, half on top of Nina, almost crushing her under his weight.

Nina trembled. It wasn't she who had taken the shot. Juan groaned in pain as he lay there beside her. He began to move. Nina felt his breath. She opened her eyes and came nose to nose with Juan, inches away. She felt his warm breath and saw blood flowing from his mouth. He struggled to move his arm and she saw him reach for his gun only inches from his hand.

Seeing the intruder was still alive, Nina had no choice. She shoved her handgun against his chest, shut her eyes, and pulled the trigger. Then she pulled it again.

She turned away from his face before opening her eyes. Brian still lay unconscious, his face buried in the green waxy leaves of the philodendron, and his body littered with shattered glass.

Unknown to Brian and Nina, two Interpol agents arrived early with a sniper. The two were now inside, searching for the other intruder while outside, the sniper reloaded his rifle. *One down, one to go.*

In a car less than a mile away, Interpol Senior Section Director Pieter Van Deusen turned and spoke to the local police chief sitting next to him. "As we suspected, Katrina's nurse is Paolo's occasional girlfriend. Yesterday, when we tried to move Katrina before the party, we noted her strong feelings toward Paolo, and she initially objected. Recognizing the issue, it forced us to consider moving Katrina further down the street. Then we arranged for the nurse to have the afternoon off by sending money with a forged note from Paolo, saying, 'Go buy something pretty this afternoon. I'll see you at midnight, after the party.' She's also why we positioned two extra agents early this morning while your officers were here. And in our open discussion with Agent O'Sullivan earlier, we spoke loudly, giving her the impression only two agents would be here at five. We could tell she was paying inordinately close attention to our conversation.

"Chief, it sounds like my agents have entered the house."

Inside, Klaus turned to Paolo's girlfriend. "Did you hear that? How do we get back to the atrium?"

"This way; follow me."

The two moved slowly down the hallway. From the doorway to the atrium, Klaus glanced in and saw the shattered glass and Juan's body on the floor.

"This isn't good. How do we get to Katrina's bedroom?"

"This way. Her room's on the left. I left her in here."

The two turned the corner and entered the room. Suddenly, Klaus found two agents pointing their weapons at him. He quickly grabbed the nurse, using her as a shield pulling her in front of him. He stuck the gun to her head and demanded to speak to Van Deusen.

The second sniper, peering in from the position outside, addressed Pieter. "Director, this is Sniper One. Mueller has a gun held on the nurse. I have a clear head shot."

"Sniper One, you are authorized to take the shot."

CHAPTER FIFTY-SEVEN

Crime Ring Ends

Nina still lay on the floor of the atrium with her leg in pain and emotionally distressed. Juan's dead body lay inches away, his eyes still open and staring at her. Five feet away, the man she loved was lay face down in a plant. She was crying, yet firmly holding and pointing her gun at the doorway, waiting for the other intruder.

Then she heard another shot. Unsure what was going on outside the room, she remained steadfast and waited. But now the gun was getting heavy. Her hand shook, and she was having a difficult time pointing.

Meanwhile, several rooms away, another agent made a call.

"Pieter, we're all set here. Both targets are down. We confirmed before the kill shots were taken that they were Mueller and De Leon. We have their accomplice, the nurse, in custody. Send the EMTs into the rear bedroom for the elderly woman. She's on the floor. She may have tried to get up and fallen, and her head is bleeding. Send more EMTs into the atrium for agents von Scholz and O'Sullivan. They're still on the floor in there, according to Sniper One."

Two agents with helmets, visors, tactical chest protection, and tactical short rifles entered the atrium. Nina immediately recognized them as agents by their arm bands. One of the two, a woman, came and knelt beside her. She asked if Nina was okay and shared what had happened in the other room. Nina pointed to Brian and asked if he was alive. Touching his neck, the agent detected a pulse. A moment later the second EMT team entered. They went right to Brian, who was just regaining consciousness. They lifted him onto a stretcher, put Nina on another stretcher and began moving them, leaving Juan's dead body for the local police.

The police car carrying the police chief and Van Deusen arrived out front as Brian and Nina were carried outside.

"Director, your people have kept us busy the last two days. We're normally a very peaceful community, and we abhor crime. I hope it's all over now."

"Chief, I assure you, this crime ring's days have just ended. The Muellers from their perch in the Netherlands and Mallorca, Luzzi and Gozzo from their locations in Naples and Malta, the Luciano family in Rome, and Juan De Leon from Málaga operated with impunity for thirty years. Now it's over. We'll be recognizing the bravery and outstanding efforts of several current agents and a former Interpol agent when I return to The Hague, namely Kristofer Bronn, Brian O'Sullivan, and Nina Von Scholz. And we will posthumously cite Erick Schmidt, Vittorio Petrullo, and Tony Massa for their roles in bringing these criminals to their just end. I'll be sending you a note of thanks, as well. Your personal assistance, and your department's help, in dealing with this operation has been commendable."

Brian and Nina arrived at the hospital in separate ambulances and were put into adjacent rooms. Feeling much better, Brian didn't want to be admitted, but the doctor said passing out wasn't normal and he needed to have bloodwork, an EKG, stress test and a coronary angiogram.

Hours later, after finally being returned to his room, he went to Nina's room. " How are you feeling?"

"I'm tired and my thigh is throbbing. but more importantly how are *you* feeling?" Tears welled in her eyes, and she put a hand to her chest. "My heart was crushed when I saw you fall face down on the floor in the atrium."

She started crying.

"Relax. I'm fine. An EKG showed I have something called 'atrial fibrillation.' My heart was beating too fast, and I passed out. That's all. They've given me some meds and I already feel much better. They'll keep me tonight for observation and release me in the morning."

"You've been under a lot of stress… but look at what you've accomplished."

"Nina, it's what *we've* accomplished. From what Pieter said, several dozen paintings once found and stolen a second time have turned up in the three Lucianos' homes. We have no one else to worry about in this investigation, and our search for the hidden paintings in KvR's diary is complete. This Nazi mystery and thirty-plus years of art capers are resolved. Our friend Kristofer Bronn must be delighted."

"Most importantly, Brian, your elderly mother is alive, you found her and visited with her. She needs your presence."

"I'll head back there and stay for a few days. We need to spend time together. Even though Paolo was trouble, his death will come as a shock to her. In one of my discussions with Katrina, she clearly remembers the past, but she's struggled a bit with her short-term memory. She might be suffering a bit from her stroke recent stroke."

"You'll stay here tonight with your leg up. Come around noon tomorrow to meet Katrina. I'd like you to stay there with me, but you must promise you'll rest. I'm going to call Grace now and fill her in on what's happened here – and let her know I'm planning to stay with Katrina."

As he left the room, Brian looked at his watch. It was just before 10 PM in Malta, so he tried calling Grace.

***

In New Jersey, the weather was dreary. It had been raining all day. Grace was early as she pulled up to the attorney's office for her 4 PM meeting. Her mind was made up. She'd diligently filled out all the preliminary papers and now was waiting patiently to go inside and introduce herself. As her watch struck the hour, she stepped from her late-model Evoque and headed inside. The assistant said the attorney would be ready to see her in a few minutes and offered her a cup of coffee. She accepted the offer.

As the assistant went for the coffee, her phone rang. She looked at the number. It was Brian. Her heart tugged at her emotions. Brian's handsome image flashed into her mind. Her finger pressed the button to answer the call just as the lawyer's office door opened.

"Mrs. O'Sullivan, hello! I'm Attorney Shaw. Please come in."

Grace immediately shut the flip phone and followed the attorney inside.

***

Brian momentarily thought his call to Grace had connected, but a moment later he heard silence, as if the call had dropped. *Odd for the call to drop like that. Let me try again.*

This time it went straight to voicemail. "We're sorry, but the voice mailbox of the person you are calling is full. Please try again later."

He decided to step outside to the hospital's rose garden courtyard. Last night's full moon was just beginning to wane, but it still cast his shadow on the sidewalk. He sat on a bench and reflected on the past week's events. It had been such an exhilarating—yet harrowing—time. A flood of emotions took him by surprise. *I need to stay with my mother a few more days. We've got so much catching up to do! But what about when I get home? What then? A good night sleep will help me decide what to do next about Grace... and Nina.*

CHAPTER FIFTY-EIGHT

Goodbyes

Brian was up early the next morning. He checked himself out of the hospital and arrived at Katrina's house by 8. He met the new nurse, who'd been recommended by the chief of police. He asked about his mother and was told she was still asleep in her bedroom. Brian asked if the facial injuries she'd suffered in her fall yesterday had been serious. The nurse said the bleeding from her fall was from superficial scratches and nothing was serious.

The weekly housekeeper had already arrived and made coffee. She also brought almond pastries. He was delighted to see them. He sat at the kitchen's island, plugged in his laptop, and enjoyed a pastry as he reviewed his emails from the past week. One caught him by surprise. It had been forwarded by Nina minutes earlier. The original email was a response from a woman in Leipzig, the one who'd sold Kristofer Bronn KvR's diary. Nina had emailed her shortly after Bronn had given her the woman's contact information.

Brian read the woman's responses to Nina's questions. Nina had sent several questions, this time blind copying Brian. Moments later, Nina forwarded another email response from the woman.

"Yes, I'd like to meet you at the antiques shop in Leipzig. Any time in the next two or three weeks is convenient."

Brian smiled. *She's always trying to solve a puzzle.*

Then he emailed Nina.

Nina, I was thinking last night. I feel I need to stay here at least a week with Katrina. I tried reaching Grace again last night without any luck. I'll try her again later, when it's morning in New Jersey. When my week is up, I'm heading back to New Jersey. I need to tell her about Interpol, apologize, and explain why I had to keep it a secret all these years. I'm also going to try one last time to learn the underlying cause of her depression. She'd told me she's planning to divorce me. I need to see where that goes. It's been a tough road with her the last dozen years. I just need to see what she's decided to do.

Just then, the nurse walked in. "*Signore* O'Sullivan, your mother is asking for you."

He jotted a last line — have to run. I'll see you here later. — then hit 'Send' and followed the nurse to Katrina's room.

Their conversation again focused on her life — it was a review of what he'd heard the day before. Eventually, Brian turned the conversation and gently revealed what had happened two nights earlier.

Having a sudden change of heart, he opened by saying Paolo had been a terrific Interpol agent for many years and had been involved in an important undercover position in a special operation to identify and capture a ring of art thieves. Without further explanation, Brian said the undercover role was intense and became quite dangerous. Paolo found himself in a difficult situation and was killed during a shootout with the thieves.

Looking at Brian, Katrina understood. Mothers know when their children are lying, and she knew Brian had whitewashed Paolo's criminal past. She'd suspected as much for many decades. But she loved that Brian covered Paolo's faults and corrupt past the way he did. She didn't want to say aloud she'd known for certain Paolo had murdered Luca. It pained her heart to recall the moment her darling husband had reached for her hand as he lay dying.

Mother and son talked for a short while, then Katrina asked to go to her room for her nap.

As Brian returned to his room, he checked his watch. 1:30.

His phone rang.

"Hi Brian. I'm feeling so much better today. I had a really good sleep."

"That's terrific, Nina!"

She sounded hesitant. "I've been thinking. I'm going to head back to Amsterdam today, on a five-o'clock flight. I've got a few things back there I need to look into."

"Really! I thought you wanted to meet Katrina and stay here a few days."

"I think your time with her should be just your time," she replied diplomatically.

"Okay. Are you still curious about the diary?"

"Yes, I'd like to meet Elsa, the woman who brought it in. If I get to meet her, I'll let you know."

Brian nodded. He was silent for a moment. "I was thinking about your apartment this morning. It's beautifully decorated, but it's so tiny. I recalled Erick mentioning his lease was coming up soon and the owner was putting the building up for sale. I'd like to buy the building as a gift to you. You can have the building all to yourself. And then you can decorate it any way you like. I'm sure it'll be gorgeous!"

"W-what?" she stammered in astonishment. "Brian, that's so nice of you! But it's an awful lot of money!"

"Ha! I couldn't spend all the money in my Swiss bank account in my lifetime, even if I tried!"

"You're such a sweet man. I accept! When I return to Amsterdam, I'll speak to a real-estate agent, do some research, and let you know what I find out."

"I won't see you again for a while, Nina. I'll be here with Katrina, then I'll head back home. I spoke with Pieter Van Deusen this morning. Given my pending retirement, there's no need for me to return to Amsterdam. We just need to trust that things will happen for the best."

"Oh, Brian, I'm going to miss you so terribly!"

"Just take care of yourself. I do plan to go see Massimo about acquiring some of his art, and I promise I'll come see you in Amsterdam, probably in ten to twelve weeks. Maybe you'll be in your new place by then."

"Brian, I love you. Please think of me."

"Nina, you know how I feel about you. But I have to work through everything with Grace."

As they hung up, Nina wondered if she'd ever see him again.

CHAPTER FIFTY-NINE

The Freedom Club

Grace woke feeling relieved. Her decision late yesterday to go ahead with the divorce was what she had come to believe was best for her. She sat at the kitchen table, drinking instant coffee with two sugars and looking over her calendar. She planned to meet four of her friends for lunch today to celebrate. All four were divorced. They'd been encouraging her these last few months to take the leap into being single once again—even before Brian made his latest trip. They openly joked with Grace about her joining them in what they called "The Freedom Club."

Grace finished her coffee, showered and was getting dressed when the phone rang.

"Grace, I'm so glad to finally reach you! I've finally found my birth mother, Katrina. I'm in Malta with her now. She's absolutely beautiful. Despite her age, hair is still almost black, and she has the most beautiful blue eyes. We've had several wonderful conversations. Her long-term memory is pristine, but she has issues with what happened a few days ago. I'm planning to stay here for a few days, then I'll fly home. I have so many things to tell you, Gracie! What's happened in the last ten days is unbelievable. I've even become a—"

"Brian, let me stop your enthusiasm right there. I filed for divorce yesterday. Don't bother coming back to the house. A local company is packing your clothes tomorrow and bringing all your belongings to your mother's house in Staten Island. When you come back, you can go and live where you grew up. Brian, I am through with you and your traveling. I'm through with your goddamn secret life in the art world with your secret gay partner Erick, and that woman Solie, his make-believe CIA girlfriend. Now, I've got a few things to get in order and I have lots of planning to do now that I don't have to worry about *you* any longer. Good-bye, Brian."

"Grace, hold on a second!"

Brian heard the click, and the line went dead.

He leaned against the wall and peered out the window. *I can't stay here a week. I need to get back there right away.*

He took a deep breath and let it out slowly. Then he went inside to see Katrina.

"Brian, it's so good to see you again. What happened here? They said I can't go into my lovely atrium because of a broken window. Who were those people with my nurse yesterday? I didn't like the looks of them. Where is my nurse? And where has Paolo been? His birthday is any day now."

Brian spent the rest of the afternoon with his birth mother. Then he explained he'd need to return home the next day. She understood.

"Is your wife okay? She must miss you. Are you happily married? How many children do you have? Some things are hard for me to remember. Did I already ask you these questions?"

He smiled. "Mother, you're right on top of things for your age and you know how to get to the heart of the matter. Grace and I have been married a long time, and we still have some issues that are hard to fix. I need to go home and spend time there, to see if we can mend our relationship. It's been broken for a long time."

Katrina patted her son's hand and offered him a tender smile. "Go home. Talk. Make things right. Then bring her here. I'll wait for your return, but don't take too long."

Brian knew her short-term memory was slipping, and that saddened him. But he so enjoyed having found and speaking with his mother these last few days. His search to find Katrina had been an incredible journey.

Back in the spare bedroom, Brian went online and bought his return airline ticket. He placed a call to the Interpol office in The Hague to clarify his retirement arrangements and ask that someone in Amsterdam reach out and pick Nina up at the Schiphol airport that night, since she still needed crutches. He called for a car to pick him up at Newark Airport for his ride home. He wanted to see Grace face to face and share everything about his career and what had happened on this trip.

After Katrina retired for the night, Brian stepped outside. The night was clear, with a soft breeze. He returned inside and composed an email to Nina, who would soon arrive in Amsterdam.

Dear Nina, I have bad news from Grace. It's making me leave here in the morning. She's filed for a divorce. I'm not sure she's serious, but my gut tells me that tomorrow we both begin new chapters in our lives. You have so many years ahead of you. You'll accomplish so much. Hopefully, you'll soon have a beautiful new home. If you stay with Interpol, you'll surely be promoted, and may even have your own team of sleuths!

Nina, I have such special feelings for you. You must know I'm going to miss you terribly. I truly hope I'll get to visit within a couple of months. – Brian

He went to the kitchen pantry, and he found a bottle of scotch. He looked for a small glass, got an ice cube, and then poured two fingers' worth.

He sat in the kitchen, daydreaming about how things would be when he returned home. Just minutes later, Nina's reply popped up on his screen.

Dear Brian, I just arrived home. Thank you so much for these past ten days. What began as a challenging search for stolen art turned into an incredible story of your search to find Katrina. Our time together has given me so much to remember.

I understand you need to return to New Jersey. But I want you to know I love you. I've always dreamed my relationship with a man would be with someone special. While working with you this past year, I began to realize you were that man. My love for you has helped me mature. I can say I feel more 'grown up' now than I did even a few months ago. Yes, there's definitely a new chapter in my life. You've been so important to me, and you will always have a special place in my heart.

Brian, I'm going to miss being with you day in and day out. I sincerely hope I see you again, and I hope we get to spend some time together. Love always, Nina

Brian finished his scotch while reading her email four more times. Then he poured another and read it a fifth time.

The next morning, Brian entered the veranda room to say goodbye to Katrina. He promised he'd return as soon as possible. He leaned and gave her a hug and a kiss.

"My son, I've missed you for so long. Your life has been wonderful and adventurous, and you finally came back to see me. Thank you. I feel like you've forgiven me, and I can be at peace now. Please visit me again soon."

With tears in his eyes, Brian turned and climbed into the waiting cab.

Katrina clutched her rosary and prayed for his speedy return.

CHAPTER SIXTY

Back in the Garden State

The flight to Newark via Barcelona arrived later that afternoon. Brian went through customs quickly, then headed for the exit. The chauffeur was waiting and holding a sign: O'SULLIVAN. Brian acknowledged the driver with a look and quick nod. He took Brian's bag and asked if that was all he had. Brian nodded.

The spring rains, warm air, and a few days of sunshine in the past week was greening up the grass along the Garden State Parkway. The ride south to Spring Lake seemed quick.

When Brian arrived home, the front and side doors were locked. So, as he'd done in the past when traveling, he opened the garage and found the house key hanging on the tiny brass hook he'd installed twenty-five years earlier. Inside, the house was warm. He walked around and immediately noticed his Impressionism collection, weren't hanging where they'd been. In his den, his collection of signed photos of New York Yankee baseball players was missing from the wall. It surprised him. Then he made his way to his bedroom—he hadn't slept with Grace for the last two years. He took off his tie and jacket and opened his closet and saw all his clothes were gone. He found the house just as she'd threatened. He shook his head. *She's serious. All my things must be at my mother's, like she said. Can she really be going through with this?*

It was three o'clock when Grace returned home. She pulled into the garage and, holding the small box with her half-eaten lunch, stumbled into the house, giving no concern to that fourth glass of Chablis at lunch. She stowed the food in the refrigerator and as she closed the door, noticed Brian standing at the end of the kitchen island.

"Well, it's Mister Art Expert. And what brings your ass to the fair state of New Jersey?" she taunted, emboldened by the alcohol.

"Grace, we need to talk."

"There's— be right back." She ran toward the bathroom. When she returned, she wasn't looking well.

"There's nothing to talk about Mister Art Expert. It's all over. There's a pile of mail for you somewhere around here. Oh, here it is. And that top piece – yep, the thick one – it's from my lawyer."

"Grace, I need to tell you something. It's a secret I've kept from you for the last twenty years."

"Oh? This must be the scene in the movie where the husband admits to the wife about having another woman. Or maybe it's where you tell me about being in love with your gay partner. You know, the one called Erick something or other."

"Grace, it's nothing like that. Please let me explain."

"Oops. I'm gonna be sick. I need to go."

Twenty minutes later, when she didn't return, he went inside to her bedroom and found her lying on the king-size bed, asleep. He returned to the den, and seeing his recliner missing, rested on the couch and fell asleep.

The next morning, Brian suggested breakfast at a local diner.

Still feeling bad from yesterday's lunch with the Freedom Club, she nevertheless agreed.

The battery in his Saab was dead, so they took the Range Rover Grace had bought when she was pissed at him for being away an extra week two years ago. Neither spoke during their brief three-minute drive. She parked her shiny silver Evoque, and they went inside. They sat in a booth at the rear of the restaurant, as he had so many times before. The old Greek owner greeted his regular breakfast guest – the professor – with a smile and the morning paper. He brought two cups of coffee to their table.

It was the first time they'd been face to face in two weeks.

Brian began by sharing how Interpol had recruited him. He explained that he'd been approached at a prestigious event and invited to be part of a unique team recovering lost art. He told her how there'd been more activity in Europe in the past decade, how he and Erick Schmidt had become a team, and about the change in leadership. Then he mentioned how the SS soldier's diary was found.

Grace listened in absolute silence.

His coffee grew cold while he spent another ten minutes explained his search for art in Andalusia, seeking information in Rome, and his search for his birth mother, whom he learned was still alive, on the tiny island of Malta. He didn't share the discovery of Luca's business, its value, Luca's will, or the contents of the safe-deposit box. Nor did he disclose the traumatic events at the birthday party or the next day in the atrium of Katrina's home.

Grace took it all in but was outright indifferent about what she heard. Toward the end of Brian's lengthy account, she absorbed little of what he'd said, focusing only on deciding what she would say in response. As a result, she overlooked most of Brian's joy at finding his birth mother.

"Are you finished, professor?" she mocked at last.

"Well, I'm fully retired from the college, and there's more, but what do you think about what I just told you?"

Grace folded her arms and frowned deeply. "Frankly, Brian, I'm not sure I can believe your explanations. You've been so involved in your life as a professor and traveling overseas to all those conferences all these years, you've completely neglected our marriage – and me. There are so many things you could have done differently – including being more affectionate. Why should I believe you now? But that's all in the past now.

"I tried for years to have a child. It crushed me emotionally, Brian, trying and trying to get pregnant, all those years. And when all those *in vitro* techniques failed, and I fell apart, you weren't paying attention to me. No. Instead, you were off to your art conventions. While I was an emotional wreck, and our marriage was falling apart. You were busy teaching or flying off to yet another conference in Europe. You weren't here when I needed you most. For years, I watched your sisters have child after child. And having to go to all those baby showers and baptisms! Those times were so difficult for me, Brian! But you never even noticed! I've been depressed for years, and the damn medications haven't helped me at all."

Grace sipped her coffee. Then she looked at him again. "Listen to me now, Brian. It's over between us. I've decided to put it all behind me. It's time we parted ways. Our marriage has been broken for a long time. A long time, Brian. And now, for my mental health, it's time I started over. I'll be healthier without you in my life. I've got my girlfriends. They're always supportive of me. We share common interests. We enjoy doing things together and being with each other. They think you've been extremely self-centered, and they're all convinced you must be seeing someone overseas. My girlfriend Sue believes you never travel but are seeing someone right here in New Jersey. Ha!

"So, Mister Art Expert, go home to Staten Island. Your fancy art, those signed baseball photos, your clothes, your stupid recliner and all your art books are at your mother's house, in the garage. Go visit your happy place at the Point. Go spend time thinking about what happened to our lives, our marriage, and what you might have done differently if you truly loved your wife the way you should have."

The server came to the table. "More coffee? And are you ready to order?

"Not for me. I'm leaving."

Grace squiggled to the edge of the booth, stood, and left. Through the diner's wide windows, Brian watched her walk to her car, get in and drive away.

"Sir, will you still be having breakfast?"

"Uh… yes. Two eggs over easy, bacon, no potatoes, and please burn the edges of my English muffin. Tell Alex in the kitchen it's for the professor. He'll know what to do."

CHAPTER SIXTY-ONE

Leaving the Diner

Brian opened to the sports page and started reading the article about how New York's two baseball teams were looking. Only a moment passed before he put it down and stared out the window. He'd thought long and hard during breakfast about Gracie's comments. Revisiting her words, he began to understand how she'd struggled all those years. He recognized how self-centered he'd been – but it was only because he enjoyed his work so much and spent so much time away. A pang hit him right in the conscience. *She made a lot of good points. I was too focused on my own career and my own successes that I didn't pay attention to what was going on with her. I should've been more aware of her struggle. I need to let her know I was wrong and hope it's not too late to try to make it up to her.*

He recognized how she could have viewed his career as a one-sided decision to constantly travel and enjoy a great social life. He began to see how his frequent absence was at the root of their ruined marriage. But he hung onto one idea: Her inability to conceive and carry children was a far deeper issue for her and became the single issue that ultimately crushed her spirit.

Brian drifted back to when he was much younger and was deeply concerned about his income. He worried about saving enough money in his retirement. So, despite having a great income from his college professorship, when Interpol approached him, he felt it held the answer to his financial goals.

But now he reflected how the commitment to his 'part-time Interpol job' sucked away one-on-one time from Grace and inevitably hurt his marriage.

He was so deep in his thoughts of figuring out ways to fix things with Grace, he had yet to think about how he'd get home. Realizing that, he reached for his phone to call his sister for a ride. Shawn was probably home. He was about to punch in her number when his phone rang.

"Hi Brian. It's Nina."

"Nina! Hi! How's your leg feeling?"

"I'm feeling much better today. Thanks for asking. I have a question for you, Brian. Were you serious about buying Erick's building? You weren't teasing me, were you?"

"Of course not! And yes, I was serious. I want to buy it for you."

"Well, I've investigated the details. Erick's lease ended while we were in Andalusia. He told me he planned to get a place near his sister in Zaanse Schans, near those beautiful old windmills. I'll email you the information I found. Are you somewhere you can look at the message?"

"Not at the moment, but I should be in about an hour."

"Okay, please take a look and let me know what you think."

"I will."

"Uh, how are things with Grace?"

"Well, she's still terribly upset with my being away so much. And I'm sure her time in jail in Amsterdam didn't help matters. I'll look at your information and get back to you."

"Thank you. I miss you."

"Thanks, Nina. I miss you, too."

Brian finished his breakfast and deciding not to impose on Shawn, called a cab for a ride back to the house. His second call was to the local garage to have a mechanic come to the house and have his car battery jumped or replaced. The cab driver said he'd unexpectedly encountered traffic and was rerouted. He took the long way back to the house, but Brian didn't care.

He found the house empty when he returned. Grace had either returned and left again or driven to her friend's house directly from the diner. Going inside to look around, their splitting up became more real and finally hit him. He was devastated. He sat on the couch and began to cry, knowing it could have been much different, and knowing it was largely his fault. *When she gets back, I'll sit her down and share the news about the fortune left to me by Luca and Katrina. I'm sure it'll open her eyes and make her reconsider. We can travel or, if she wants, we can stay here and go to the beach in LBI – or even build a new house in LBI.*

I've made a huge mistake and I need to fix it. Nina will be fine. She's young and beautiful and will have a wonderful life ahead with some lucky man. I'll set up a fund for her so she can retire early if she wants. She means a lot to me, but I know I need to be here.

The mechanic arrived an hour later. "Hi professor. Sorry for being late."

"Hi, Billy. How's Dad?"

"He's good. What's with your old Saab? I bet you've got over two hundred thousand miles on it by now."

"Good guess. Just over two hundred three thousand, and a dead battery from lack of use. You might need to put a new one in. I have no idea when it was replaced last."

Billy worked in silence for a moment, then started chatting again, just to make conversation. "Gee, professor, you shoulda seen that accident. That's why I'm late getting here. You might remember I'm a volunteer fire."

"Sure. I remember. So was your dad. You guys do great work. It's why we donate regularly."

"I appreciate that, professor. Anyway, there was this awful accident an hour ago. This little SUV got hit broadside by a tractor trailer and it rolled over four or five times. Apparently, the driver must not have been paying attention and ran a red light. One of the state troopers said the driver was killed instantly. "

"Billy, where did the crash happen?"

"At the intersection of Allaire Road and River Road."

"What kind of SUV was it?"

"Gee, professor, it was all mashed up. I could see it was silver and a complete mess. It was one of those smaller, foreign SUVs. I was finishing up an oil change and the customer was waiting. So, by the time I arrived, our volunteer engine company was finishing sweeping the roadway and leaving. A towing company from Belmar was loading the vehicle onto a flatbed. It was all chopped up to get the body out. The cops were still taking pictures and marking up the road."

As they chatted in front of the garage by his service truck, a state police patrol car pulled up. Two troopers got out. After putting their hats on, they walked up the driveway. Brian suddenly froze in fear.

"Excuse me, sir, are you Mr. O'Sullivan?"

CHAPTER SIXTY-TWO

The Cemetery

The accident was so severe, Grace's body was in a closed coffin during the three-day wake. Now, after the morning's funeral Mass at the Catholic church in Spring Lake, more than thirty cars with their lights joined the funeral procession heading over the Outerbridge Crossing to the Resurrection Cemetery at Mount Loretto on Staten Island.

Brian stared out the window as the funeral car crossed over the Kill van Kull. He thought of the words *déjà vu* and shook his head as he looked down on the water and saw a container ship enter the narrow passage way. *How many times have I been across this bridge to visit my parents' house, to visit Dad's grave, to go sit with Mom for an afternoon? And now this. I just can't believe this happened. Gracie's gone.*

Brian's three sisters rode in the car with him. Each took a turn with the box of tissues. Their husbands and all the children followed in the next three procession cars. As car after car arrived at the cemetery, they parked, and family and friends trod solemnly toward the freshly dug grave.

They waited for the casket to be removed from the hearse and set above the grave. All the flowers were then put in place. The priest and the funeral director moved into position and then motioned the mourners forward to stand graveside.

Everyone attending was in shock, still not believing what had happened just days ago. Not one divorcee from The Freedom Club came. After the priest blessed the casket one more time, the graveside service concluded and Shawn's husband, Stephen, invited everyone back to a restaurant near Brian's home.

The return trip to Spring Lake seemed surreal. Numb, Brian gripped Tricia's hand in the limo. His other sisters had gone on ahead to oversee the setup at the restaurant. Without much to say, the siblings stared out the limo's window.

"T, it's all just so unbelievable. Breaking up is one thing," – he shook his head – "but what's happened to Grace… it just couldn't be any worse than this."

"Brian, we all love you. You need to look forward. Seven of your nieces and nephews are in high school right now. They're at the age where your positive influence as their favorite uncle can really help as they head toward college." Squeezing his hand, she forced a smile for her big brother's benefit.

"Yes, Tricia, that's certainly something to think about."

At the restaurant, Brian's nieces and nephews went to a table set for them, and Brian and his sisters and brothers-in-law sat together. Shawn, who'd been the one to discover all of Brian's things at their mother's house five days earlier, asked him for the first time what had happened between him and Grace that had her move everything of his out of the house.

"Let me summarize in a page what could be an entire book. Gracie was extremely depressed and at a real low point. While she'd initially been proud of my career as a professor, she ultimately felt neglected, because I traveled so much. Also, her inability to carry a pregnancy to term devastated her. She was being treated for depression. It worsened over the years and yesterday, at the house, I discovered she hadn't been taking her depression meds. Plus, she'd just filed for divorce."

Shawn's eyes widened and filled with tears. "Oh, Brian!"

"It seems my latest trip after Mom died put her over the edge. I never told her – and I never told any of you – that besides being a professor at Rutgers, I've been an Interpol agent for many years."

"Oh, my God, Brian! You've been traveling overseas as a secret agent?"

"Yes. Well, not exactly as a secret agent. But the day Mom was buried, and we found that Bible in her hope chest, I got an unexpected phone call. A case my team had been working on for over a year became hot. My Interpol partner in Amsterdam called about a lead on two pieces of stolen art in a recently obtained Nazi SS soldier's diary."

"Brian, that's amazing. I understand why you never mentioned it to any of us, but you never even told Grace?"

"No. But an incredible thing happened as we dug deeper in that case. One of my associates saw a pattern in the SS soldier's diary that not only mentioned stolen art, but also a woman named Katrina. I'd told them about finding the letters in the Bible in Mom's hope chest. Other passages in the SS soldier's diary matched Katrina's words from her letters. After the art was discovered, I went searching for Katrina, and found her in Malta. She's 94 years old! There's no doubt she is my birth mother and get this – the SS soldier whose diary was discovered was my father."

"Oh my God, Brian! You found your birth mother? You actually found the lady in those letters?"

"Yes. Our Interpol team helped recover the stolen paintings. Then I went to Malta to meet Katrina. After meeting her, I flew back here and found all my belongings moved to Mom's house. When I went back to the house, Gracie said I neglected her." Brian paused, reflecting on her words. "The thing is, she was right about much of it. I slept on the couch that night.

"The next morning, we went to the Greek diner near the house. She reiterated and drove home my marital failings. She said she'd be healthier and better off without me, and said she was divorcing me. Then she walked out of the restaurant without eating and drove away leaving me there. I imagine she was distraught, anxious, and confused when she blew through that red light and was hit broadside by the tractor-trailer. Please God, she didn't do it on purpose."

CHAPTER SIXTY-THREE

June Arrives

Springtime in the Netherlands is always exceptional, but even the experts said this year's spring crop of seven million-plus tulips at the Keukenhof botanical garden in the town of Liss surpassed those in years past. Millions of visitors who visited during the early-April to mid-May tulip season were not disappointed.

Three blocks from colorful Vondelpark, Nina was fixing up her new home. Not only had Brian given her the money to purchase the building, but threw in a generous allowance to buy new, contemporary furniture and an assortment of high-end collectible art. In effect, his gift to Nina to fix up the place was carte blanche.

Erick's sister arrived a few weeks later to pick up Erick's belongings. Nina struggled with her emotions as she helped Monica pack his memorabilia. Their time together was pleasant but sad. Although they sometimes teased each other, Erick had been a good friend. Few knew it was he who initially interviewed Nina and selected her for the team.

Nina's on-the-job injury and the mandatory recuperation period to heal her thigh muscles gave her time to do all the decorating she wanted. But now, as everything was coming together, Nina thought about returning to work. She was excited about her promotion, which included a generous salary bump, and she looked forward to having a team of her own. But she also wondered whether that was best for her right now.

Solie visited Nina's house frequently during the renovation, and they became friendly. One afternoon, as they walked home from a large open-air market blocks away, Solie asked Nina about Brian.

Nina shook her head. "The entire situation has been terribly upsetting. Brian was devastated about what happened when he returned home to New Jersey. He emailed me about her filing divorce papers. He wrote that despite their problems, he loved her and wished things had been different between them – with him being more attentive. He said she'd become really difficult in the last few months, but he wanted to recommit to his marriage again, and try to help her. He said he hoped she'd see a new doctor and try new meds.

"He was crushed – *heartbroken* – when Gracie died. Then two weeks ago, his birth mother Katrina died of a heart attack. That *really* hit him hard. It's unthinkable to have that happen so soon after he found her. I know he had planned to go back to see her, but at least he got to meet her and spend time with her."

Solie sighed deeply. "What Brian's been through in such a short time can really break a person's spirit! Losing his mother Sheila in a car accident, the divorce filing, Grace's death, then his birth mother's death! My gosh, it's enough to buckle most people."

"And don't forget Erick. Over the years, he and Erick had become close friends."

"You're right. I've only been here two years, but I'd see them laugh a lot when they were coming or going from the apartment. I admit I'd wondered about Brian for a while because I knew of Erick's… lifestyle."

Nina gave a coy smile. "Well, I'm here to confirm you don't need to wonder about Brian. But here's another thing that makes this situation all even worse. And Brian's still torn up over it.

"A few weeks after Grace passed, Brian's sisters helped him go through their house. Among Grace's things was her journal. Tricia, the older twin, looked through it and discovered a letter addressed to Brian tucked into the back. Grace had written it five months before Sheila died, but never gave it to him.

"In it, she wrote about having terminated a pregnancy a few years before they met. She wrote, 'They botched my abortion and made me sterile. I'm so sorry for never telling you.' She said her insides were a mess and the scarring kept her from sustaining a pregnancy. She admitted her inability to conceive was the absolute cause of her depression and said through their entire marriage, she felt guilty for being unable to give him a child – and even worse for never telling him the truth. She wrote that she sincerely regretted what she'd done, and felt her emotional instability as she aged was completely her responsibility for their marriage's falling apart. In the letter she also admitted she could have been more involved and engaged in his career if it hadn't been for her constant sorrow over not having kids. Brian said her letter was filled with *mea culpa*s."

Solie dabbed at her tear-filled eyes. "Oh my God, Nina, that's so sad! Look at me – I'm crying just hearing this. Brian must be an emotional mess. Why didn't she ever share that with him?"

"I don't know, but I know it's bothered Brian terribly since he found out."

"Nina, that's awful. I feel so sorry for Brian! I hope he can close that chapter of his life."

She gave a pensive nod. "It takes time. Sometimes a huge distraction can help. So, I have news for Brian when he comes. And I'm hoping it'll provide the distraction he needs."

"What's that?"

"First, the woman in Leipzig, Germany, who got the diary from her mother has been back in touch with me. She's taken one of these genetic tests and, as I suspected, it's certain now that she and Brian are half-siblings. The SS soldier, Karl von Richter, who wrote the diary was her dad. He must have been with her mother in the Bendlerblock building during the war."

"Wow! That's amazing."

"And Solie, that's not all."

"Oh?"

"When Brian visits, I have special news for him."

Solie leaned forward. "Can you tell me?"

"Remember you asked me about all the color choices in the house? And why I had the spare bedroom upstairs painted bright yellow?"

"Yes."

"Well, that room will be the nursery. Brian's going to be a father."

"Oh my God! Nina! You're pregnant! How wonderful!"

"I'm so excited! Brian's been in Malta the last two weeks for Katrina's burial and to take care of legal matters there. Her oceanfront villa is now his. He had already learned he was given houses in Capri and Sorrento.

"Brian also wrote he'd stop in Sicily to spend a few days with his friend Massimo. It has something to do about buying some art he liked when we were there. He'll be arriving here late tomorrow morning. He said he'd stay a few days, but I'm hoping he'll stay longer when he hears the news.

Despite everything, he finds time to email me every day, telling me his plans for the day. Sometimes it's a brief note. And sometimes his words… uh, well, it seems like he misses me. He is so sweet. I think he really… well, you know what I mean."

"Does he suspect anything yet?"

"Not yet."

"How do you plan to tell him?"

"When he shows up, first I'll show him how Erick's old place looks with a woman's touch. Then we'll have dinner down the block at Restaurant Bellavista. When we sit, he'll order a bottle of red wine. Then I'll tell him, 'I won't be having any wine.' He'll ask me why, and I'll just smile. Then he'll know."

"Oh, Nina. You're making me tear up. I'm so happy for you!"

As they arrived at the front steps of Nina's new house after their walk, Solie looked at her watch and said she needed to go inside to get on a call.

Not far behind, a tall, white-haired man had been following for the last five minutes. He saw them stop, talk and say goodbye. When Solie entered her apartment, Nina took a few steps but before she could open the door to her place, the man caught up to her.

"Miss von Scholz, good afternoon!"

Frightened by the sudden voice over her shoulder, she turned.

"Oh my, Senior Director Van Deusen! You startled me. Good afternoon to you, as well!"

"Please, call me Pieter."

"What can I do for you, Pieter? Would you like a coffee?"

"No, thank you. I'm here to check up on your health. I'm glad to see you're walking without a limp."

"Thank you. The long walks have been good for my leg. I'm feeling much better."

"Miss von Scholz, uh, Nina, I tried reaching Brian earlier today. I know he stopped in Sicily after leaving Malta."

"Yes. He's in Siracusa to see a friend and buy some paintings. He'll be here tomorrow morning. I expect him to arrive here at the house around eleven thirty."

"Nina, I have two pieces of news to share with you."

Her eyebrows rose. "Oh?"

"First, we learned only four days ago Erick Schmidt is alive. He was shot in the lower back and left to die. Fortunately, an elderly couple found him in a deep ditch on the side of a road. The bullet somehow missed his vital organs, but he almost died from excessive blood loss. In addition to the gunshot, he also suffered a severe concussion from a head injury. He endured memory loss for several weeks while he was healing from his back and head injuries. He was nursed back to health in a small veterinary clinic in a remote area southeast of Seville. His papers were missing, and his identity wasn't immediately known, not even to himself. Our all-points bulletin hadn't been seen by those in the small farm-animal clinic. Over an eight-week period, Erick regained his health, but his memory returned more slowly. He was lucky the doctor at the clinic took care of him so well. Once Erick remembered who he was, he feared contacting our agency. Then, as his memory continued to improve, he remembered his old friend Kristofer Bronn in Leipzig and reached out to him four days ago. Bronn told him about the Muellers, Luzzi, Gozzo and the fixer of the gang being killed. Bronn's wired him money and he made his way back to his sister's house late last night. Erick called me this morning, saying he's feeling well and is eager to return to work."

"Oh, Pieter, that's wonderful news! I'm going to cry! I recently met Erick's sister, when she picked up his things. She was planning to have a small memorial set up for him. I'll call him at his sister's house when I go inside."

"Next, Nina, you know the agency sent Brian a letter a few months ago. It was a demand notice saying he must retire within ninety days. Well, yesterday I ordered his retirement notice withdrawn. I'm extending Brian's commitment to the agency by two years. Interpol has the right to extend an agent's obligation to serve under Section Fourteen-point-four."

Nina looked perplexed. "Why?"

"I'll explain why in a moment. Now, I've come here today to find out for myself how you're feeling. I watched you and your neighbor walk back from the market and I'm delighted to see you doing so well. So let me get to the point – the real reason I'm here.

"Something unusual came up a few days ago, and few agents have the talent to deal with this challenge. So, given your recent promotion to team leader, Brian's extension, and Erick's miraculous return, I'm assigning your team to the case. It involves several international agencies. Your above-average problem-solving skills, intelligence and perseverance will allow our agency, together with the others, to unravel what we know and get to the bottom of this situation. I'm delighted to have the three of you together again!

"After Brian returns, bring him to my office tomorrow afternoon. I've set up a meeting at three. I've invited Erick to attend, as well. That's all for now. Good day, Miss von Scholz."

"Wow! Yes. Good day, Director. We'll definitely see you tomorrow."

As Pieter walked away, Nina stood for a few moments, taking in what had just happened. Then she sat on the porch steps to think some more. *Working together again with the team would be great, but I wonder what this is all about. What will Brian think? With all that's happened, and his new fortune, will he even want to stay on? Maybe I should wait to see his reaction at the meeting before I tell him I'm pregnant. And even if he is interested, will he still want me to do this once he finds out about the baby? Maybe I should tell him when I see him...*

Suddenly nervous, Nina leapt to her feet and hurried inside.

— *To Be Continued* —

Fictional Characters – Alphabetically and by Role

Interpol

Kristofer Bronn – Retired Interpol agent; formerly part of the Interpol team searching for lost art stolen by the Nazis in World War II. Owns an antiques store in Leipzig.

Antonio Gozzo – Interpol agent.

Paolo Luzzi-Luciano – Interpol agent. Also Katrina and Luca Luciano's adopted son.

Tony Massa – Interpol agent, acting as first mate aboard Paolo's new yacht.

Klaus Mueller – Former director of the Interpol Art Research Unit; father of Wilhelm Mueller.

Wilhelm Mueller – New director of Interpol Art Research Unit.

Brian O'Sullivan – Interpol agent. Son of Katrina Amorino-Luciano. Art-history professor and department head at Rutgers University in NJ. Part of the Interpol team searching for lost art stolen by the Gestapo and Nazis during World War II.

Donna Padula – Interpol agent.

Vittorio Petrullo – Interpol agent doing a deep internal investigation, acting as captain of Paolo's new yacht.

Erick Schmidt – Interpol agent, part of the team searching for lost art stolen by the Nazis in World War II.

Ursula – Secretary to Wilhelm Mueller.

Corina Varrichio – Interpol agent.

Nina von Scholz – Interpol agent, part of the team searching for lost art stolen by the Nazis in World War II.

Other Characters

Katrina Amorino-Luciano – Brian's birth mother.

Elsa – Received Karl von Richter's diary from her mother, Hilda; sold it to Kristofer Bronn.

Juan De León – "Fixer" for the Mueller family when they need people eliminated.

Gianni Giordano – Childhood friend of Paolo Luzzi; yacht salesman in trouble with the law.

Dominic Luciano – Luca Luciano's nephew; runs the Luciano family bank in Rome.

Karl von Richter (KvR) – Brian O'Sullivan's biological father. German SS soldier who misplaced his diary, which contains information on stolen art and his nefarious deeds.

Luca Luciano – Katrina's husband. Owned thriving wine-export business. Uncle to Dominic, Maria and Stefano Luciano.

Maria Luciano – Luca Luciano's niece; works with her brother (Stefano) and cousin (Dominic) at the Luciano family bank in Rome.

Massimo Marini – Brian's college friend who lived in Greenwich Village.

Monsignor Giorgio Borrelli – Manages the Vatican art collection.

Solmaz, a.k.a. Solie – Neighbor of Erick Schmidt.

Stefano Luciano – Luca Luciano's nephew; runs the Luciano family bank in Rome.

Grace O'Sullivan – Brian's wife, fed up with his frequent trips to Europe.

Tricia, Kathy, and Shawn – Daughters of the O'Sullivans. They discover the German family Bible in their late mother's hope chest.

Historic Locations and Events of Interest

Hartford Circus Fire – Occurred during an afternoon performance of the Ringling Bros and Barnum & Bailey Circus, attended by an estimated 6,000 to 8,000 people, on July 6, 1944, in Hartford, CT. One of the worst fire disasters in United States history. In all, 167 people died in the fire from burns and by being crushed as people tried to flee. Over 700 injuries were reported.

Mount Loretto, Staten Island, NY – Orphanage established on farmland in Staten Island by Father John Drumgoole, an Irish Catholic priest. Founded in 1882 to help poor or abandoned immigrant children from Manhattan. Eventually the orphanage expanded and covered over 700 acres of land.

Outerbridge Crossing – One of three bridges between Staten Island and New Jersey. Originally named the Arthur Kill Bridge, it was later renamed for George Outerbridge, a structural engineer and the first chairman of the NY and NJ Port Authority.

The Alhambra – A palace-fortress complex located in Granada, Andalusia, Spain. One of the most famous monuments of Islamic architecture and one of the best-preserved palaces of the historic Islamic world. Contains notable examples of Spanish Renaissance architecture.

The Alcázar de los Reyes Cristianos – Also known as the Alcázar of Córdoba, a medieval castle (or alcázar) in the historic center of Córdoba, next to the Guadalquivir River. Served as one of the primary residences of Isabella I of Castile and Ferdinand II of Aragon. Christopher Columbus had his first meeting with Queen Isabella in this castle, seeking her financial support for his expedition to find a new trade route to India by heading west across the Atlantic.

Mosque-Cathedral of Córdoba – Also called the Mezquita, in the city of Córdoba. Now known as the Cathedral of Our Lady of the Assumption and the cathedral of the Roman Catholic Diocese of Córdoba. Also known as the Great Mosque of Córdoba. Constructed on the orders of Abd ar-Rahman I in 785 AD, when Córdoba was the capital of the Muslim-controlled region. Converted to a cathedral in 1236 when Christian forces captured Córdoba during the Reconquista.

Málaga – City in southern Spain along what is referred to as the "Gold Coast."

Seville – City in southwestern Spain.

Roman Bridge of Córdoba – Originally built in the early 1st century BC, crossing the Guadalquivir River in the city of Córdoba, Spain. For two thousand years it served as the city's only bridge across the river. Most of the present structure dates from the Arabs' reconstruction in the 8th century.

Staten Island Ferry – A passenger and vehicle ferry service operated by the New York City Department of Transportation. Its 25-minute route runs 5.2 miles between the southern tip of Manhattan to St. George, Staten Island. Service originated in 1817 when the Richmond Turnpike Company started a steamboat service from Manhattan to Staten Island. Cornelius Vanderbilt bought the Richmond Turnpike Company in 1838 and merged it with two competitors in 1853.

69th Street Brooklyn Ferry – Established in 1817, the ferry serviced people and vehicles traveling between Brooklyn and Staten Island. Made obsolete after the construction of the Verrazano-Narrows Bridge, which opened in the fall of 1964.

Sources:

Wikipedia commons; http://en.m.wikipedia.org/wiki/ Wikipedia:Copyrights

Hartford Circus Fire – 1944; Wikipedia commons; fair use

Miranda Warning Equivalents Abroad May 2016; The Law Library of Congress, Global Legal Research Center law@loc.gov • http://www.law.gov

About the Author

Peter J. Marzano is the son of Italian and Irish families, immigrants to New York City in 1908 and 1928 respectively. Born in Manhattan's Greenwich Village, he grew up in Staten Island. After attending Staten Island Community College, Peter worked in construction and eventually migrated into sales with divisions of General Dynamics, United Technologies, AT&T, and an American division of Air Liquid.

His broad business experience spanned 45 years, allowing him to travel nationally and internationally in Europe for work and pleasure while living in NYC; Atlanta, Georgia; Orlando, Florida; Hartford, Connecticut; and Wilmington, North Carolina. His unique skills, knowledge and technical experience allowed him to help customers in a variety of industrial settings.

Father of four and grandfather of eleven, Marzano has been married to his high-school sweetheart, Kathleen (Coyle) Marzano 50 years. An avid photographer, he loves capturing family, friends, outdoor scenery and wildlife. He currently resides in Connecticut.

Search and Deception is his second novel.

CPSIA information can be obtained
at www.ICGtesting.com
Printed in the USA
JSHW051932131122
33110JS00003B/9

9 781736 682722